When the White House Was Ours

Books by Porter Shreve

The Obituary Writer

Drives Like a Dream

When the White House Was Ours

When *the* WHITE HOUSE Was Ours

Porter Shreve

A Mariner Original
Houghton Mifflin Company
BOSTON • NEW YORK
2008

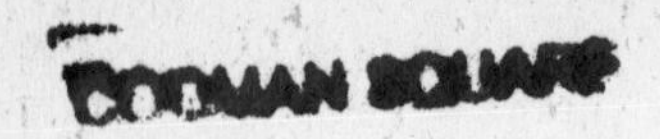

FOR MY FAMILY

www.houghtonmifflinbooks.com

Library of Congress Cataloging-in-Publication Data
Shreve, Porter.
When the white house was ours / Porter Shreve.
p. cm.
"A Mariner Original."
ISBN 978-0-618-72210-5
1. Parent and child—Fiction. 2. Eccentrics and eccentricities—Fiction. 3. Alternative schools—Fiction. 4. Washington (D.C.)—Fiction. 5. Domestic fiction. I. Title.
PS3569.H7395W47 2008
813'.54—dc22 2008011432

Book design by Melissa Lotfy

Printed in the United States of America

DOC 10 9 8 7 6 5 4 3 2 1

Prologue

FOR YEARS WE LIVED IN BOXES. Box rooms at the end of narrow hallways. Box houses so small we drew shallow breaths. We moved so often we didn't bother to put the boxes away. They grew flimsy from overuse and slumped against our living room walls. We piled into the old tan van, a moving box on wheels, and scribbled across the Midwest like bewildered pioneers.

We left six places before I had turned thirteen: Duluth when my father's baseball career ended with a play at the plate, Bloomington after my parents pursued their teaching degrees, Cincinnati where my sister was born. We lived long enough in Indianapolis that I thought we might settle down, but then we packed up for the north side of Chicago and my father's first private school job.

Maybe we shouldn't have been surprised when, two years later, in March 1976, Lake Bluff Academy fired him. He'd lost work before, but this time he knew that my mother was at the end of her patience. He kept saying that he had trouble with institutions, and my mother reminded him that marriage was an institution, and this one was heading for trouble. At breakfast two weeks after Lake Bluff had let him go, my father announced his new plan: he was going to start a school of his own, a forward-thinking one, he said, where no one would be hemmed in by rules. My mother laughed, but he said he was serious. "Where?" She pressed him on it. "How are you going to get funded, Pete?" When he admitted he hadn't thought it all through, she shot up from the table. "You've finally lost your mind," she said. She packed a duffel bag, rounded up Molly and me, and told our father that we were leaving for a few days, long enough for him to come down from his cloud. We spent the Easter weekend at our grandparents' house in Wausau, Wisconsin, and returned to find my father smiling broadly at the apartment door.

"We've got our school." He opened his arms. "You didn't think I could do it, did you, Val?"

My mother didn't believe him at first, but over the course of a month he convinced her. As if by magic he even produced pictures of the place: a magnificent white Victorian house on the corner of 16th and Hill streets in Washington, D.C.

"Is it a mansion?" Molly asked.

"Better," he said. "A free mansion, and it's all ours."

Later, my father told me that the house wasn't free. We were alone in the apartment. My mother was off walking Molly to the elementary school where she was teased for her bargain-bin clothes. "Your mother would kill me if she knew this," my father said. "So you'll have to give me your oath." We had a ritual whereby I'd place my hand on the head of Chester, our indifferent gray tabby, and pledge by the earth, sea and stars that I would not reveal the secrets of the Fellowship of Chester, on pain of tumult and general unhappiness. Then we'd each take a piece of loose fur to keep in remembrance of our vow.

My father confided in me because he was running out of second chances, and he knew that I'd do anything to help him hold the family together. He wasn't the only person who bent my ear. The kids at school gave me grief for my sticking-out ears, which I hid by growing my hair into wings. "Tell them that Buddha and the Pope have big ears, too," my father used to say. "Those chumps are jealous that you're privy to the secrets of the universe." I did seem to be a magnet for secrets, and liked to imagine that I had bionic hearing. I used to sit at my desk, pretending to divide fractions, and listen to my parents argue in the next room. If I really concentrated I could hear the whispers of the dormitory kids down the hall saying, *Mr. and Mrs. Truitt are headed for divorce.*

My father had told my mother that his old friend Bailey Dornan, from the University of Wisconsin baseball team, was giving us the house rent-free for as long as we wanted it. Bailey's family owned entire blocks of downtown Washington, and he had once said that if my father ever needed anything he should just call. But my father was proud and stubborn, and he knew that his friendship with Bailey had always been tinged with distrust. So he'd kept the offer in reserve, to be used only in case of emergency. And he was selective about what he told my mother. By sharing the truth with me, he was passing on the burden. "Bailey's not asking for rent for the first four months," my father admitted. "But after that, we have to pay."

"Is it expensive?" I asked.

"He said he might cut me a deal, maybe half the going rate, but I figure four months is a long time. We'll have this school up and running by fall. Mark my words, Daniel."

Even then I could have imagined my father picking up the phone after yet another disappointment. He wouldn't have said he was fired. He'd have spoken in the bantering way he always used with his old baseball friends. "So whaddya say, Bailey. I've got this idea I've been kicking around." He wouldn't have used the words "alternative school," though in fact that's exactly what he'd had in mind. Hands-on learning, a free and open laboratory for kids to explore their own interests. My father had written his master's thesis on democratic education, where students and faculty have equal say. And though he'd taught only in traditional schools, he had talked about going to innovative places like the Free School in Albany, the Sudbury Valley School in Framingham, Massachusetts, or even the seminal Summerhill, in Leiston, England. But money and timing had stood in the way, and he'd never felt bold enough, raising two kids and still clinging in times like these to the safe and familiar. Now, with a résumé of short-term appointments and haphazard zigzags across the map, finally aware that his marriage was on the line, perhaps he felt he had one last chance.

Besides the house he'd arranged with Bailey, my father did have another ace in the hole: a small inheritance from a godmother who had married a Ford executive. She was the only person of means with any tie to our family. A widow with no children, she used to send a Christmas card each year with a crisp fifty-dollar bill folded inside it. "For the Truitts," she wrote in her crabbed hand. "Affectionately, Aunt Natalia." My parents had come to count on that fifty dollars; it paid the credit card bill at the end of the holidays. Molly and I used to draw crayon self-portraits on our thank-you notes, addressed to Mrs. Malcolm McRae of Bloomfield Hills, Michigan.

The inheritance, my father explained, could cover operating costs and salaries for a year, and by then the school would be running on its own.

"Three thousand dollars is a lot less than you think," my mother said.

"So we'll save," my father promised.

"We've never saved a dime in our lives."

And on went the argument until my mother tired of asking questions and finally acquiesced. We had no other prospects, after all. So one June morning in the bicentennial year, we assembled the boxes again and left the Midwest. "Just for the record," my mother put in, "this was your idea."

Like Jimmy Carter's presidency, our years in Washington began with hope then slid into crisis. Three administrations and more than two decades have come and gone, and this year we marked the millennium. But there was a time, back in our own white house, when every possibility seemed to open up for us.

I

OUR HOUSE

1976

1

We drove all day from Lake Bluff, Illinois, twelve hours in the old tan van. I rode in the back, flipping through pictures in *Life* magazine of the tall ships docked in New York Harbor and the Freedom Train drawing red, white and blue streaks across America. My father sat patiently at the wheel while Chester meowed in his cat carrier and my mother and sister sang campfire songs out of tune. Ordinarily, I would have longed for the peace and quiet that I'd yet to find in twelve years of following my parents from one shared space or thin-walled apartment to the next. But today I couldn't complain: we were moving to a six-bedroom house in the capital city.

The sun sat like a fiery gem on the fingertips of the trees. It was two weeks short of the Fourth of July, 1976. Though we'd heard D.C. would be a madhouse, approached from the top it seemed a quiet city of neighborhoods, full of tall oaks and colonials set back from the road. I popped open a window; the humid air swirled around the van, dust motes scaling the wall of boxes stacked to the ceiling in the back seat. Fishtailing behind us in a U-Haul trailer was much of what we owned: beds, chairs, a turntable and stereo, a black-and-white TV, my father's records, my mother's books, Uncle Linc's pottery and dreamcatchers wrapped snugly in old clothes.

I couldn't wait to move. I'd had my eye on Washington since

fifth grade, when I began writing mini-biographies of the American presidents. My mother taught English part-time; my father taught social studies and always had some administrative job. They'd worked primarily in public schools, and Molly and I enrolled wherever they taught: Eagle Elementary, Dakota Meadows Middle School, Henry Wadsworth Longfellow, Lake Bluff Academy. We never stayed long enough in any one place to form real friendships. So I sought out the company of Dell Yearling biographies, while Molly read her Nancy Drews, imagining herself in smart suits on daring adventures with her fellow sophisticates. Molly had done well in public school, but envisioned our family in grander circumstances, and I'd been happy enough camping out in the library or shooting baskets at the empty playground in our neighborhood. I loved the hard pop of the chain nets and how, after I made a shot, the hoop would seem to hold the ball for a moment, then let it go. I felt as if I was playing catch with a tall, silent friend.

But at Lake Bluff Academy for Boys, the basketball courts were all indoors and crowded with kids stronger and more aggressive than me. So I bought a Nerf hoop and set it up in my room at the corner of the dormitory, where our family shared space with the boarding students. I'd gotten straight A's in public school but at Lake Bluff I fell behind, and my teachers were not impressed that I knew more about the presidents, from George Washington to William McKinley, than they did:

James Madison's secret disease? Epilepsy.

Andrew Jackson's favorite foods? Milk, cheese, blackberries, partridge and venison.

John Quincy Adams's form of exercise? Swimming in the nude, every morning at 5 A.M., in the Potomac River.

I got a D+ in American history. On my first test I had little to say about the Articles of Confederation, but I did write that Thomas Jefferson's favorite pet was a mockingbird named Dick that used to ride through the White House on the president's shoulder. Jefferson had been known to feed the bird from his own lips at state dinners. "This is trivia," my teacher wrote in the margins. "Trivia, by definition, is unimportant."

So I checked out, pulled C's and D's throughout my two years at Lake Bluff. I stopped writing my biographies and instead fell asleep listening to the Indiana Pacers and their star, George McGinnis, tear up the ABA. My free tuition had been one of the perks of my parents' jobs, but the powers that be had threatened to hold me back for eighth grade or not let me go on to the high school. Being a scholarship kid and faculty brat was bad enough. It didn't help matters that I was small and easily pushed around. But worst of all was my father's inability, as dean of students, to follow the headmaster's directive and "make young Daniel get up and fly right."

No one was happier than I to be flying right out of Lake Bluff. I would have settled for a hovel in the sticks. But here we were with keys to a mansion in D.C., ready for a fresh start far from the taunts and diminishments.

We were closing in on downtown now. People streamed into apartment buildings and strode the sidewalks with brisk self-certainty. The streetlamps bore red, white and blue flags—*1776–1976: Happy Birthday, USA*—and I pretended that 16th Street had been decked out just for my family's arrival. A one-van parade.

We stopped at a light next to a city bus with a Virginia Slims ad on the side—a picture of a wispy woman in a sheer blouse, her cigarette poised over the words *You've Come a Long Way, Baby.*

I'd been quiet for much of the trip, trying to play it cool, but now I asked my parents where Molly and I would be going to school in the fall. I was pretty sure I knew the answer—my parents had fought about it already.

My mother turned around, and I noticed that she looked a lot like the Virginia Slims lady, with the same shoulder-length chestnut hair and languid way of holding herself. She didn't smoke, but she did have a habit of eating whole boxes of orange Tic Tacs while admonishing Molly and me against sugar.

"You'll have to talk to your father about that," she said and turned back around.

My father looked at me in the rearview mirror. He wore the kind of glasses that went from amber in the daytime to clear in low light. The outlines of his eyes were growing more visible. "You're going to be our very first students," he said.

"Guinea pigs," my mother put in, over her shoulder.

"You know the D.C. public schools are terrible, Val. We've gone over this already."

"Not long ago all of our meals were paid for. Free room and board," my mother said. "Someone else picked up our health insurance. And we both had jobs."

My father shifted into gear and the van lurched forward. "We can talk about this some other time," he said. "Trust me."

In a matter of months Jimmy Carter would win the presidency on this very slogan, triggering my lifelong fascination with the thirty-ninth president.

"'Trust me'?" my mother said. "I've heard that line before."

"This is the last move for a very long time. I promise." He took a right-hand turn, the muscles quavering up his shirtsleeves. He'd played third base for the Wisconsin Badgers and the Duluth-Superior Dukes, and still had the thick, compact forearms of a power hitter. I used to glimpse his arms from the back seat of the van as we drove long distances, and feel that nothing bad could happen to us.

He pulled over and stopped at the curb. I waited for my mother's reply, but she let the atmosphere thicken with a caustic silence. My father rolled down the window, looking up toward the row of houses. "Do you see what I see?" He smoothed his sideburns and broke into a smile. "White Victorian. Corner of Sixteenth and Hill." He opened the door and stepped out, the rest of us fanning behind him. We were parked in front of a fire hydrant that had been painted to resemble Benjamin Franklin, with rectangular glasses and rosy cheeks and nozzles for arms.

Molly climbed the steps and pressed her face to the window. I held back to take in the view. The sun had fallen beneath the trees, the flattened clouds fringed with pink. Sixteen Hundred Hill was the grandest house on the block by far, looming brightly over a long line of uniform brick row houses. Our last apartment had had one window per room, but this house had a dozen just along the front, and it was three stories high with two chimneys and elaborate spindlework along the porch and gables. But best of all, rising at the corner from the base to the top was a round tower, cantilevered out at the second floor and with large curved windows on the third.

"The tower is mine," I announced and grabbed Chester's cat carrier.

"No, I want it," Molly yelled down from the porch.

I ran up the steps, which thudded under my Adidas high-tops.

My father studied the house key that his friend Bailey had sent. "The princess always gets the tower," he said.

My mother turned from admiring the lace-like brackets along the porch supports. "Our daughter is not a princess. Haven't you heard? We don't lock girls in towers anymore."

"I heard an old lady died up there." I followed my parents into the darkness of the shuttered house.

"You're lying." Molly flipped her horsy braid off her shoulder.

"A long, slow death." I trembled. "With convulsions. Soon after sundown, on a night just like tonight . . . up in the tower."

Ten years old but still afraid of the dark, Molly hugged our father's waist.

"Cut it out," he said. Then, "Shhh. What's that?"

My mother flipped a switch and the hallway light came on. I heard a creaking on the floor above us, then what sounded like footsteps on the stairs. When a voice called down, "Hello," I nearly dropped the cat carrier and ran out the door.

"Bailey?" My father sounded worried.

"That you, Pete?"

Then a pair of bowlegs and a battery-shaped torso, in a charcoal suit and red-striped tie, appeared on the stairs. Bailey had been a backup infielder, a walk-on for the losing Wisconsin team on which my father had been the only star. Bailey looked stockier than he did in team pictures I'd seen in photo albums. He had pale, thin lips and a square jaw. His jet-black hair was parted in the middle and set so low on his brow that when he crinkled his forehead his whole scalp moved.

He gave my father's hand a vigorous shake. When he hugged my mother, he stood on his toes. He asked Molly and me if we remembered him, and we both said yes, though in fact I couldn't recall ever meeting Bailey Dornan. I knew him only from still photographs and from my mother's warnings to my father: *Bailey has never wished you well.*

As my mother liked to tell it, Bailey and my father had been inseparable in college. Roommates their junior year, they signed up for the same classes and took sorority girls on double dates to the garden patio at Lombardino's. Bailey, the eager but untalented bench player, was drawn to my father's cachet as a campus athlete; my father, a brewery foreman's son from La Crosse, had never known anyone from Washington, D.C., and the way Bailey dropped names you'd think his father was the vice president. He'd gone to prep school with the sons of senators, congressmen, secretaries in Eisenhower's cabinet, and saw my father as a protégé, a heartland innocent whom he thought he could shape into a young Republican. He even talked of bringing my father to Washington, setting him up in the family real estate business.

"But then I entered the picture," my mother had explained. During the summer after his junior year my father stayed in Madison and took a course in American political thought. The professor liked to break the class into groups, and my father often sat near the bright and attractive Valerie Gearhart so he could work with her. It turned out that she was trying to sit near him, too. The daughter of Wausau High School's baseball coach, she knew all about Pete Truitt and would call her parents after class to say, "You'd think he'd be so confident, but he's shy. He doesn't know how smart he is." They studied together and she helped him write a term paper on the progressive reforms of "Fighting Bob" La Follette. My father got a rare A in the course—he had never studied so hard in his life—and later volunteered with my mother for Kennedy's campaign to win Wisconsin in the 1960 election.

When Bailey returned from Washington he found his protégé a changed man. They still roomed together the fall of their senior year, but my father was off at rallies or poetry readings with Valerie, and often spent the night out. After Bailey was cut from the baseball team, he rented his own apartment and stuck my father with the lease. It would be months before Bailey would make his gesture of apology, in the form of a standing offer that only now, fifteen years later, my father had finally taken him up on.

Now Bailey was shaking my hand. "Let's see your grip," he said.

I gave his blockish mitt a squeeze.

"That's all you've got? I thought you'd have your daddy's muscles."

"He's a basketball player," my father said. "Isn't that right, sport?" He nudged me lightly on the arm. My father never called me "sport." With his strong jaw and stiff-backed posture he could have been cast as one of Caesar's guards. But the way he hunched his shoulders and twisted the reddish-blond curls at his temples, he looked to be bracing himself for the moment when Bailey would spill the details.

"What's your kitty's name?" Bailey asked my sister.

"Chester Alan Arthur," she said a bit haughtily, as if having a cat with such a name gained us entry among the elite.

Bailey rattled the gate of the carrier. I thought of the Fellowship of Chester, the secret that only my father and I knew, and felt a twinge of dread. I glanced at my mother, who was hugging herself, though the air inside the house felt close and hot, much warmer than outside.

When I set the carrier down by the stairs, Chester turned in a circle then lay back down. "*Mrrrow,*" he complained.

"We didn't expect you here," my mother said to Bailey.

"I wanted to make sure that the place wasn't haunted." He

smiled at Molly, his teeth as wide and pearly as Chiclets. "Just kidding, kids. It's an eviction property."

My mother looped her arm around my father's waist. It had been a while since I'd seen her do that. "What happened to the former tenants?" she asked.

"Someone in my office dealt with that, so I have no idea," Bailey said. "But whoever used to live here couldn't afford it. Look at this place. It's huge."

He stepped into the living room and we all followed him. I was wondering how *we* could afford it, and was surprised that my mother didn't pursue this line of thought. I glanced at my father, who gave me a conspiratorial look.

"So when are the movers arriving?" Bailey's scalp shifted forward and back.

My father laughed uncomfortably.

"Movers?" my mother said. Her hand slipped from my father's waist.

"You did it yourself? I'm impressed." Bailey went over to the window and looked out toward the street. "That's all you've got? Just that little trailer? There's a lot of space to fill here."

When my mother had asked my father if the place would be furnished, he'd told her *of course.* He'd said that Bailey had scores of properties and kept a warehouse full of furniture. But the room was mostly bare—just an old coffee table, a few rickety chairs and an upholstered bench with the stuffing coming out of it.

A tarnished brass fixture in the middle of the ceiling cast a feeble spotlight on my father. "It's just a misunderstanding." He turned to Bailey. "You have some furniture lying around, don't you?"

"Who do I look like, Fred Sanford? I run a business here, not a junkyard. I take old properties and turn them around." Bailey stepped away from the window. His eyes had the opacity of dark berries in a dubious patch. "I was going to let the former tenants do the work themselves—the guy was a housepainter, handyman type—but he flaked out on me. Didn't do a lick of work, and he fell behind on rent."

My mother had wandered over to the cast-iron fireplace. Though she was tall and willowy, she looked petite under the twelve-foot-high ceilings, framed by the ornate Victorian mantel. "You told me there'd be furniture, Pete."

"You'll have to excuse us, Bailey," my father said. "We've had a long trip. We're weary from the road."

"That's not why we're weary," my mother shot back.

"Let's not bother Bailey with this." My father apologized for the confusion. "You know how stressful moving can be. Thanks for checking in on us, though. How about I call you in the morning." He took his friend's elbow and steered him toward the front door. "You've been such a great help already."

A slight smile played at the corners of Bailey's lips. He paused as if savoring the moment, then checked his watch. "I should probably get back to the house. My daughter, Cleo, has a basketball game tonight. She's the star of the team."

Bailey drove off in his champagne Cadillac, long and low, with a supercilious grill. My father closed and double-locked the front door. "Okay then." He clapped his hands together as if all was well.

"So is Bailey going to come around every day?" my mother asked. "Letting himself in anytime he pleases?"

My father opened the hallway closet door and peered inside. A paint-speckled denim shirt hung on a hook and toward the back sat a box of old toys. Molly dug around in the box—a random assortment of costume jewelry, building blocks and a couple of soiled dolls with eyes that snapped shut—while my father tried on the shirt: a little long in the sleeves and tight in the chest, but not a bad fit. "Bailey just wanted to look in on the house. I thought it was a nice gesture."

"You lied to me, Pete," my mother said.

My father nodded toward Molly and me to indicate *we shouldn't talk in front of the kids,* a familiar escape that never worked. "It's been a long day. Can't we go over this later?"

"I'm tired of your surprises," my mother said.

"This is Bailey's surprise, not mine. He told me the place would be furnished."

Molly, on her hands and knees, drew her name in the dust on the closet floor. Ordinarily, she'd be echoing our mother: *Where are we supposed to sit? Why is the house so filthy?* Asking questions was my sister's favorite pastime. But bleary-eyed and disappointed, she resorted to other means of attracting our parents' attention. When she stood up, her white knee socks were black at the shins.

"For God's sake." Our mother took the bait. She shut the closet door and pulled Molly into the living room, where she brushed off the dirt under the light.

I noticed that parts of the living room floor looked clean, patches of polished wood here and there, where a rug, another sofa, tables and chairs might have stood. "There used to be furniture," I said, and thought of adding something more to scare my sister, like *the ghosts took it and they're having a garage sale, all proceeds for a ticket back among the living.* But suddenly I felt uneasy too, unprotected in this strange city in a room that was nearly as large as all the rooms put together in the apartment we'd just left.

The place smelled of dust, old plaster and something musky and humid, like an animal pelt. I didn't want to think about animals at the moment: rats under the floorboards, raccoons in the alley, who-knew-what at the top of the stairs. The room in Illinois I'd shared with my sister had not been so bad. I thought of the simple life we'd left in the cozy dormitory apartment and the hot meals that awaited us each day in the refectory. I was hungry. I'd never gone hungry at Lake Bluff Academy, where my father, as one of the dorm masters, had a key to the kitchen and I could gorge on Ritz crackers, peanut butter and grape jelly, Cheetos and

John's frozen pizza, Frosted Flakes and milk. Giddy with anticipation through the whole drive here, I'd hardly eaten all day.

"Come on, Daniel," my father said. "Give me a hand opening these windows."

Behind the shutters, dead bees lined the sills and sashes. Some of the bees were so desiccated they looked like tiny houseflies. I wondered how long it had been since these shutters were opened. Then the odor of the insects hit me, that pelt smell plus something vaguely metallic. I stepped away and let my father open the windows. The screens had all rotted and sagged.

"We know nothing about this neighborhood." My mother slammed shut one of the windows. "We can't keep the house open all night."

My father swept the bees off the sashes, and they skittered to the floor.

"You told us this was a mansion. It sure doesn't look like one," Molly complained.

"If Nancy Drew were here, she'd take her trusty flashlight and check the place out," my father said. "I thought you were supposed to be brave, Molly."

"Nancy *investigates* houses like this." My sister crossed her arms. "She doesn't have to *live* there."

"So what are we going to do?" I asked.

"We're spending the night in a hotel," our mother announced. When our father protested she raised her voice—"I don't want to hear it"—then headed for the front door.

From the porch I watched my mother swipe a parking ticket off the windshield wiper of the van. My father shambled down the steps, and she thrust the ticket at him. "Was it so hard to pull up another ten feet?"

"You could have moved the van, too." He folded the ticket and shoved it into his back pocket. "We can go to a hotel, get a decent dinner. Then we can come back tomorrow and start over again."

In our haunted house with no furniture, I thought, but I was too hungry to speak. I sat on the top step and Molly joined me. Her socks drooped at the calves like spent balloons.

"I've changed my mind," our mother said. "We can't afford that ticket *and* a hotel. We're staying here tonight."

My father pulled the van well ahead of the fire hydrant then wandered up the street into the darkness. My mother grabbed a broom from the U-Haul and ripped off a box top to use as a dustpan. Molly swept the living room floor while our mother collected bees with the box top, tossing the carcasses into the garden bed. I dragged the mattresses up the steps and dropped them in the living room, dug out linens and pillows from the van and made the beds.

I was locking up the trailer when my father rounded Hill Street with an extra-large pizza on his shoulder. After running the rust out of the water in the downstairs sink and washing the dirt off my face and hands, I sat with my family on the edge of my parents' mattress eating slices of the most delicious pepperoni pizza I'd ever had.

It was too hot that night to climb under the sheets. My mother switched off the overhead light. My father kissed Molly on the cheek and rubbed my arm—I had passed the age of being tucked in. "Goodnight," he said. "Sweet dreams." Then he crawled into bed next to our mother, who turned away from him.

I lay on my back listening to my father's sibilant breathing and the water settling in the pipes. I felt small and huddled in that vast room, just the four of us. As waves of headlights crossed the ceiling and banked down the walls, I wondered if one of those cars was the president's limousine, headed home late after a state function.

I tried to close my eyes but found it impossible. I was wide awake at the very center of the world.

2

FROM INSIDE THE third-floor room, the turret looked like the big top of a spider circus. Webs stretched across the rafters; gauzy nets sagged with flies and bees, mostly dead but some still struggling, while the spiders hung from tightropes awaiting their next strike. “Step right up,” I said, and Molly ran screaming out the door.

Just like that, the turret was mine.

“Good things come to those who like insects,” I said to my father.

“It’s still Molly’s room, if she wants it.” He squinted up into the rafters, where dust and gossamer flecks drifted through the morning sunlight.

“I don’t want it!” Molly yelled on her way downstairs. “I want to go back home!”

“We are home,” my father said. He shot me a disapproving look and left the room.

For the rest of that week I helped my family clean the house and move what little we had into its cavernous spaces. No matter how much elbow grease we put into it, the place never seemed to get clean. We’d scrub the living room, dining room and kitchen, and by the time we finished the bedrooms, the first floor would be grimy again, as if we were living in a farmhouse on an unpaved country road.

"I thought Bailey bought places and turned them around. I guess we're the ones who have to do all the work," my mother protested.

"We're getting the house for free. What do you want for nothing?" my father said.

"At this rate we'll never get the school off the ground, unless you're planning to start a training academy for maids. And who's to say Bailey won't kick us out after we've spruced the place up?"

"He wouldn't do that. He gave me his word."

"I want to see a contract."

"Come on, honey. We're old friends."

"He's always been jealous of you, Pete. No telling what he'll do. We need a lease and some furniture. You're going to have to call him, or else I'll do so myself." Then she headed off on another run to the Adams Morgan Safeway for cleaning supplies.

While she was gone my father announced to Molly and me that he was going to paint the whole interior. The outside looked fine—a bright white that seemed to gleam after a rain shower—but inside was dingy, many of the rooms covered in moldering wallpaper trimmed with floral borders. "The whole place will be done by the Fourth of July," he promised. "And then we can start rounding up students. Democratic education for all!"

But as much as I wanted to have confidence in my father, to imagine him sweeping through the rooms in the next ten days like a superhuman handyman, I was too aware of his history of grand ideas followed by shaky execution.

Molly must have been thinking the same, because she pointed to a piece of plaster buckling at the corner of the living room ceiling and asked, "Should we be worried about that, Dad?"

"Oh, it's nothing," he said. "Just a couple leaking pipes. I'll fix them."

My sister and I shared a commiserative look, knowing that our father had never fixed a thing in his life. Until now, we'd had a reliable landlord or a number to call for building services, but the more we'd see of this house, the clearer it would become that the problems went deeper than a few small leaks.

One afternoon only a week after our arrival, when my father was at Hechinger's buying screens for the downstairs windows, my mother announced that she'd had enough. It was sweltering and she'd just banged her thumb with a hammer while hanging her Edward Hopper print above the mantel.

"Bailey needs to send a crew over now," she said. "And I want a formal lease. We can't live this way."

I took her place on the milk crate and hammered in the nail and picture hook. She handed me the print, *Compartment C, Car 293*, the painting of a woman in black traveling alone on a train. "What if he makes us pay rent?" I lined up the print level with the mantel.

"Then we'll have to leave."

"But I like it here. I want to stay. Dad will be done in no time; then we can go out looking for students." I stepped down from the crate and followed my mother into the dining room. The walls around us had been stripped and sanded, nail holes and pockmarks filled. I adjusted the rotating fan so the air would speed the spackle to dry.

"Your father has no idea what he's gotten us into. This house is falling apart, and I'm beginning to wonder if he was clear with Bailey about the kind of school we're starting. Bailey thinks education should be about drill sergeants and shivering plebes. But a school like ours? Your dad calls it democratic education. Bailey would call it anarchy."

"Well I, for one, am excited," I said. A school where I didn't have to face dismissive marks on my papers, where I could learn what I wanted when I wanted to, in a city that was a museum of American history. Lake Bluff and the rest hadn't known what to do with the independent thinkers besides belittle us. Though I'd never meant to cause trouble or bring home bad grades, I wanted to make my own mistakes, my own discoveries. Perhaps here I'd finally be free to do so.

The phone rang and a minute later Molly summoned our mother into the kitchen. I figured it was our father at Hechinger's, having forgotten something. He had a habit of rushing off without checking the fridge, measuring the windows, making a list. But when I asked Molly who was on the phone, she said it was Uncle Linc. "He sounds bad."

Uncle Linc was my mother's kid brother, her only sibling. He'd been a pudgy, awkward kid, easily picked on, and she had always been his protector, walking him to school, somehow materializing just as his enemies closed around him. After she went off to college in Madison they wrote frequently, often about politics and the increasing gulf between themselves and their old-line parents. Linc fled to Beloit College around the time that we were packing to leave Duluth, and my mother felt a counselor's pride when he joined the college Democrats and became active in student causes.

In the summer of 1968, between his sophomore and junior years, he went down to Chicago with his girlfriend, Cindy, and a group of other Beloiters to protest the Vietnam War at the Democratic National Convention. He was on Michigan Avenue near the Hilton Hotel when the protesters failed to disperse and the police went in with billy clubs. After Cindy was sprayed with Mace, Linc shook his fist at a cop and had his head bloodied. He spent the night in jail and the next several months helping to organize a chapter of Students for a Democratic Society at Beloit. Not long after SDS broke into radical factions, Linc quit school a year early and left for northern California, then Baja, then the mountains outside Tucson. In the past seven years he'd lived all over the West, married Cindy, who changed her name to Cinnamon, and now was hunkered down on a commune somewhere in the mountains of Washington State. He had told my mother that he was writing a book called *How to Live for Free in America.* Molly and I used to fantasize that he'd make a million dollars and the whole family would be rich. What a triumph it would be if Linc, after all his bumbling, had the last laugh.

When my mother got off the phone she was shaking her head. "I can't stand to think of your uncle out there hitchhiking to town so he can root through restaurant dumpsters. They can't grow enough food. They don't know how to farm." She'd told me over the years that the commune had been thinning out, but now apparently it had fewer than half of its original members; those who knew anything about growing vegetables had moved or, in hippie parlance, *sold out to the plastic bourgeoisie.* "He needs money again. And we have nothing to give."

"What about his book?" Molly asked. "Can't he try to sell it?"

"Oh, sweetheart. I thought you knew. He stopped working on that a while ago. There's this guy named Abbie Hoffman. He led the protesters in Chicago when Linc got beaten up. Hoffman's a hero of the counterculture. A few years ago he wrote something called *Steal This Book*, which gives tips about how to survive on the cheap. That put an end to *How to Live for Free.*"

I was disappointed for Linc and for us, but then I thought of my father and how useful such a book might be if our money ran out. "We should get a copy," I said distractedly.

My mother leaned on the edge of the water-stained dining room table. Chester jumped up and rubbed his whiskers against her arm. "Hoffman has some good ideas, but he's also a rabble-rouser. He talks about stealing clothes and food, anything to get by. And he's all for making bombs, as long as you turn them on the cops. Your uncle's no revolutionary, but that doesn't stop him from finding trouble."

My mother talked about Linc's terrible timing. Of course he was in the melee in Chicago; of course he couldn't profit from his one big idea. She had said many times that he'd been born too late for the sixties, just as she had been born too soon. "It's 1976. No one lives on communes anymore." Her eyes welled up. "I don't know what to do."

My grandparents, who had little savings to begin with, had cut

Linc off years ago when he was busted for marijuana possession in Vancouver.

I fiddled with the rusty pull of the pocket doors at the entrance to the dining room. "Don't you have some money from Aunt Natalia? You could give Linc some of that." But as soon as I made the suggestion, I worried about putting my father in a bad spot. Money was too tight already.

"That's Dad's sole inheritance. He needs it for the school," she said, to my relief. "And, really, when will it end? We can't keep sending checks to a P.O. box in Mazama, Washington." With the toe of her Wallabees she scratched at a cloud-shaped spot on the floor, then her eyes brightened for what seemed the first time since we'd arrived. "I'll tell you what I'd like to do. I'd like to get your uncle out of that place."

Molly, who was cooling off in front of the rotating fan, stepped back and gave an audible groan. "How?" she asked.

"We could bring him here," my mother said.

"Linc and Cinnamon are coming to stay with us? So much for having friends over." I could see that Molly hadn't recovered from the news that Linc's book would not be our salvation. She was embarrassed by our uncle and aunt, who went around barefoot looking like castaways, slept late and left rings around the tub and strands of hair and breadcrumbs in their wake. We hadn't seen them in two years, but that wasn't long enough for my sister, who wanted to be a normal kid with polite, wholesome relatives. Or, better yet, like Nancy Drew, with fabulous handbags and a mansion outside the city where her charming friends could gather over tea and strategize. I didn't blame my sister for being too ready with her complaints. She was ten and didn't fully recognize the delicate balance in our household. Eventually, she would move beyond this prim stage into messy adolescence and come to appreciate Linc and Cinnamon, as I did—laugh at their bawdy stories and crank calls that cracked me up no matter how dumb they could be:

Is Mrs. Wall there?

No.

Is Mr. Wall there?

No.

Are there any Walls there?

No.

Then how does your roof stay up?

They climbed trees and built sheet forts, and unlike Molly, who longed for the fast track to adulthood, they refused to grow up. At times I'd worried that I, too, was taking life too seriously, and wondered if it might be good for me to have a couple of grown-up kids around. But at the same time I knew that my father would hate the idea of my uncle and aunt crashing his party. He had already burned enough money on Linc and couldn't stand the way my mother rushed to his aid every time he got into a scrape.

Linc was also accident-prone, and my father believed that his bad luck was contagious. Once, on a hike in Saguaro National Park, Linc had encountered a mountain lion and on the way back to his car that same afternoon was struck by lightning. But he survived. "Just fried a few more brain cells," he'd said at the time. I remember him telling me when I was eight or so: "Don't ever take acid." I didn't know what acid was, but I swore off vitamin C for months before my mother explained that I could go back to drinking orange juice. "Acid is a drug," she'd said. "Like beer and cigarettes and marijuana. Unless you want to be like your uncle, who spent a week in the hospital seeing pink elephants, you'll stay away from drugs."

"Don't worry, Mom," I said then, and I meant it. I didn't need to be warned off the path of Linc.

But now my mother wanted him to come to Washington. As much as I loved my uncle, I feared that his mere presence might bring catastrophe and spoil my father's plans.

"All Dad needs is a month or two," I said. "He's going to fix up the house and recruit a bunch of students and the school will be ready for fall classes. Just give him a chance, Mom. This is the first time he's gotten to start something of his own, with no one looking over his shoulder." I could just as well have been speaking for myself.

Molly and I followed our mother into the kitchen, where she took out a tray of ice, loosened the cubes and dropped them into glasses. "Bailey is watching. As much as your father would like to think this is a perfect situation, you know it's not."

"How many people get a house rent-free?" I asked.

She filled glasses with tap water for the three of us and leaned against the copper countertop, tinged brown with green rings where old Mason jars used to be. With one thin eyebrow slightly raised, she repeated "Rent-free," neither a statement nor a question, and I wondered for a moment if she knew. But before I could feel guilty she was talking about Uncle Linc again. "He'd be a great teacher. Remember, Molly, how he showed you how to make candles and pottery?"

"He made the dreamcatcher that hangs over my bed," Molly said. "It's supposed to catch bad dreams in the web so only good ones pass through. But it doesn't work. I've been having more nightmares than ever."

My mother ignored this and turned to me. "Remember the time your uncle took you whitewater rafting, Daniel? He knows all about the outdoors. He's been living off the land since the sixties."

I thought of that weekend trip with Linc along the Wolf River in Wisconsin, when it rained every night. It had been just the two of us, and each evening as the sunset bronzed the rapids, Linc said, *Just a little bit further now. I know the perfect camping spot.* But it started to drizzle and we had to moor on some brambled bank. Then the rain came pouring down, too heavily for us to put up a tent. We waited out the storm huddled under the raft, the ground too wet for a fire, both of us too tired or demoralized to unpack the stove. So we drank our Chunky soup cold from the can and slept in our rubber cave. When the sun came up Linc stretched his arms and promised: *I won't make that mistake again.*

Over dinner on the night of Linc's call, my mother brought up the idea that at our new school he could teach art or wilderness skills or maybe religion, which was his major before he dropped out of college. We sat gingerly in the mismatched chairs that my father had found in pieces in the back yard and glued together. He'd had more than his usual two glasses of Gallo Chablis. Paint and dry plaster dusted his hair and arms, and he looked worn out from all the scraping and sanding, a little lightheaded perhaps from the wine and turpentine fumes. The hot air seemed trapped in the dining room, and he drank in gulps as if to quench his thirst. He set down his fork on his plate, still piled with tuna casserole, and slid his seat away from the table. "You're not serious. Linc? The Midas of Mayhem? I thought we were trying to get qualified faculty. I don't want this to be amateur hour."

"He's artistic," my mother said. "In high school he carved an eagle from a log and gave it to my parents. It took him a whole year."

"Would you like me to repeat what you just said?" my father asked. "*He carved an eagle from a log. It took him a whole year.* I'm sorry. I've seen that eagle, Val. It's still perched in your parents' dining room. It looks like Howard Cosell with wings. Your brother is not an artist. He's a late-blooming hippie, and I know he's a lovable lunk, but he hasn't done a damn thing with his life."

"He's never had the opportunity," my mother said.

"Well, he shouldn't have squandered his education."

"He could go back to college. He only has one year left."

I watched my sister across the table take the top off her grilled cheese sandwich, roll the bread into pieces of dough, then pile the dough like little cannonballs on the side of her plate. Molly was a vegetarian, had been since she came home from third grade one day and asked if meat really came from animals. Whenever we ate a nonvegetarian meal, my mother had to cook her a separate grilled cheese or bowl of buttered noodles.

Molly was trying to get our mother's attention—to no avail.

"I hate to say this," my father said. "But I don't want Linc on the faculty. In fact, I don't want him here at all." He picked up the Gallo—he always bought the $3.99 jug that you had to pour with two hands—and topped off his glass. "You know he'd just bring his friends. I'm a McGovern progressive. I'm for giving every American a thousand bucks and a pat on the back." He set down the bottle. "But Linc and his merry band don't work. They don't even try to make an honest living. They just take whatever they can. You remember the last time they visited? The savings bonds that disappeared from our closet? Your grandmother's missing brooch?"

"Linc didn't steal those things."

"Well, if he didn't, one of his friends did. Probably that gypsy, Tino, who's always telling him what to do."

"We have nothing to steal anyway," my mother said.

"Oh, they'll find a way."

"I'm only talking about bringing Linc and Cinnamon. You wouldn't have to pay them. They'd be glad to teach for room and board." The shadows in the room made a bolt across my mother's face.

Molly stood up and slipped into the kitchen.

"You know what'll happen," my father said. "Even if it's just the two of them, they'll turn this place into the ultimate crash pad. He'll bring his old hippie and protester buddies here all the time. Do you really want this school—the place where we live—to become a shelter for vagrants, have the kids wake up to a bunch of strangers on the floor?"

As if in answer to the question, there was a shriek, then a loud crash in the kitchen.

My mother shot up from her chair. "Molly, are you okay?"

My father and I gathered at the kitchen doorway. Molly cried against my mother's shoulder. "I just wanted some yogurt. But there was a cockroach on my spoon."

When my mother finished comforting Molly, she grabbed the broom and dustpan and swept up the broken dish. "We can't live like this. Cockroaches in the cupboards. Peeling lead paint." She tossed the shards into the trash. "We have no money. No furniture. No jobs." She tore off a sheet of aluminum foil, covered the leftover casserole and put it in the fridge. My father watched, still leaning in the doorway, while my mother cleared and rinsed the plates. After she'd sponged down the whole kitchen and dining room, she went upstairs to her bedroom and slammed the door.

My memory of those first weeks in Washington is of heat so thick we tried to swat it from our faces, the astringency of Top Job and Murphy's Oil Soap, Paul McCartney and Wings on my father's transistor radio, the taste of zucchini bread that my mother baked, worrying over Uncle Linc and our futures. As if to make up for lost time, I caught bicentennial fever and persuaded Molly to help me paint my room red, white and blue. On one wall we pinned an American flag with gold tassels next to eight-by-tens of the twenty-five presidents—from Washington to McKinley—about whom I'd written biographies. The other walls we filled with magazine cutouts of George McGinnis, Mel Daniels, and the rest of the Indiana Pacers, who wore gold uniforms that matched the tassels of my flag.

I liked working with Molly, who had been my sidekick through years of packing up the covered wagon and starting over. Though she could be petulant and I had my own difficulties with "flying right," we were easy kids, as I look back on it now. We could burn whole days with our books and backgammon, our games of German Whist and Spite & Malice. Our companionship was born of necessity, of being thrown together in narrow confines, and I assumed we would stay as close as always in this house of seemingly endless spaces. But I didn't anticipate what might happen to us, to our family, once the spaces began to fill.

It was the morning of the Fourth of July when we put the finishing touches on my patriotic room. My father had painted most of the downstairs, but had fallen short of his goal of completing the house, and I figured I'd make myself scarce so I wouldn't be around for the fallout. I unpacked my red, white and blue basketball, and slipped on my gold wristbands and matching headband, which promised me good luck on the court and a surefire shooting touch. I hadn't had a haircut since we'd left Lake Bluff. My hair bloomed around my headband like a tight-cinched bale of hay.

My mother liked to remind me of the story of Samson. Long hair was a sign of strength, she said; girls liked boys with lots of wavy hair. For the first time I'd found myself lingering at the checkout over the cover of *Cosmopolitan,* noticing the long trim legs of storefront mannequins, the heaving cleavage of corseted-up actresses in the period films my mother dragged us to. In this new city I felt released from the Alcatraz of that boys' school and all of its frustrated energy.

Surrounded by the peeling walls of the third-floor bathroom that I had all to myself, I looked closely into the mirror. I pulled my hair away from my eyes and tucked it under my headband, lifted my shirt to check on the downy patch of blond hair sprouting above my solar plexus. Maybe one day I'd put some muscle on these bony shoulders and become Wonder Woman's secret consort, the invincible passenger in her invisible plane.

On my way out the front door to the basketball court I had what seemed like a vision. Headed up our steps, in avocado-green running shorts and a purple tank top, was a girl about my age who looked almost familiar in the way attractive people often do. She was carrying a '76 edition American flag, wreathed with the thirteen stars and folded in the tricornered shape symbolic of the hats worn by Colonial revolutionaries.

"Hello," she said.

"You surprised me," I started. I could think of nothing more to say. I wasn't used to standing within five feet of a girl, particularly one so pretty. She had dark brown eyes and feathered bangs and a braided macramé bracelet, the kind that didn't come off unless you cut it free. I felt like the cartoon coyote that had run past the edge of the cliff and would soon fall from midair. "How are you?" I managed to ask. But I was thinking *Who are you?*

Her smile slid to one side, an imperfection that made her face all the brighter. "I'm fine. How are you?"

"I'm Daniel," I stammered. "Daniel Truitt." I shook her hand.

"I know." She had a strong grip. "I'm Cleo. My father owns this house."

I froze. The basketball felt like a weight under my arm.

Cleo turned to look over her shoulder, and that's when I noticed the champagne Cadillac parked out front and Bailey rummaging around in the back seat.

He pulled out what looked like an unwieldy tool then shut the car door. "I like your outfit," he yelled up to me. "Getting ready for the NBA?" He chuckled.

"Are you on a team?" Cleo asked.

"I just got here." I felt the blood rushing to my face. "I'm not on a team yet, but I like to play."

"I'll put my money on the girl," Bailey said on his way up the steps. "So do me a favor. I need a drill and some Phillips-head screws. And I could use some help putting up this flagpole."

I should have rushed inside and warned my father that Bailey had returned, or found some polite way to shoo him off the property—*don't worry about the flagpole, we can put it up ourselves; great to see you again; have a wonderful Fourth*—but something about his fixed gaze and the authority with which he gave commands made me forget about the Fellowship of Chester. And it didn't help that his daughter, cradling the thirteen-star flag in her tanned arms, was such an unexpected standard-bearer. Caught off guard, I stepped inside the house and yelled, "Mom! Dad! Mr. Dornan's here!"

3

It had to happen sooner or later. There I was in the middle of the fray, that irresistible place where I always thought I wanted to be until I got there. I had been my father's confidant, his hand-selected vice president, but more and more I would begin to feel like his co-conspirator.

My mother and Molly came down the staircase just as my father rounded the living room corner. Bailey was placing the flag-pole bracket on the right-hand column of the porch. Cleo introduced herself and handed my mother the flag.

"Happy Fourth!" Bailey said over his shoulder. "We thought we'd help you get into the spirit."

Glowering, my mother passed the flag to my father. Bailey asked about tools, and my father sent me into the house to check the utility drawer. We didn't have a drill or anything beyond a hammer, one or two screwdrivers and a monkey wrench. When I returned to the porch with a Phillips-head and a small paper bag full of nails and screws, Bailey was giving my family a speech on flag etiquette: "It should be raised and lowered slowly and ceremoniously. Take every precaution that it does not become soiled. Never fly the flag upside down except as a distress signal. On Memorial Day fly it at half-staff from sunrise until noon and full staff from noon until sunset, and when a national figure dies and the government flags are flying at half-staff, comply with due haste and the utmost respect."

Out of the corner of my eye I saw that Cleo had her hands tented over her mouth, hiding her expression. I wanted to know what she thought of her father, his voice broadcasting over the whole neighborhood. The stoic widower next door, Mr. Unthank, stood up from his gardening and leered at us from the frame of his tidy yard, and Jackie Clarke, the divorcée in the row house down the street, folded her magazine and went inside. My father nodded attentively, as if by moving his head up and down he could hasten the afternoon along.

When Bailey took a breath, my mother jumped in. "I'd rather not fly a flag at all."

"Come on, Val," my father said. "It's the bicentennial."

"What if I don't like what the flag stands for?" my mother asked, and my father winced.

"It's not a political symbol." Bailey's scalp shifted forward. "It represents everything that makes America great. Honor, courage and sacrifice, our national heritage of good deeds and accomplishments."

My mother opened her mouth to speak but I interrupted. "You didn't have a problem with Molly and me painting my room."

"They painted his room red, white and blue," my father boasted to Bailey.

"That's the spirit." Bailey clapped my shoulder with his meaty paw.

"The flag is not political? Ha!" My mother laughed to herself.

My father asked me for the screwdriver and screws. I tried not to look at him as I traded the tools for the flag, but his eyes flashed for a moment. Bailey stepped aside as my father took over securing the bracket on the porch column.

"It's high time we went over the rental agreement," my mother began. My father explained that he'd already worked that out, but her voice rose over his: "I want to see a lease."

"Trust me," my father said, but when he put his hand on her arm, she shrugged him away.

Bailey seemed to be enjoying the volley. He wore blue jeans so stiff they seemed never worn and a red safari shirt with the collar turned up. His thick chest hairs swirled at his neck like a black gurge.

"You promised we'd have some furniture." My mother turned to Bailey. "Did you tell Pete this place would be furnished?"

"I don't furnish my properties. Too much of a hassle."

"We can talk about this later," my father broke in.

"You always say that," my mother hissed. "We're talking about it now."

I glanced at Cleo, who raised her eyebrows as if to say *Parents!* then nodded in the direction of the front door. Taking her cue, I gathered Molly and invited Cleo into the house. We sat in the rickety chairs at the dining room table, and I apologized for the dropcloths and paint-spattered newspapers that had dried and stuck to the floor, though I knew I should have said sorry for the state of my parents' relationship. Even now, as I cast about for something to say, my mother was probably discovering that my father had been lying to her about the deal he'd cut with Bailey. I wanted to distract Cleo, so like a fool I opened my mouth and let whatever words happened to be there tumble out.

Only two subjects had come to mind: the Indiana Pacers and presidential history. Hoping to sound smart, I launched into the bicentennial, explaining that today also marked the 150th anniversary of the coincidental deaths of John Adams and Thomas Jefferson. Jefferson, the best writer among the founders, had drafted the original Declaration of Independence, and Adams, the most eloquent speaker, had defended it brilliantly before the Continental Congress. But in the election of 1796 Adams defeated Jefferson by three electoral votes, and in the rematch in 1800 Jefferson won, causing long-term enmity between the two men.

As I was speaking I had the parenthetical thought that the story of these Founding Fathers resembled the rivalry between Cleo's father and my own. But not wanting to stir the waters I was quick to note that Jefferson began writing Adams late in life about the future of the nation, and though Adams would always tell his friends that he would outlive Jefferson, their rift, for the most part, healed.

Molly had been growing impatient, and finally interrupted. "Would you like a snack?" she asked Cleo.

"I'm fine," Cleo said.

"You should go to the kitchen and get something for our guest," Molly suggested to me.

"Why don't you go yourself," I snapped back. Then it dawned on me that Molly was only being a decent hostess, like a proper girl sleuth, and also wanted to make sure that Cleo didn't see the roaches stalking our kitchen cabinets.

"Fine." Molly disappeared for a minute, and Cleo encouraged me to continue. She crossed her arms under her breasts, small plums snug in her tank top. I worried that she'd think I was rude to my sister, or worse, a know-it-all, droning on about dead men in wigs and knee breeches. Still, I couldn't leave the story unfinished. "On July 4, 1826, the fiftieth anniversary of the signing, John Adams died; his last words were 'Jefferson still lives.'" I paused a moment to let this sink in. "But here's the amazing thing: two hours earlier, *Jefferson* had expired!" I looked down at my Adidas high-tops, white with royal-blue stripes. "His last words . . . 'Is today the Fourth?'"

I couldn't tell if Cleo was listening, but I asked if she wanted to hear the clincher, and she said, "Sure."

"After Adams died, the messenger sent to deliver the news to Monticello actually crossed paths with Jefferson's messenger, who was headed on horseback to Adams's house, also bearing sad news."

"I never heard that story before," Cleo said, with less intonation than I'd hoped.

"Well—" I shrugged. "History is full of surprises."

Molly returned with an ice tray filled with homemade popsicles stuck with toothpicks.

"We have two flavors." She set the tray on the dining room table. "Orange juice and apple sauce."

Except for those two years at Lake Bluff when we had the run of the school kitchen, my mother never allowed us to have real snacks. We ate Roman Meal bread with ketchup and cheese instead of frozen pizza, cinnamon toast or, if we were lucky, graham crackers in lieu of cookies. For dessert we had Dannon yogurt, which we froze in the cup, or popsicles made out of Minute Maid concentrate—the kind where you have to mix the orange glop with water and stir it into a juice that's always too weak or too strong and tastes like the slotted metal spoon you used to stir it. When we'd tired of having only one flavor, my mother suggested we try freezing applesauce. I could see from the effort in Cleo's lopsided smile that her pantry at home must have been stocked with Fritos, Chips Ahoy, Marshmallow Fluff and soda, her freezer a storehouse of Stouffer's pizza, Breyer's Neapolitan and Klondike bars.

She plucked an orange juice pop from the tray. "My dad can be a pain," she said out of nowhere. "He likes to boss people around. I told him he should call first before coming over, but that's not his way." She held her toothpick like a tiny umbrella. "I hope you don't think we're rude."

"Of course not," I said. "If anything, my mom was the rude one. I think she'll be better once we've settled in. She always gets cranky when we move."

Cleo asked about the move, and I said it wasn't bad; we were used to it. We'd lived in six cities, and I hoped this would be our last.

"I've never been anywhere." She licked the corner of her popsicle where the orange juice was dripping. "Some family trips, that's about it."

She wanted to know exactly where we had lived, so Molly and I went over the list.

"Bloomington. That's a pretty name." Cleo combed her feathery hair out of her face. "I bet it's full of flowers."

"I was three years old when we left there," I said, surprised that she would find anything to recommend a city in Indiana.

"Our grandparents live in Wausau, Wisconsin," Molly piped up.

"Wisconsin. That's where our fathers met," Cleo said. "I know your dad was a big baseball star. I've heard stories about him since I was a kid."

I admired my father for never talking about his baseball career. His reticence only made the myth grow. When people urged him along, he said, *No sense living in the past.* My grandfather—the baseball coach—had saved all of his clips, and anytime we visited Wausau I'd dig into boxes of yellowed newspaper articles about my father's game-winning hits and towering home runs, his barehanded pickups and bullet throws across the diamond. I remembered one article in particular, written the year of my father's career-ending concussion, after a neurosurgeon in Duluth said he should never play again. It was by the baseball columnist of the *Milwaukee Journal Sentinel.* The headline read, "What Might Have Been."

But I wasn't going to bring this up with Cleo. She had probably heard enough from Bailey. "Your dad was a good player, too," I offered.

"All I know is he hates to lose." Cleo chewed what was left of her popsicle, now nothing more than a pale block of ice. "So, should we check on the adults?" she asked.

With a sense of dread I followed her and Molly to the door, but when we stepped outside all was quiet. My father had screwed in the bracket and was angling the flag into it. Bailey stood on the top step with his hands in his back pockets and his belly out.

"How's this?" my father asked.

"A little higher," Bailey said.

Molly scanned the porch. "Where's Mom?"

Our father adjusted the bracket and slid in the flag. "Your

mother took a drive down Livid Lane." He mopped his brow with the back of his hand.

"When did she leave?" I asked.

"About five minutes ago. We had a misunderstanding about the terms of the lease."

Often in the middle of a fight my mother would round up Molly or me or both of us and go for a drive to let off steam. She rarely went alone, so this time she must have been especially infuriated.

Livid Lane was one of many street names my father had made up. He'd imagined a whole map of my mother's escape routes, including Angry Avenue, Stormy Street, Bitter Boulevard, and Hoppin' Mad Highway. He had been taking my mother's disappearances less and less seriously, sometimes encouraging Molly and me to play along and treat the situation as a joke.

For a while I thought nothing of it, but looking back I realize that the map of my mother's escape routes would turn out to be real, not imaginary, and part of me must have known, even back then, that we were laughing only to avoid the threat that none of us wished to face.

I had a pretty good sense of where my mother might be—somewhere near the Potomac River—because every time I went along on one of her drives she found a park bench looking out over the nearest body of water. In Cincinnati she went to the East End riverfront, in Indianapolis to the Canal Walk downtown. Lake Michigan was less than a quarter mile from Lake Bluff Academy, so it was just a short drive to Sunrise Park, where she could gaze at the expanse of water that on a bright day seemed Caribbean blue and in winter could cool her most jagged nerves.

It used to be that she'd take off for only a short while, but lately her time away dragged on. I recalled the trip to our grandparents' house a couple months ago, after my father first announced his plans to start the school. As usual, my mother drove Molly and me to Sunrise Park. But that time, on a surprisingly warm April day, she wasn't satisfied looking out from the bluff to the wavering boundary of sand and shore. So we piled back into the car and drove to another body of water, Lake Wausau, two hundred and sixty miles to the north, where as a teenager she used to go to bonfires with friends. On some level I must have recognized that my mother was no longer kidding around, because from that moment on I'd been keeping a close watch, determined to stop the fissures in our family from growing any wider.

After my father had finished installing the flagpole, Bailey said he and Cleo had better be on their way. "I've got my own old lady to worry about. Good luck with yours." He winked. "We've got a party at the club tonight. I'd invite you, but it's members only. Maybe Ann and I will have you over to the house one of these days."

"We'd like that," my father said.

I told Cleo that it was nice to meet her. She held out her hands, an invitation to catch a pass, and I threw her the red, white and blue ball. As she walked down to the sidewalk she bounced it once on each step then swung around and threw me a perfect chest pass.

"We should play sometime," she said.

"Sure."

"What playground do you go to?" she asked.

"Pierce Park," I said, and since I couldn't help myself, added, "I believe it's named for Franklin Pierce, our ineffectual fourteenth president." I left it at that, though I could have said that his campaign slogan was "We Polked you in 1844, we shall Pierce you in 1852," or that he was a terrible drunk who, while in office, was arrested for running over an old woman with his horse and carriage. "Maybe I'll see you there," I said, playing it cool.

But as Cleo waved and the Cadillac drove away, the mini-flag on its antenna rippling, I realized that I wanted nothing more than to shoot baskets with the daughter of our treacherous landlord.

I wouldn't always enjoy the Fourth of July, and before long I'd have good reason to hate anything that pops, including cap guns,

M-80s, balloons, champagne bottles, snaps—and especially fireworks. But the papers were promising a spectacular display that evening, and I hoped to be on the Mall downtown to watch it with my own eyes. By midafternoon, however, my mother still hadn't returned from Livid Lane, and we all started to worry.

I remember my father calling a cab and our inching through bicentennial traffic, looking up at the kites—red, white and blue jewels in the sky above the Washington Monument. We'd never seen so many people in one place before, tens of thousands bordering the Reflecting Pool, sitting on the steps of the Lincoln Memorial, wandering the kiosks and bandstands, or just basking in the bright sunshine. We passed a parade of Uncle Sams walking on stilts along Constitution Avenue and the Freedom Train on its final stop in front of the Smithsonian. In the distance I thought I saw the masts of the tall ships moored along the Potomac, and in the Tidal Basin, the boat—cannon angled skyward—that would launch the national fireworks over the city.

Convinced that our mother would be somewhere by the river, we had the cabbie drop us off at the Southwest Waterfront. We wandered along the wharf to where some rundown houseboats were docked, and found a salty septuagenarian couple in deck chairs reading raised-letter pulp. Their wrinkles bunched together at the eyes in the same fan pattern, as if they'd been gazing at each other since the Great Depression, and I wondered if my own parents would stay together that long. I sensed they were at the beginning of the one true test of their marriage, without a guidebook, a thousand miles from home, and I wanted to believe that if they survived this trial they could make it through anything.

We described my mother and asked the couple if they had seen her. The wife lowered her book—*Nurse Harriet Goes to Holland*—and shook her head no. We continued down the docks, amidst the broken bottles, clamshells and fish parts, the air redolent of offal, stale beer and gasoline. Molly stopped at a bench with a hole in the middle slat, sat down on the edge and refused to go farther. "This is dumb," she said. "Why can't we be like other families, having friends over for a barbecue?" My father reached for Molly's hand, and after a moment, during which her eyes never left the ground, she allowed him to pull her up from the bench.

We arrived home late in the afternoon to find my mother on the front steps, reading over a lease. While Molly and I had been sharing popsicles with Cleo, our mother had demanded that Bailey draw up a formal agreement, so he grabbed a blank lease from his car and wrote in his terms: three and a half months for free, then, beginning October 1, a one-year renewable term thereafter, at four hundred dollars per month. I'm glad I wasn't there when my mother and Bailey simultaneously discovered that my father had been lying.

"I want to talk to both of you." She gestured at Molly and me. Our father threw up his hands and went inside the house.

"Have a seat," my mother said. I slumped with my back against the porch column and Molly sat on the step below me. She picked up a twig and drew invisible pictures on the flaking wood steps.

"How long have you known that we weren't getting this house for free?" my mother asked me.

I was wearing my headband, which felt like a vise. I pulled it off and my hair fell into my eyes. "This house?"

"Yes, this house. Tell me the truth, Daniel."

My mother had an uncanny ability to see right through to my motives. At the time I wondered if she had ESP, because I couldn't keep a secret from her without it flashing over my face like an electric news ticker. She knew me far better than I'd realized. We had both spent years protecting my father, and now that she was giving thought to bowing out, I had to work twice as hard to compensate.

I admitted that I'd known about the deal with Bailey since before we'd left Lake Bluff, but said Molly had nothing to do with this. "When the students sign up, we'll have plenty of money to pay the rent. We're getting a good discount."

"That's not the point. Your father lied to me, and so did you." She stood over Molly and me, the fading sun in her eyes. Her pupils contracted into tiny ellipses.

Molly broke her stick as she was drawing and asked, "What are we going to do?" She dropped her shoulders and looked up, like a street urchin from *Oliver Twist,* the movie we'd seen at the American Film Institute.

"I'll tell you what we're *not* going to do. We're *not* going to go to the fireworks tonight."

I started to protest but my mother interrupted. "You'll have other Fourths of July," she said.

"But not in 1976!" I threw down my headband.

"You know better than to lie to me, Daniel."

"I didn't lie."

Strands of hair blew across my mother's face. "Yes, you did." She tucked her hair behind her ears. "Secrets and lies are two sides of the same coin. Only, one is hidden and the other is face up."

My mother leaned down and kissed the top of my sister's head. "It's not your fault, Molly. Your father and brother did this." She headed toward the front door then stopped and turned around. "And another thing you both should know: as soon as I walk in the house I'm going to pick up the phone and call your Uncle Linc and invite him to come live with us. Either Linc moves to Washington or I'm not going to sign this lease. Forget the school. I'll throw our stuff in the van tomorrow morning and take you kids to Wisconsin. And if your father doesn't like it, well, he can stay here all alone with his dreams and his secrets and lies and his so-called generous friends." My mother reached into her purse and tried to shake some orange Tic Tacs into her hand, but the candies had glommed together in the heat. She tossed the box back into her purse and marched inside.

That night, Molly yelled at me for denying her the world's greatest Fourth of July. I knew she didn't care about the bicentennial; she just hated to be left out, expunged from the guest list of the nationwide party. She also knew that by throwing a tantrum loud enough for our mother and father to hear, she might win an unseen voucher for some future reward.

After Molly had harrumphed offstage, I listened at the top of the stairs to our parents arguing in their bedroom. They used to shut the door, but over the years they'd grown careless and now no longer bothered. My mother had already spoken to Linc, and it sounded as if he didn't need much convincing. He would head to D.C. as soon as he could hitch a ride or sneak onto a bus or whatever you did to get clear across the country without a dime to your name. My father called Linc a quitter, and I knew exactly what my mother would say even before she responded: *You're one to talk.*

I didn't understand then why my father couldn't keep a job, but if you looked back over the course of his life, you'd see where his trouble began. His own father couldn't step out of the role of brewery foreman, drinking too much at home and parenting by the proverb *Spare the rod, spoil the child.* It didn't matter that the *La Crosse Tribune* called my father the town's next big leaguer or that he was the first in his family to go to college, on a full ride. My mother knew this and on some level must have grasped why my father's first instinct, at even mild criticism, was to flee. Throughout our wayfaring, my mother endured his failures and sacrificed her own prospects, determined to be the one person who would support him through and through.

But the tables were turning; I could hear it with my own ears:

Linc will ruin the school, my father predicted.

Welcome him with open arms or I'm leaving, my mother shot back.

Spare me your threats.

These are my terms, she said, and repeated this phrase until the sun fell, and in its place the Fourth of July fireworks shot into the sky.

In my red, white and blue room, I tried to forget my parents' quarrel. I took the tasseled flag off the wall and hung it outside my window. I turned off the lights and kneeled down so I could see through the scrim of trees. To the south and east the aerial shells screamed high over the Washington Monument, exploding in wide streamers to the ground. I clapped with each new flash and pop, each bloom and flourish of fireworks, and told myself that I didn't need to be among the masses on the Mall for the bicentennial spectacle because here I was up in the tower, watching a thousand stars rain over my own little kingdom.

4

I REMEMBER THE EXACT DAY that Linc and Cinnamon arrived—July 13—because the night before, my family had gathered around the television to watch Texas Democrat Barbara Jordan become the first black woman to deliver a keynote address at a major party convention. "My presence here is one additional bit of evidence that the American Dream need not forever be deferred." I know this quote by heart; her ringing speech and the whole spirit of the '76 convention still give me chills. This period when we lived in Washington, in a white house not far from the real White House, will always live in my memory as the pivotal moment for my family, but it also marked my dawning awareness that our lives were converging with something larger than ourselves, a whole country at a crossroads.

I remember where we all were sitting, too. My mother had given up on any furniture materializing so she'd bought a dusty brocade sofa and a couple of faded-to-pink butterfly chairs at an estate sale so we could have somewhere to sit and watch the speeches. She was anxious that we hadn't recruited a single student for our school, but my father promised that as soon as the convention was over he was going to hit the pavement like a salesman on a tight commission. The hope that a Democrat might win back the presidency had stirred some good feeling in our household, and we were tuned to the *NBC Nightly News* with John Chancellor and

David Brinkley, looking forward to a couple nights from now when Jimmy Carter would officially accept the nomination.

We had finished our dinner of sautéed mushrooms on toast—it was a rare treat for Molly and me to eat in front of the television—when a roving reporter stopped in the hive of the Wisconsin delegation and, to my mother's surprise, interviewed an old college friend of hers, Linda Silvers, whom she hadn't seen since my parents' wedding. Linda and my mother used to picket for labor and hand out campaign flyers at county fairs and farmers' markets around Madison, but had lost touch during our many moves. According to the caption on the screen, Linda was now chief of staff for Wisconsin Senator Gaylord Nelson.

"I knew she'd do something with her life, but chief of staff?" My mother's enthusiasm carried what seemed like a tinge of regret. "She's not even forty."

"She sure looks it, though," my father said. "Too many late nights on coffee and cancer sticks."

"That's not my point."

"Maybe you should look her up, Val. I bet she has a bunch of D.C. contacts, and could help us."

"Maybe." My mother stood up and cleared the plates, the television casting her in a platinum glow, then left to clean up the kitchen. The rest of us were watching a profile of Amy Carter, who was Molly's age and devoted to the family housecat, Misty Malarky Ying-Yang, when three taps of a car horn sounded from the street in front of the house.

Linc had made one brief call from the road a day or so before, so we'd been expecting him and Cinnamon at any time. But he had run out of coins before my mother could ask when they'd arrive or how they were traveling. Hearing the car horn, I wondered if they really had managed to hitchhike all the way from Mazama, Washington, to Washington, D.C. But when we all gathered on the porch to greet them, Linc unfolded himself from the back seat, and Cinnamon got out on the passenger's side, of the strangest-looking VW Bug I had ever seen. It was plastered with Salem cigarette ads. White, sea green and gold, with the words SALEM, MENTHOL FRESH, SMOOTH, REFRESHING, FILTERED CIGARETTES splashed on the doors and curving along the roof and hood.

And instead of some friendly stranger dropping off our aunt and uncle and waving goodbye, to our surprise the driver's side door opened and out stepped a third member of the Freelandia commune, my father's least favorite of all: Uncle Linc's best friend, Tino Candelaria.

My mother, Molly and I gave Linc hugs. He wore an *All-Temperature Cheer* T-shirt and was sweaty and ripe from a week in a Bug without air conditioning. My father slapped him on the back hard enough to make him cough. "I didn't know there'd be three of you," he said, barely acknowledging Tino. "Just you and Cinnamon are staying, right?"

Linc's beard had grown down to his chest, and he'd gone balder since I'd seen him last, two years ago. He had a patch of black hair like an Oreo cookie at the top of his forehead; behind it stretched a cap of sallow skin. And he'd lost weight. He used to look like Sancho Panza: short, potbellied, the happy gnome, with a malleable face that made me smile. But now he seemed diminished, as if dried in a toxic sun.

"No, it's going to be three of us," Linc muttered. "Hope you don't mind."

My father started to object, but my mother's voice rode over his. "So where did you find this car?"

"I didn't tell you about that?" The question seemed to jolt Linc to life. "Some Seattle adman gave it to me for free." He fished a pack of Camels from his shirt pocket, offered a cigarette to my parents, who both refused, then lit up. "I don't even like Salems, but I agreed to drive the car around Seattle and park it at ball games and conventions and down by Pike Place Market, all the touristy places."

"They gave him a green outfit with Salem across the front," Cinnamon said. "And a trunkful of free smokes."

"Those menthols will kill you." Linc inhaled deeply. "Eventually I blew out of Seattle and took the VW to the commune. It's a junker, but we got here all right."

"So basically you stole the car," my father said.

"The adman was shady, a real slick talker. He told me to cruise the Washington hot spots, and that's what I'm doing." Linc adjusted his black-rimmed glasses. "Washington State. Washington, D.C. Same deal."

Cinnamon cut in, "So this is your crib?" Unlike Linc, she seemed ageless. A band of freckles dappled her cheeks and shoulders, and she had long straight hair the color of her name.

My father's light-adjusting glasses had turned an ocher hue in the dusk-lit early evening, but I could tell from the way he stood, his arms at a right angle, his chin resting on his fist, that he was feeling put out. "Bet this beats a shack in the woods," he said.

Tino had been uncharacteristically quiet. But now he tightened his ponytail, wiped his hands on his peasant shirt—white, stained gray around the collar—and gave my father a soul handshake. "So what's the scam?" he asked.

"No scam," my father said defensively, his forearms tensing.

"It's just lingo," Cinnamon explained. "Hippie talk for 'What's up?'"

"Thanks for the translation," Tino said. "But I know you're working some kind of magic here, Pete. Who died and gave *you* a castle?"

My mother told the hippies about Bailey Dornan and the special lease they'd signed. She admitted that we'd gotten a good deal. "But we need to get students under the roof ASAP if we have any hope of making it." She didn't go into her reservations about Bailey except to say, "Our landlord is a pill. You're not going to like him. But at least he hasn't been coming around too much." Nor did she mention the money from Aunt Natalia, which I'm sure my father appreciated, since he didn't want the hippies rifling through his drawers.

Tino and Cinnamon hauled sleeping bags and foam pads, burlap sacks and milk crates full of tapestries, records and paperbacks up to the front hallway. Linc pulled out a guitar case bedizened with advertising stickers—*You Deserve a Break Today; Nothing Sucks Like an Electrolux; First to Sears, Then to School*—and showed us his beat-up guitar, which someone passing through the commune had abandoned. Molly strummed it and I did a few bars of "Smoke on the Water," the one song I'd learned in the Lake Bluff dorms, and Linc said he was a beginner, too. This drew an eye-roll from my father, who was no doubt dreading the discordant fits and starts of a novice guitarist under our roof.

We helped the hippies sweep out the car, which was littered with empty Shasta cans, cigarette butts, plastic thermoses with faded gas station logos and Burger King and Jack in the Box bags. I knew that my uncle and his friends had been living off the land for the past few years, so I was surprised by how much fast food they'd put away on the trip.

"You probably shouldn't park there," my father said to Linc.

Tino laughed when he saw the painted fire hydrant next to the car. "Who's that supposed to be?"

I piped up, "Benjamin Franklin. They did it for the bicentennial."

"Ben Franklin, huh? Aren't you a sight for a full-bladdered dog." Tino gave the fire hydrant a kick with his huaraches. "Go fly a kite, bro."

My father was not amused. "I got a twenty-dollar ticket for parking there."

"And you paid it?"

"I didn't want to get towed."

"You gave your money to Jerry Ford?"

"D.C. government, actually," my father said, visibly annoyed that this reedy guy, with the rolling Mick Jagger walk and Zapata mustache, had come to live with us. Tino liked to flirt with women, my mother included, and my father had a territorial nature.

Linc dug his own set of keys from his pocket. "I'll move the car," he said, turning sullen again. He slumped into the front seat of the Bug and reparked.

My mother and Molly were talking to Cinnamon about the cross-country trip. I half listened, but mostly gawped at this woman in the floral-print babydoll dress. When I was eight, she made me ring bearer at her and Linc's wedding and whispered in my ear, "Just bring *me* the ring, and you and I can run off together." She was the first woman ever to enter my dreams.

Smoothing her feather earrings with her fingers, she talked about the attrition at the commune in the past several years. "Hot Plate Peterson crapped out and joined the System in Portland. He used to work bareass in the orchard, but last I heard he's wearing a suit. Cheeba Viti found an heiress girlfriend, who bought him a plane ticket and set him up in Taos. Rudy Wentzel moved to town and now sorts mail at the Mazama P.O. After the drought last year a whole caravan blew the scene and headed to Yellow Springs, because 'at least there they know how to fucking farm.' And then we had that bummer with Maryjane. You remember Maryjane?" Cinnamon asked.

I'd never heard of a Maryjane, and though my mother nodded, she didn't look as if she had either.

"Tino's ex? The cheerleader? She couldn't get her hands dirty. She laid a serious trip on us when Tino and I got together. She went crazy, like Anita Bryant. What did she call us, honey?" she asked Tino.

"Libertines."

"Libertine, Ovaltine. She took a scissors to every last piece of clothing we owned and went running back to her mom in Tallahassee. How do you like that?"

My mother didn't like it, and neither did I. Molly, picking up on the scandal, looked as if someone had sped by and ripped a lollipop from her mouth.

Tino was counting the money in his wallet. He seemed to have a large wad of bills, but by the way he shook his head, they must all have been ones.

Cinnamon grabbed the side of his belt. "Maryjane's loss," she said.

My mother turned to Linc in dismay. "You didn't tell me about this."

Linc scratched the Oreo cookie on his head, which stuck out over his forehead like a phylactery. "You never asked."

My father had an I-told-you-so look on his face as he watched the numbers play out before his eyes: not two but three unwelcome guests. And if that weren't enough, a triangle: my uncle, his best friend, and his best friend's new girlfriend, who only recently had been my uncle's wife.

"It's cool." Linc shrugged. But I wasn't convinced.

"So you're separated? Divorced?" my mother asked.

Cinnamon acted as if it were no big deal. "We're still married, but marriage isn't a contract," she said. "We still love each other, but it's not like we have to wear straitjackets."

I didn't know what to make of this. As much as I wanted to see Cinnamon as an earth goddess, an ever-replenishing gift to the world that no one man could keep, I couldn't help feeling that she and Tino had betrayed my uncle.

"It's not my business. As long as you're all okay with it." My mother waved the matter away, though apprehension lingered in her eyes. "We're just glad you're here."

"Us too." Cinnamon stretched and her dress rose to the very tops of her thighs. "You kids have grown since I last saw you." She hugged Molly and me at the same time. She smelled sweet, like honey and patchouli oil with a hint of nicotine. "You're pretty as springtime, Molly. And look at you, Daniel. I love your hair."

Tino pulled the last box from the trunk. "Look what I brought, kids." He lowered the box so Molly and I could see it. There must have been fifty fireworks in there. "How do you like this stash? They were practically giving it away—post–Fourth of July sale—at a roadside stand near Intercourse, PA. Intercourse is *the* place for fireworks, kids." He smiled at my mother, who looked away.

Tino pointed out each one as if he were working the counter of a candy shop: "This is a pinwheel. That's a cherry bomb. Here's the fizgig, the whiz-bang, the snake, the squib, the flowerpot. We've got sparklers for the ladies." He handed a box of these to Molly. "And Roman candles for the gents . . ."

I was about to take the Roman candles when my mother intercepted them. She grabbed the sparklers from Molly and returned the fireworks to the box. "Thanks, but no thanks," she said. "The Fourth of July is over, and I don't think this is a good idea."

Tino pointed to the '76 flag hanging in front of our house. "What's the prob, Val? A nice patriotic family like yours, how can you not want some discount pyrotechnics?"

"They're dangerous, for starters. And that's our landlord's flag, not ours."

"Let's ask one of the Founding Fathers what he thinks about all this. So, what do you say, Ben?" Tino leaned his ear in the direction of the fire hydrant. "Ben says light 'em up!"

With visions of me and Cleo watching the fireworks from the windows of my room, I pleaded with my mother, "You didn't let us go to the Mall on the Fourth."

"And you know perfectly well why," she said.

But my father, Cinnamon, Linc and even Molly, who'd been on the verge of righteous indignation, ten-year-old style, over the suggestion of adultery, weighed in on Tino's side. Realizing that she was outvoted, and also that she was asking a lot of my father to put up with these recent arrivals, my mother said, "I'll tell you what I'm willing to do. If Jimmy Carter beats Gerald Ford in November, we'll throw a party here at the school and you can have your fireworks."

That night I lay under the turret's pointy nipple while Tino and Cinnamon moaned and thumped against the wall. On the commune Tino had built an elaborate tree house, so he and whoever shared his bed were used to sleeping close to the stars. He didn't bother to grab his stuff from the hallway. Instead he hauled his sleeping bag straight to the top floor and, seeing that I had taken the turret room, tried to talk me into handing it over to him. I'd never been good at defending my turf, but luckily my mother had come upstairs, too—and she wasn't about to give ground again.

On his way out of the room Tino flicked the fringes of my American flag. "You a Nixon fan, Danny? You sure have a lot of red, white and blue in here. Maybe you should wear Tricky Dicky's favorite pin: AMERICA, LOVE IT OR LEAVE IT." Tino was annoyed not to have his room of choice. He seemed the type who got what he wanted. "You've raised quite the little nationalist, Val." He laughed then dragged his sleeping bag and pad to the other top-floor room, right next door to mine.

Lying awake to the moans and love sounds of Cinnamon, I decided my life could be a lot worse. I'd have to see more of Tino than I'd bargained for, but I could get used to drifting off this way. Out of the darkness Cinnamon took shape, as if materializing from a nearby planet onto my starship. She hovered in zero gravity, a weightless blanket over my chest. I twisted in the sheets, nuzzled my pillow until the hologram beside me shifted and rearranged itself: feathered hair framed her face; a braided bracelet clung to her wrist as she reached out to touch my cheek. But soon the noises in the next room turned to talk then silence, the face beside me disappeared, and I was alone again.

All around me I heard a faint clicking in the walls and a rustling sound that seemed to rise slowly from the house's foundation. I'd only been trying to spook my sister when I'd said that an old lady had died on the upper floors, but on cloudy nights like this one, when no moon or starlight brightened my room and after the whole house had gone to sleep, I almost believed that the place was haunted, that a former owner was out to chase us away. Or perhaps Aunt Natalia had spirit-traveled from her mausoleum in Detroit. I remembered reading about a clerk in the White House who saw the ghost of Abraham Lincoln sitting on a bed and pulling off his boots. Eleanor Roosevelt, who used the Lincoln Bedroom as a study, said that she often sensed that a strange presence watched her while she worked. And several White House staffers over the years had felt a cold rush of air and seen chandeliers flicker and doors snap shut inexplicably, certain that Lincoln's restless spirit drifted about them.

That night I tossed and turned, repeating "It's just an old house" over and over until I fell asleep.

At breakfast the morning after the Democratic Convention ended, I hatched a plan to get back at Tino. As though his theft of my uncle's wife weren't enough, he'd also spoiled Jimmy Carter's acceptance speech by imitating his soft, folksy accent and calling him a slave-state Jesus freak. Molly and I were eating Cheerios on the window seat of the living room when I saw that Tino and Cinnamon had still not moved their records, paperbacks and bags of clothes out of the front hallway. I looked around at our mostly empty house and thought of the word "naked," picturing the couple asleep under the covers right now, yesterday's clothes tossed on the floor.

I recalled the familiar nightmare of showing up at school without a stitch on. "Wouldn't it be nice," I said to Molly, "to embarrass Tino in front of everyone?" My sister had a daredevil streak that came out only at transitional times, so I figured I'd try to exploit it. I told her to sneak into the third-floor room next to mine and steal the couple's clothes—"just like Tino stole Cinnamon from Uncle Linc," I said, appealing to her sense of measure for measure.

And with only the slightest hesitation—"Go on," I urged her; "think of Linc"—Molly put down her Cheerios and rushed up the steps. The little o's in her cereal bowl looked like a chorus of schoolkids crying "ooooooo" after a dare. A minute later she returned, giggling, and dropped a paisley bandanna, hip-hugger jeans, a peasant shirt, a floral dress and underwear at my feet.

"Did they see you?" I asked.

She was laughing so hard her cheeks were red as a child's wagon. "Tino yelled, 'Come back, you little Sprite,'" she said. "Who calls someone a can of pop?"

"That guy's weird." I picked up Cinnamon's dress; its threadbare softness tickled my arms. "Quick. Let's hide the rest." We grabbed their remaining clothes, and were stuffing them into the kitchen cupboards when my mother came in from the back yard.

"What are you devils doing?"

"Nothing. Just putting away the cereal." I closed the cupboard door and thought of ways to distract her from checking. I had seen a copy of *Steal This Book* at the top of the pile of Cinnamon's and Tino's stuff, so I fetched it to show to my mother. "Remember we were talking about this book?" I said. "The one that ripped off Linc's idea?"

My mother took the paperback from me and leafed through it, reading the table of contents out loud: "Free Food, Free Clothing and Furniture, Free Transportation, Free Land, Free Housing, Free Medical Care, Free Communication, Free Play." She turned to a chapter called Free Education. "This one starts out fine. He's talking about auditing classes. I see nothing wrong with sitting in the back of a huge auditorium and listening to a lecture. Even if you're not paying for it, that doesn't hurt anyone." My mother flipped the pages. "But then listen: 'The only reason you should be in college is to destroy it.' That's vintage Abbie Hoffman. He makes sense for a second and then says something crazy." She showed me a page titled People's Chemistry, then read the subheadings: "Stink Bomb, Smoke Bomb, Molotov Cocktail, Sterno Bomb, Aerosol Bomb, Pipe Bomb. See what he's calling for? Out-and-out revolution."

I wondered if the communards had ever been revolutionaries or if they'd bring chaos to the school. Now that they lived at the seat of government, they could plan something radical and drag our students into it. I imagined Cinnamon dressed up like Patty Hearst, in a slick beret, her top buttons undone, an heiress to billions storming a bank with an assault rifle on her hip. Sexy, I had to admit.

But my mother took the look on my face as concern. "Don't worry about these guys, if that's what you mean. They're hippies. They're into peace and love and Janis Joplin. The yippies, Black

Panthers and Weathermen—they were a different story. They were guerrillas."

Molly laughed at the word "gorillas," and I seized the opportunity to ask for the book back. "I don't want this around my house," my mother said, slipping the paperback into her Naugahyde purse.

Molly was standing in the doorway closest to the living room, a look of excitement on her face. "Someone's coming down the stairs," she squealed, and ran out the back door.

"What's wrong with your sister?" my mother asked.

"I don't know," I said.

But it was only Linc, in cutoff jeans and a *Jersey Maid Yogurt* T-shirt. Somehow he managed to get all kinds of free stuff by writing companies and saying, "I love your product." *I would be honored if you'd send me any promotional items so I can tell all my friends about . . . the stunning brightness of All-Temperature Cheer . . . the healing power of Curads . . . the incredible suction system of Electrolux vacuum cleaners . . . the delicious taste of Jersey Maid!* Tino liked to tease him and call him a sellout, but I thought the idea was ingenious.

"How'd you sleep?" My mother poured my uncle a cup of black coffee.

"I might need a different room." He nodded dolefully toward the ceiling. "I'm right under the lovebirds."

"Oh, dear," my mother said and turned to me. "Why don't you go give your father a hand, Daniel. He's cutting back the ivy."

For the next several hours I helped weed, rake and bag our jungle of a front yard. I couldn't believe how fast the greenery grew in this city. I knew that George Washington had chosen D.C. for its strategic location along the Potomac and at the intersection of north and south, and I could feel what the city must have been like then, a hardship post built on swampland. By lunchtime Molly had gone back inside to help Linc and my mother clean the downstairs, while my father and I went out to Roy Rogers to pick up boxes of fried chicken.

We were all sitting in the den, paper napkins spread in our laps, when Tino and Cinnamon appeared. They stood hand in hand at the threshold between the den and front hall, framed like a painting of the Fall of Man, only minus the fig leaves and the looks of disgrace.

Molly screamed and covered her eyes. My mother fumbled a biscuit and nearly dropped it. My father stood up, as if to offer this Adam and Eve a refuge. Linc sedately finished his drumstick and wiped his beard with the back of his hand.

"Afternoon." Tino waved. His private business looked like a Groucho Marx mask flipped upside down. "What's for lunch?"

"How about some clothes?" My father checked behind him to see if Molly and I were watching. Molly had turned her chair around, her eyes on the floor. I looked down too, but under the V of my brow I glimpsed Cinnamon, pale and hipless, her hands half concealing the russet triangle of her crotch, her small nipples peeking through her curtain of hair. Before I lowered my head completely I could have sworn she smiled at me.

"We usually come to supper in proper attire," Tino said. "But a certain wood nymph visited our room this morning and made off with our clothes."

"And why would someone do that?" my father asked.

"Perhaps you should query your children. It's youth that keep company with sprites and fairies."

"Daniel?" my father said.

I had no skill for pranks, and couldn't remember a single instance when I'd gotten away with something. I knew that Tino and Cinnamon could have come downstairs wrapped in their bed sheet or shielded with pillows; they could have grabbed towels from the second-floor bathroom, or at least made some effort to cover themselves. But since Tino, especially, had no shame, he could stand before us all, bare as the day he was born, and in so doing claim his victory. Molly and I had not avenged Uncle Linc; we'd only worsened his despair by arranging this portrait of infidelity. Tino didn't have to say "Enough is enough"—he had already won—so without a word of explanation I ran to the kitchen, opened the cupboards and brought back the box of clothes.

But when I returned, Tino had gone out to the front porch for all our neighbors to see.

"Get back in here," my father demanded.

"Take it easy, bro." Tino flashed a peace sign. "I was going to make a bathrobe out of that American flag. But no can do."

I threw him his clothes, and he took his sweet time climbing into his underwear and hip-huggers.

Across 16th a young black woman stood on her porch looking in our direction. But she was too far away to catch an eyeful. She yelled at someone inside her house, and a moment later yanked open her screen door and disappeared.

Cinnamon slipped her babydoll dress over her head and came out to join us. "Looks like someone took your flag," she said to my father.

The flag and flagpole were missing. Only the bracket remained.

My father turned to me, his face flushing. "Is this another one of your pranks, Daniel?"

I looked to my mother, Molly and Linc, gathered at the door, a troika of expressions: anger, disapproval, resignation.

"I'm innocent," I said, but I knew no one believed me.

5

By JULY 20 WE STILL had no students, no income, only a rough sketch of what our school would look like; and we were sluggish from the heat, exhausted from the task of putting our enormous house in order. My mother counted the days on her Illinois Bank & Trust calendar, which she taped to a wall beside the fridge, and announced that only fifty-five remained before our targeted first day of classes. "I hope you realize that's less than two months away," she said, prompting my father to call our first official meeting in the living room.

Linc had discovered a construction site around the corner and had gone there late at night to grab an empty telephone cable spool, which he rolled back home and converted into a table. We sat on the hard floor in a semicircle in front of the cable spool, and my father pulled up a chair behind it, the ostensible headmaster, though no such term of authority would be used at our still unnamed school.

My father had said little about his specific plans, and I can see now that he must have been avoiding the subject, which my mother had been trying to discuss with him ever since we'd arrived. He'd never started something from the ground up any larger than a lemonade stand, and he must have been fighting the voice in his head, of his own father telling him, *You're not good enough* and *Who do you think you are?* But with time running down he could no longer delay.

I knew he planned to apply some of the free-school model of A. S. Neill, the founder of Summerhill and the subject of my father's master's thesis. Students would not be divided by age, and the school would be run as a democracy, with kids and teachers on the same plane. Like Summerhill, a key component would be the council meeting, where rules were established or broken, complaints aired, and plans made. Council meetings could be convened at any time, by anyone, for any reason. My father explained all this to the hippies, and they thought it was a cool idea.

"Sounds like a commune for kids," Cinnamon put in.

"More like a mini-government, right here in the house," my father said, and quickly added that he didn't buy into all of Neill's philosophy, particularly concerning curriculum. Summerhill had none to speak of; in fact, students were not required to attend class. My father had spent too long in traditional schools to allow that much freedom. "I'm all for democracy, but we have to have *some* structure."

Tino sniffed at this, but just as he raised his voice to object, Molly spotted an earwig scrambling across the floor. She screamed and shot to her feet.

"They're not going to hurt you." Cinnamon let the bug walk up her finger before taking it outside and tossing it into the garden bed.

"I hate this place." Molly refused to sit down again and instead leaned against the living room wall, pouting and keeping a lookout for the bugs that had only multiplied the farther we'd marched into summer. "I don't want to go to this school." She dusted off her skirt and checked the pockets of her kangaroo socks to be sure the quarters she stashed in each one hadn't fallen out.

It was clear that Molly wanted everyone to know just how short of her expectations this so-called mansion had fallen. Where was the central air, the bright wall-to-wall carpet, the private bath with monogrammed towels and faucets so polished she could see her reflection? My sister could be persnickety, but I'd come to understand how the bugs and strangers that were always letting themselves in made her feel as if she lived in a house without boundaries, in a room too large and transitional-seeming to call her own. She needed furniture and pretty things in order to anchor herself in a place. In this way she and I had the same desire: once and for all, for our family to settle down.

My mother was stirring a glob of honey into her Red Rose tea. "So let's talk about the structure. We need a humanities program and an arts program, and since we're giving the students freedom of choice, the courses have to be broad."

Everyone brainstormed while Molly and I took notes. Tino paid no attention to what my mother had said as he came up with his own course ideas—the History of Rock-and-Roll, Coyote in Native American Myth, *On the Road* in Novel and Film, Utopia Through the Ages—each so specific that my mother, father and Linc voted them down one by one.

"All right." Tino tried again. "I say we dedicate a class to Mao, the greatest world leader of the century. He broke the imperialist stranglehold and rallied the people. He took an ass-backwards country and drove it into the modern age. From Beijing to the countryside they're parroting Mao's example: '*Wei ren min fu wu*'—'Everything you do, do for others; do it for the people.' If that's not a lesson, I don't know what is."

My mother put down her cup so hard the brimming tea sloshed on the floor. She rubbed the spill into the worn hardwood floor and dried her hand on her patchwork skirt. "Mao puts a lot of people off." She spoke with an effort to keep an even keel. "I don't think his name is going to win us recruits."

"Oh, come on. Who are we recruiting? John Birchers? The Daughters of the American Confederacy? Loosen up, Val. Kids want hip courses. You talk about making this school like family. That's Mao's whole objective. The world is one family."

"Sure, if you're into fratricide," my mother said. "How many tens of millions died in the Great Leap Forward's forced labor programs or the purges of the Cultural Revolution? Mao's a megalomaniac who rules like every other dictator, with brutal force. And don't tell me he's a man of the people. During the Long March he didn't march, didn't even ride a horse. He was carried on a litter."

"Okay, okay," my father interrupted. "No need to get political."

"Starting a school *is* political." My mother's eyes flickered, as if animated by the thought. "You said it yourself: we're making our own little government. So, what's government without politics?"

"Fine, but arguing won't get us anywhere." My father gripped either side of the cable spool like a driver steering an unwieldy truck. "A course on Mao is too narrow. I thought we'd been over that. But if you insist, we could take another vote."

"You've already torpedoed all my ideas." Tino glared at Linc, who, as the fifth faculty member at this charter-defining meeting, held the deciding ballot. "Looks like three-to-two every time, with me and Cinn on the losing end. That's bullshit and you know it."

I tried not to catch Molly's eye, because I knew that if she saw me smile she'd crack up. Finally, justice for Uncle Linc!

"I vote as I see it." Linc reclined on his side, leaning on his elbow. When my mother called "All in favor?" he didn't raise his hand.

Cinnamon shook her head, the beads in her braided hair clinking together like tiny china cups. "You're not voting with your heart."

Linc paused for a moment then fixed his wife with a meaningful look. "Sure I am."

So my parents got their way. The students would take a broad, open curriculum in the humanities and arts, the classes would be run not by "teachers" but by "tutor-collaborators," and our motto would be drawn straight from the free-school handbook: "Act first. Ask permission later."

Almost twenty-five years after that meeting, I still have the brochure that Cinnamon designed. It hangs in a rustic frame by my writing desk, near a collection of Jimmy Carter's campaign buttons.

On the second page, under the words "Humanities Program," the brochure reads:

GOVERNMENT: Man & His Institutions, Peter Truitt, M.Ed., Indiana University

RELIGION: Thought & Belief Around the World, Lincoln Gearhart, M.A., University of Arizona

ART: Everywhere a Canvas, Cynthia Vandermeer, B.A., Beloit College

NATURE: Earth, Man & Animals, T. Candelaria, B.A., Florida State University

LITERATURE: Beyond the Page, Valerie Truitt, M.Ed., Indiana University

"'Earth, Man and Animals'? What the fuck?" Tino said.

"We just need a name for the course. You pretty much do whatever the kids want." My father gestured for me to hand him the notepad so he could look over the list of classes.

Cinnamon was annoyed that my parents wanted her to use the name Cynthia on the brochure, but my father talked her down. "Washington's not like Seattle and San Francisco. They say it's an old-fashioned Southern town. We've got to trick people into thinking we're a bunch of squares."

"Good luck with that," Cinnamon said.

My mother was more worried about the phony credentials. After all, she had not gotten around to writing a thesis, so hadn't finished her M.Ed. My parents never discussed the subject, and I had no idea at the time that my mother had gone into education ambivalently. Later I'd learn that she'd wanted to get a Ph.D. in political science but my father had persuaded her to go into his own field. I still don't know why he was so insistent that they both pursue teaching degrees. He hoped one day to open a school and perhaps he only wanted her to be his partner in this. Then again, maybe he worried about what might happen if his wife's career overshadowed his own. Could he accept a supporting role? Would she exhaust her sympathies and leave?

My mother didn't put up much of a fight because she was young, with an infant and another in mind, and she was caught in that borderland between fifties convention and sixties reform and could never commit to one side or the other. So she wavered back and forth, here the voice of rebellion, there of restraint, here of self-reliance, there of codependency, keeping house and teaching part-time, while her eyes threw out sparks of her smoldering ambition.

She was not the only one claiming a degree she hadn't earned. Tino had dropped out of Florida State his sophomore year, and Cinnamon and Linc had left Beloit before graduating. Linc's "M.A." from the University of Arizona in fact amounted to a couple of religion courses that he'd audited while living in the mountains outside Tucson.

"No one's going to check," my father assured my mother.

"All it would take is one nosy parent to bring everything crashing down," she said.

Once again, like Jimmy Carter, my father smiled sincerely and trotted out his old refrain: "Trust me."

It was the July of Hank Aaron's 755th home run, which would turn out to be his last; Elizabeth Taylor's sixth divorce, from Richard Burton, again; Gerald Ford's insurmountable lead over Ronald Reagan for the Republican nomination. By the end of the month my father had made a perfunctory round of phone calls to local schools, all of which told him, *You should talk to so-and-so, but he's gone for the summer.* My mother demanded that my father start showing up in person, and he claimed he was busy applying for tax-exempt status and researching grants and other opportunities. When my mother tapped her watch, he promised, *Okay, first thing tomorrow,* but then tomorrow came and he said *First thing* again.

Through all of this, no one returned the flag. Enough time had passed that I seemed a less likely suspect, so consensus in the household turned to Tino. But he continued to deny the theft. Frankly, none of us would have cared, except my father worried that Bailey would drive by and see the absence of his flag as unpatriotic, and with our rent-free months winding down we needed to stay on his good side. So my father asked if he could fly the tasseled flag from my room on a broken broomstick. "Just for show," he said, and I consented.

When the Bank & Trust calendar showed forty days to go and my mother looked ready to storm down Livid Lane again, my father gathered himself and took me along on a tour of local schools, parking the van out front and telling me to wait while he went inside and spoke to the head honchos. Usually he came out a few minutes later declaring the place a ghost town. He'd take a quarter of an hour, sometimes even a half hour. But I pictured him seeing the closed door of the administrator's office, answering the secretary's *May I help you?* with a polite *Just looking around,* then wandering the halls with his hands behind his back. He'd stop for a cold slurp from the water fountain, glance at the student art on the walls, killing time so when he returned to the van it would appear to me that he was giving it his best shot, and had no doubts, no fears that his dream might be folly.

After three days of visiting schools in D.C., Arlington and Montgomery County, he had met face to face with just two headmasters, and both said, no doubt unconvincingly, *We'll keep you in mind.* I remember our going home that last day and my parents fighting and my mother taking off with Molly for Raging Road, Conniption Court and points in between. While they were gone my father called me into the den for another tête-à-tête. The house was empty, since Tino, Cinnamon and Linc had fanned out across the city to post recruitment flyers. Cinnamon had spent days on the design after we'd already burned precious weeks prepping the house, working the phones, debating names for the school. My father had resisted the hippies' names—"Eternal Harmony" and "Kaleidoscopia"—but could come up with only dry ones of his own, like "The Tower House School." Finally, in frustration, my mother had turned up the Crosby, Stills, Nash & Young record that was playing on the turntable. "Here's the name, calling out all along—"

And so the flyer that went up in grocery stores and community centers, on telephone poles and bulletin boards around the city took a line from the song that even now, when I catch it on a classic-rock station, calls back the whole picture of my family's one great adventure:

OUR HOUSE

IS A VERY VERY VERY FINE HOUSE

ENROLL NOW

IN THE SCHOOL THAT CELEBRATES YOU

My father sat on the brocade sofa and called Chester into his lap. I pulled up a butterfly chair and asked what was wrong.

"It's about the Aunt Natalia money." He plucked a piece of loose fur from the cat, who looked languorously over his shoulder and yawned a halfhearted *Mrrrow.* "You swear not to tell your mother about this?"

I showed him the pinch of Chester's dun fur.

"So I went to Riggs Bank to move our savings from Illinois to here, and I must have had the numbers all wrong." He took off his light-adjusting glasses and rubbed his eyes. "I thought we had three thousand. It's more like eight hundred."

"What happened?"

"Well, there was the U-Haul, the loose ends we had to tie up back at Lake Bluff, the money we give your uncle whenever he puts out his palm. The price of scrapers, rollers, brushes, paint, the tools I had to buy, cleaning supplies, new screens for the windows, new glass for the broken panes, standing fans, the electric bill, all the hidden costs of fixing this place up. Your mother and I don't have jobs, Daniel. Nothing's coming in." He stroked Chester too vigorously. The cat jumped off his lap onto the floor and settled in a patch of sunlight. "And it's not going to get any better. Gas prices are going through the roof, and winter's mere months away. I don't want to think about the heating bill for a place like this. Everything costs more these days, and they keep talking about inflation, how it's only going to get worse. Your mother just *had* to buy this furniture, didn't she?" He picked up a round chenille pillow then dropped it on the sofa.

I had gone with my mother to the garage sale and knew the furniture didn't cost more than fifty dollars, total. And where else were we supposed to sit? I could see how a few hundred dollars could have escaped my father's notice. But more than two thousand?

"Just do me a favor," he said. "You've got to keep this from your mom. Do I have your pledge?"

"Of course."

"And not like last time, Daniel."

"I promise," I said. "So what are we going to do?"

My father thought about this for a minute, and I could sense another *Trust me* coming on, but instead he sat forward on the couch, his eyes locking on mine. "I don't care what it takes. The other day I drove by the Rent-A-Man office on Seventh Street. Hell, I'll do odd jobs, night shifts. I used to work construction all afternoon in the hot sun during high school summers and then played ball at night in the union leagues. We're going to make Our House happen," he said emphatically. He had a way of inspiring confidence that had always made him a great interview. *Getting* jobs had never been his problem.

I felt heartened by my father's resolve—at last I could go to a school of my own—but not long after our conference I was already thinking that I'd heard this speech before. I wondered how we could possibly correct our money woes. Cooling off with an applesauce popsicle, I watched my father in the back yard remove his shirt and bend his pale muscular frame toward the weeds in the garden.

It occurred to me that I had never been alone in the house. I thought about ghosts patrolling the upstairs halls, the flag thief casing our property. When I shook off the jitters I found them replaced by a different sensation, a frisson of opportunity that I couldn't identify. Then I remembered the radical guide my mother had confiscated, Abbie Hoffman's version of *How to Live for Free in America.* As if summoned to carry out some secret mission, I went upstairs to my parents' room to find the book.

The spackle and paint had run out before my father had reached the second floor, so the walls of their bedroom looked jaundiced and patterned with cracks like lightning bolts crashing above their bed. They had stored their box spring and bed frame—little more than flimsy strips of metal on wheels—in the basement, and now slept on a rumpled mattress, with upside-down milk crates serving as side tables. Of all the rooms in the house, my parents' looked the least moved into.

My father had fashioned a bookcase out of pine shelves and cinderblocks, and I checked there first. The books were out of order, many of them still in stacks on the floor: my father's graduate school texts, like *I Learn from Children* by Caroline Pratt; city guides and maps of Cincinnati, Indianapolis and Chicago; *I Never Had It Made* by Jackie Robinson mingled with my mother's poetry collection; poli sci books, biographies of Elizabeth Cady Stanton and Ida B. Wells and, at the top, looking unread, with the famous cover of a zipper opening to a woman's naked torso, *Fear of Flying* by Erica Jong.

I pulled myself away to look out the window for my mother and Molly. The shadows had lengthened over Hill Street, and the van was still gone. I checked the closet, which went deep along the rise of the stairwell, but it was dark and empty, save for my father's clothes and shoes, briefcases and the bag of bats and gloves that he took everywhere we moved, but as far as I knew hadn't opened since 1966.

Claiming the continual press of chores, my mother had not bothered to unpack her wardrobe box. It stood next to the closet, canting to the left, as if it were tired but had no place to lean. It occurred to me that my mother didn't believe we'd be in this house for long, that she wanted to keep the box packed in case she had to make a hasty exit—with or without my father.

I opened her Naugahyde purse, but besides the stray penny, bleeding ballpoint, Tic Tac, M&M and Werther's butterscotch candy wrapper, the purse was empty. I checked her red bamboo purse and the denim one with the rainbow appliqué, plus every dress and coat with pockets, and found only a napkin with an address my mother had looked up of her old college friend Linda Silvers, in a Senate office building on Capitol Hill. When I'd been through all of my mother's clothes, I turned the box upside down.

And onto the floor spilled *Steal This Book.*

So I did.

Up in my tower I read the pages ravenously, stopping only for a moment when I heard a thud on the first floor and called downstairs. But no one answered, and I was too engrossed to wonder much about the sound. Probably my mother and Molly coming back from their drive, or my father grabbing a glass of iced tea before returning to the back yard. After some minutes passed without another noise, I went back to reading.

Abbie Hoffman was a rabble-rouser, as my mother had said, but I thought his book might help us. I didn't need to know where to find free dope or a gas mask for demonstrations. I could have done without Abbie's diagrams showing how to break a cop's knuckles or aim a decisive judo chop at an enemy's Adam's apple; and I wouldn't need "People's Chemistry" either, in which he explains where to buy butyric acid for homemade stink bombs or how to turn a glass bottle filled with gasoline, Styrofoam and a gas-soaked tampon into a first-class Molotov cocktail.

But his advice for day-to-day living was like money falling from the sky. I would come to think of *Steal This Book* as my own "Dear Abbie" column for survival in a city that my family couldn't afford, following a rainbow that desperation had led us to.

Dear Abbie,

We have almost no furniture. How can we start a school when we don't have money for desks or chairs?

Worried in Washington

Dear Worried,

Hit the dumpsters. Landlords are always throwing stuff out when they renovate. You can score tables, chairs, lamps, all kinds of shit to trick out your pad. Call the sanitation department and learn the bulk pickup day for the fancy neighborhoods, then cruise the streets after-hours looking for treasure. Check out the backs of the big department stores for floor models, window displays and the nicked-up crap they're trying to get rid of. Be inventive. Go to construction sites and look for scraps. Doors make a nice base for a couch. Nail kegs are great for stools. And the price is always right if you're in the market for a cable-spool table or a cinderblock bookcase.

Linc could have written this himself, and my father was on his way with the bookcase he'd built. But we needed more, and not just furniture. Winter clothes to bundle up in when our parents would turn the thermostat low. Food. And, most of all, money.

"No book on survival should fail to give you some good tips on how to rip off bread," said Abbie on a page I bookmarked called "Free Money." "Really horning in on this chapter will put you on Free-loader Street for life, 'cause with all the money in Amerika, the only thing you'll have trouble getting is poor."

By the time I had read and tabbed all the pages that I knew I'd return to, the sunlight had migrated from the middle of the room to my bed beside the windows. I sat up, feeling a head rush, and stashed the book in a niche in the turret where I knew my mother would never look.

Monkeying down from the rafters, I saw that our van had pulled up to the house. I dusted myself off, grabbed a biography about my latest subject, Theodore Roosevelt, which I'd recently checked out from the Mount Pleasant Library, and sat in bed to read and take notes.

I handwrote my presidential biographies and put them in order on my bookshelf in marbled green composition books. Each entry was at least fifteen pages long, with the requisite timeline at the end. William McKinley had not been the most captivating subject, though like Jefferson he had kept a bird in the White House, a parrot who could whistle "Yankee Doodle." I liked that McKinley wore a red carnation on his lapel for good luck, though it ran out on September 6, 1901, when he was shot by the anarchist Leon Czolgosz with a concealed revolver. After his security detail beat the shooter to the ground, McKinley cried out, "Don't let them hurt him." Eight days later the twenty-fifth president died.

While I was skimming pages about Teddy Roosevelt's childhood as an asthmatic cipher whom older kids bullied, I heard my mother scream from the first floor. A second later she called my father's name then mine. I ran downstairs and found her and Molly in the parlor.

My mother was hysterical. "What's going on here? Would you look at this?" She pointed to the corner of the room by the built-in bookcases. Our television stand had fallen on its face and our TV was gone. Molly was holding Chester, hugging him close. When he jumped down from her arms she started to cry. "Can you tell me what's happened here, Daniel?" my mother asked.

"I have no idea. I've been up in my room reading."

"Where's your father?" she said through her teeth.

I rushed out to the back garden to grab him. He had the transistor on; his Top 40 station played the song of the summer: Elton John and Kiki Dee's "Don't Go Breaking My Heart."

"Did you hear Mom call?" I asked.

He rinsed off his hands at the garden spigot, dried them on his shorts and turned off the radio. "No."

"The TV's missing," I announced.

Back inside, my mother yelled at him for playing his stupid music and not paying attention.

Molly wiped the tears from her eyes. "What if the robber is still in the house?"

None of us had considered this, and I shuddered at the thought that I could have run into him, armed and dangerous, on my way downstairs.

My mother grew nervous, too, herding Molly and me out to the sidewalk. "Call the police," she commanded.

"You're being ridiculous, Val." My father stopped halfway down the front steps. "No one's in there."

"So who took our television and knocked over the stand? Who's been stealing the flags? Look—" She pointed up to the porch, where we saw that the second flag, mine, with the gold tassels, was gone.

My father wiped his forehead with his shirtsleeve, his eyebrows yellow dashes across his florid face.

"How do you explain that?" my mother asked.

"Had to be Tino. Who else could it be?"

"Tino's putting up flyers with Cinnamon and Linc. They've been gone all day."

"That doesn't mean they didn't come back and help themselves."

"Are you calling my brother a thief?"

"I wouldn't put it past him or any of that troupe. They could be pawning the TV off right now."

"That's outrageous," my mother said. "I'm calling 911."

Molly tugged on her arm and told her to stay.

"There's no one in there," our father assured us. "But I'll check if that'll make you feel better." Molly started to say no, but our father puffed himself up and stomped into the house. We watched the first-floor windows, then the second-floor windows, as he combed each room. The minutes slowed and I kept looking over to 16th Street hoping a cop would drive by. My father was still up there, and Molly had broken into gentle sobs, when the Salem Cigarette Car whipped a right onto Hill and pulled up to the curb.

Cinnamon hopped out, all excited. "Man, we went everywhere, put up boo-koo posters. I can't tell you how many kids we talked to who said they hate their school and might check us out."

"Have you been gone all day?" my mother asked.

Cinnamon started counting off the places they'd been: the Safeway in Adams Morgan, Fields of Plenty on 18th, Vital Vittles at Georgetown University, the Mount Pleasant Community Center, coffee shops and bulletin boards all over Dupont Circle. "We got as far as the Giant in Cleveland Park before we ran out of leaflets," she was saying when my mother interrupted. "So you haven't been back to the house?"

"Nope." Cinnamon's braids jangled as she pulled back her hair. "We're on a quest to save the post-Nixon generation."

I told Linc and Tino about the robbery and said my dad had been up in the house for a while checking rooms. Tino's expression—surprise giving way to pique—convinced me right then that he wasn't the thief. He bounded up the steps into the house to help my father search.

My mother turned to Linc. "You swear to me once and for all that you guys didn't take anything? I have to know."

Linc wore the same sad-eyed countenance he'd had since his arrival. "I already told you, Val. We never take from pawns, only kings."

Before long, Tino and my father had returned to the porch, assuring us that they'd checked every nook and cranny. My father still appeared suspicious of Tino, and wary of looking like a fool. We followed them hesitantly back into the house and were all standing in the living room, which still echoed in its emptiness, when Cinnamon noticed that the far window, on the mantel side, was wide open, with the screen missing. My father had bought new screens for all the windows because we didn't have air conditioning, and since Molly squealed at the sight of any insect, my father made a special effort to seal off the windows thoroughly. But the house was ninety years old, and no amount of battening down hatches could keep the cockroaches away or the potato bugs, earwigs and varieties of beetles from rising through the earth to wander our desolate floorboards.

"That's how they got in," Cinnamon said.

Everyone gathered at the window and we saw that the screen had not been removed. Someone had ripped or cut it out of its frame and left it lying on the ground in the side yard.

My mother blanched. "Oh, my God. We really have been robbed."

Tino twisted the ends of his long mustache. "They got in here, but if they were lugging that old black-and-white, they must have let themselves out through the front door. Was it open when you came into the house?"

"Only slightly," my mother said. "And Chester was standing there, about to bolt."

Molly held tight to our mother's hand as we retraced the thieves' steps into the parlor. No amount of Nancy Drew books could awaken her inner detective, and I felt sorry for my sister: when faced with an actual mystery, she lost all courage.

Tino pointed to the lower shelf of the bookcase next to our record collection, and there, beyond the toppled TV stand, sat the Kenwood receiver and turntable my father had given my mother two birthdays before, one of his notoriously self-serving gifts.

"What amateurs. They ripped off the idiot box but left your primo stereo just sitting there." Tino switched the receiver on and off and turned the knobs. "Smooth," he said, to my father's annoyance. "What were they thinking?"

"It probably wasn't 'they.' Could have been 'he,'" Cinnamon put in. "Why else wouldn't he grab the stereo? He ran out of time and had no backup."

"Shit, I bet you're right," Tino said. "Listen to me good, kids. If you're going to live a life of crime, there's something you've got to remember." Like an officer showing his badge, he grasped his big oval belt buckle, embossed with a tangle of roses and vines. "If you want to be successful you've got to work with a partner. Butch and Sundance, Bonnie and Clyde, Leopold and Loeb, Nixon and Haldeman. Time-tested, tried and true."

"This isn't helpful," my mother said.

But I was thinking I'd gotten this same advice earlier from Dear Abbie Hoffman in his chapter "Steal Now, Pay Never." Little did I know that right under our noses, someone was turning the tables on all of us.

6

IT WAS ONLY AFTER we'd settled in, adjusted to the arrival of the Freelandia communards, and made a series of bootless efforts at attracting students to our school that we realized our house sat in a no man's land at the convergence of three separate and economically distinct neighborhoods. It would be a while before I'd understand the layout of the city and the social complexities of these neighborhoods' encroachments upon one another, but for now I knew only this: we were on the border, and every direction we turned seemed like a new front.

To our south and west stood Dupont Circle, with its Beaux Arts mansions, neoclassical embassies and lavishly appointed townhouses, while to our east, across 16th, lay Shaw and Logan Circle, the longtime home of the black bourgeoisie, most of whom had left midcentury for the northern tip of the city. The grand Romanesque and Italianate homes had been converted into apartments and boardinghouses, and the poverty that once pressed at the neighborhood's flank had now spilled over, bringing with it vandalism, burglary and drug-related crime.

From my bedroom I could see the northwestern edge of Shaw and the lower half of Meridian Hill Park, where my mother said I could never go. "Think of Sixteenth Street as the Berlin Wall. You're not allowed to cross it," she decreed after reading in the

Washington Post that the park had become a marketplace for heroin and other drugs. So when I left the house on my own I could only head west toward 18th and Columbia Road, into the heart of the closest neighborhood to our house. My mother assumed that Adams Morgan was a lot like Dupont Circle: prosperous and benign. After all, Bailey himself lived on its far west side, across from Kalorama Park. But I would discover that in this city of clear divisions between rich and poor, grandeur and decay, Adams Morgan was a true mélange, resistant to the power brokers' attempts to homogenize the neighborhood.

After the break-in my mother went on high alert. Less than a month remained before our supposed opening day of September 13, and though a few parents had made calls of interest we still had no commitments. But my mother had more immediate concerns than recruitment. Every article she read in the *Post* only confirmed her fear that we lived in a war zone. The hippies assured her she was overreacting, and my father said, "Don't pay attention to the papers, they just print bad news."

Unconvinced, my mother turned our house into a citadel. She sent my father to Hechinger's for deadbolts, window locks, floodlights for the porches, hundred-watt bulbs for every room. She kept the downstairs lights on through the night. From the street our house looked like a theme-park castle—all lit up and on display.

"We have to be safe," she said.

"By drawing as much attention as possible?" My father had grown short with her, tired of doing her bidding and more anxious than ever that we wouldn't have a class for fall term. "It's like we're on stage here. Anyone driving by can see exactly what we're doing. We have no curtains in the windows."

"So go out and get some," my mother said. "In this neighborhood we need to be visible."

My father looked up and squinted, as if he were calculating how much remained of the Aunt Natalia nest egg. He bought curtains anyway, sheer panels that made our house seem abuzz but less conspicuous. After a long weekend of putting up curtain rods he told my mother, "Enough."

She ignored him. "There are all kinds of ways to break in. We need bars on the basement windows."

"Someone else can do that." My father opened the utility drawer, tossed in the screwdriver and slammed the drawer shut. "I'm finished."

To escape, I grabbed my basketball and headed to Pierce Park, at 18th and Kalorama. The court was blessedly empty, under a powder-blue dome of sky. I tightened the laces on my high-tops, adjusted my Pacers headband around my hair, which spilled down my neck in staticky waves. What a relief to be out of the house—as big as it was, it could feel like a trap.

I pulled up from the top of the key and did a reverse lay-up off the *swish.* I shot around the world—corner, side, elbow, free throw, lay-up, elbow, side, corner—then ran out to fifteen feet and did it again.

I was starting to break a sweat and had just flipped in a lefty underhand scoop when I heard someone call my name. "Daniel, check this out."

I wheeled around to see Cleo on the other side of the eight-foot fence. She had her own ball, a standard orange Spalding; she launched a shot, missing the rim by a couple of inches. She asked for the ball back, and on her next try she sank a high-arcing thirty-footer. "All luck," she said, joining me on the court.

She wore green shorts with white piping and a gray practice jersey with the letters *OLPH,* for Our Lady of Perpetual Help.

"Fancy meeting you here," she said, rolling her ball aside and asking for my red, white and blue one.

"It's the ABA model," I pointed out.

She spun the ball in the air, making a lavender blur. I talked about the demise of the ABA and how the Pacers would be joining the NBA in the coming year. But Cleo wasn't much of a basketball fan. "I just like to play," she said.

And play she could. It didn't matter where she stood on the court; nearly every shot she attempted went in. She had a feathery touch, and my heart thrummed when I noticed that, like me, she was left-handed. I was the only lefty in my family, and maybe because little else at the time set me apart from the hoi polloi, I liked to think that my left-handedness gave me membership in a tribe of the preternaturally gifted.

"You're a lefty, too." My free throw clanged off the front of the rim.

"Yeah," she said.

I thought of reciting the roster of our exclusive club—Julius Caesar, Michelangelo, Queen Victoria, Paul McCartney, Presidents Garfield, Hoover, Truman and Ford—but she seemed neutral about the coincidence, so I made nothing of it. Retrieving the ball, I dribbled hesitantly to the top of the key, and in a herky-jerky motion tossed up another miss.

Cleo snatched the rebound and sank a sweeping lefty hook across the lane.

"You're good" was all I could say.

She stopped at the baseline and held the ball under her arm. "So I haven't seen you since the Fourth of July."

"What's been up with you?" I asked.

"My dad bought a beach house in Bethany, on the Delaware coast. He sent me, my mom and my moody brother to live there for a month. It was a total surprise. I'm sure he bought it to get us out of his hair."

"I wouldn't mind having a beach house," I said.

"I know. I shouldn't complain. I guess I must sound like a spoiled little rich girl."

"No you don't."

Blushing, she changed the subject. "So, how's your school coming along?" She flipped the ball up and in and caught it under the basket.

I didn't realize Cleo knew about the school, and wondered if her father had made fun of our quixotic scheme. I thought of lying and telling her we had a full enrollment, but at some point Bailey would show up again, to check on the flag or remind us that free rent would soon be ending. I couldn't tell her that we'd been robbed. She'd think of us as easy targets, midwestern hayseeds who couldn't make it in the big city. But I knew I had to say something, even if it wasn't a hundred percent true. "The school could be going better. We have like a dozen students. But we definitely need more. My parents are kind of stressed."

"Have they talked to my dad? He knows lots of people."

"They'd rather not get him involved. He already found us that house," I said, and could have added *with the cockroaches and carpenter ants, the buckling plaster and rotting rafter tails, the sirens wailing up 16th in a neighborhood under siege.* Free rent was free rent, and I didn't want to seem like a charity case. "He's been generous already."

"I don't know about that," Cleo put in. "He can be an A-number-one jerk. Maybe I should talk to my mom, or better yet, I could set up an appointment with Sister Donovan. You shouldn't have a problem getting students. Lots of kids I know are sick of the same old schools. I'd probably go myself if my parents would let me."

She fed me a bounce pass and I stumbled in for a lay-up.

We decided to play a game of H-O-R-S-E, and shot free throws to see who would go first. We'd barely begun before I was down three letters.

To distract her from noticing that I couldn't sink a shot, I asked if she knew who used to live in our house. She said her father had only recently started to take her around to see his properties. "The Fourth of July was one of the first times. He's overprotective, to say the least, and a lot of his buildings are in iffy neighborhoods." She banked a twelve-footer off the backboard.

Though my next shot didn't feel good leaving my hand, I managed to rattle it home.

"Nice one," she said, and launched a rare miss. "I never met the people who used to live in your house, but I heard some rumors. They had a huge family and my dad kicked them out for unpaid rent. He said they were doing a number on the interior of the place, too. They had something like ten kids in there."

"You're joking."

"Two to a room, according to my dad." Cleo missed a corner jumper.

"Opposite-hand finger roll," I called, but blew the lay-up.

"My mom always flips out when Dad evicts people. She worries they're going to come after us, which is why my father hired a guy full-time, almost like a security guard. He calls him Factotum Frank."

Cleo stopped dribbling, shaded her eyes with her hand and surveyed the panorama. "Frank sometimes picks me up at school, and I've seen him spying for Dad when I'm out with friends. I once caught him looking down from the balcony when some girls and I went to see *The Return of the Pink Panther* at the Uptown Theater. He could be watching us now, on my father's orders. I guess a factotum is a personal assistant, but Frank's more of a bodyguard. So don't do anything funny." She faked like she was going to pass me the ball, and I flinched. "Scared ya." She laughed. "Anyway, Dad claimed he had no choice but to evict that family. I think it's terrible, but his attitude is: if you can't make the rent, you've got to go."

I shot an air ball.

"Don't worry about Factotum Frank," Cleo said. "He's totally harmless."

But I wasn't worried about someone spying on me. We had less than a month to start a school, and only weeks after that our first rent check would be due. Then what?

Cleo gave me an S on a gorgeous rainbow *swish* from twenty feet away.

"Do you know when the family was evicted?" I asked.

"I'm not sure," Cleo said. "I think they moved out right before you got here. D.C. law says tenants have thirty days to vacate if they've violated their lease. My dad's always quoting tenant law at the dinner table. He's so *boring*."

"That's weird," I thought out loud, then stopped myself from saying anything more. It occurred to me that Bailey might have kicked this family out to make room for us. It was a wayward notion, and maybe I was wrong, but the timing of the eviction seemed uncannily close to when my father called up Bailey to cash in on his favor. "Does your dad own a lot of houses?" I asked.

"Only a few," Cleo said. "Mostly it's apartment buildings, where he can have a manager and an on-site maintenance crew. He hates to do the upkeep, so he's been selling off his houses one by one. I guess yours is one of the last he owns. But it looks like you've done a lot of work on it. You're old friends, right? So it's a perfect arrangement."

"Right," I said.

Cleo dribbled the ball at the free throw line. "Opposite hand," she called, lining up her shot.

Her form and follow-through were flawless. She extended her right arm and wrist up and over, like a swan's neck. As I watched the ball drop through the net with a whisper, I knew I didn't stand a chance.

At dinner that night, I announced that we finally had a lead: Sister Donovan at Our Lady of Perpetual Help. But the weekend passed without a phone call from Cleo, and when my father tried the main number at OLPH, the sisters must have been in their cloisters, because no one was answering.

I'd been debating calling Cleo, had even planned to hang up in case Bailey answered, when the doorbell rang and on the other side stood a lanky man with a high-bridged nose, boyish cheeks and a patchy beard that looked pasted on. "Name's Frank," he said after I cracked the door to the length of the chain. "I work for Mr. Dornan. He asked me to deliver this." I unchained the door and he handed me a sheet of paper with instructions for how to fly a flag.

"Mr. Dornan noticed that your flag's not out, so he wanted you to have this reminder." Frank spoke in elongated vowels and had a phlegmatic way about him, as if it were a hundred in the shade and it was all he could do just to stay on his feet.

My father, who had been filling out a grant application at the dining room table, came over and apologized for the misunderstanding. "It's been a dusty summer. We took the flag to the dry cleaner. Very patriotic folks—they're cleaning it free of charge." He spoke rapidly, his voice cracking, and though he'd always been a clumsy liar, Frank seemed to buy the BS, or perhaps didn't want to expend the energy of asking questions.

"I'll let Mr. Dornan know," Frank said. But turning to leave, he stopped himself. "I almost forgot something. I have a message from Mr. Dornan's daughter." He didn't look like a bodyguard. I had pictured him as a James Bond henchman like Oddjob, from *Goldfinger,* with his lethal bowler hat. But Factotum Frank was too tall and deliberate for a spy, and he seemed an unlikely fit in Bailey's employ. I imagined him sipping a pop through a straw on the front porch of a country store, or blissed out on a hammock at Freelandia commune.

"Cleo wanted you to have this." He passed an envelope to my father. "Don't know what it's about. I'm just the messenger." He scratched his beard and gave a little wave then packed himself into his yellow Dodge Colt and took off.

Cleo had written my name on the envelope in her adorable looping cursive. My heart quickened as my father passed me the note and I imagined the declarations of love it contained.

> Daniel,
>
> I can't stand it any longer. Meet me tonight at Pierce Park. Frank will have the car running, and I'll be in the back seat waiting for you. My parents are out of town . . .
>
> The beach house in Bethany is open, and Frank is going to chauffeur us there. We'll drive all night and take a moonlit walk on the beach, the waves lapping at our toes, calling us into the ocean . . .

"Go ahead," my father said. "Open it."

I stepped into the parlor for privacy and gently unsealed the letter. "Do you mind?" I told my father as he approached.

But it was not a confession of the heart. "Daniel," the note read. "Don't tell my dad about this, but here's the phone number for our dean of students, Sister Catherine Donovan." After the number she wrote: "I happened to be at school today and spoke with her. She told me she'd be happy to talk to your parents. She's a nice lady. Just try not to stare at her forehead. Basketball was fun. Sincerely, Cleo."

My father was ecstatic about this opportunity. He called upstairs to my mother and the entire household that we still had a fighting chance. My mother pointed to the Illinois Bank & Trust calendar, which showed a little over two weeks to go, but my father kept up his enthusiasm, figuring a dean of students at one prominent school would only lead to more meetings. "A lot can change in a couple of weeks. Just watch."

The next day he finally reached Sister Donovan—Cleo had given us her direct line—and set up an appointment. "She sounded very nice, though I thought I was talking to a child," he said when he got off the phone. "She has a tiny voice and she kept giggling for no reason. But we're on for tomorrow at ten A.M."

Over a pasta dinner that Cinnamon made with fresh tomatoes, garlic and basil—among the many vegetables, I'd come to learn, that Tino was stealing from community gardens—my parents went over their strategy. Since our school would welcome all ages, they decided to bring me along to play the role of sample student. My father said my hair was too long and suggested that my mother cut it that night. She refused, but we did agree not to tell Sister Donovan that I was their son. We didn't want to sound like a mom-and-pop operation, though that's exactly what we were—plus uncle, uncle's wife and uncle's best friend, now shacking up with uncle's wife. This last bit was not likely to endear us to a nun, which is why my parents encouraged the hippies to stay home.

Tino didn't care, and Molly was content to help Cinnamon

decorate an Our House banner for the living room. But Linc had a moue of disappointment on his face. "It's fine," he said, when my mother tried to be solicitous.

"Are you sure?"

"Of course he's sure," my father answered for him.

My mother shot a dark look across the table after Linc excused himself and went up to his room, no doubt to play "Blackbird" on his guitar.

My mother and Linc had been latchkey kids before that term was much in use. They'd come home from school and wait for their mother to return from her nursing job at Wausau Hospital and their father to arrive for dinner, having stayed hours after baseball practice to rake and line the diamond and mow the outfield grass. While Linc was getting into scrapes with other kids on their block of two-bedroom ranches and split-levels, my mother would read *Anne of Green Gables* and the *Little House on the Prairie* books, stories of small towns and neighbors pitching in, and imagine herself in similar communities.

Sometimes I wonder if she got into politics back in college more to be among people joined in a cause than for the cause itself. When she gave up on graduate school she talked about having a bigger family than the one she was born into. But Molly's was a difficult birth, money was always tight, and so, probably to my mother's own surprise, she stopped at two children. To widen the circle she sought out strangers. In Cincinnati we rented a four-bedroom Craftsman and sublet two of the rooms, as much for the company as for the small break in rent. And at Lake Bluff she took on the den mother role, much to my embarrassment, often leaving the apartment door open and inviting kids I didn't even like to come in and sit down.

As for my father, Our House was a chance for redemption. At each new job, he had arrived with great plans. He began a social service program at Henry Wadsworth Longfellow, an under-funded inner-city public school in southwest Indianapolis. But the students weren't up for doing free labor when a lot of them already had jobs. Parents grumbled that their kids shouldn't be asked to pick up litter in the parks or ladle soup for the homeless when their school was always last in line for new books and equipment. My father argued that the program was only voluntary, and said something along the lines of *You need to learn to help yourselves.* But the faculty pulled his words out of context, some of the parents took offense, and soon my father looked like a privileged upstart, out to tell everyone how to run their lives. Instead of explaining himself or fighting back, he gave up on Longfellow, the state of Indiana, all public schools for the time being, and moved the family to Illinois.

By his second term at Lake Bluff Academy he had licked his wounds and was back to thinking about the public good again. He put on a fundraising drive and collected enough money to bankroll three full scholarships, room and board included, for the incoming freshman class. But he never stipulated to the donors that the money would be used for minority students only. He went ahead and recruited some of the brightest eighth-graders from Chicago's South Side. Then, at a banquet in the fall, he introduced the new scholarship kids to the alumni board. I knew just the type who sat on that board: they went to country clubs and wore kelly-green wide-wale pants and belts printed with nautical patterns. Their wives subsisted on white wine and oyster crackers and were a genus of exotic insect sent into the world to complete one task: get their sons into Yale. They didn't like my father's *Guess Who's Coming to Dinner* stunt. So it came as no surprise the following year when the headmaster asked another faculty member, an old tie from the class of '53, to take over the school's new scholarship program. By that point the handwriting was on the wall.

Now, despite our difficulties hoisting the school up on its feet, my father was at least free of interference. No parents lining up at his door. No board members telling him what he could and could not do. Only himself to account for—or so he wanted to believe.

• • •

The next morning Sister Donovan greeted us at the ivied entrance to Our Lady of Perpetual Help, a gated school set amidst the rolling hills of Woodley Park between the vice president's mansion and the National Zoo. She led us back to her spare, windowless office at the end of the main hallway of the upper school. I sat between my parents on a hard wooden chair with a head-on view of the nun, whose voice was exactly as my father had described: giggly and childlike and with a flat nasal sound that I thought I recognized from visits to Wisconsin. Wherever she came from, her voice did not match her appearance, and the unsettling combination caused me to shift in my chair and sit on my hands. I'd pictured a small, bubbly woman in a white habit, like Sally Field from *The Flying Nun.* But Sister Donovan wore civilian clothes—a violet turtleneck under a black blazer—and she was cube-like, with an underbite and a wen in the middle of her forehead.

Cleo had warned me not to stare at the pale cyst, exactly the size and shape of a third eye, but the warning was all I could think about as my parents made their pitch and the nun scanned our brochure. I worried that if I kept staring, the wen would open up like the eye of Polyphemus awoken from his drunken sleep. So I fixed my gaze above and beyond Sister Donovan's head, to a Byzantine print of the Madonna and Child wearing crowns of gold, and tried to tune in to the conversation.

"You have an acceptable curriculum," the nun was saying in her cheerful voice. "But I'm not sure what you'd like me to do. We cover most of these courses, in some form or another, and our students are happy."

My father had not worn a tie in months. He tugged at his wide collar where the top button pinched his skin. "We have a fine crop of young learners, like Daniel here," he said. "But we're trying to build a larger student body. Perhaps you know some underachievers who might benefit from our more open approach."

"And what do you mean by 'open approach,' Mr. Truitt?"

"Peter," my father said, trying to be casual. "Take Daniel, for example." He put his arm around my shoulder and I smiled on cue, my eyes trained on the Madonna and the skinny baby Jesus. "Daniel was unhappy at his former school because the rigid structure made him feel he had no control over his course of study. When students are in control they feel they can handle the work. It's like being a driver versus a passenger. Passengers can't steer; they're just along for the ride. Drivers, on the other hand, control their own destinies."

Sister Donovan asked me how old I was, and I told her thirteen in December. "So you think that twelve-year-olds should drive?" she asked my father, chipper as can be.

My mother answered for him. "What he's saying is, not everyone responds well to traditional education. I'm sure you've seen some students like Daniel, smart kids who get restless sitting in a classroom, where they can't see how to apply the ideas in practical terms. Our students play an important role in the school's decision-making process. They're part of a democracy, invested in all we do."

Without changing her demeanor Sister Donovan questioned my parents' preparedness, said it was impractical to think they could increase their numbers so close to the first day of school. She asked about teacher qualifications, which my father only further embellished, claiming that Linc had gone to a seminary after earning his degree at Arizona.

"Do you have a lawyer?" Sister Donovan asked.

"Of course," my father said.

"How do your neighbors feel about the school?"

Caught in a lie, he had to lie again: "They're one hundred percent behind it."

"And how many students do you have?"

My father hesitated and with a lilt of defeat said, "Eight."

I wondered how he came up with that number, then counted the occupants of the house: Mom, Dad, me, Molly, Linc, Cinnamon, Tino. Seven teacher-students, plus the cat, made eight.

Sister Donovan clasped her large-knuckled hands together. "What you've described sounds more to me like a learning center than an alternative school. Perhaps a couple of years from now you might have the funding and infrastructure to be autonomous. But in my opinion—and don't take this as a discourtesy—you're not ready for that yet."

The barometer in the room dropped, and I felt terrible for my parents, whose pitch had turned into a lesson. They didn't argue. They listened dutifully as the nun explained that they should summon together a few schools willing to accept credit from their students who wanted to take courses at Our House. "We're not interested in such a partnership, I'm afraid, but I do thank you for coming in to see us," she said, the skin on her forehead wrinkling around the wen. "Our mission is to educate the whole child, to instill compassion and a love of learning in the hearts, minds and spirits of all of our students, so they will live according to the teachings of Jesus Christ."

As we stood up to go, I couldn't help saying something to Sister Donovan. I'd had an urge to ask her a question, to resolve the incongruity between how she looked and sounded. "I think I recognize your accent," I said. "Is it Wisconsin? That's where my parents' families are from." My mother and father looked at each other, unsure about whether to admit I was their son. "I go to Wausau every summer," I continued, "and sometimes up to La Crosse, too. Wisconsin's a beautiful state."

The nun's crimped smile loosened. "I'm from Minnesota," she said. "Rochester, not far from La Crosse."

She sat back down in her chair, and I felt we might be on the verge of a breakthrough when she screwed up her eyes, looked directly at me and asked, "Are these your parents?"

My role in the family had been as a vessel of secrets. But glimpsing the Madonna, her ear tilted toward the baby Jesus, his right hand flashing a peace sign, I asked myself what there was to lose by confessing to a nun whose worldview depended on sin and pleas for forgiveness. I wondered how the system worked. I had yet to read Saint Augustine or Thomas Aquinas or learn the difference between mortal and venial sin, but I knew that lying was a no-no in this hyper-self-conscious faith. Still, I conveniently dismissed some of my and my housemates' other transgressions—impure thoughts, lies and loss of patience, petty theft, gas siphoning, taking the Lord's name in vain, adultery, not to mention my collusion with Dear Abbie Hoffman, whose ideas would rattle the bones of ten thousand martyrs.

"Yes." I came out with it. "These are my parents." I figured a single confession was enough for one day. I couldn't afford to overwhelm her.

Sister Donovan nodded with self-satisfaction.

My father spoke up right away. "We're just at the beginning of this project, and we could use all the help we can get," he pleaded. "Yes, Daniel is our son, but he's also a student at Our House—and he needs classmates." My father went on to say that all he'd wanted since finishing his master's at Indiana was one day to start his own school. He didn't mention our peripatetic life in the Midwest, the failed volunteer and scholarship programs, or the fact that Lake Bluff had fired him. But as he talked in an unbroken stream that at first seemed an effort to obscure his deceit, he veered off, telling this stranger about his childhood in La Crosse, his domineering father, how his mother's voice grew so soft toward the end of her life that she spoke in a whisper.

He said he'd come closest to pleasing his father as a schoolboy athlete, and for one of the first times in my memory he recounted his glory days at Wisconsin and his doomed career as a minor league baseball player. "I batted .308 with fifteen homers and seventy RBIs my first year with the Duluth-Superior Dukes. Have you ever been up to Duluth?" he asked Sister Donovan.

"The North Shore is beautiful country," she said.

"I was on the radar of the Detroit Tigers back then," my father continued. "We were their single-A team and they were looking to bump me up to double- or triple-A. That was in 1965, the year after Daniel was born. Sometimes I think about what might have happened—the Tigers won the World Series in '68, the year of Denny McLain's thirty-one wins—but one of the weak spots on the team was at my position. They had a guy named Don Wert, skinny for a third baseman, and if I had stayed healthy, who knows? I could have cracked the lineup." My father adjusted his tinted glasses, the lenses almost clear in the nun's dark office. "I don't know why I'm maundering on like this."

"So what happened?" Sister Donovan asked.

"I tried to score from second base on a routine double. The center fielder threw a bullet, and I saw the ball in the catcher's mitt as I went for home. I wish I had stopped right then, just let him tag me out. So much can happen in a moment. It was an early-season game. We were up by four runs already and we had our best closer on the mound. We would have won if I had stopped at third—we didn't need to pad the score. But I liked to play hard, and I was better than everyone else because when coaches used to say 'Never quit,' I took them seriously. So I lowered my head and tried to bowl the catcher over so he'd drop the ball. A few years ago Pete Rose did the same thing in the All-Star game to a guy named Ray Fosse, who hasn't been the same player since. As fate would have it, the catcher made out just fine, but I got a concussion that ended my career."

My mother had told me this story before, but I'd never heard my father recall it in such detail. One key fact was missing, though, something I've thought about more than once as I look back on the knotty weave of my own relationship with my dad: at the time of the collision, his father had lung cancer, soon to follow his wife, who had died two years before of the same disease. I tend to resist baseball-as-life analogies, though I can't help seeing my dad's racing toward home as an attempt to unite with his impossible-to-please father, or at least to make him stand up and take notice, once and for all.

Whatever might have compelled my dad to round that base, the story contains a host of minor tragedies beyond his injury. It occurred not in the major leagues, but in single-A ball; it didn't happen in the bottom of the ninth of a crucial game where he represented the winning run, but late in an early-season blowout; and the lug of a catcher held on to the ball, so unlike Ted Williams, who homered in his last at-bat, my father was called out on his final play. It carried no drama, no gasps from the fans, because almost immediately after the collision, he got up, lightheaded, and walked to the dugout without any help. It wasn't until he sat down on the bench, out of view of the crowd, that he blacked out and tumbled over. A teammate drove him to the hospital, where my mother and I met him—I was a little over a year old, so I have no memories of Duluth—and though my father threw up several times that night and complained of dizziness and blurred vision, he stayed in the hospital for only twenty-four hours, for observation, before the doctors said he was okay to go home.

But he had sustained as serious a concussion as one could without suffering permanent damage. His ears rang for months; he had severe headaches that made him short-tempered and often sent him to bed; and his vision went blurry at times, so he had to get glasses. The season ended without his suiting up for another game, and sometime between September and the Dukes' home opener the following April, my father, still feeling the side effects, decided to try Plan B. He and my mother applied to graduate schools, and because only one accepted both of them, we packed our boxes for Bloomington, and a new beginning.

"I could always play again," he'd told my mother during the move. "Maybe after the degree I can make a comeback." But the desire to "Never quit" had been jarred loose, and in my parents' worst arguments my mother would unleash her most withering insult: *You're not the same since that collision.*

My father finished his story and once again asked Sister Donovan to contact him if she could think of any way to help.

"I'll do that," she said. Her face had softened; the room felt less claustrophobic. "If I were starting my own learning center, I would talk directly to the parents and listen to their concerns. I can't remember a more distressing time than the one we're living in now. The world is full of dangers. Crime. Temptation." She touched the silver cross that hung outside her turtleneck. "Parents are terrified of outside forces corrupting their children, or worse. We've seen what happened in California with the Manson family and Patricia Hearst. But the cults, these spiritual counterfeits—like the Moonies and the Hare Krishnas—are running rampant, threatening our young people with brainwashing and mind control, steering them off the path of Christ. Parents want to know where their children are throughout the day. At schools like ours we can tend to the flock until three in the afternoon, or five if you include athletics. But what happens between the middle of the day and dinner, when the sun goes down and the streets begin to stir with devilment? I'm concerned about those hours, and I think parents and partner schools would be interested in a safe haven. So"—Sister Donovan stood up from her chair and reached across her desk to shake hands with my parents and me—"think about holding your classes in the afternoons and evenings. Your learning center could be a place where kids go to stay off the streets."

My parents looked puzzled by this unexpected outpouring of advice, but they smiled and thanked the nun for the meeting.

"You'll keep us in mind?" my father asked as we were leaving.

"I will," she said. She clasped her hands together and pointed them in our direction, either in prayer or dismissal. I couldn't be sure.

7

WHEN MY MOTHER FLIPPED the Illinois Bank & Trust calendar from August to September she must have known we had little chance of opening the school by fall. Sister Donovan hadn't called, nor had my father's other leads, and the kids Cinnamon had talked to while putting up flyers never materialized. No doubt the boys had merely been flattered by her attention and the girls had gotten nowhere when they'd said the words "alternative school" to their parents.

We did get a few phone calls, but only one turned into a visit —and that was a fiasco. My father got the time wrong and was out of the house when the prospective student and his mother arrived. The teenager was tall and stoop-shouldered with a starter beard, his face half hidden under a swarm of corkscrew curls. His mother wore a tailored military-tan pantsuit, and after Tino answered the door and invited her inside she kept her Jackie O sunglasses on. My mother was upstairs at the time, so she couldn't do damage control when Tino attempted to melt the woman's icy casing by touching her elbow and squeezing her shoulder as they toured the house.

Up on the second floor she asked where the classrooms were, and my mother, who had stepped into the hall, said we had three downstairs but in fact the whole city was our classroom, then she quoted from an article she'd read about an alternative school in

Minneapolis: "We're not a college-prep school. We're a life-prep school."

In the dark hallway the woman took off her sunglasses, revealing small, close-set eyes that diminished her effect. My mother switched on the light.

"But you don't have desks or chalkboards or anything," the woman sneered. "What do you do? Sit cross-legged on the floor?"

"Mom?" the teenager muttered, his hair backlit by the overhead bulb.

"I'm handling this, Lachland."

And that was the last we'd hear from Lachland, who retreated under his frizzy shell.

My mother said we had furniture on order that would be arriving within the week. I'd never heard her lie before, and couldn't decide if this was a good or bad development. "We have a dynamic faculty, including visiting lecturers from Georgetown and other universities. We have lots of equipment on order, but since our students take responsibility for their own education, we wait to see what their interests are so we can help them toward their goals. Our House is like an extended family—we're less teachers than guides. We tell our students, 'Act first. Ask permission later.'"

"I don't know how I feel about that," the woman said. "You could be asking for trouble."

My mother tried to smile. "Our House is built on trust. By trusting our students we ensure they'll act responsibly."

She asked Lachland what his interests were, but his mother answered for him, saying he had few interests other than whatever happened to be going on in his head. "And you can't get inside there, can you?"

Tino chose this moment to pipe up, "Sure you can, with the right pharmaceuticals."

"He's only joking." My mother froze Tino with a look and handed the woman a brochure. She barely glanced at the piece of paper before slipping it into her purse and clamping her Jackie O sunglasses onto her face.

When the woman and her son had left, my mother told Tino to cool it with the drug references.

"I was just buttering her up," he said, then praised my mother for her performance. "Didn't know you had it in you, Val. Visiting lecturers from Georgetown?"

"I bet there are some old radicals who'd drop in for a talk. It's something to look into. Not that we'll ever see Lachland again."

Two good things resulted from the icy woman's visit. I noticed that my mother was beginning to stake a claim on the school. In the first months she'd mostly gone along, watching and waiting, not wanting to bail my father out, still talking on occasion about finding some new career. But since the hippies' arrival she'd been getting more involved, showing signs of her old community spirit. The burglary had been a setback and she still fretted too much, but somewhere along the way she must have recognized that our project—to build our own mini-commonwealth—tapped into something she had always craved.

Also, though the interview had not gone well, it did spur me to get Our House more furniture. My accomplice in the task was Uncle Linc. Since he'd arrived as the third wheel on the Cinnamon and Tino love wagon, he'd spent most of his time sleeping late, smoking Camels on the porch while reading Robert Musil's *The Man Without Qualities,* or fumbling through the picking patterns of "Blackbird." At least Tino was handy, and had set himself to finishing the work on the second floor. I asked my father who was paying for the paint, and he told me that Tino kept talking about some mystical thing called The Flow, how whatever you needed would appear out of the blue. "Sounds like shoplifting to me, but that's none of my business," my father said. "If they throw him in jail, maybe your uncle can get his wife back."

Cinnamon was as sweet to Linc as ever, though that didn't stop her from thumping the wall next to my bedroom or running her hand through Tino's hair at the breakfast table for all to see. To make a little money she parked the Salem Bug downtown and sold every box of smokes that Linc had gotten with the car, plus a slew of extra cartons that she claimed she picked up wholesale. Next she started to turn up with clothes, some used, some with the tags still on them. And over Labor Day weekend she hung a banner across the porch that read *Hip Replacements: Supercheap Clothes Sold Here.* Tino fashioned a sandwich board for Molly, who stood on the corner on the West Berlin side of 16th Street waving cars toward our house. We made over a hundred dollars, and on the Wednesday after Labor Day—bulk trash day in the ritzy neighborhood of Wesley Heights—I went out in the van with Linc on a scavenger hunt for furniture.

"So where'd you get this idea, Daniel?" he asked, without a trace of suspicion. None of the hippies had noticed that *Steal This Book* had gone missing, or at least they hadn't said so. Perhaps the idea of theft, like possession, didn't exist on a commune. Just as Tino hadn't *stolen* Cinnamon but was merely enjoying her company for an indefinite period, I hadn't *stolen* the Abbie Hoffman book but was partaking of its wisdom, with an eye toward the common good. Though these ideas were as foreign to me as living in the heart of an unpredictable city, far from the safe middle where I'd grown up, I was more than willing to go along, for the thrill and the sake of survival.

"Mom told me this was something you liked to do," I said. "Didn't you talk about free furniture in your book?"

Linc swung a right onto Massachusetts Avenue and passed the embassies of South Africa, Iran and Great Britain. It was a humid night, a little after ten o'clock, and the streets were mostly empty. Linc rolled his window down to let in the warm breeze, and I did the same. "Oh, yeah. *How to Live for Free in America,*" he said, as if he'd forgotten all about it. "Ancient history, man."

I could sense that my uncle was about to get heavy on me. It had happened once before, on our camping trip, when Linc was going through one of his existential crises, but I was too young to understand what he'd been saying—something about material worth and the body and spirit. I recalled only that it was over my head, and as much as I appreciated him never talking down to

Molly and me, I could contribute nothing more than a smile and a nod.

"I know you guys have been wondering what happened with Cinn and me. That *issue* has been hovering around the house like Casper the unfriendly ghost." Linc punched the lighter on the dashboard and reached into the pocket of his OshKoshes for a Camel.

Soon after they'd arrived, I'd diagrammed the Tino-Cinnamon-Linc triangle in the margin of one of my green notebooks:

```
t c i n n l
 i a m o i
  n n n
   o c
    ,
```

But recently, with all our other worries, I hadn't given much thought to my uncle's problems.

"When that book went bust I kind of gave up. I was like Ulrich from *The Man Without Qualities.* He tries to be a great man three times in his life: when he joins the cavalry, as a civil engineer, then as a mathematician. But each time he gets tired of the work, until he finally says forget about it. He decides to take a year off so he can 'seek an appropriate application for his abilities.' I'm in the middle of volume two. There are three volumes, each like a thousand pages, all about this guy's vacation from life." Linc pulled the lighter from the dashboard and pressed it to the end of his cigarette, brightening the van with a tiny orange star point. "Hell, I've been on vacation for about three years now."

I was wondering what this had to do with Cinnamon, but my uncle had a roundabout way of getting to the heart of the matter. "See that house up on the hill." He pointed to our left, at a large white Victorian far beyond the iron gates that separated the property from the street. "That's where the vice president lives. Nelson Rockefeller. I guess you could say he's a great man, especially if you measure greatness by a name. My folks gave me a great man's name—Lincoln—but a lot of good that's done."

We crested the hill at Massachusetts and Wisconsin avenues and continued on toward Wesley Heights. I knew enough not to stop Linc when he loosened up like this. He'd mostly kept to himself in the two months since he'd arrived, and even my mother had been having difficulty getting through to him. I didn't know why he'd decided to start talking now, to his nephew whom he'd seen a half dozen times in the past ten years. He must have thought I was too young to understand what it felt like to run out of options.

"Yep, I had three shots," he said. "As a political activist, working on a commune, and as a writer, I guess, with *How to Live for Free.* But they all came up lame, and that last time, when Abbie beat me to the punch, I dug a hole and climbed in. That didn't sit too hot with Cinnamon. She's got the fire, and I'd gone contemplative on her. Not a good combination. It was only a matter of time before she'd find someone else with the fire and I'd be stuck in my hole alone."

I pictured Cinnamon with her hair aflame dancing with that devil Tino on the banks of a river of fire, while poor Linc shivered off in the distance, in his hole in the cold ground. "I don't know why I'm going on like this." He leaned into the wheel and merged into yet another traffic circle with the statue of a horse-mounted general in the middle.

We were both quiet for a minute, the only sound the mysterious click in the engine that never failed to set my mother off on a series of nervous questions about car diagnostics that my father couldn't answer.

"Maybe you have another shot coming up," I said to Linc. "What if the school takes off, and you, Mom, Dad and everyone become great teachers?" I told him about Thomas Jefferson's founding and building the University of Virginia, how on his gravestone he didn't even mention he'd been president, but made a big fuss about UVA because along with the Declaration of Independence, starting that school had been his proudest achievement.

"You're a good kid, Daniel. You always keep your head up. But don't worry about me. I'm on the mend." Linc turned onto Foxhall Road then a smaller street. "So here we are," he said. "Wesley Heights, land of plenty."

The houses were enormous: Tudors, Georgian manors, Colonial Revivals with elaborated entrances and high fences, no doubt enclosing swimming pools and manicured back yards. Driving slowly over the rolling hills, we could see that it was bulk trash day from the hedge clippings and lightning-struck tree limbs at the curb, but the wealthy of Washington were mostly parsimonious with their valuable trash. We did snag a couple of brass standing lamps at the bottom of someone's driveway, and Linc plucked a toaster oven and some perfectly good pots and pans from a metal trash can. We also made what might have been the score of the night when we grabbed an old TV with faux wood paneling. But I worried that the rush of adrenaline I spent lifting that monstrosity, all the while terrified of being caught, would be wasted if the tube no longer worked.

"Done better, done worse," Linc said as we headed back toward Mass. Ave. "I have to be honest, though. I'm tired of living like a raccoon. I'm not bad at it, but when your mom called and said she had this big house and did I want to move in, I jumped at the chance. I thought I'd come here and try the straight life again. Cinn and Tino are purists, so don't tell them this, but I've been writing jingles on the guitar, even sent a few to the companies that gave me free stuff." He twisted to show me his red *Hey, Kool-Aid!* T-shirt, with the smiling pitcher rushing to the rescue. "You know my Electrolux bumper sticker? 'Nothing Sucks Like an Electrolux.' The company is Scandinavian and had no idea what it meant to 'suck' in America, so when they brought their ad campaign here it was a total failure. A couple days ago I sent them a new jingle I wrote: 'Your house will look like a million bucks if you get an Electrolux.'"

"That's good!" I said, with visions of royalty checks dancing in my head. "When will you hear back?"

"Dunno." Linc showed me his crossed fingers. "But for now, a raccoon's work is never done." And just as Dear Abbie had suggested, we soon found ourselves rooting through dumpsters in the back lot of the Lord & Taylor up near the Maryland border. To my relief the area behind the department store was only dimly lit, no security guards in sight. Linc took his sweet time rustling through the garbage, naming each goodie in the trash and asking if we might have use for it: no to a box of hair rollers, yes to slightly bent flatware; no to a shower head marked DISCONTINUED, yes to button-down shirts marked FLAWED. I thought we were done for the night, but Linc pointed to the Woodward & Lothrop across the way.

The back lot at Woodies was as bright as a prison yard, and our van sat under a flickering light for anyone to see. Still, Linc hopped into the garbage without a care, as if he were climbing into bed for the night.

He'd been in the trash for a good fifteen minutes, and I could no longer see the top of his head. When he gave me a running play-by-play his voice had a rusty echo.

"Mom's going to start getting worried," I said.

"I need a hand." He seemed to be straining, but I didn't want to leave my post.

When I cautiously approached the dumpster he said, "Hop in." He was pulling with all his might on the end of a very large bag.

I shimmied up and over the lip, nearly kicking Linc in the face as I tumbled in. Holding my breath from the wet earth and new plastic smell, I pulled the smaller bags and boxes out of the way. I tried not to think about the police and the family of rats that would be strolling over any minute now, after dinner in the alley of the Magic Pan.

Outside a voice shouted, "Hey!" and I stopped what I was doing. Then another voice—or was it the same one?—shouted "Hey!" again. I considered diving under the trash and not making a sound until the voices went away. But there was our van, like a fat thumb pointing in our direction.

"Let's go!" I whisper-shouted to Linc and sprung out of the dumpster like a jack-in-the-box. I jumped in the passenger side of the van, ducked low and listened. I heard voices—it sounded like two different people. But now they seemed farther away.

For a minute that felt like an hour, I waited until a huge plastic bag spilled over the side of the dumpster, followed by Uncle Linc. He wiped his hands on his OshKoshes then dragged his prize toward the van. I opened the doors and we hauled the surprisingly light bag up and in. On our way out of the Woodies parking lot I saw two bedraggled men on the corner, one with a grocery cart piled high with junk, talking in loud voices to each other.

When Linc was safely back on Mass. Ave., he said, "Looks like you got the heebie-jeebies."

I wanted to seem brave, but had to admit that I'd thought the homeless guys were cops.

Linc burst out laughing and pulled a half-eaten sub out of his pocket. "Stick 'em up." He pointed the sandwich at me.

"Gross. Are you gonna eat that?"

"Free food is free food. It'll do for now." Linc unwrapped the wax paper from the sub and took a bite.

When we got home, my mother was waiting at the window. I could see her parting the curtains as Linc and I struggled up the steps with the TV. "Jesus Christ, it's about time," she said. "I'm never going to let you do that again."

The television was too big for the stand, so we set it on the floor in the corner of the parlor by the built-in bookcases. Chester jumped up on the TV, rubbed his face on the top corner and lay down.

"Maybe you'll like some of our other merchandise." Linc headed back to the van.

While he was gone, my mother scolded me. "I was five seconds from calling the police."

"That would have been a good idea, Mom. 'Hello, Officer, could you help me look for my son and brother? They're behind a department store digging through the trash.'"

Linc shouldered open the door dragging the huge bag. He hauled it to the living room and spilled its contents on the floor.

Nothing but pillows, in every size and type of material. There must have been fifty.

I brought in the rest of the stuff as Linc was explaining why pillows were just as good as furniture. "You've seen drawings of Confucius. His students sat on pillows on the floor. Snug as bugs."

"Just promise me you won't get in trouble," my mother said, calming down.

"Only if you promise me to stop flipping your wig." Linc headed back to the parlor and plugged in the TV. Chester licked his paws, his eyelids lilting as if he were enjoying a treat. Linc turned the switch and the TV hummed. Then, like an eye opening, it came on. In the light of the last minutes of *The Tonight Show,* a smile stretched across Linc's face and I wondered if he did have another shot at greatness, after all.

I believe that it wasn't until the last Friday before our alleged first day of school that we managed to schedule more visits from prospective students. Sister Donovan sent us two of her charges, and though they were only interested in part-time classes, at least it was a start. With such an operation as we were running, our breakthroughs rarely occurred before the eleventh hour.

That morning coincided with the announcement by the Chinese Communist Party of the death of Chairman Mao. I won't forget the wounded look on Tino's face when he saw the banner headline in the *Post,* or the sight of him dashing out the front door, barefoot, and vanishing into the rainy morning. The rest of us gathered in front of our salvaged television to watch news clips of throngs of Peking residents looking bleak and dazed as the party's message washed over them from loudspeakers above Tiananmen Square. When the prospective students arrived, the visits went well, thanks to the absence of their parents and the obtrusive Tino.

Dawn and Stephanie were best friends, and they hadn't found a creative outlet at Our Lady of Perpetual Help. "Unless you include Chant Choir with Sister Mary Kuplinski," said Dawn. "I want to learn to play the guitar like Joni Mitchell." My father pulled out the worn cover of *Blue* from the hippies' record collection and put the album on the turntable. Dawn shared a passing resemblance to Joni Mitchell, with the same pale hair and hollow cheekbones. My father pointed out Linc's guitar, propped in the corner, and told Dawn she'd come to the right place, then bounded upstairs to tell Linc, who was in his room reading, to pretend to be a master guitarist.

Stephanie explained to my mother and Cinnamon that OLPH didn't have a darkroom, and art met only one day a week. A redhead with constellations of freckles under her eyes, Stephanie wore a tiny Band-Aid on her cheek that from a distance looked like a scar. "I take a lot of pictures, but I have nowhere to develop them," she complained. And my mother, apparently willing to say anything at this point, claimed that we were planning to build a darkroom, then introduced Cinnamon as our "artist in residence." "She teaches photography, painting and drawing, anything you're into."

"You bet," Cinnamon went along.

"What kind of camera do you use?" Stephanie asked.

As far as I knew, Cinnamon didn't own a camera. She was mostly a collage artist, an assembler of found materials. But before she could answer, my father and Linc rumbled down the stairs. "You must be Dawn," Linc said and shook the pale-haired girl's hand. Joni Mitchell was singing "My Old Man" and Linc bobbed his head to the music and told Dawn a story I hadn't heard before, about how Graham Nash wrote the song "Our House" when he was living with Joni Mitchell on Laurel Canyon's Lookout Mountain Road. "She's one of my favorite singers," Linc said. "Sure, I could teach you to play like Joni."

Later, in college, when I grew nostalgic for this kind of music, I'd learn that Joni Mitchell was not your classic three-chord folksinger. Her technique, involving experimental tuning and complicated picking styles, was nearly impossible to imitate. But Dawn shook Linc's hand and said, "Great. When's our first lesson?"

Not wanting to be left behind, Stephanie asked the same of Cinnamon. Tuesday and Thursday afternoons became the agreed-upon meeting times. And with that, only three days before our scheduled opening, we had enrolled our first students.

After the girls left, a cheer went up at Our House. "This is only the beginning," my father predicted, and went to the kitchen, with new resolve, to work the phones. We dispersed to our various chores and projects, and I swept any questions and doubts to the back of my mind. Was it only the beginning? Why was my mother suddenly lying? How long could Linc and Cinnamon fake it? Where had Tino gone, and what might he do, let loose in the city?

On the way upstairs to get back to my biographies I passed Linc's room. He was sitting cross-legged on the floor, playing "Blackbird" again and looking melancholy.

"Worried about giving lessons?" I asked. He must have felt he had no business teaching guitar when he was little more than a beginner himself.

"No, it's not that." Linc scratched the Oreo cookie on his forehead. "I was thinking about 'Our House.'" He played the opening bars of the song: *I'll light the fire, you place the flowers in the vase . . .* "It's sweet but sad, because Graham Nash and Joni's romance didn't last long," he said. "Back at the end of the sixties, we all had this dilemma about loving 'the one you're with' or settling down with the one you love. You're too young to understand this, Daniel, but every wandering soul longs for a house of his own —you know, a stable life. The song was written in an hour, but that picture, that scene of domestic harmony, it never goes away."

By the end of the day and on through the next two afternoons we still had no word from Tino, and among all but one resident of Our House the tacit hope seemed to hover that he might never return. "He'll be back," Cinnamon promised. "He goes underground when he needs time to think." I pictured Tino descending into the Inferno, on his way to pay respects to the Great Dictator, Hell's latest arrival.

With Tino out of the picture, we enjoyed some rare tranquility. Good news arrived in the mail that our application for tax-exempt status had gone through. Though we had only two customers so far, at least we were officially open for business. My father helped ease my mother's worries by installing bars in the basement windows and joining the Metropolitan Police Department's Neighborhood Watch. "I told Officer Mazzocca about the robberies. He promises to keep a close eye on the house." My parents took turns leaving messages on the answering machines of school administrators in the hope of setting up more meetings. Even Linc seemed to shake free of the blues, trimming his hair and beard, throwing out his last pack of Camels and driving the Salem Cigarette Car to SmokEnders to pick up some quit-the-habit brochures. He brought home boxes of grape Bubble Yum, sneaking a stash for Molly and me, and sat on the front porch playing the Beatles' "I've Just Seen a Face," blowing purple bubbles until a huge one popped and webbed his beard.

Cinnamon didn't bother to go out looking for her paramour. "As my grandma used to say, he'll come back when he gets hungry." With the smiling eyes of the faithful, she settled into a butterfly chair to read the basic photography books she'd checked out of the library. And on the evening of the twelfth, the night before our first day, Tino returned. We were finishing a chili and cornbread dinner that my father had cooked. He always overspiced his food, which my mother complained was his way of getting out of cooking. I had tempered the chili with cheddar cheese and gobs of sour cream, but the air was so thick with cayenne pepper that when I breathed too deeply I fell into a coughing fit.

We almost didn't notice Tino. He barely made a noise as he walked into the house. He had found a pair of socks and mud-caked moccasins, and he wore a long-sleeved waffle shirt and a black band around his left arm. Though he'd been gone only two and a half days, he looked and smelled as if he hadn't showered in weeks.

Cinnamon jumped up from the table, threw her arms around him and kissed his dirty face. "Where have you been?" she asked.

"Here and there." He had hauled a trash bag with him, and now he unpacked it on the dining room floor. "I grabbed the Little Red Book from a shop on Dupont Circle and spent a couple nights under the aquaduct." He pulled Mao's manifesto out of the bag and read a few lines about overthrowing the bourgeoisie, then unrolled a poster of the dictator, in Zhongshan suit and cap, looking boldly into the future. "I found one other little thing, too." His face brightened. "Or, I guess you could say it found me." He dug into the bag and pulled out a tiny black kitten, lifting it toward the candlelight. The kitten lowered its ears and tensed its famished body. It couldn't have weighed much more than a pound, but it looked fierce, ready to spring. Chester, in the dining room trolling for scraps, came bounding over, and the kitten hissed like a rattlesnake, sending our tabby into a hasty retreat.

"Just what we need, a feral cat," my father said.

Tino ignored him. "I was sitting under the bridge in Rock Creek Park the other night giving glory to the Great Teacher when I felt this weight in my lap. Little guy hadn't eaten in days. So him and me, we hit the dumpsters along Connecticut Avenue and scored some pretty good snacks. The kid needs fattening up, though."

"What should we name him?" Molly asked.

"His name is Chairman Mao." Tino lowered the kitten into the crook of his arm and cooed, scratching the urchin under its chin with his index finger.

"Chairman Me-ow," Molly said, satisfied.

"The cat has to go." My father stood up to clear the table, and thus began an argument that lasted much of the evening about whether we should keep the kitten. My father worried that a feral cat would make Chester sick and the vet bills would put us in debtors' prison; Molly and I both knew that a helpless creature like the Chairman didn't stand a chance back in the wild. "So let's take him to the pound," my father said. "He'll find a nice home."

My mother entered the fray. "They'll just put him to sleep."

In the end my father was outnumbered. On our way up to bed, Cinnamon led us in a chorus:

Our house is a very, very, very fine house
With two cats in the yard . . .

8

....

BY THE NEXT DAY the sing-along was over. Tino had gotten up early and made a shrine above the mantel to the fallen Communist leader, taping the poster of Mao over my mother's Hopper print, laying yellow chrysanthemums next to a white candle, and standing the Little Red Book face-out. When Molly and I came down that morning for breakfast we expected a confrontation, but our parents had more pressing concerns. With Dawn and Stephanie not due to arrive until the next day and many schools now opening their doors, our recruitment efforts redoubled. Our father wore his brown check pants and Sears jacket, and our mother had on her best black and white wraparound dress.

"Your uncle's going to take care of you while we visit some headmasters," my father said. "We can worry about *this*"—he pointed to the mantel—"when we get back home."

But just as they were headed out, the doorbell rang, and before any of us could answer it, the deadbolt clicked open and in walked Bailey in a houndstooth blazer, with Cleo a step behind him.

"Thought I'd drop in on the school," he announced in his stentorian voice.

My father blocked the entrance to the living room and herded Bailey and Cleo into the parlor, saying, "What a pleasant surprise." My mother looked alarmed that Bailey had let himself into the house. We hadn't seen him since the Fourth of July, and had almost forgotten our initial concerns that he'd be the worst kind of smothering landlord. He said what I already knew: that he'd bought oceanfront property in Delaware and had been running back and forth all summer, "busier than a one-armed paper-hanger," trying to finish work on the Bethany Beach house while also completing a development project near Fell's Point in Baltimore.

"But we're wrapping that up now, too," he said. "Daddy's going to be home more." He hugged Cleo, who gave a half-smile as she leaned away.

Cleo wore a green plaid skirt, white blouse and saddle shoes, her hair pulled back in a short ponytail. She must have noticed me assessing her uniform, because she explained that it was her orientation day at OLPH. I wanted to thank her for setting up the meeting with Sister Donovan and ask if she had anything to do with Dawn's and Stephanie's interest or if she'd heard of other leads. But Cleo's note had said not to tell her father. So we talked about the pleasant weather instead.

Tino, Cinnamon and Linc joined us in the parlor.

"Are these your students?" Bailey asked.

My father hesitated for a moment, as if considering another lie. "No." He exhaled. "This is the rest of our faculty." He introduced the hippies, giving their fake credentials.

"Interesting." Bailey cast a long look—at Linc and his *Uneeda Biscuit* T-shirt and the stray bits of gum in his beard; at Cinnamon, braless and chiming with amulets; at Tino, in ginger corduroys ripped at the knee, his eyes trained, I noticed, on Cleo.

My mother must have signaled Linc, because he announced, "We're going to run some errands," then shepherded Tino and Cinnamon outside.

"That's a motley crew," Bailey said.

"They clean up well." My father twisted his hair where his part used to be. "They have lots of teaching experience."

"So where are the students?" Bailey looked around.

"Can I get you something to drink? Maybe a coffee?" my mother asked.

"I don't drink coffee. Makes me irritable," Bailey said, barely looking my mother's way. He had a habit, when talking to my parents, of only addressing my father. My mother had commented on this before, and I'd noticed that she made a point of stepping into Bailey's line of vision to force him to take her into account.

My mother offered Bailey a chair, which he refused, saying he had to get going soon. "The truth of the matter is, we have only two students so far, and they're both part-time." She launched right in. "We got way behind on recruitment because, frankly, there was a lot to fix up here."

Bailey raised a thick eyebrow. "I guess I could stay a minute." He sank into one of the butterfly chairs. "What else have you got to drink?"

My mother sent Molly to the kitchen, and my sister reported back. Bailey asked for a glass of milk, and I helped Molly gather milk and cookies for everyone. I was glad Cleo hadn't joined us, because the dishes had piled up and a family of roaches, with long, expressive antennae, had gotten an early start on their day and set up camp on the edge of the sink. We opened the cupboards and they scuttled away.

When we returned, our mother was asking Bailey if he had any ideas about where to find students. "We're not from Washington," she explained. "We have no connections here, so we keep getting the brushoff." My mother tended not to lay her cards on the table, and she usually let my father deal with his dubious friend, but lately she'd been trying a more direct approach, sometimes even taking charge.

But Bailey ignored her. "So what happened to the flag?" He dipped a Chips Ahoy cookie into his milk and took a bite. "Are you making some kind of political statement?"

"I've been meaning to tell you," my father jumped in. "I know this is going to sound ridiculous, but we had a burglar." He went on to tell the story of the missing flags and the theft of the television.

Bailey set his empty glass on the floor and wiped his lips with the back of his hand. "You're saying someone stole *two* different flags."

"That's right."

"If they stole the TV, what's that?" Bailey pointed across the room.

"It's a replacement."

"That's a mighty old replacement."

My mother intervened again and talked about the crime reports she'd read on the neighborhood and all the time we'd spent securing the house. Cleo tried to reassure her, saying, "We've never been robbed, and we don't live too far from here." But Bailey confirmed that 16th Street straddled the border between the haves and the have-nots. I wondered where my family stood. We had a house, yet at any moment our landlord could take it away. We had a school, at least in name, but hardly any students. My parents were out of work, subsisting on a dream, and someone had been casing our house, perhaps thinking we were rich. And yet we had no more than a few hundred dollars, with a wave of expenses building just beyond our view.

My mother passed the plate of cookies to Bailey, who took the last two. "We're sorry about the flag," she said. "I don't know why someone would want to steal it."

Bailey polished off the cookies. "Some of your neighbors have flags. No one has stolen them."

"I'll grant you, it's strange. More milk?" my mother asked. Bailey declined, and for a wild moment I wondered whether he might have taken the flags himself.

"I'll tell you what," Bailey said. "I'll drop off another flag tomorrow, but this time keep a better eye on it."

My mother agreed, then got back to the subject of Bailey's connections. "I remember when we were in college you said your father used to drink with Senator McCarthy. I know this is a lot to ask, but we'd love to sit down with some people who could help us. Do you know anyone?"

My father added, "We've already talked to the dean of students at Our Lady of Perpetual Help. She sent us two terrific girls."

Bailey's scalp did its little dance. "And how did you find out about Sister Donovan?"

Seeing that Cleo's pretty neck was flushing, I answered for my parents. "We've been up and down the yellow pages and all over the city. Isn't that where you go to school?" I turned to Cleo.

She said yes and asked which of her classmates had enrolled, and I told her Dawn and Stephanie. "They're nice," Cleo said. "Artsy types. But I don't really know them."

Bailey got up to go, a hint of suspicion leaving his blunt face. "Well, I wish you'd consulted me first. I'd rather not mix the nuns up in this enterprise."

My mother wasn't getting any help from my father. He cleared the glasses and cookie plate and took them back to the kitchen. "So you'll give us a few contacts?" My mother opened the front door.

"I'll see what I can do," Bailey said. But as he turned to leave, he caught a glimpse of the poster above our mantel. "What the hell's that?"

My father hurried back from the kitchen. "Nothing at all. Just a silly school project."

Bailey stepped into the living room. "How can you have a school project when you don't have students?"

My father blew out Tino's mourning candle.

The tips of Bailey's ears turned bright red. "What's this? Some kind of shrine? I knew you had lefty inclinations, Pete, but you can't be serious."

"It's not mine," my father said.

"Mao Tse-tung?" Bailey squinted out of the caverns of his sunken eyes. "That S.O.B. made Hitler look like a libertarian."

"I don't disagree." My father swiped the poster off the wall, nearly knocking down the Hopper print beneath it.

"Hold on a minute," my mother said. "That poster belongs to Tino, who's teaching a course in social behavior. And it's not a shrine—it's a display. We're not going to ignore current events here. Mao died. There's a power vacuum in China. We have to talk about these things."

Bailey was unmoved. "Do you light a candle and lay a wreath anytime you discuss a topic? That's a shrine. I've got Maoists living under my roof."

The thin veneer of my mother's patience fell away. So much for trying to turn on the charm. "There's nothing in our lease stipulating what we can and cannot put on the walls." She raised her voice. "Yes, this is your roof, but you have no right to let yourself in whenever you please. We live here now, and what happens inside this house is none of your business as long as we abide by the terms of the contract. So forgive me for troubling you. I shouldn't have bothered to ask."

"I've helped you folks plenty," Bailey said. "Sorry if I hadn't planned on contributing this year to the Communist Party."

My father tore the poster into a dozen pieces. One swatch—of Mao's lower lip and the mole on his chin—floated to the floor.

"Tino's gonna be maa-ad," Molly said.

"You shouldn't have done that," my mother added.

"We're not Communists," my father declared.

Bailey turned to go. "I'm disappointed, Pete. That's all."

Trailing a few steps behind her father on her way out the door, Cleo mouthed the words "I'm sorry."

After the champagne Cadillac pulled away, my mother scolded my father. "Why do you have to cave in to him every time? He's not the head of this school. You are. We all are."

My father slumped on the brocade sofa, springing dust spores into the slanted light. "I don't want a Mao poster on our living room wall. Sorry if I'm not a fan of genocidal dictators."

"This isn't about the poster and you know it. Bailey's going to try to control everything we do."

"But he's not controlling us. We haven't seen him in months."

"You heard him. He wanted to check in on the school. He's only coming around now because he thought classes had begun." My mother hovered over the sofa, too restless to sit down. "That bully let himself into our house. We need to change the locks."

"I'll talk to him. We're getting a good deal, remember?"

"It's not worth it." My mother dug a butterscotch candy out of her purse, unwrapped it and popped it into her mouth.

"Be reasonable," my father said. "Do you think we can run a school out of a two-bedroom apartment? Hell, we couldn't afford a two-bedroom apartment. We need Bailey on our side. Why don't you let *me* deal with him. You two are like fire and gasoline."

The black kitten stepped cautiously into the room, and Molly, standing just inside the threshold, snatched him up. The little gremlin struggled, pawing at the air, and Molly let him go. "You tore up Tino's poster, Dad. What's he gonna do when he finds out?"

"He's not going to find out," our mother broke in, the candy clicking her teeth. "We'll tell him that Bailey tore up the poster because he hates Chairman Mao."

"I don't know if that's a good idea," my father said.

"Well, it's what we're going to do, and that's final. Now why don't you stay here and take care of the kids. I'm going to try to get us some meetings."

My mother did manage to get meetings that day, and over the course of the next few weeks my parents had drawn up a list of nearly a dozen students whom administrators had labeled "candidates for a change of scenery." But since the fall term was already under way, it was unlikely anyone on the list would enroll before January.

When Dawn and Stephanie arrived for their first tutorials they were surprised to find the house empty of students, so we all rushed around trying to seem busy. Linc and Dawn sat in the parlor listening to *Blue,* and by the end of the first two weeks they had gone over tuning, how to hold a pick, how to play a chromatic scale, and were working up to "Greensleeves." Cinnamon and Stephanie had been on a field trip to the National Portrait Gallery, and since Cinnamon was still studying shutter and aperture, exposure and film speed, from basic photography books, she sent Stephanie out into the city to shoot images based on the seven deadly sins, then had the pictures developed at a discount camera store. Thus far Stephanie had covered three of the sins: Lust was an evening exterior shot of Good Guys, a strip club in Glover Park; Gluttony was a still life of a Quarter Pounder, fries and Coke on a Formica dinette; and Greed was an aging socialite in a department store mirror trying on an ermine coat. The photos were predictable and technically unversed, fuzzy blends of gray with little sense of composition, but Cinnamon promised, "At the end of the year, you'll have a one-woman show."

Whether we wanted it to or not, October 1 arrived, and my father sat at the dining room table writing a check for four hundred dollars to Dornan Properties. It had taken Bailey a couple of weeks to call and say he was stopping by with the new flag, and my father wanted to have the check ready and to make sure that Tino was out of the house. When Tino had found his Mao poster in shreds on the living room floor, the self-proclaimed peace activist had vowed revenge on Bailey: "I'm going to cloud up and rain fist and heel all over that fucking Nazi." My parents had tried to reason with Tino, but the gauntlet had been thrown down, and he wasn't the type to turn and walk away. So the best we could hope for was enough time to pass so that he'd forget about the incident. But after two weeks he hadn't let it go.

"You need to send him on an errand," my mother said in a low voice. "Bailey could be here any minute."

Tino was lying on the sofa in the parlor, reading *Stalking the Wild Asparagus* and listening to Big Brother and the Holding Company on the stereo. My father put his fingers to his temples, as if trying to concentrate, when the black kitten rubbed against his leg and let forth a rusty meow. The urchin's bowl was empty, which gave my father an idea. He went into the pantry and threw away what was left of the Purina Kitten Chow, then told Tino that Chairman Mao was hungry and out of food. Tino shut off the music and came in to investigate. "I could have sworn I just got some." He yawned and stretched. "He's got some appetite," my father said, without batting an eye.

After Tino had driven off, my mother tried to persuade my father to ask for an extension on the free rent. "Just two more months, so we can call it an even six." But Bailey had a limited number of favors to offer, and my father wanted to keep one more in reserve just in case, down the line, things got truly desperate.

"That time's going to come sooner than you know," my mother said.

"Trust me, Val." My father avoided eye contact with me. "We have more than fifteen hundred dollars left over from Aunt Natalia. That should take us well into next year. And I'll get a second job, if it comes to that."

In truth, we had six hundred in the emergency account. My father had confessed to me that we had less than two months' worth of rent, with three months remaining before the start of the spring term, January 10.

I'd done my part to keep expenses down, consulting Dear Abbie as often as I could. Linc and I were regulars at the Adams Morgan McDonald's, where we used coupons to buy hamburgers and on the way out filled our pockets with packets of sugar and creamer, salt and pepper, ketchup and mustard, napkins and cups. Often we visited the restrooms for toilet paper and cleaning supplies. Though I wasn't proud of taking what I could, Linc told me that McDonald's exploited cheap labor and often shut down franchises when employees threatened to unionize. "There are good corporations and bad ones." He wiped Big Mac "special sauce" from the corners of his mouth. "If you take from the bad, you help even the scales."

Linc had made friends at other restaurants, too, and was known to come home at midnight, after the Omega, El Caribe and Millie & Al's closed, with a satchel full of leftovers for our next day's meal. My father said he was probably trading pot for food. I'd seen Linc tending his marijuana plants in the side yard, but my parents looked the other way, so long as he was making a contribution.

Cinnamon had worked her charms on a stock boy at Fields of Plenty, who each Tuesday morning gave her a box of dented cans and slightly bruised produce. Added to the bounty from Tino's late-night raids on local community gardens, we had no shortage of fruit and vegetables. Veggie stews, veggie lasagnas, tabouli, moussaka, and big salads with sautéed onions, zucchini and potatoes had become our nightly staples. Molly was so pleased by the rare abundance of vegetarian meals that she stopped asking how the food had arrived at our table. "It's all part of The Flow," Tino had explained. When Molly and I would look back on this period in our family, she'd tell me that by a certain point she cast aside her rectitude and began to feel entitled to anything we could get our hands on. And I knew exactly what she meant. Good fortune had been slow to arrive in our childhoods, which made right over wrong a less appealing notion than *whatever it takes.*

Thanks to a scam straight out of *Steal This Book,* we had plenty of baked goods, too. One day we were all sitting down to breakfast when Tino appeared in a black hat and coat and a white clerical collar that he'd picked up at a Goodwill in Seattle. With his Zapata mustache and "Keep on Truckin'" strut he looked like a debauched version of Father Guido Sarducci. "How many years do you get in Purgatory for impersonating a priest?" Tino laughed. But the costume actually worked: he found a bakery near Georgetown University that was only too happy to hand over day-old bread and pastries to feed the urban poor.

So we were scraping by, though the problem remained that we needed cold hard cash.

By dinnertime Bailey had still not shown up, and I worried that he'd arrive any minute. Tino was back with more kitten chow and winding himself up for another diatribe. He was reading the *Washington Post* at the table, going on about a recent *Playboy* interview in which Jimmy Carter admitted that he had lusted in his heart for many women. As a born-again Christian, Carter believed that his sinful thoughts counted as adultery. "You want this guy to be president?" Tino said. "He's going to fill the White House with Scripture-quoting nut cases and sanctimonious pricks. Have you heard of anything so stupid?"

He looked around the table, but no one spoke up. Cinnamon certainly wasn't going to encourage an exegesis on biblical adultery and coveting thy neighbor's wife. "Maybe you should put your newspaper down and eat your salad," she suggested.

Tino folded the *Post* and tossed it on the floor. "All I know is, if I had a dime for every woman I lusted after, I'd be on easy street right now."

As much as I disliked Tino, I had to admit that he did serve a purpose: his presence alone gave my parents someone to rally against. They disagreed with nearly everything he said, and along with Bailey he provided a common adversary that helped bring them together. For the first time in a long while I sensed that my parents were getting along. They didn't snap at each other as much, and now that everyone had a specific role at the school, they were less at odds and more bound by a need to cooperate if we had any hope of succeeding. Though my mother had her anxieties, she felt empowered in ways she never had as the trailing spouse of a secondary school administrator. She seemed to be looking forward to teaching in this new way, and open to the possibility that Our House could make room for her aspirations, too.

After dinner I went out to the front porch with my parents and, to our relief, found a new flag in the bracket. Bailey must have sent his furtive factotum. The night was crisp and cool, football weather; the linden trees that lined our street rustled in the breeze, their leaf-like bracts pulling free and helicoptering to the sidewalk. Sitting down to go over their list of students to follow up with, my parents waved at Mr. Unthank, who relaxed on the porch next door with a scotch and the *Washington Star,* Sarah Vaughan drifting out of his open window. He gave a two-finger salute, more obligatory than friendly, and I wondered how he'd feel about a swarm of kids filing in and out of our house at all hours.

As we were getting ready to go back inside, a police car sped past on 16th Street and swung a left on W, just beyond Meridian Hill Park, across the border in Shaw. The squad car stopped where we could still see its lights whirling around the neighborhood houses. Two policemen got out and knocked on one of the row house doors. A large woman in a cornflower-blue robe stepped onto the front porch and gestured down the street. The officers had left the siren on, so we couldn't hear what the woman was saying, but my mother grabbed my arm and pulled me inside the house, where we watched from the parlor. Mr. Unthank had gone inside too, shut his door and windows and drawn his curtains. But my father wandered toward the squad car to see what was happening. No one else had appeared on the street. For a neighborhood of tight-packed houses, we were surprised that we'd met only the tidy Mr. Unthank and Jackie Clarke across the street with her overgrown yard. My mother took this as further evidence of people's fear.

When my father returned twenty minutes later he reported that the woman had not been robbed. She lived alone and had heard noises in the house, but there were no signs of a break-in. "Officer Mazzocca was one of the cops. Apparently she's called in false alarms before. I could tell she's batty."

My mother pressed him. "If she's a regular caller, why haven't we seen the police there before?"

"I've seen cops around here," I offered. "The neighborhood's well patrolled."

"This is between me and your father." My mother pulled the curtains closed and locked and latched the front door.

"I told you Mazzocca's watching out for us. But apparently that's not good enough for you," my father said.

So that night he slept on the brocade sofa with one of his old baseball bats. He had been exiled to the couch before, but this time he went voluntarily. "I'm going to stay right here until I catch a thief," he announced.

"You're being ridiculous, Pete," my mother said. "But suit yourself."

I figured this was another of my father's chivalric stunts to win my mother's affection. I doubted he'd last long before heading back upstairs.

9

ON THE THIRD NIGHT of my father's self-imposed exile on the couch, I was sitting in bed before midnight reading about Teddy Roosevelt. I had amassed a large collection of trivia about the twenty-sixth president:

> His first wife and his mother both died on Valentine's Day, 1884.
>
> At his inauguration he wore a "mourning ring" containing a strand of Abraham Lincoln's hair.
>
> He was the first president to fly, on a four-minute ride in a pusher biplane designed by the Wright brothers.
>
> He was the youngest president, at forty-two, ever to serve, and he changed the name of 1600 Pennsylvania Avenue from the Executive Mansion to the White House.

Unlike some of my past biographies, I found myself not so much skimming for trivia but actually reading entire chapters about Roosevelt's presidency. Here was a guy who got things done, leading the charge at the Battle of San Juan, breaking up trusts and railroad monopolies, connecting the Atlantic to the Pacific Ocean, leading a "life of strenuous endeavor" as he cordoned off 230 million acres of land for national parks.

I was so absorbed that I didn't hear the shouting downstairs.

But I caught a glimpse of Cinnamon, half naked, throwing on a shirt as she rushed past my bedroom door.

By the time I'd made it to the first floor, Tino and Linc had formed a barricade between the hall and the parlor, Tino in a "fists for hire" position, looking like *The Street Fighter*'s Sonny Chiba, and Linc in an awkward semicrouch, holding a Louisville Slugger as if it were a fishing pole. Cinnamon locked the front door, and my father stood over a black kid who looked not much older than me, yelling, "What the hell do you want?"

Pinned on the sofa, the kid held up his palm to shield himself, as if preparing for my father to strike him.

"He was about to break in. He came right up to the porch and peeked in the window," my father said to the rest of us. His eyes flashed white, like the Incredible Hulk thrown into a rage.

My mother and Molly had gone to the kitchen to call the police. The kid retreated to the corner of the sofa. "Let me explain."

"There's nothing to explain. You robbed us, and now you're coming back for more. Empty your pockets," my father demanded.

The kid wore a metallic-green parka with a fake-fur-lined hood encircling his face. His black knit cap, pulled low on his forehead, might have looked menacing on someone else but on him seemed more like an ill-fitting shell. When he unzipped his coat and pulled rabbit ears from his dungarees I could see that he was a wisp under all that armor, with remarkably clear skin for an adolescent, and a piano player's hands. Sweat formed a V on his brown velour shirt and along the top of his lip, where he had the vague trace of a mustache. Something about him—his starry eyelashes, his fine, almost pretty features—seemed familiar. "I'm here to *return* your stuff," he said. "I live down the street, and I know who broke into your house."

"What are you talking about?" my father asked.

"A friend of mine did it. He's got a secret hideaway where he keeps his loot, so I know where your flags and TV are. I could get them right now if you want."

Tino stepped out of his *Street Fighter* pose. "That sounds like a crock."

"I'm serious," the kid said. "Give me ten minutes."

"So you can disappear? I don't think so." Tino took the bat from Linc and brandished it. "You're not going anywhere."

My mother sent Molly and me upstairs, but we stopped and crouched just below the landing, where we could watch the drama as if from balcony seats.

"You can't keep me here." The kid turned defiant. "I came over to do you a favor, and this is the thanks I get?"

My mother asked if he had actually broken in, and my father said, "Not exactly. He was snooping on the porch."

"Snooping?" The kid's voice cracked. "I was about to knock on your door, that's all. Is knocking on doors a crime?" He lowered his hood and wiped the sweat from his lip with his coat sleeve. I concentrated on his face, trying to place him somewhere. Hill Street? Pierce Park? Was he a bagger at the Safeway?

My mother said, "He's right. We can't keep him here," and though Tino protested and shook the Louisville Slugger—"I know what you're up to. You can't bullshit me"—my mother apologized to the kid and let him stand back on his feet and walk out the door, just minutes before the red lights of a cop car pulsed across our ceiling.

My father answered, and Officer Mazzocca walked into the parlor. He had a cop name, but didn't look like a cop. He was small and wore Buddy Holly glasses. His well-muscled partner, in a uniform so tight it seemed part of his skin, leaned in the doorway, one thumb in his belt, the other hooked over the handle of his billy club.

"Thanks for coming," my father said, "but we've sorted it out. I heard some activity in front of the house and thought we were being robbed, but it was just one of our neighbors."

Mazzocca took off his glasses and wiped them with a handkerchief. "Pete, right?" He turned to his partner. "Pete's a member of the Neighborhood Watch."

"I haven't been on patrol much," my father explained. "We've been kind of busy around here." He introduced everyone. The hippies barely looked at the cops and kept their hands in their pockets so Mazzocca's partner, Officer Trammell, couldn't crush their fingers with his action-hero's grip. I looked on from the landing, trying not to think of the marijuana plants in the side yard, *Steal This Book* and its opinions about the police ("Pigs have small brains and move slowly") stashed in my tower, Cinnamon's poncho hiding her morning's cache of shoplifted over-the-counter drugs.

"You folks have a good night," Mazzocca said and followed Trammell out the door.

The cops hadn't been gone five minutes when the kid in the fur-lined coat rang the doorbell, this time carrying the stolen television and flags in his arms.

Sweat beading on his forehead, he poured through the open door like a river through a sluice and set the TV down heavily in the hallway. "Satisfied?" he asked Tino.

"And why should I believe your story?" Tino cocked his head back. "Who's to say you didn't snatch our shit in the first place?"

"Why would I bring it back?" The kid stuffed his hands into the pockets of his dungarees.

"To get in good with us."

"For what reason?"

"Because we live in the biggest house on the block, and you think we're rich. But take a look around." Tino pointed toward the living room, where the pillows lay strewn about the floor and the only decorations on the walls were my mother's Hopper print and Cinnamon's hand-designed banner:

WELCOME TO

OUR HOUSE

ACT FIRST. ASK PERMISSION LATER.

My mother intervened and apologized for Tino's rudeness. She asked the kid his name and where he lived. He said Quinn, and that his place was close to here, a little ways across 16th.

Tino asked, "And who's this friend of yours, the amateur thief?"

"I can't tell you," Quinn said. "He's got it bad enough already. And I don't dime-out my friends."

Tino tried to press the matter, but my father told him to go easy on the kid. "The important thing is we know who broke into the house."

"You're looking at him." Tino pointed to Quinn, who shook his head.

My father defended him, but did want some assurances that we wouldn't be robbed again. "What's going to happen when your friend finds out you've returned our things?"

The fur of Quinn's hood surrounded his head like an aureole. "He left town for good a month ago. His folks split and he moved to Cleveland. He was going to get caught sooner or later."

"And where's this so-called hideaway?" Tino asked.

"Why would I tell *you* when you've been treating me like a criminal?"

Cinnamon took Tino's hand and wrapped his arm around her shoulder. The freckles along her clavicle looked like grains of brown sugar falling into a cup. "Let's go upstairs," she said. On his way out of the room Tino glared at Quinn. "I know your scam. Don't think you can fool a yippie."

Tino and Cinnamon brushed past us on the stairs, her peasant skirt tickling the skin of my arm, her sweet tobacco and patchouli scent a fleeting intoxication.

My father dug for more about Quinn's friend and their secret hiding place. "As a member of the Neighborhood Watch, it's my duty to report unlawful activity." But Quinn had no reason to trust us, and though my father had changed his tone, only a half hour ago he'd been teetering over the kid, his slugger's arms tensed to strike.

Quinn said he couldn't give away that information, and my father reminded him that even knowing about such a place made him an accessory.

"Don't threaten him, Pete," my mother put in.

"I'm just letting him know."

Quinn headed for the door and zipped up his coat. "Some thanks I get," he repeated.

Before he stepped into the night and walked away, I took one last look at his face and remembered where I'd seen him. He'd been a regular all summer at the Mount Pleasant Library, and always sat at the same table, near the military history shelves. More than once I'd seen him napping there, his head resting on a stack of books.

After Quinn had left, Molly and I climbed up to our rooms. I tried to return to Teddy Roosevelt, but couldn't concentrate as my parents' voices rose up to the rafters. My mother laughed at my father for claiming it his duty to report criminal activity, but he said he never would have joined the Neighborhood Watch if she hadn't been so paranoid about where we lived. She blamed him for getting us a house in a dodgy part of town, and he blamed her for inviting the hippies. "You want to talk about criminal activity," he said. "Most of it's going on under our roof."

"Is that my fault?"

"It's not mine."

"Did you have to pull him into the house and act like such a tough guy?"

"I didn't lay a hand on him. He followed me in on his own."

"You were being threatening, Pete, pushing your weight around. Would you have been so suspicious if he was white?"

The house went silent for a moment, just crickets playing their violins outside my turret window. "It was Tino, not me, treating him like a criminal," my father said. "What would you do if someone in a big coat stood on your porch at midnight, peering into your house? And where do you get off asking such a question? You're the one who made me put bars on the windows and extra locks on the doors, and who's always telling Daniel and Molly they can't cross the street into the black neighborhood. Have you forgotten the scholarship program at Lake Bluff, everything I tried to do for those South Side kids?"

"No, I haven't forgotten. It got you fired. We're in this mess because you got fired, Pete."

"And what have you done besides complain? I slept on the couch for three fucking nights. Some thanks I get, indeed."

That comment would put my father on the couch for three more nights, and drive my mother to look up her long-lost friend Linda Silvers, chief of staff for Wisconsin Senator Gaylord Nelson. I was in the kitchen eating Cheerios while my mother thumbed through the white pages and wrote down Linda's number. "Your father says all I do is complain. I wonder how he'd like it if I got off his back and started working full-time. You think this house is falling apart now. Wait till I'm not here to do damage control."

But when she reached the main office of Senator Nelson, a secretary told her that Linda was in Milwaukee getting out the vote for Jimmy Carter during the final election push. Asked if she wanted to leave her name and number, my mother said she was a constituent and would try again later. But something in her voice made me doubt she would anytime soon.

It was also around this time that Tino announced at dinner that he'd convinced a pair of twins and two of their friends to sign on for spring term. "They're stuck at a tight-ass prep school for now, but they'll be ready to start full-time in January."

"How did you find them?" my father asked.

We had eaten the last of the co-op and garden tomatoes a few weeks before, so I was struggling to choke down our dinner of roasted acorn squash buttered and salted in their skins and bulgur wheat so dry it parched my throat.

"Does it matter?" Tino shrugged off the question. "Gotta take what we can get."

"I'm just curious," my father said.

"I tripled our enrollment, bro." When Tino ate, he held his fork in his fist, like a baby in a highchair. He put down the fork and wiped his mouth with his shirtsleeve. "The twins are the headmaster's sons at that goose-stepping St. Sebastian Prep, up in Cathedral Heights, but they can't take the mind control. They're *this* close to blowing up their daddy's school, so we're doing everyone a favor. And you'll get a kick out of this, Pete: their best chum is the bishop's son, and he's trying to blow up the cathedral."

"Great." My father topped his glass with red wine. "Just what we need, a bunch of baby anarchists."

"They're not literally blowing shit up. These kids are mellow in the right environment."

Cinnamon, helping herself to seconds of bulgur, laughed and added, "You mean the right state of mind."

My father swung an accusing look at Linc, who had been minding his own business. "So you sold drugs to these kids? Is that how you found them?"

Linc dug into his OshKoshes for an after-dinner stick of gum. "A piece for peace?" he offered, and my father said no thank you, he was starting a school here, not a smoking circle.

"This isn't my racket," Linc said. "I've just been strumming my guitar. If you're asking about the cannabis, I put it in pots for winter and donated it to my friends here. I'm out of the business."

"It's true," Cinnamon said, with a disappointed lilt in her voice. "Can't you see he's Mr. Clean?"

My father looked at the bald, earringed icon on Linc's T-shirt and said he didn't care who was selling the dope. It had to stop. "I don't want another visit from Trammell and Mazzocca, let alone the DEA."

My mother got up to clear the table. "The important thing is, they recruited four students."

Tino licked the ends of his mustache, which curled over the top of his lip. "For the record, *selling* is a disputable term. Sure, I was enjoying some high-grade Hawaiian Indica, and the young men did pack a steamboat with me. And perhaps green paper exchanged hands, but I never named a price. The payment was voluntary, a suggested donation, as you'd find at any museum or church. It's like trick or treat for Unicef. You don't have to slip a dollar into the box, but you know it's the right thing to do."

It wouldn't be long before Tino would carry actual Unicef boxes from house to house on Halloween, leading Molly and me around the same Wesley Heights neighborhood where we'd picked up the big TV some months before. Our parents stayed home that night to hand out candy corn, while Molly and I dressed up as hippies—I already had the hair, so to complete the look I wore one of Linc's dashikis and a matching headband. Molly disappeared under a Janis Joplin–style hat that she found in Cinnamon's closet, a pair of moccasin boots and plenty of bead jewelry. Linc and Cinnamon dressed as they probably had on a typical day at the commune—overalls and an army jacket, floral dress under a shearling coat—and pretended to be our parents; it was nice to see them looking like a couple again. And Tino broke out his Father Guido Sarducci costume, playing priest and reformer to our ragtag band.

We filled our bags with candy, most of which Cinnamon would later sell to worker bees downtown, masquerading as a volunteer with New Dawn drug treatment center. By the end of the night we had knocked on enough doors to stuff six Unicef boxes full of bills and change. Linc drove the van home, with Cinnamon in the passenger seat and Tino in the back with us kids, counting up our earnings.

"A hundred and fifty-eight dollars and twenty-five cents," Tino announced. "Take us to easy street, driver."

"But it's for Unicef," Molly said.

Tino laughed. "That money's ours. Unicef's a bunch of wolves in sheep's clothing. They skim that money for themselves."

"But we said 'Trick or treat for Unicef.' That means we were lying." Molly took off her floppy hat and fixed her hair.

"Oh, please." Tino turned to me. "Tell your sister how the world works, bro."

I remembered Abbie Hoffman's chapter on "Free Money," how he said that charities are one of the biggest swindles around, and something like eighty percent goes back into the organization, for fancy cars, big salaries, or tax write-offs for Jerry Lewis. "We need that money for rent," I said. "We have to give it to my dad."

"I didn't see *him* trick-or-treating. We earned this bread fair and square." Tino lifted his fake cross from his chest and shook it at me. "I could use a coat. They say we're looking at a brutal winter."

Cinnamon turned around in the front seat. "Come on, sugar. All for one and one for all. Put the money in the pot so everyone's happy."

In the rearview mirror I caught a glimpse of Linc; the trace of a smile rustled his beard.

Back at home, we walked into the parlor startled to find my mother, father and Quinn in casual conversation. Quinn was dressed up for Halloween in an old-fashioned pilot's outfit, complete with wings on his jumpsuit, a quilted flying cap and goggles.

"I'm William J. Powell," he volunteered. "A pioneer of aviation. You've heard of Charles Lindbergh, but Powell could have crossed the Atlantic backwards. Too bad he was a black man."

I was surprised to find Quinn in a talky mood and would come to hear he'd been at the house for a while. He'd gone out trick-or-treating alone, and my father had invited him inside, perhaps to make up for their first encounter. Once Quinn had gotten comfortable, he'd grown garrulous, as if no one had sat down and listened to him in a long time. He said little about himself, but he did tell a long story about his friend Anthony, the amateur thief who had moved to Cleveland, and who, in fact—and this was only half the story; the rest I'd learn months later—had lived in our house.

Anthony was six years old when child services took him away, after his mother died. She'd been drinking Cisco, and climbed up on the railing of Duke Ellington Bridge. He had been walking with her and witnessed it all, tried to call out but the wind picked up and she fell. Before long he was in foster care, and over the years would stay with six families, all but the last of them the same song: a dollar would turn up missing from someone's wallet, and he'd be blamed all the way back to Horizon Foster Home to start over again. But one day when the city was trying to place him, the Kurtzman family called, and Anthony moved in with them, right here on the corner of 16th and Hill. So many years of waiting for a family, and it looked like Anthony had finally found one. They gave him the tower room, across the hall from his foster sister, Rachel, whom he adored. The rest of the Kurtzmans occupied the second floor. The kids—Rachel, Josh, Adam and Becca—called their parents by their first names, Sol and Joy.

For over a year, according to Quinn, his friend was "living *The Brady Bunch,* in black and white." Quinn and his older sister, Angela, used to come over for dinner and for sing-alongs in the living room. The Kurtzmans grew wildflowers in the garden and sold them at the Eastern Market on Saturdays, and Anthony went out in Sol's van on his first real job as a housepainter. He did the taping and sanding, Sol did the rolling and Josh and Adam did the trim. Anthony made three hundred dollars and worked through August as if it wasn't hot at all, even painted the outside of this house and was getting ready to do the inside when school started up again. But winter came around and Sol had debts that made him slam doors and put cracks in the walls. Around Christmas Joy's mom in Cleveland went into kidney failure, so Joy and the girls packed up for Ohio. And when the grandmother died, the boys went, too. Sol and Anthony stayed and held down the fort through January, February and March, and there was talk of the rest of the Kurtzmans returning to Washington by summer. But all that changed when Bailey sent a notice in the mail: they had thirty days to move out.

Now Quinn was helping himself to more candy corn. Molly and I showed our parents our Halloween take of Milky Ways, Hershey's Kisses, Sugar Daddys, Mary Janes and SweeTarts. My mother confiscated the candied apples and pocketed a large handful of Smarties for herself, but we knew we couldn't keep the candy anyway so didn't raise a fuss. Linc handed my father the Unicef boxes, grabbed his guitar and headed for the back patio to practice. Shooting Quinn a Mephistophelean smile, Tino took Cinnamon's hand and led her upstairs, where I pictured them stripping out of their priest and hippie clothes and frolicking like dolphins.

"Good news," my father announced to Molly and me. "We have another recruit."

And so it was that in the space of the few hours we'd been out trick-or-treating Quinn Simmons had gone from onetime suspected thief to our latest enrollee. Fed up with being the pestered freshman at Cardozo High, he seemed eager to join Our House, and right away.

"You're sure it's okay with your parents?" my mother asked again.

"They let me do what I want."

In time I'd learn more about Quinn's parents, and why he made all his own decisions, but for now I only cared that he was our newest student, our lucky number seven.

"Well, I ought to be getting home." Quinn lowered his goggles over his eyes. "Time to 'fill the air with black wings.'" He saluted us on his way out the door.

After he'd left, my father explained that Quinn would be our first scholarship student, on a work-study program. "I'm going to take him under my wing, so to speak. You should have heard him go on about flying machines. He's obsessed with zeppelins," my father said to me, and because I must have looked confused, having only heard of Led Zeppelin, often at high volume in the Lake Bluff dorms, he added, "You know, blimps."

Not that my dad had a clue about aeronautics, but this was probably far from his mind on a night that would mark the beginning of our first good run.

We hadn't had a trick-or-treater in the hour since we'd returned, but then we heard a knock on the door, and to my delight it was Cleo and two friends, dressed as Charlie's Angels, with Factotum Frank their stolid Bosley. In Wesley Heights we'd passed several versions of "the eye-popping, crime-stopping trio" in the same getups. Cleo was tomboy Kate, with a sporty vest over a wide-collared shirt, jodhpurs and knee-high boots. Her friends, whom I didn't recognize at first, had voluminous wigs—blond and brown—and carried cap guns in their silver-studded belts.

Farrah and Jaclyn took off their wigs, and we all had a good laugh when we recognized Dawn and Stephanie under the disguises.

"I didn't know you were friends," I said.

Cleo twirled her cap gun. "When the Townsend detective agency calls, we answer." She waggled the gun at me. "Any funny business going on around here?" I was still in my hippie costume. "Illegal narcotics, perhaps?" she asked. "Come on, girls, let's pat him down."

I blushed and backed away while the Angels ran up and tickled me.

After I'd recovered from this most welcome assault, Stephanie reported that Sister Donovan was delivering four more students for the spring term who wanted to do special projects that weren't offered at OLPH. "They're mostly poets," she said with a sneer. "They do rhymey, performancy stuff, not my cup of tea." I didn't mention that the only book of poetry I could recall ever opening was *The Prophet* by Kahlil Gibran. My father had bought it for my mother, and inscribed it with the lines from "On Marriage":

Love one another, but make not a bond of love.
Let it rather be a moving sea between the shores of your souls.

"Oh, and I almost forgot," Cleo said as she and the Angels dropped candy corn into their bags, preparing to leave. "My dad wanted you to have this." She handed us an invitation. "We're throwing an election party. Hope you all can come."

10

THE 1976 PRESIDENTIAL RACE was a nail biter. Carter's "trust me" campaign had catapulted him to a thirty-point lead after the Democratic Convention, and he had successfully positioned himself as a Washington outsider, a clear-eyed moralist hundreds of miles removed from the lying and thieving of the Nixon administration. He brought tradition and modernity together, a peanut farmer who replaced shacks in Atlanta with skyscrapers, a Sunday school teacher with a graduate degree in nuclear physics, a Southern governor with a progressive's heart. Ford and his running mate, Bob Dole, known around our house as Bozo and the Pineapple, had tried to restore dignity to the Republican Party by asking Americans to "look at the record," but even moderates couldn't forget that Ford had pardoned Nixon for Watergate.

Yet into September and October Carter had made his own missteps, promising a "blanket pardon" to Vietnam draft dodgers during a speech at the American Legion, alienating women and conservative Christians by admitting that he'd "lusted in his heart," and outright losing the first presidential debate. Though Ford stumbled in the second debate, by Election Day he had closed the gap, and most polls were divided over who would win.

On that Tuesday morning, Bailey called to make sure we were all coming to his party. As a bonus, he'd reportedly told my father, a number of parents with junior-high- and high-school-age kids would be there. "But I need you to promise that you won't be teaching *The Male Machine* or *The Liberated Man* or any of that other fluff at your school. We guys have enough problems with Gloria Steinem taking whacks at our privates." My father had assured him that no such course was on the books, and Bailey promised that he'd make a round of introductions. "Don't forget your rent check," he'd added. "We're past the first of the month."

This reminder prompted a meeting of the Fellowship of Chester, only we couldn't find our tabby so had to settle for Chairman Mao. My father closed my bedroom door behind him and plucked some fur from the scruff of the kitten's neck, causing the Chairman to hiss and spring to the floor.

I was hoping the superstition about black cats wasn't true when my father confessed that the Aunt Natalia fund had dwindled to less than five hundred dollars. After raiding the Unicef boxes and collecting Dawn's and Stephanie's money from guitar and photography "lessons," we'd still be down to three-fifty after paying November's rent. Take away four hundred for December, and we'd be lucky to have fifty dollars for the opening day of school. "It's going to be a meager Christmas," he said.

"But won't you get tuition?" I asked.

"We still only have twelve students, half of them part-time, and you, Molly and Quinn are freebies. I made the mistake of charging those four poets thirty bucks a course. Your mother and I had planned on fifty a course, but they drove a hard bargain. Look at this production: a leased house, no supplies, teachers with sketchy credentials. Maybe I could have gotten more, but I've never been a good negotiator. Please don't tell your mother."

I hated to see him this way, lines creasing his face. "I won't," I promised.

He clasped himself, as if to keep from falling apart. "I've applied for something called a Braitmayer Grant, but I only just got around to finishing the application. It's a long shot; we can't depend on anyone but ourselves. So listen—you'll have to keep this from your mother, too, but I told the hippies that whatever contribution they can make, I'll take it. At this point I don't care where they get the money from."

After our meeting adjourned, the adults went off with Molly to vote for the man from Plains. I shot baskets at the playground to shake off my nerves then sat on my trundle bed revisiting *Steal This Book:*

> Dear Abbie,
>
> Our stockings are empty. What should we do?
>
> Broke in the Nation's Capital
>
> Dear Broke,
>
> What better time to shoplift than the upcoming Christmas season? Every year the sleigh bells start their ring, ring, ring-aling, ding, ding, ding-aling earlier and earlier, so why not get into the spirit? Sew extra pockets to the inside of your longest, roomiest coat. Pick a cold, rainy weekend when everyone's shoulder to shoulder and looking the same. The best times for the five-finger discount are when the security guards are taking lunch, or right before closing when the retail stiffs are thinking it's Miller Time. Don't forget to practice at home. Case the store so you'll know its blind spots. And work in a team: one can bullshit the salesman while the other packs a fat bundle into his Santa's sack.

I put away my book, dabbed some of my father's English Leather on my neck, and slipped into my Toughskins and the only Izod shirt I owned: a blue-and-white-striped rugby with a red alligator. I blow-dried and brushed my hair in the mirror so that the wings fluffed out and the ends nearly touched my shoulders. Cinnamon said she loved my hair, and I almost believed that if I grew it out as long as Samson's, the brawn and the admirers would follow.

I joined the others downstairs as they gathered for the party. The election fell in the same week as my father's thirty-sixth birthday, and he'd said the only gift he wanted was to get through this night without any trouble. Though he'd tried to make the hippies stay home, Linc and Cinnamon had complained, and my mother had taken their side. Knowing the fuss was mostly about him, Tino assured everyone he'd behave. He said he'd put the incident with the Mao poster aside and would try, for the good of the school, to forget what a fascist pig our landlord was. My father warned him that the party would be crawling with Republicans, so if Carter won we couldn't celebrate until we came back home.

"I dig it," Tino had said.

"And one other thing," my father had added. "You're going to need to look presentable."

Downstairs in the hallway I couldn't believe the hippies' transformation: Linc wore corduroys and an oxford shirt he'd borrowed from my father; Cinnamon had pinned her hair in barrettes and ironed her floral dress; even Tino wore freshly laundered clothes, his hair tied back in a ponytail, and he'd trimmed his Zapata mustache just short of traffic cop.

As we were getting ready to leave, I reminded my mother that she said we could shoot off Tino's Fourth of July fireworks if a Democrat regained the White House. She winced before agreeing. "I guess a promise is a promise." She picked cat hairs off the sleeve of Molly's red jumper. "But like your father said: only after we come back from the party."

Not wanting to pull up to Bailey's house in the Salem Cigarette Car, all seven of us climbed into the van: my parents up front, Linc, Cinnamon and Molly on the first bench, and me stuck in the back with Tino. We added an eighth when we picked up Quinn at the Mount Pleasant Library. My father had been impressed with his knowledge of airplanes, and planned to show him off as a model of self-directed education. As for me, I'd practiced a mini-speech about Teddy Roosevelt's mediation of the Russo-Japanese War. Given the crowd, I planned to remind them that Roosevelt was a Republican, though I knew that he was really a man of the people, like Lincoln, a Democrat at heart.

Quinn was waiting for us on the ruptured steps of the library. My father complimented him on his suit—a brown polyester blend, short in the sleeves—as Quinn stuffed himself into the back seat. "It's my Sunday best, but I haven't been to church in a while." He fixed his collar over his fat-knotted clip-on tie and settled in next to Tino and me. The suit smelled like mothballs.

We headed down 16th toward Adams Morgan, and as my parents and Cinnamon talked in the front seats about the good weather auguring a high voter turnout, Tino opened one side of his Afghan coat, and I saw that he had the same sewn-in pockets recommended by *Steal This Book*. "I'm predicting fireworks at Bailey's house," Tino whispered. He dug into his coat and showed us a handful of squibs and bottle rockets.

"Damn!" Quinn's eyes lit up.

"Shhh, it's contraband." Tino put his finger to his lips. "We're smuggling incendiaries across enemy lines."

If 16th Street divided the haves from the have-nots, Connecticut Avenue, between the southwest corner of Adams Morgan and the eastern edge of Kalorama Heights, separated the haves from the have-it-all-and-then-somes. Bailey Dornan and his family lived in the largest privately owned home I'd ever been invited to. A French Eclectic mansion with balustraded porches and multiple balconies, it had four flagpoles, flying the American, District of Columbia and Irish flags plus one other that I couldn't identify —black, red and green with a shield-and-spear coat of arms.

My father said it was the Kenyan flag, and that Bailey had told him he'd bought the place from the Republic of Kenya three years before, when the sub-Saharan drought had devastated the country's economy and forced the diplomats to move to a more humble residence, across Connecticut on R Street. I could see how this place had once been an embassy. It had all the splendor of the grand manors along Embassy Row.

A stocky maid with mannish hands answered the door and let us into the great room, where Bailey was holding forth to a coterie of narrow-hipped women and smock-faced men who looked like many I'd seen on homecoming weekend at Lake Bluff Academy.

All the downstairs rooms were decorated in an African safari motif: zebra throws over black leather couches, wicker tables on giraffe-print rugs, teak shelves holding leather-bound volumes between ebony hippo bookends. And on the walls: masks, wood carvings, priceless-looking artifacts and shadow boxes filled with tribal figurines. Thick candles burned in handcrafted candlesticks, scenting the rooms with wild sage and woodsmoke. I was surprised not to see rifles on the walls and the mounted heads of cheetahs, wildebeests, reedbucks and sables. I thought of the photos of Teddy Roosevelt from his big-game hunts in Africa, his large square teeth flashing as he planted the barrel of his shotgun on the carcass of a rhino.

Bailey left his conversational circle and greeted us by a standalone table, on top of which sat a soapstone chess set. "Pretty authentic, huh," he said. "We wanted to keep the African flavor." He picked up the king and handed it to my father. "These guys are Masai warriors. They used to dominate East Africa until the English showed up. Even today they're still so proud and stubborn that they refuse to Westernize." He took the chess piece back from my father and placed it behind its regiment of pawns.

My father gave him the rent check, and Bailey slipped it into his hacking jacket then shook everyone's hands in a perfunctory way. "So, who do you think is going to win this election?" he asked no one in particular.

"It's going to be close," my father offered. "Ford has run a smart campaign."

"Are you kidding?" Like many of the partygoers, Bailey wore a Ford-Dole button on his lapel. He waved at Factotum Frank, who was crossing the room with a tray full of drinks. "We should have nominated Reagan," he said. "Ford's basically giving away the Panama Canal. And he was a fool to sign the Helsinki Accords; you might as well hand over the whole of Eastern Europe to the Russkies. No sense bullshitting me, Pete. I know you folks voted for Carter. Hey, it's a free country." Without acknowledging Frank, he took glasses of wine from the tray and passed them to my parents, Tino, Cinnamon and Linc. "A toast." He raised his glass. "To democracy."

Frank moved on, and soon we were joined by Bailey's wife, Ann. The tallest, thinnest woman in the room, she had straight blond hair, dark at the roots, and wore a tight-fitting pink top under her blue blazer. The cross around her neck hovered incongruously over her surprising cleavage. "I can hardly believe how many years it's been," she said, as tight-lipped and mechanical as a ventriloquist's dummy. "And these are your children? How wonderful." She shook my hand as I imagined a praying mantis might, with the ends of her long fingers.

"I understand you're starting a school. Isn't that something," she said to my mother, acknowledging the hippies and Quinn with a passing smile that ended on a note of suspicion. "Here, let me introduce you to some new friends."

She walked us into the preppy gyre that Bailey had earlier abandoned, and we met a mortgage broker and a couple of lawyers and their wives. One of the lawyers introduced himself as Dawn's father, and asked which of us was Lincoln Gearhart. Linc gave a little bow and went on about how lucky he was to teach such a talented young guitarist. In truth, he had told me that he thought Dawn would never realize he was barely an intermediate player himself because she was making such slow progress. She'd mastered "Greensleeves" and "House of the Rising Sun," but was struggling with the capo in "Nowhere Man." She had skipped two lessons in a row, complaining that her fingers hurt.

Her father said, "If she keeps this up, we're going to have to build her a studio in the back yard. No offense to you, but she's always banging on that guitar and playing her Janey Mitchell records."

"*Joni* Mitchell," his wife corrected him. She sported a wealthy bohemian look, with her gauzy cotton tunic and Navajo jewelry. "So who's in charge?" she asked, and my father stepped forward. "We have another daughter, Brie," she said, rolling her eyes. "You want to talk about a handful? She broke records for demerits at Pilgrim Hill, and this term she's at Woodrow Wilson, the *public* school. We don't like the influences there. I think we might be giving you a call." She glanced at her husband, who looked away. "Brie is tough to keep an eye on, let me tell you. She's—how best to put this?—*adventurous.*"

"Well, we're all about adventure," Tino offered, to my mother's annoyance, then excused himself along with the rest of the hippies to watch the election coverage in the TV room. Bailey followed in their wake, to point the way—or to keep an eye on them. Meanwhile, the adults in our circle talked about upcoming vacations. One was going to Breckenridge, another to Bermuda; and Ann said her family was going to Ireland for Christmas, and later, over the kids' spring break, to Kenya on their second safari. As she was talking about their previous trip, a sour-looking teenager skulked by. Ann grabbed his sleeve and pulled him over. "We're going to have a great time, aren't we, Troy?"

Cleo had seldom mentioned her brother, and I could see why. The kid looked a few years older than me, probably a junior in high school, and had the same pugilist's features and surly demeanor as his father. "Ireland's okay, but Africa sucks. It's dirty and boring. At least in Ireland I can drink."

Ann smiled as if her son had said something charming. "He could do without the jet lag," she spoke for him, then turned to Quinn. "Have *you* ever been to Africa?" Quinn was helping himself to a canapé of some kind of cheese and relish. "You must want to go," Ann said. "Isn't that the fashion these days? Everyone celebrating their heritage and wearing the traditional clothes?"

My mother looked at Ann in disbelief, but Quinn flicked cracker crumbs from the lapel of his suit and answered the question as if it were perfectly reasonable. "I do want to go to Kenya someday, but not overland in jeeps and tents. When I go, I'll have my own zeppelin. I'd like to run a zeppelin safari company, where we can follow herds of elephants across the savanna and stop in midair to watch from the observation deck while lions sun themselves on rocks and hyenas pace and carry on. My zeppelin would be incredibly maneuverable; we could park it on a tree and stop for the night and sleep above the animals."

Quinn went on for a while about zeppelins and flying machines, and when he took a breath my father introduced him to the group as one of the many bright students at Our House whose interests we were fostering. One of the lawyers mentioned the new Air and Space Museum on the Mall, which had recently opened, and Quinn said he couldn't wait to go.

He seemed to be disarming the crowd when I spotted Cleo across the room and wandered over. She wore gray gabardine pants and a white bell shirt, loose at the waist, and a silver-banded watch where her braided bracelet had been. With that outfit and makeup and her meticulously applied burgundy nail polish, she seemed more adult than before. I felt my courage slipping and looked for a way to sneak off or turn back. But then she noticed me and we were face to face, and again I could come up with nothing to say, so I asked about the bracelet then worried that she'd think I'd been watching her too closely.

"Oh yeah, my anti-shark bracelet," she said. "I wore it to keep Jaws away. But that was the summer. No sense watching for sharks now, so I cut it off."

I couldn't tell what she meant by this, but I wondered if, somewhere between basketball, Halloween and now, she'd changed. Maybe she had a boyfriend.

"So are your friends here?" I asked.

"No, just their parents. All my friends are Democrats. They wouldn't be caught dead in this place on election night. Look around." She gestured toward a crowd of people spilling out from the edge of the TV room—strident men in loud shirts talking over each other, stiff-backed women refilling lipstick-clouded glasses of wine. A voice I recognized as Harry Reasoner's floated from the television into the hallway. *The nation is split between West and South this year,* he was saying. *We're waiting on Ohio and the midwestern states to see who will be the thirty-ninth president.*

“Can you tell what network they’re watching?” Cleo asked.

“Sounds like ABC,” I said.

“That’s right. And you know why? Because ABC stands for Anyone But Carter.” Cleo smiled, and my heart leapt. That same sweet, lopsided smile.

“Word’s traveling fast about your school,” she said. “And not just from people at OLPH. You might be hearing from Dawn’s older sister, Brie. Watch out, she’s a real wild child. She got booted from Pilgrim Hill for sending notes to one of her teachers.”

Cleo paused and I thought of asking her about what the notes said, but her face had turned scarlet and, intrigued as I was, I didn’t want to embarrass her further.

“Even a lot of normal kids are frustrated,” she continued, “because most of the schools around here just don’t get it. You’d think the civil rights movement or women’s lib never happened. We use old-fashioned textbooks, and forget about taking courses like World Religions or Native American Myths or getting to read books that you care about. I brought *Forever* by Judy Blume to OLPH one day—it’s about a senior in high school who goes on the pill—and I was reading the book in the library when one of the nuns snatched it from me. She probably took it back to her bedroom,” Cleo leaned in to whisper. “Anyway, I think it’s so cool what your family is doing. A school where you can study whatever you want. Why can’t they all be that way?”

I couldn’t tell Cleo that we were out of money and completely disorganized, so I went in the opposite direction and said we’d received a huge grant—which of course hadn’t happened, nor likely would—and that we had a fabulously wealthy aunt who’d left us a pile of cash. “Her husband was Henry Ford’s right-hand man,” I said, though in fact Uncle Les had been in sales and detested Henry Ford. “He designed a lot of the great cars. You know, the Corvette, the Mustang.” I couldn’t remember if Corvette and Mustang were even made by Ford. But then, to my relief, I felt a tug on my sleeve, and there was Molly.

But instead of bailing me out, she sniffed the air and said, "Are you wearing Dad's cologne?"

"No." I blushed, then stepped back so Cleo wouldn't catch the scent.

"What are you guys talking about?" Molly asked.

"Daniel was saying that you have a rich aunt." Cleo wore the same bemused look that I'd seen on Bailey's face. It was the first glimpse I'd had of her even vaguely resembling her father.

"Aunt Natalia wasn't *that* rich," Molly said matter-of-factly. "Mom thinks we need to save the money in case of emergency."

I tried, futilely, to correct her. "Uncle Les had a special account," I lied. I hated for Cleo to think of my family as pathetic, unable to get by on our own. "It's the school account. There's a ton in there."

"I've never heard of it." Molly crossed her arms. "Mom would have told me."

Years later when Cleo's name would come up I'd ask Molly why she went out of her way that night to call my bluff and make me look foolish, but all she remembered from Bailey's house was what happened afterward, and how, in this actual mansion, the kind of place where she'd always imagined herself, she felt small and inconsequential.

A chorus of boos resounded from the television room, and we wandered over to check in on the election coverage. Carter had just won Missouri, and though he was expected to lose the West, he had locked up nearly the entire South, including the biggest prize of all: Florida. Now, with sixty percent of precincts reporting, he led by three percentage points in Pennsylvania, and was in a dead heat in Ohio. To win the election, all he had to do was capture one of these two states.

"Christ!" Bailey said, and the crowd quieted. He'd been right up close to the television, but now he turned and headed back toward us.

A charge of anticipation ran through me, the likes of which I hadn't felt since the closing minutes of Game Seven of the 1973 ABA Championship, when George McGinnis and the Pacers were putting away the Kentucky Colonels. But I knew I had to bottle up my excitement.

Bailey stopped and zeroed in on me. "Are you ready for four years of tax-and-spend?" he asked.

Cleo answered for me. "He doesn't pay taxes, Dad."

"That's right. And his family doesn't pay rent either."

I wanted to say *Yes we do* or speak up for my father, but I froze.

After Bailey had continued on past us, Cleo said, "Don't listen to him. He's just a sore loser."

I remembered my mother once telling me that in my father's sophomore year at Wisconsin he and Bailey had both vied for the starting third-base position. My father had won and gone on to lead the team in every batting category, while Bailey languished at the end of the bench. It seemed as if that competition nearly twenty years before had never gone away.

"Do you want to see the rest of the house?" Cleo asked, and soon we were touring the downstairs rooms, my sister a bothersome hanger-on.

Crossing the threshold from the original structure to an addition on the east side was like taking a giant step from Africa to the United Kingdom. The Kenyan motif gave way to a folk-Irish assemblage of Celtic-inspired tapestries and antique pine furniture. We ducked into a room off the hallway—"the glory days room," Cleo called it—crowded with baseball memorabilia: team pictures from the 1950s of the Washington Senators, aerial shots of the old Griffith Stadium, a photo of Senators star Harmon Killebrew signed "To Bailey: Keep slugging," and posed pictures of Bailey himself from high school, glove down as if fielding a grounder. He had the same OLPH letters across his chest, and I thought of asking Cleo about this—I hadn't known she went to his alma mater—but then she pointed to a team picture of the Wisconsin Badgers from 1961, and next to it a photo of my father posed with a bat on his shoulder, his muscular forearms tensed in the vernal light.

"My dad still idolizes your dad." Cleo stood on her tiptoes to look closely at the picture.

I was thinking that he sure had a funny way of showing it.

"You look like him, you know. Around the eyes," Cleo said. "You have nice eyes."

I caught a glimpse of Molly, who opened her mouth to speak then mercifully refrained. She lifted the end of her ponytail as if it were a pet and rested it on her shoulder.

In the room at the end of the hallway, a capacious library with high shelves and a ladder on wheels, we found Tino, Cinnamon and Linc curled up on a plush sectional sofa watching the returns. Linc was tossing a handful of cashews into his mouth, and Cinnamon laughed as she read aloud from a book of limericks. The room had the dungy sweetness of Tino's high-grade Hawaiian Indica, a smell that had become familiar ever since the hippies arrived from the West Coast. On the library television, set into a wall of shelves, John Chancellor was saying that with seventy-five percent of precincts reporting, Carter was a percentage point ahead in Ohio and four points up in Pennsylvania.

This news inspired Tino to come up with an impromptu limerick of his own, which he recited loudly, leaning toward Cinnamon:

There once was a Georgia gov
Who used to be tight as a glove,
But he won the election,
Then got an erection,
And now he believes in free love.

While Cinnamon giggled like a schoolchild, Tino got up from the couch and said he wanted to talk to me for a minute. I followed him back into the hallway. Molly and Cleo stayed for Chancellor's analysis.

"I've got something to show you." Tino squinted as if peering through smoke. "I gave your uncle the fireworks because I wanted to make room in these pockets." He opened his coat and pulled out a handful of knives and forks. "This is some serious antique silver. See these mother-of-pearl handles and this little insignia on the back?" He flipped over one of the knives and showed me the elaborate D monogrammed at the base of the blade, below a hall-mark of symbols including a crown and a lion waving its paw.

"You can't take those," I said.

"They won't even notice. This place is a gold mine. They had drawers and drawers full." Tino rubbed his red eyes with the sleeve of his coat. "Bailey's lackey, Frank, kept following us around, so we had to divert him. Who knew the guy was a doper? Linc distracted him with the pipe and I went in for the kill."

I wondered why Tino had pulled me aside, and figured he was just being his exhibitionist self. Then he lectured me on Bailey's colonialism and how most of the stuff in this house was stolen from Africa or the U.K. or somewhere else in the first place, and it was only right that we steal some back.

"Not only that," he said. "But if someone fucks me, I'm going to fuck them back. Bailey trashed my shrine to Chairman Mao, and that was irreplaceable. So I'm taking some of his chattels. Here's today's lesson: when the world's out of whack, it's up to you to set it right again."

I was thinking about Tino's logic when the maid with the mannish hands came down the hall and said that dinner was about to be served.

The hippies made short work of their carved roast beef, scalloped potatoes and asparagus with hollandaise sauce, and had gone through the line a second time before most others had gotten firsts. Tino still had his Afghan coat on, and I worried that people could hear the jingle of pilfered silver in his pockets. But he seemed cool as a fan as he piled his plate high.

I caught up with my mother, who raved about Quinn and said she was sure after tonight's performance that we were going to attract more students. Quinn had yet to eat; he was busy working the room.

It was just after dessert—a yellow cake with white frosting, topped with icing in the shape of an American flag—that the house fell silent and Harry Reasoner announced that ABC was now ready to put the state of Pennsylvania in the Democrats' column. *Ohio is leaning toward the challenger, but it's academic now. James Earl Carter Jr. will be the thirty-ninth president of the United States.*

Some gasped, others said "Can you believe it?" and I held my breath to stifle a reaction. During the tense quiet that followed I sneaked a glance at the hippies, and had never been so proud of them. They stood solemn-faced watching the coverage. Except for their long hair and relatively dressed-down appearance, they could have passed for three more crestfallen Republicans.

Bailey broke the silence. "So what do you think, Pete?" he called across the room to my father. "Looks like you backed the right horse."

My father's face turned crimson. "Close race," he said. "Hard-fought." He tried to dismiss the topic.

"This is my friend Pete Truitt, everybody," Bailey announced to the crowd. "Maybe some of you have met him and his colorful friends. Pete's new in town, and I thought we'd show him some hospitality." Bailey's scalp shifted forward and back and he blinked rapidly, as if he were going on the fritz. "I hope Pete won't mind me saying, but he's needed some hospitality lately. What do you do when you get fired from your job? You count on friends not to turn their backs on you. Jerry Ford got fired today, and we're not going to turn our backs on him, are we? Even if he did run a stupid campaign. Come on. Everyone get a glass." The guests put down their dessert plates, emptied the caterers' trays of champagne, and when enough glasses were raised in the air, Bailey made his toast: "To losers," he said. "And to the winners who give them a second chance."

People seemed confused at first. They turned to each other with odd looks on their faces, then shrugged and clinked their champagne flutes. I didn't know what to think, though I was pretty sure that my father had just been terribly insulted. The blood drained from his face; he turned toward my mother and they seemed to huddle in the corner of the room.

Molly went over to join them. Linc walked by, licking icing from his finger. "Can you believe that sonofabitch?" he said as he passed, not waiting for a reply or seeming to care that Bailey's daughter was standing right next to me. Linc continued on through the crowd. Trailed by Cinnamon and Tino, he walked out the French doors that led onto the back patio.

Cleo touched the sleeve of my shirt. "Do you want to go upstairs?" she asked.

I felt like I'd walked onto the set of a movie where the pretty, modern girl, dispensing with ceremony, invites the near stranger up to her apartment. "Sure," I said.

When we got to her room, on the third floor, the lights were out and she didn't bother to turn them on after we stepped inside. All I could see was the outline of her face, backlit by the copper glow of the light-polluted city. She took my hand and squeezed it, and neither of us spoke, as if we held an ineffable truth between us that words would shatter. I closed my eyes, the room went dark, and I could feel her stepping toward me. I'd been kissed only once before, in the parking lot after a tea dance at Lake Bluff Academy by a girl named Carly Manning, whose father had financed half the buildings in the Loop. She stuck her tongue in my mouth, a sensation that reminded me of the time a group of schoolmates had dared me to swallow a goldfish. It swam up from the back of my throat and bumped against the lining of my cheek until I lost my nerve and spit it out. But I couldn't spit out Carly Manning's tongue even if I had wanted to.

Outside, the sound of fireworks interrupted Cleo and me. When I opened my eyes she was walking toward the window.

"Did you see that?" she said after a bottle rocket shot up through the trees, popped and flared in four directions.

She opened the window.

Soon we were standing hip to hip, looking down. A small crowd had begun to gather on the back patio to watch Tino launch his fireworks high into the clearing between the house and the trees. Another bottle rocket rose above us and burst into the night. Then came a series of squibs with their cackling, witchy cries. Cinnamon and Linc oohed and aahed. This was so close to what I'd imagined—Cleo and I up high in a perch watching fireworks rain over our own little kingdom—that I forgot about any trouble that might follow this display.

"I want to see two at a time," Cleo said, and I leaned out the open window to call down the request to Tino. For a minute the skies were clear. I thought I heard my mother yell, "Stop. You can't do this. I told you to wait until we got back home," but I couldn't spot her in the crowd, so ignored any warning. All I could see was Tino and, crouched next to him, my unlucky Uncle Linc, fumbling with a box of matches. Linc yelled, "This one's for Jimmy Carter!" He struck a match and the flame grew large and I heard a sound like a psychotic bird flying directly toward my ear. Then it seemed as if the bird's beak had struck a bull's-eye in the middle of my scalp. I felt a sharp pain, like alcohol spreading to the corners of an open wound.

"Oh, shit," I heard Linc say. "His hair's on fire! Someone do something!"

I reached toward my head but the heat made me drop my hands. I thought of calling for help or jumping from the window so the air would blow out the fire, but the patio seemed a long way down and that crowd of figures, as still and dumbstruck as chessmen, couldn't save me now.

The room went black again, a cool burn washed over my scalp, and a pair of hands with burgundy fingernails lifted a blanket slowly over my head.

"It's okay," Cleo said. "The fire's out."

I turned toward her, her shirt glowing like the moon. Tears pooled in the corners of her eyes.

II

OUR SCHOOL

1977

11

....

GOVERNMENT

A FEW FACTS about Jimmy Carter's inauguration:

> He swore the oath of office on a Bible given to him by his mother, Miss Lillian, who, when he first told her of his plans to run for president, asked, "President of what?"
>
> Rejecting the pomp and circumstance of his office and setting a tone of modesty and frugality, he served peanuts and pretzels at his inaugural ball.
>
> He was the first president since Thomas Jefferson, in 1801, to walk the mile-and-a-half route along Pennsylvania Avenue from the Capitol to the White House after his swearing in.
>
> And I was there.

On that cold and sunny Thursday in January, I stood with the inaugural class of Our House at the corner of 10th and Pennsylvania, waiting for what we assumed would be the presidential motorcade. The entire school had come—all twenty-eight of us—on what would be the first of our many field trips into the city of Washington. We had heard Carter's earnest, sermon-like speech over loudspeakers from the National Mall—"together, in a spirit of individual sacrifice for the common good, we must simply do our best"—then we'd migrated en masse to the parade route. Across the street from us stood the Department of Justice, and just behind us the FBI. "We're surrounded," Tino said to his group of charges. "One false move and we're done for."

We hadn't anticipated that twenty students would sign up for Our House, and despite Sister Donovan's belief that parents would want their kids only in after-school programs, twelve had enrolled full-time. My father had been under the illusion that the school would attract serious, self-motivated students, but from early on it was clear that we had assembled a version of the Sweathogs, à la *Welcome Back, Kotter*, a woolly band of underachievers who figured they'd pulled the ultimate scam on their folks, signing up for a pressure-free school that catered to their very own interests.

Unfortunately, few of them had interests, and many of those who did were up to no good. On that first day we'd all sat in a circle in the living room under Cinnamon's banner: WELCOME TO OUR HOUSE: ACT FIRST. ASK PERMISSION LATER. My father went over the format of the school, which my parents and the hippies had continued to revise. Instead of having students take various classes at once, we decided the whole school should focus on one subject per month, but within that subject each student would have complete freedom of choice. The faculty served as tutor-collaborators, each taking a turn leading the focal subject and otherwise being available to lend expertise. Students could claim a specialty field at any time and work closely with a faculty expert, or they could free-float, more or less doing as they pleased. Since the school opened with the inauguration of a new president, the subject for the end of January and the short month of February was Government: Man and His Institutions, with my father as guide.

Though my parents had tinkered with their original mission, we were still at the core like Summerhill. Its founder, A. S. Neill, believed that traditional schools sought to break the student's will. Progressive schools, by stressing freedom, put kids back in touch with their natural "goodness," allowing them to grow into more thoughtful members of society. We'd be self-governing and democratic, and a council meeting could be called at any time, but my father added a new wrinkle by asking everyone to participate in one voluntary community-building project per month that would benefit the whole school.

That opening meeting, we went around the room, each of us talking about our obsessions. The first to speak, Senedu, a recent immigrant from Ethiopia who was taking ESL lessons with my mother in exchange for dinner vouchers at his parents' restaurant, said, "Abscessions? Do I know this word? Is that not some kind of swelling?" And everyone laughed. Quinn said flying machines of all sorts, dirigibles especially, and the next guy made fun of him: "I'm into intergalactic travel and mind control." The four poets read from Ginsberg, Ferlinghetti, Rexroth and Bukowski. Dawn and Stephanie said guitar and photography, but Dawn's sister, sixteen-year-old Brie, the castoff from Pilgrim Hill and Woodrow Wilson, had a one-word answer, "Men."

"Any other interests?" my mother asked.

"Just men. Not boys," said Brie, who looked like a younger Cinnamon, only with flaxen hair. She cast her eyes brazenly around the room for possibilities, landing for a moment on Tino, who tightened his bandanna.

I told the group that I was into presidential history and had just begun research on William Howard Taft, "our heaviest president. Taft kept a cow on the White House lawn so he could always have fresh milk, and he drank a lot of it, because he weighed over three hundred and fifty pounds." I pulled the knit cap I'd worn every day since the accident lower on my head. "He kept getting stuck in the White House bathtub, so he had to get a new one custom-made. It took four large men to haul the tub up to his bathroom, and it was wide enough for all of them to fit in there."

My story got a better response than it ever would have at Lake Bluff. But soon the conversation went downhill. The next student said he didn't have obsessions; the one after him said "Cartoons," and the bishop's son cupped his hands under his chest and said, "Racquel Welch's tatas." My father let the comment go. As dean of students he'd been known as a softy, so running a free school made him even less inclined to play the scold. And what was the point with this kid? He had probably been determined since birth to get a rise out of the bishop.

"And how about you two?" my father prompted the identical twins, who had the ghostly translucence of laboratory workers.

"We like anything that explodes. Pop Rocks. Atomic bombs." They said they'd recently detonated an explosive device on the ninth hole of the Greater Potomac Country Club. "Our father didn't like that," they said impassively. As headmaster at St. Sebastian, their father must have had some explaining to do, since his entire school board belonged to the club.

"We'd rather you not blow up anything here," my father said in an anxiously jocular way.

"We've got nothing against you," the twins said. "We just hate golf."

The very word "explosion" gave me chills. I could still hear the bottle rocket screaming toward my ear, and smell the fetid burn of my own hair, like the Gary steel mills we'd passed on the highway leaving Chicago. I ducked at loud claps, sudden yells, slammed doors, popped balloons, and knew how Samson felt, his head shaved, the strength drained out of him. Every day since the accident, I'd stood at the bathroom mirror rubbing in a salve of causticum, calendula and cantharis that Cinnamon mixed for me, and felt the warm tingle of the poultice doing its work. Cantharis was made out of crushed Spanish flies, Cinnamon told me, and had been used since ancient times as a love potion. She said too much of it would drive me wild, that I should use only a little at a time. But the idea of love and romance, of reaching for Cleo in the darkness, now seemed impossibly far away.

The minor burns on the crown of my head and around my ears had nearly healed, but my hair had been slow to grow back. A nurse in the George Washington Hospital emergency room had trimmed around the torched parts at the top, so that I looked like a Franciscan friar, and the following week I'd gone with my father to Tony & Camillo's barbershop. No sooner had I sat down in the barber's chair than the shop began to fill with people.

"What happened to you?" they asked.

I faltered. "Just an accident."

But my father told them everything. He was at his wit's end with Tino, and I sensed that he blamed me, too, for sticking my head out the window and bringing an abrupt end to the election-night party, which he'd been banking on for recruits. "Bottle rocket," he said. "Can you believe it?" Even Camillo, shaving away my wings with his quarter-inch electric clippers, couldn't hold back a smile.

I was furious with my father for humiliating me, with Linc for his awful luck, and with Molly, who had watched the accident unfold from the patio then ran inside and announced to the party that my hair had gone up in flames. Before I could comprehend what had happened, my whole family, Bailey, Ann and a host of strangers had rushed upstairs to Cleo's room.

"I can't bear to look," my mother cried.

One of Bailey's friends was a physician. He inspected my scalp and declared that the burns were first degree. He led me to the bathroom and ran water over my head as the guests crowded in the doorway.

"What's all this crispy stuff?" My mother sounded panicked.

"Just burnt hair," the physician said. "He's going to be fine."

But my mother wasn't having it, and before I could object or say anything to Cleo, I found myself riding in the back seat of our van, then lying on a steel table in the emergency room under a doctor's reproachful gaze. Back home, after midnight, I stood for a full hour in front of the bathroom mirror, getting up the courage to peek under my bandages.

In place of the bandages I now wore a knit cap the same tawny color as my hair, and had been avoiding Cleo for the past two months. She'd called a couple of times during the busy Thanksgiving and Christmas holidays; she'd tried on December 15, unaware that it was my thirteenth birthday, but I had my mother tell her I was off running errands, and I never called her back. Dawn and Stephanie reported on the first day of school that Cleo felt terrible and thought the fireworks mishap had been all her fault. But who knows how badly I might have been burned had she not grabbed the blanket off her bed and thrown it over me? I realized I was only making her feel worse by ignoring her, but I was afraid she'd want to meet, and I couldn't bear her seeing me this way.

As the presidential motorcade came crawling up Pennsylvania Avenue, Dawn and Stephanie began to cheer, followed soon after by the rest of our school. At first all I could see were police cars and a staggered line of Secret Service agents in trench coats, then, in the distance, a bright spot of blue. Anticipation washed over us like a wave. "It's Rosalynn!" someone yelled. Then, like a news show come to life, there they were walking toward us: Rosalynn in her cerulean wool coat waving to the crowd; Amy in big round glasses and mukluk boots, holding her mother's hand; and Jimmy, the thirty-ninth president of the United States, flashing his famous smile. The rest of the Carter family trailed behind: sons and grandkids, brother and sisters, nieces and nephews, the whole lot out for a stroll on this wintry day, just an ordinary family, too much like the rest of us for limousines. Doing research many years later, I'd learn that Rosalynn had packed her own picnic lunch that morning, and that the flaring wool coat, which seemed so bright and new buttoned tight over her trim figure, was in fact six years old.

The Carters crossed 9th Street, and when they were no farther away than the distance from our front porch to the street, Molly yelled out, "Hi, Amy!" Then "We love you, Amy!" As she passed, the First Daughter turned and waved in our direction and the whole school erupted in cheers.

We were in the midst of one of the coldest winters on record. A string of subzero days gripped the Great Lakes, and parts of the

Mississippi River froze, stalling barge traffic from Minneapolis to St. Louis. In Michigan, to offset the steep rise in energy costs, Detroit Edison reduced voltage, and lights dimmed across the state. Even in Miami, snow fell on the beach and the temperature dropped to 31, the lowest ever, killing orange, grapefruit and avocado crops. And in our drafty house in Washington we bundled in long underwear, corduroys and wool sweaters and wandered the cold floor with blankets wrapped over our coats. Every day when we didn't have a snowfall my father and I would collect wood from the back yard, and once a week we'd take the van to Rock Creek Park and load up with twigs and frozen branches which we stacked on the porch to dry. We couldn't afford to buy a cord of wood, so we counted on Tino and Linc to turn up whatever they could, and we didn't ask questions when they popped the trunk of the Salem Cigarette Car and marched up the steps with armfuls of cut logs.

My mother had thrown a fit when on the first freezing night of the year my father discovered that the flues of the fireplaces on the second floor had all been mortared up. Only the hearth on the first floor worked, and the house was so immense and poorly insulated that the heat barely radiated beyond the living room. So every morning before school my father would build a fire and feed it logs throughout the day. At least the students were keeping warm, since in essence we'd become a one-room schoolhouse, but the upstairs and the rest of the rooms were arctic, and we couldn't afford to turn up the heat beyond 50 for fear that the gas bill would run our funds down to zero.

A little less than two weeks into his presidency, Jimmy Carter made his first televised address, and it gave my father an idea. He had told our students to watch the speech and take notes, and the next day we all gathered around the television. We had moved the set to the corner of the living room, and Chester and Chairman Mao were already spooning on top of the console. They used to fight, but since the onset of winter they clung to each other like departing lovers.

In between the TV commentary, my father gave mini-lectures about the makeup of the new government and the role that Carter expected to play as chief executive. Since 1973, when OPEC placed an embargo on oil sales to protest U.S. support of Israel, the price of gas and heating oil had risen steeply, until even Molly knew the meaning of "energy crisis." Carter wore a cardigan when he gave the speech, in part to seem like a regular guy but also to lead by example. He promised that his administration would propose a dramatic new energy policy in the coming months, but the time was now to start practicing conservation at home.

"We must face the fact that the energy shortage is permanent," he said. "There is no way we can solve it quickly. But if we all cooperate and make modest sacrifices, if we learn to live thriftily and remember the importance of helping our neighbors, then we can find ways to adjust and to make our society more efficient and our own lives more enjoyable and productive."

Turn your thermostats no higher than 65 by day and 55 by night, he suggested. These numbers seemed a luxury to those of us who lived on the upper floors of Our House, where at night the wind whistled through the turret's cracks and trapped me in a cylinder of bone-cold air.

"You heard the president. It's up to us," my father said, and announced that he had a challenge for the entire school. "Your first major project for government class is an energy conservation assignment: I want you to go in groups to the library, the hardware store, anyplace where you can read books or talk to experts about home insulation and energy efficiency. Then come back here tomorrow and share what you've learned."

To my amazement, no one asked for further discussion. The school split into groups: some walked to Mount Pleasant Library with Tino, Cinnamon and Molly; some caught a ride to Hechinger's with my father, Quinn and me; the twins and the bishop's son stuck around the house "to take notes" under Linc's and my mother's guidance. The next morning, so frigid that we burned four logs at a time, we reconvened in the living room to compare our findings. The twins and the bishop's son had been adept at locating the draftiest parts of the house, and drew up a room-by-room plan of attack, and as a group we decided on a list of supplies that we'd need for the task.

"Think of this as your own White House," my father said. "The work we do here is for the good of the country." He spoke as if he believed it, which has always been his greatest gift. But I couldn't help thinking that our school assignment was just a home improvement project in disguise. My father would never admit it, but necessity had pushed him to be more like Abbie Hoffman every day.

The students didn't seem to mind. Restless teenagers, they were all too happy to get the blood flowing and feel that they were making a contribution to a community that wasn't in their parents' control. Just as I began to wonder how we'd pay for supplies, Brie said she'd gotten twenty extra dollars from her dad "for lab fees." Leaning toward Tino, who sat next to her in the circle, she slipped the money into his shirt pocket and said, "Daddy's little girl always gets what she wants."

The next day, other students brought in a few extra bucks, and I was relieved that we wouldn't have to shoplift at Hechinger's. Before my hair had caught fire, I'd planned to take Dear Abbie's advice and stuff my coat for the holidays, but after the accident I didn't have the nerve and couldn't rally myself to go out in public, so I spent the end of the bicentennial year under blankets, reading about Teddy Roosevelt, post-presidency, and his brushes with death in the Amazon.

As my father had predicted, we had a meager Christmas. I got some ballpoint pens and bound notebooks for my biographies and a pair of cloddish, discount-bin high-tops. Molly had pleaded for a Casio Biolator, an overhyped novelty item. Mostly a calculator, it had a band across the top that supposedly measured one's health through some mysterious math based on date of birth.

Molly would pull the gimmicky thing from her pocket, consult the waves across the band and announce, "It seems I'm feeling fine today" or "Drat. I'm under the weather."

Tuition fees had made us briefly solvent, but with rent and the heating bill looming each month I knew it wouldn't be long before my father took me aside to say, "Our nest egg is a goose egg." Still, my mother managed to put dinner on the table: crock pot stews, lasagna, potato-leek soup. I had no idea where the money was flowing from and didn't ask, but I figured as long as Tino had yet to pawn Bailey's silver, we hadn't hit rock bottom. Every few days I'd sneak into the room next to mine and check the closet floor, where Tino kept the stolen silver wrapped in a sock and tucked into his huaraches. I'd count to make sure all twenty pieces were still there, and I'd consider grabbing the stash and returning it to Cleo. But I didn't want her to think that I lived among thieves. I imagined inviting myself to her house and stealthily returning the pieces to Bailey's credenza drawer. But that would mean facing Cleo too soon. So I left the silver where it was and crossed my fingers we wouldn't get caught. Thanksgiving, Christmas and New Year's had passed, traditional days to break out the good silver, but even into the first week of February, Bailey hadn't darkened our door.

I have a clear memory of the students coming back from Hechinger's with supplies, and over the next few days winterizing the house. My father divided us into three groups: basement, living spaces and attic. Senedu and the boys from St. Sebastian were assigned to basement detail, and with Tino's help girded the water heater with insulation blankets, slipped foam sleeves over the pipes and stuffed insulation into the crawl space where the floor joists met the rim joists. My mother complained about the division of labor by gender, and turned it into a lesson about Rosie the Riveter and the women who worked in shipyards and factories during World War II. Then she handed out plastic tape and self-stick foam to Molly, Dawn, Stephanie, Brie and the poets so they could seal the windows, and she and Cinnamon installed sweeps and weatherstripping around the outer doors.

My father and Linc pulled up the attic floorboards and filled the spaces between the joists with fiberglass insulation, and Quinn and I cleaned out the ridge vents to help the air flow through the roof. Quinn wore his metallic-green parka, with the hood up as usual, and as he toweled dust out of the vents told me he used to play hide-and-seek up here. I had almost forgotten that he'd been inside Our House well before my family had moved to Washington. I'd been meaning to ask more about his friend Anthony, who used to live in my room, but amidst the din of school I hadn't had a chance.

"I used to hide over there." He pointed behind him, but the attic was so dark and cavernous that I couldn't see much of anything. "There's a door across the way, and behind it is a little room. I'd go in there and wait, sometimes for an hour or more. But no one ever came up until one day Anthony was 'it' and he found me. We promised not to tell the others about our spot. Here—" Quinn paused from cleaning the vents and led me slowly through the murk to the room.

When he flicked the switch the single bulb cast an eerie light over the cardboard-sided walls. Hidden from prying eyes, this seemed the kind of place where government agents passed secret documents or paranoid presidents hatched schemes to take down their enemies. Washington must be full of rooms like this, I thought, as Quinn opened the closet door and said that Anthony used to stash some of his spoils here.

Fishing around in the closet, Quinn pulled out a trash bag dusted with plaster. I jumped back, afraid of who knew what, as he spilled the bag's clanking contents onto the floor.

"What are they?" I coughed at the dust that had kicked up.

"Hood ornaments." He polished one—the Cadillac crown within a gold laurel wreath—and handed it to me. "Anthony liked to hit up all the fancy cars. He used to go around with wire cutters and free these suckers loose. 'To even the score,' he liked to tell me. Man, he had quite a collection," Quinn said. "But then he got bored, which is how it always went with Anthony: he'd go on about one thing for months, then wake up and be into something new."

As I sifted through the hood ornaments—some of them beautiful, like a silver Jaguar—I tried to get Quinn to fill in Anthony's story. In particular, I wanted to know what had happened to the Kurtzmans after Joy's mother had died. Why didn't they move back to this house? Quinn said he assumed that the parents' marriage was on the rocks, and when the old lady died it gave Joy an excuse to make a clean break and stay in Ohio for good. But Sol didn't get the hint, because after the eviction he and Anthony packed up the furniture and drove to Cleveland. When they arrived they found the rest of the family stuffed into three bedrooms in the old lady's house.

"Sol stayed, but Anthony saw there wasn't room for him," Quinn said. "He took the first Greyhound back to D.C."

"So why do you think Anthony broke into our house and took the flags?" I asked, though I was pretty sure I knew.

Quinn offered me more hood ornaments but I only pocketed the Cadillac's. "I guess he thought this was his house. He was happy here, then someone took it away. He told me that people put up a flag when they're trying to claim something. He must have thought you were trying to claim this house as yours."

"Well, we did sign a lease," I said haltingly.

"So you had nothing to do with the eviction? Seems your dad and that Bailey go way back." Quinn sounded like neither an adult nor a kid. His small voice seemed to come from a deep well. He was a little older than me, but I sensed that he'd seen twice as much as I had in his fourteen or fifteen years. I hate to admit it now, but anytime I was around Quinn, even later when we became friends, I was always aware that he was black and lived on the other side of 16th Street, a different world. Perhaps because of this I felt an urgent need to bridge the gap, to give him something, and the truth was all I could offer.

"My dad and Bailey knew each other in college," I began, and told the whole story of my father's baseball and teaching careers, how we had moved so often that we'd kept our boxes in the living room. I said our family was a lot like the Kurtzmans, barely getting by and having no business living in a place this grand. I said I sometimes worried about my parents and wondered how they'd survive if the school didn't make it. I finally got around to answering Quinn, saying, "I'm pretty sure we had nothing to do with the eviction." But as I uttered the words, I recalled what Cleo had told me on the basketball court months before, that the former occupants had ten kids, when in fact it sounded as if they had half that many. I wondered if Bailey had been lying, and had kicked out this family to make room for ours.

Quinn slid the rest of the ornaments into the bag and returned it to the closet. "It doesn't matter." He shrugged. "The Kurtzmans weren't coming back here anyway, but that didn't make it any easier on Anthony. That summer, he asked if he could move in with me. But my mom already lost my sister to a gang and wasn't going to see me running with a bad element. So Anthony went back to Horizon Foster Home and started breaking into houses, and I swear he was a second from getting busted when Sol called—it must have been August or September—and said, 'You want to come to Cleveland?'"

"So they made room in the old lady's house for him?" I asked.

"Not exactly. Sol and Joy got divorced, and Sol moved out on his own."

This stuck with me for the rest of the day while I helped insulate the attic. I had the bizarre thought that the clicking in the walls and the rustling I'd heard since we first moved into the house were not the sounds of Aunt Natalia's ghost or of the restless spirit of a former occupant, but something more like a premonition, a ghost of the future.

We finished sealing the house on the very day that the gas bill arrived. My father stood before the entire school, opened the letter and showed it to us. "Outrageous!" he said. Even with the thermostat set at 50, we were looking at a $248 bill, nearly a full month's rent.

"Throw it into the fire!" Tino yelled.

"We can't do that." My father gathered himself. "Now just you watch," he said. "I'll bet with all the hard work we just did, we'll cut the heating bill in half by next month. We're going to make President Carter proud."

The next week, more bad news arrived in the mail, not from the gas company this time but from the adman in Seattle whom Linc used to work for. I found out about it during our second field trip in as many days. White House tours had been so popular that we couldn't get a reservation, so we'd gone to the Supreme Court, and the day after that to the Capitol. We were in Statuary Hall, the Old House Chamber up on the second floor, when Linc pulled me aside and said he had something to show me. My father had just given a talk to the students in front of the Robert La Follette statue. "If it weren't for 'Fighting Bob,' I might never have met Val," he said. "We were in a history class in college and worked on a paper about La Follette's reforms." The girls cooed, the boys rolled their eyes, and I felt momentarily hopeful again about my parents.

"Hey, Daniel." Linc nudged me as the rest of the group moved on to other statues. "I need some advice." He took two letters out of his coat pocket and handed the first one to me. "I've been holding on to this thing for months," he said. "I didn't think much about it, but then a follow-up arrived today, and it gave me the willies."

The letter had a coffee cup stain around the date, June 23, 1976:

> Dear Lincoln Gearhart,
>
> I've been all over Seattle looking for you. I called the number you gave me, and the guy who answered said he'd never heard of you. I've asked fishmongers, ticket takers, street performers and

vendors if they'd seen the VW Beetle advertising smooth, filtered Salem cigarettes. And only one guy, a bartender, said he recalled such a vehicle.

But you know this car, because you signed a binding contract agreeing to drive around the city distributing sample packs of Salems on certain highly trafficked street corners. You were to report to me weekly for restocking, gasoline reimbursement and strategy sessions. We met three times in May, but after I returned from a business trip in Las Vegas, you missed the June 4 meeting. Thus began my efforts to locate you and the vehicle that my client, the powerful R. J. Reynolds company, expects me to use for the promotion of their menthol-fresh tobacco product.

I stopped by the group house in Fremont that you listed on your contract and spoke to several residents, who claimed not to know you. When I offered free cigarettes, one of your friends coughed up a P.O. box in your name out in Mazama. I'm sending this letter now expecting you to contact me immediately to explain where you've been the past six weeks and when you'll return my car. I'd hate to pay you a personal visit in Mazama. That's a good four hours from here, and I've been known to grow impatient after a long drive.

Sincerely,
Rex Brisbee, President
Sound Marketing of Greater Seattle

"This letter's more than six months old," I said. "What did you do about it?"

Linc unwrapped two pieces of grape bubblegum and popped them into his mouth. "It freaked me out at first, but I wasn't about to turn around and drive all the way back to Seattle just to return the car. That guy Rex is a sleaze merchant. He only deals with hot cars, which is why he said nothing about calling the cops. He runs a cash-only business, and you should see his office: bars on the windows, barbed wire along the fence. Rex doesn't care about that car; it's a suicide machine with ninety thousand miles on it. I figured after a while he'd forget about it, and that's exactly what I did, too."

When I returned the letter to Linc he handed me a second one. It was written in a chicken scratch that I could barely make out. "From the same guy?" I asked.

"No, this one's from Rudy Wentzel. He quit the commune during the mass exodus and moved to town to sort mail. He's the only person in the Mazama post office who knows where I am, and I gave him our forwarding address with the instructions not to tell anyone. I've known him for ages and he's loyal as a yard dog."

Linc blew a purple bubble and a Capitol guard came over and asked him to throw the gum away. Reluctantly, Linc stuffed the half-chewed gum into his pants pocket. I asked him to summarize the new letter for me, since I was having trouble deciphering it, and he said that Rex had called the Mazama P.O. several times and Rudy had told him that someone named Lincoln Gearhart used to live in the area but had moved and never left a forwarding address. Rex had asked where Linc's house had been in Mazama, but Rudy said he didn't know, and even if he did, it was against policy to pass on such information. A week ago, however, the adman called again, this time to say he'd heard Linc was now living on the East Coast, around D.C., and did the post office have a new listing? Rudy repeated that he had no forwarding address, though he did try to send Rex down another trail, saying that someone had told him Linc had moved to California.

The rest of the school followed a Capitol guide out of Statuary Hall and toward the Old Senate Chamber. We walked a short distance behind them, our footfalls echoing in the marble hallway. Linc leaned close to my ear. "So here's the advice I'm looking for, Daniel. I guarantee that Rex has a friend or two on this side of the country. I pissed him off and he's not going to let it rest. He's probably already put out an APB for his cronies to be on the lookout for a Bug with Salem splashed all over it. If I keep driving that thing around I'll be a sitting duck. Just when my world is starting to come together, this has to happen. Did I tell you, by the way, that I got a handwritten note from Electrolux?"

"Are they going to use your jingle?" I asked, my heart leaping at the thought.

"No, but they said they liked it, and I got a coupon for free belts and bags. Too bad we don't have a vacuum cleaner." Linc dug into his pocket and popped the linty gum back into his mouth. "Anyway, here are the options, and I want you to decide." He held out four fingers:

"Ditch the car.

"Sell it.

"Take it back.

"Paint it black."

My first instinct was to say, Take it back, but I didn't like the sound of this Rex Brisbee and had no idea what forms of torture might be awaiting my uncle if he returned the car to Seattle. Then I thought, Sell it, because we needed the money, but my already muddled conscience intervened—or perhaps I realized that if we sold the car and Rex's friends saw it, the road would eventually lead back to Our House. Ditching the car made no sense when it still worked perfectly fine. All it needed was a fresh coat for winter. "Why paint it black when we've got all the colors of the rainbow to choose from?" I looked up ahead at the students in the Old Senate Chamber, gathering around Rembrandt Peale's portrait of George Washington. "And we've got a school just waiting for a new project."

"I like what I'm hearing," Linc said.

I slapped him five, then joined the rest of the group, ready to share our plan.

12

....

ART

Overnight, a dozen inches of snow fell on the nation's capital, hiding Linc's stolen car beneath a powdery mask of white. Plows barreled up 16th and down Hill Street and by the end of the day the Bug was buried in foot-high snowdrifts. Temperatures dropped below zero and held steady for more than a week, encasing the snow in ice. My father canceled school, and Linc and I had to put our art project on hold for the time being.

With little to do but wait for the students' return, I grew increasingly concerned that at any moment a group of thugs would show up at our door. I went to the window and made sure that none of the lettering on the Salem Cigarette Car was visible. If a patch of green or gold emerged, I put on my boots, trudged to the sidewalk and patched the visible spaces with handfuls of snow.

In the excitement of the first month of school I'd had little time to notice that at last my hair was growing back. I still wore my knit cap on the upper floors of the house to keep my ears from getting frostbite, but in the living room, in front of my father's four-log fires, I took it off and slipped it into my back pocket. I missed Cinnamon's homeopathic treatments, the hot-ice sensation of the balm tincturing my skin. But how much better it felt now when she ran her fingers through my new-sprung hair and proclaimed me cured. I was free again to see Cleo, but the very thought of her made me worry all over again about the stolen car, the stolen silverware, the Robin Hood existence we'd been living that I knew would catch up to us if we didn't do something to narrow our odds. It was only a matter of time before Tino would pawn or fence the silver, so I decided it was up to me to take it back.

Recalling what Tino had said about thieves working best in pairs, I enlisted Quinn as my scout and partner in crime. We waited until the first temperate day, when the snow began to melt and the students were getting ready to return to school. Linc and Cinnamon were down in the living room helping my father make the fire, and Tino was out front shoveling the melting ice and salting the steps and sidewalk. As always, Quinn had been the first to arrive at school, and he kept a lookout at the top of the stairs. I wasted no time slipping the silverware out of Tino's sock then fluffing the sock and returning it to his huaraches. I wrapped the silver in a sock of my own and hid it in the closet of our secret attic room.

When we got downstairs the students had begun to file in. Linc pulled me aside and showed me that much of the snow had melted off the Salem car, and he was going to spend the day digging it out, drying it and covering it with two coats of primer. We had already talked to the residents of Our House about our idea to paint the car. Linc said nothing about the letters he'd received, and he lied to my mother when she asked if he was going to get in trouble for breaking the contract. She'd been annoyed with him and Tino since the bottle rocket accident, and Linc didn't want to test her patience. He said the car was an old tin can, he'd put in more than enough time for R. J. Reynolds, and if the adman had taken issue he'd have gotten in touch during the past eight months. "He had my address and phone number," Linc said, "but I haven't heard a word."

Since we'd reached the end of February, my father called a council meeting to discuss which subject to pursue next. I proposed art, and though the twins and the bishop's son argued for science, and caused the meeting to drag on for hours making their case, the residents of Our House formed a solid voting bloc, so Art: Everywhere a Canvas won the month of March.

I remember my father's turning the reins over to Cinnamon, who had Stephanie pass around some of her photographs. I was amazed by how much her work had changed. In the fall she'd complained when the darkroom my mother had talked about never materialized, but Cinnamon had convinced her she should master the camera before getting into developing. Stephanie was still laboring over the seven deadly sins and had stopped hanging her old pictures in the living room, calling them obvious; she'd even declined the promised one-woman show, saying she just wasn't good enough yet.

Since Cinnamon had little experience with photography, she'd kept bringing her teaching back to what she did know: collage When she lived out west she used to go on long hikes in the Cascades collecting wildflowers, sedge grasses, arrowheads and stones, and she'd combine them with maps, magazine ads, candy wrappers, coins, toothbrushes and plastic figurines. She'd glue the pieces on poster board and paint over them, then leave her collages nailed to trees on nature trails, pinned on bulletin boards in public spaces, so others could discover them, add to them, take them home if they liked.

Now she was holding up *Lust*, from Stephanie's deadly sins project—a collage made of parts of various photographs. Cinnamon pointed out the pieces from some of the earlier pictures—Good Guys strip club at night, a teenager in a cutaway Rolling Stones T-shirt, the Washington Monument angling toward the sky—and explained how Stephanie had counterposed these scenes of lust with images of chastity—an icon of the Madonna, a lock and key, a pink bow in a flower girl's hair—and cut up all the photographs into geometric shapes, assembling them into one large composition.

"So what does it mean?" one of the OLPH poets asked.

"You tell me," Cinnamon replied.

"The nuns would say it's about the destructive power of sin, and how lust shatters everything into pieces."

"That's good, but it's only half the picture. Don't forget that chastity is thrown into the mix. In other words, there's no such thing as pure sin or pure virtue. We're all a puzzle of contradictions. But the cool thing is, when you step back from the collage, it looks like a unified picture. That's how it goes with lust, gluttony, greed, sloth, wrath, envy and pride—all those so-called deadly sins. From a distance they seem like absolutes, but look closer and the story is much more complicated."

I had never seen this side of Cinnamon, whom I'd always considered a gift of the earth, too grounded for high-flown ideas. In college I'd learn that she and Linc used to make Ken Kesey's recipe for acid-laced venison chili when they lived in the Freelandia commune, and had gone through a trippy philosophic phase. But here at Our House, her insights did not seem random or improvised, and I recalled the times I'd seen her at the library cramming over photography books. On my last trip there, just before the snowstorm, when I checked out some biographies of my new subject, Woodrow Wilson, she was so immersed in her art books that she barely looked up to acknowledge me.

After Cinnamon had gone on for a while about collage and passed around some art postcards of Kurt Schwitters, John Cage, Joseph Cornell and Robert Rauschenberg, she said that we had a decision to make. She wanted us all to participate in a special collage project, but first we had to go out looking for ideas. The bishop's son groaned, "Not another field trip," and my mother snapped back, repeating her mantra, "The city is our classroom." We all talked about where to go: the Phillips Collection, the Basilica, the Freer Gallery of Asian Art. Tino said he wanted to study graffiti. "Some of the world's best artists paint on walls and subway cars but never get the spotlight. That shit's more than calligraphy, man. It's a protest against the plastic bourgeoisie. It's about pride and self-expression. I want to talk to graffiti artists and get the lowdown on their symbolism."

"Cool," said the bishop's son. "That's got my vote."

"I'm in too," added Brie.

"Two more makes five," the twins chimed in.

Quinn laughed.

"What?" Tino asked.

"You think a graffiti artist is going to talk to you?" Quinn said. "My sister Angela has run with some taggers and bombers, and they're not about to give away the goods to a white dude in a T-shirt that says *Born to Compost.*"

Tino looked down at his shirt. "So we'll talk to your sister."

"I wouldn't recommend it. She's got a tongue of fire." Quinn shook his head. "You'll find better graffiti at the King Tut exhibit. I saw it with my class at Cardozo right after it opened."

"Good luck getting in now," three people said in unison.

"I've been," bragged guitar protégée Dawn. "I nearly got crushed to death, but it was worth it. You've never seen so much gold!"

"The Treasures of Tutankhamun" had been at the National Gallery of Art since November and would be leaving D.C. for Chicago in a matter of days. We had tried to get tickets months ago, without any luck. I figured we didn't have a chance to see the most popular museum show in U.S. history, until Stephanie piped up: "How many tickets do we need?"

It turned out that her uncle was on the board of the Smithsonian, and the following day she produced a dozen tickets at our morning meeting. Tino, Brie, and the St. Sebastian kids talked a reluctant Senedu, the ESL student, into going along with them to look at graffiti, and tried to convince Quinn as well, but he said he wasn't interested and chose instead to stay home with my father and Linc to finish priming the Bug. My mother took Molly and the poets to the Basilica and the Phillips, which left enough tickets for the rest of us to go to King Tut. We even had one extra, which I asked to give to Cleo. Stephanie said okay, but she thought her friend had already been. I told her it didn't matter, and at the end of the school day, after most of the kids had gone home, I went upstairs to make the phone call I'd been putting off since election night.

When I picked up the phone in my parents' bedroom, there was an odd crackle on the line that wouldn't go away even after I unscrewed the earpiece and screwed it back on. I tapped the receiver but the crackle remained. Then a rush of cold air swept through the room, and the door, which I had left ajar, slammed shut. When I picked up the phone again, the crackle was gone.

I sat down on my parents' unmade bed, suddenly depressed at the sight of my mother's wardrobe box, which still stood unpacked by the closet, leaning toward the door. The day had gone well, and so far the school was surviving, but I couldn't help but think of Sol and Joy Kurtzman living in this very room not so long ago, probably sitting up in bed late at night arguing over the bills, their voices drifting across the hallway and up into the turret room, where Anthony would have heard them and started counting the days.

I opened the bedroom door, letting in the chatter of the remaining students, and reminded myself that throughout my thirteen years I'd had little chance for real friendships, and now a school full of kids was coming to my house every day. I picked up the phone and dialed Cleo.

"You sure dropped off the face of the earth," she said.

"I know. I'm sorry. I meant to call you back. But we were so busy with the holidays, then getting ready for school." I knew it was a weak excuse.

"Your mom said the burns weren't serious. So you're okay?"

"I'm fine. My uncle told me about a place in Turkey where they cut hair with flame. Who knew my uncle was a Turkish barber?" I tried to laugh but it came out high-pitched and forced.

"It wasn't your uncle's fault. It was mine," Cleo said. "I'm the one who asked him to shoot two fireworks at the same time. If I hadn't been so stupid, this never would have happened."

"But you saved my skin. Literally."

"I threw a blanket over your head. Anyone would have done the same."

"As a token of my gratitude I'd like to give you the gift of gold," I said. "Any chance you can go to King Tut tomorrow at three?"

Cleo paused long enough for me to realize that she'd definitely been before. "Your timing's perfect. I usually have basketball practice then, but I broke my wrist. I'm out for the season."

"How did that happen?"

"Last week during that freeze I slipped on the ice in front of our house. My dad almost fired Frank on the spot for not shoveling the walk well enough. But it wasn't his fault. I'm just clumsy."

"That's terrible," I said.

"We're two peas in a pod."

"A pod of misfortune."

"Don't worry, Daniel, our luck's going to change."

I mused over what she meant by that all the way up to the next afternoon when we met, along with the rest of the school, at the Dupont Circle Metro and descended the steep escalator into the catacombs of D.C.'s new subway system. Fat chance that Tino would ever find graffiti in this place—its walls and trains were immaculate.

On the ride over to King Tut, the rest of the students signed Cleo's cast and I sat next to her on the subway car racing backward beneath the city. Under her wool coat she had on the same outfit she wore at the election party: the gray gabardine pants and white bell shirt. She'd painted her nails burgundy to boot, and I indulged myself with the thought that she wanted to take us back to that November evening when, for an instant, anything seemed possible.

When we finally entered "The Treasures of Tutankhamun" it was like stepping off the earth into some liminal world where death was the price of gold. The rooms were laid out in the same order—antechamber, burial chamber, treasury, annex—in which the British archaeologist Howard Carter discovered them in 1922.

Excavators had scoured the Valley of the Kings for more than a century, and nearly all had given up on finding anything more valuable than a mummified cat; robbers had plundered the tombs for over three millennia, snatching every scrap of royal treasure. Carter had been digging in Egypt for thirty-one years and had promised that 1922 would be his last season, and I could imagine his determination, staking everything on one last shot at glory.

Exploring the base of the empty tomb of Rameses VI, Carter's workmen found a step that had been cut into the rock, and beneath that a door, at the bottom of which were seals with Tutankhamun's name on them. They removed the door, cleared a long passageway to another door, and there, Carter recalled, "With trembling hands I made a tiny breach in the upper left-hand corner. As my eyes grew accustomed to the light, details from the room within emerged slowly from the mist, strange animals, statues, and gold—everywhere the glint of gold."

The antechamber was so crowded that I, too, felt entombed. We shuffled along like mummies in a B movie. Cleo was right in front of me, so close that when someone jostled me, I bumped up against her. I liked the feeling of our hips colliding and slid my hand into my pocket to hide my excitement. I had brought a pad of paper, hoping to stop and take notes or sketch the crooks and flails, maces and shields, game boards and necklaces that the pharaoh's people had gathered for his trip to eternity. Cleo and I lingered at a gold shrine covered by bas-relief scenes of the daily life of Tut and his wife Ankhesenamun.

"There's a conspiracy that he was murdered. He only lived to nineteen," Cleo explained. "Some think she did it. But look at the two of them. No way. They worship each other."

"Most conspiracies are silly," I said. "Stephanie told me he died of an injured leg."

"Yeah. And later on, I bet she died of a broken heart." The gold wheels in Cleo's eyes reflected in the glass. "First she was the second wife of Tut's father. Then she was Tut's wife. And after he died she was married off to the next in line, who was probably her grandfather. Poor Ankhesenamun. She had a seriously messed-up life."

On the other side of the glass I saw our art teacher, her face in repose—not the happy hippie I was used to. Cinnamon looked portrait-still, sad and far away. I heard the echo in my mind of "Poor Ankhesenamun," realizing how much the words sounded like "Poor Aunt Cinnamon." Poor Aunt Cinnamon, wife of Lincoln the unlucky, consort of Tino the fallen angel with the wandering eye.

We waited for the crowd to peel away from the iconic object of the exhibition: the gold funerary mask found on the mummy of the boy king. I pulled out my pen and paper and did a rough drawing of Tutankhamun's face, the obsidian and quartz eyes, the nemes headdress and false beard of the gods, the broad inlaid collar. Cleo said that the vulture and cobra on his forehead and the falcons on his shoulders were meant to protect him on his journey to the afterlife, but I couldn't help wondering if this life was the only one he had, surrounded by splendor at the end of the road.

After the dozen of us students had blown our allowances on Tut posters, key rings, fake jewelry and figurines, we took the Metro back to Our House. Cleo said she wanted to peek in on the school, so she joined us on the long walk from Dupont Circle up New Hampshire Avenue to 16th and Hill. My father and Linc, in paint-speckled waffle shirts, were cleaning up after covering the Bug with primer. The Phillips Collection group were showing off their calendars, but I could see that Molly was more impressed with the Tut tchotchkes the other kids had brought back, and regretting that she'd missed out on the gold. My mother said the graffiti group had finished for the day, but we might be in for a treat tomorrow because Quinn was going to see if his sister would come by and interpret graffiti symbolism.

"Where's Tino?" Cinnamon asked.

"He took the van," my mother said. "Brie couldn't get a ride home, so he offered to take her."

"How long have they been gone?"

"Fifteen minutes or so."

Cinnamon pulled back her hair and tightened her braids, then told the rest of the class to bring in cutouts, drawings or ideas that inspired them from the exhibit, or scraps from their lives they'd be willing to donate to the project. "Keep your eyes on the ground these next few days. We're going to make a big collage, and you'll each have a corner."

After the class began to disperse I told Cleo that I had something to show her. She followed me upstairs, and I remembered the trip up to her room months before. We climbed the creaky steps to the third floor. Tino and Cinnamon's door was wide open; their top sheet lay in a pool by the mattress; the bottom sheet had come loose from the corners. Marijuana plants grew in pots in the windows; a small pipe and a full ashtray sat nearby on the floor; a homemade candle had collapsed into an unfurled tongue of wax on the cardboard-box side table. I could only imagine what Cleo made of the scene.

"Who sleeps here?" she asked.

I hadn't told her about

t c i n n l
i a m o i
n n n
o c
,

and knew there was no way to explain to a nice Catholic girl, even one who seemed inexplicably drawn to Our House, that my aunt was my uncle's best friend's lover.

"Faculty housing." I brushed off the question and flicked on the light to my room.

"You sure are into the presidents." Cleo took in the ribbon of portraits and named the first seven before tripping up on Martin Van Buren.

"Van Buren was the first chief executive not born of British ancestry," I said. "He spoke Dutch at home with his wife, Hannah.

But when he wrote his autobiography he didn't mention her even once."

"What a jerk," Cleo said.

"You'll probably make fun of me, but I've written mini-biographies all the way up to this guy." I pointed to Woodrow Wilson. "Remember that limerick book at your house? Wilson once wrote a limerick. It goes like this." I opened my latest notebook and read aloud:

For beauty I am not a star.
There are others more handsome by far.
But my face I don't mind it,
For I am behind it,
It's the people in front that I jar.

"That's a lot cleaner than the one from election night." Cleo stood at the window looking out toward 16th. "I've got some trivia for you. This one's for Democrats only. Are you a Democrat?"

"Are you?"

"Sure am."

"Me too," I said. "Does your father know you're not a Republican?"

"It's another five years before I'll be able to vote. He figures he's got time to change my mind—but no way. Republicans are liars and cheats, and they don't care about anyone but themselves. I'm tired of Washington elites, who are all about what your parents do and where you go to school. That's why I like hanging out with you, Daniel. You and your family—you're just more real."

I ran my hand over my hair and thought of telling her about Lake Bluff and Carly Manning's millionaire father, but no amount of name-dropping could compete here, among the children of power. I was amazed that she liked me at all and never questioned why. But sometimes when I hear "Rich Girl" on the radio, the single that topped the charts that year, I remember Cleo and wonder if "more real," in her way of thinking, simply meant not rich like the rest of her friends. Such a scrounger as I must have seemed exotic, just as she did to me. And I can't help laughing at the notion that my family was "more real," when in fact we were getting by on hustles and lies.

"So what's the trivia question?" I prompted Cleo.

She scratched under her cast. "There's only one president whose name contains every letter in the word 'criminal.' Who is it?"

I scanned the presidents, ran their names through the anagram scrambler in my head.

"Give up?"

I thought for another moment then shrugged.

"Richard Milhouse Nixon. The greatest criminal of them all." Cleo did her Nixon imitation. "'I am not a crook.'"

The word "criminal" and the picture of Nixon, his bejowled visage tarnishing my wall of portraits, reminded me why we had come up to my room in the first place. "Before I forget—" I told her to wait a second then ran up to the attic room and retrieved the sock.

Spilling its contents onto my bed, I asked, "Recognize these?"

Cleo picked up one of the mother-of-pearl knives.

"They're yours," I said. She opened her mouth to speak but I continued. "I know it's going to sound crazy, but let me explain." I was growing tired of carrying the burden of other people's secrets. "Someone under our roof—I can't say who or I'd get in trouble—took the silver that night at your house. This person is kind of a klepto, can't help himself. I've been wanting to return this stuff for months."

Cleo looked less shocked than intrigued. "What do you want me to do?" she asked.

"Take it all back," I said. "But can you be discreet and please, please not tell your father? I promise this won't happen again."

She gathered up the antique silverware, slid it into her book bag and stood by the side of my bed, as if waiting for something to happen. I wanted to kiss her then, but the bare bulb filled the room with a garish light. I lost my nerve and asked her if she should probably be getting home. "I wouldn't want Factotum Frank to come chasing after you."

"Maybe I can stop by once in a while for the after-school activities. Without basketball I get restless at the end of the day."

"Are you sure you can afford our steep tuition?"

"I might be able to swing it," she said, and with that my own Maid Marian made her way back to Nottingham Castle.

At the morning meeting the next day, we went around the circle and talked about our pieces of collage. I had taken scissors to an Indiana Pacers fan guide and an *American Heritage* special issue on the presidents that I'd never returned to the Lake Bluff Library, and cut out pictures to rise over the head of King Tut like a busy hedjet crown. There was George McGinnis shooting a jumper off the bald pate of Martin Van Buren, Teddy Roosevelt cantering with the Rough Riders in seeming pursuit of Pacers guard Mel Daniels, and in place of Tut's vulture and cobra I'd pasted Polaroid cutouts of Chester and Chairman Mao. When the Tut group had presented their works in progress, Cinnamon asked the graffiti group how their day had gone.

Tino shot an inquisitorial look at Quinn. "Well? Where's your sister?"

Quinn sat on a pillow, his legs pulled up under his chin. "Angela says she'll think about it, but I couldn't get her to come today. She asked me, 'What kind of school is that, going around looking at graffiti?'"

"School of life, bro." Tino turned up the collar of his Afghan coat.

For the remainder of the morning we talked about each of our contributions to the collage, and after lunch Cinnamon led us outside to the former Salem Cigarette Car, now a blank canvas of chalky gray. It was one of the first mild days of late winter, with a glimmer of sunshine and blue sky that promised spring might come after all.

Cinnamon took a felt marker and divided the car into fifteen squares: four per side, two each on the hood and back, with the roof sectioned in thirds. Then she wrote a number—one through fifteen—in the middle of each segment, put fifteen slips of paper into her Janis Joplin hat and asked each of us to draw a number. I picked the bottom half of the passenger's side door, and Quinn picked the top half. Cinnamon told us to meet in small groups—passenger's side, driver's side, front, back and roof—and discuss our plans for the composition of each part. Quinn and I shared the passenger's side with the twins, who didn't care for art and said we could do whatever we wanted; they'd throw up some graffiti and a couple of Einstein's equations. Dawn and Stephanie, over on the driver's side, began painting the gold funerary mask with KING TUT RULES in bold letters below, and had enlisted the help of Senedu, who drew words around the mask in an elegant Ethiopic script. We asked him to translate, but he just smiled.

For the sake of variety, I ditched my Tut theme and told Quinn that I was going to paste a poster cutout of the White House on my half and fit as many presidents as I could out on the front lawn, along with the Polaroids of our cats. This was fine with Quinn, so long as he controlled the airspace. He had only to decide which of the great zeppelins to choose from: the first *Graf Zeppelin* to circumnavigate the globe; the USS *Los Angeles,* the most reliable of the passenger dirigibles; or the *Hindenburg,* whose immolation, in front of thousands of spectators in Lakehurst, New Jersey, marked the end of the zeppelin era. Quinn's airships all looked the same to me: silver bullets on a slow-motion ride through the sky.

"Might as well make it the *Hindenburg,*" Quinn said. "Everyone pictures it up in flames, and that radio broadcast—'Oh, the humanity!'—but this is how it looked in its glory, longer than three 747s, with seventy-two passenger cabins on board, and a grand piano in the music salon."

At Cinnamon's urging, Quinn agreed to paint the words "Our House" in bubble letters across the blimp, and for the rest of the afternoon Quinn and I worked on our collage and talked about a recent letter Quinn had received from Anthony, who said he had started a new high school and Sol was now making good money working for a restoration company. "But you never know if you're getting the truth from Anthony. He knows how to paint a pretty picture."

By the end of the day, we had completed the blimp and the White House and I'd calculated that we had room for seven presidents on the lawn. I'd made up my mind already about the top five: Lincoln, the two Roosevelts, Washington and Jefferson. But who would round out the seven best? Woodrow Wilson? Harry Truman? A dark horse like James K. Polk, who annexed Texas and acquired California, and who took the fewest vacation days of any U.S. president? Or maybe John F. Kennedy or LBJ, heroes of my mother's for all they did for civil rights?

With the sun about to slide behind the roofs, Tino came around to harass Quinn about his sister. "So, when is she stopping by?"

"I'll keep asking," Quinn said, "but no one tells Angela what to do."

The students packed up their materials, and after everyone had left I stood on the front porch admiring the patchwork of our art car in progress. Tino threw a blue tarp that he'd nabbed from a construction site over the car to protect it from the weather, and I fretted for the first time that this project had been a bad idea. We'd covered up the Salem ads only to make the Bug more conspicuous: KING TUT RULES / OUR HOUSE. Cutouts of Redford and Newman as Butch and Sundance, dust jackets of *On the Road* and *The Catcher in the Rye,* Pink Floyd album covers, Ethiopic script and Egyptian hieroglyphics, $E=mc^2$, the *Hindenburg* and my own personal Rushmore. Perhaps we should have left the car primer gray, it occurred to me, so as not to draw the attention of our enemies.

13

SCIENCE AND TECHNOLOGY

I SHOULD HAVE BEEN worrying less about the car and more about myself, because on that same night, Cleo called and reported that there'd been a problem. "Frank caught me returning the silverware. I didn't see him, but he'd been spying on me as usual and he told my mom."

"So how did you explain it?"

"I tried to come up with some reason for why I'd take the family silver and then sneak it back into the drawer, but you have to admit it must have looked pretty weird."

"It's all my fault," I said. "I should have had a plan."

"It was my fault. I'm the only girl I know who's no good at lying to her mother."

"What did you tell her?"

"That I got it from you guys. I'm sorry, Daniel."

"You said we'd stolen it?"

"I wanted to tell her there was a misunderstanding, but that was my grandmother's wedding silver, so she didn't take it well. I have a feeling my dad's going to hear about this, so I wanted to let you know."

That night I tossed and turned, and throughout the week while we finished our art-car project I had one eye on the collage and another on the corner of 16th and Hill, where I feared that Bailey could turn up at any moment. If he knew we'd tried to steal from him, that could mean the end of our school. He'd stop at nothing to find out who had raided his silver drawer, and implacable as he was, he'd probably press charges. Sol Kurtzman hadn't crossed him half as badly as this, yet Bailey slapped him with an eviction notice. And I knew my father couldn't explain that Tino, a member of his faculty, was a petty thief; such an admission would only lead to more—the stolen food, the marijuana growing in pots upstairs, the bogus credentials of this merry band of "educators." So I decided I couldn't wait another day for Bailey to come to us. I would go to him.

For the first time, I was the one to call a meeting of the Fellowship of Chester, but instead of sharing a secret, I confided an outright lie. We were in the parlor just after lunch on the first day of April. That morning the school had voted that science and technology would be the subject of the month, and my father had made the unprecedented suggestion that Quinn and the twins take over the leadership, which was approved by a narrow vote. Tino continued to badger Quinn about Angela, and Molly complained to my mother that this school was too disorganized. Why should she have to take a class taught by a bunch of kids when D.C. was full of good schools like Pilgrim Hill and Our Lady of Perpetual Help? My mother said we couldn't afford a private school, and where was her pluck, her pioneering spirit? Molly consulted her Casio Biolator and reported that she felt fatigued, and my mother promised, as much for herself as for Molly, that life would get better soon.

Winter had nearly surrendered to spring—that was a start—and though we had yet to open the storm windows, we hadn't built a fire in more than a week. My mother and Molly had left to get group tickets to the Air and Space Museum, and the rest of the school was outside gluing plastic beads and stars to the KING TUT RULES / OUR HOUSE car and putting on finishing touches of blue, green and gold paint. I had decided on the final two presidents for the White House lawn: John F. Kennedy and, for the sake of optimism, number thirty-nine, Jimmy Carter. His term had just begun, but give him a chance, I thought: he could go down as one of the greats.

My father and I, standing so we could keep a lookout, swore our vow, and I wasted no time with my confession: "At the election party I took some of the Dornans' silver. That was before we had tuition money, and I thought we were desperate." I spoke fast and avoided my father's eyes as I told him how I held on to the cache for months, never intending to pawn it but wanting to have a treasury of silver bullion, just in case. But the guilt had gotten to me, and I'd returned the silver to Cleo, only to learn soon afterward that she'd been caught sneaking it back. "I'm worried that Bailey knows," I said. "Can you call and tell him that I did it before all of us get in trouble?"

My father looked around to be sure no one could hear us, then grabbed my biceps, pulling me down onto the brocade sofa with a force he'd never used before. "What the hell were you thinking, Daniel? This isn't like you."

I was not a practiced liar, and this was the most illogical lie, designed to get me into, rather than out of, trouble. So I stumbled over my words and could come up with no explanation other than I was trying to protect our family.

"That's my job," my father said. "Mine and your mother's. Don't you think we can handle ourselves?"

I wanted to say that they hadn't done so hot up to now. We'd been on a whistle-stop tour of the Midwest since the day I was born. We'd come east to open a school where the teachers were kids and the kids teachers, but despite our claims about democratic education, we were putting the students to work more for our own survival, and it was only a matter of time before they'd ask questions. On the bright side, my parents seemed to be cooperating, but I didn't have to be reminded that my mother had told my father, "This was your idea," his one last chance, and if the school tanked, their marriage would follow. Woodrow Wilson said, "Loyalty means nothing unless it has at its heart the absolute principle of self-sacrifice." I'd made up my mind to take a fall, to "Act First. Ask Permission Later" for the good of the community.

"I just wanted to help," I said.

"That's not the kind of help we need. You've been spending too much time with the hippies. Digging through garbage, learning how to steal. I warned your mother not to bring them here, and now look what's happened."

I hated to misrepresent myself. I was no Dear Abbie Hoffman; I'd never taken the five-finger discount. "It's not their fault, and it's not Mom's either. It was all me, and I'm sorry."

Chester was kneading my father's pant leg, digging in with his claws. My father lifted him with one hand and flung him off the sofa. "You've left me no choice, Daniel. I'm going to have to make an example of this."

I recall, later that same afternoon, how we all gathered in the living room to listen to Quinn read from a microfilm copy of the *Hindenburg*'s original brochure. It talked about the size and speed of zeppelins—nearly twice as fast as steamships—and the whisper-quiet ride, what must have been, in 1936, a revolution in luxury. I tried to concentrate, to drown out my father's threat, but as Quinn turned to a page entitled "A Day On Board," a portentous feeling, a sense of peace before disaster, came over me.

"'The enjoyment of airship travel makes people sociable, friendships are formed,'" Quinn read aloud. "'You finish breakfast and walk to the windows. Down below, you see the long shadow of the airship passing swiftly over the sparkling foam-crested waves of the blue Atlantic, and the joy of experiencing this wonderful achievement in modern travel surges through you. The air is delicious and fresh; in fact you seem to have been transported into another and more beautiful world.'"

Quinn said the *Hindenburg* used to take people on cruises over New York City, and would park on the needle of the Empire State

Building, where at the top there used to be a "Zeppelin Room." From the deck, passengers would take the flight of stairs that wound down through the needle into a huge banquet area, and there they'd have a private party, high above the rest of the world. Quinn passed around the brochure and a book of photographs. He talked about the potential for a new fleet of airships filled with helium rather than flammable hydrogen, and everyone seemed to be getting into it, until Tino interrupted. "Far out," he said. "But you told us your sister was going to school us in graffitiology, and I aim to cash in on that promise."

"I never promised you anything." Quinn scowled.

"Like hell you didn't." Tino tried to rile up Brie, the twins and the bishop's kid by threatening to march over to Quinn's house right now and demand to talk to Angela.

"You don't know where I live," Quinn said, and it occurred to me that neither did I. After school I'd watched him cross into Shaw and continue on before hanging a right down 14th. I'd asked him where his house was, and he'd said not far from here. Once or twice I'd brought up his family, but he'd spoken only in the most general terms about his mother and father, both city employees, and his hot-tempered older sister. The rest Quinn had stashed away, just like Anthony and his secret hiding place of misbegotten things.

To get Tino off his back once and for all, Quinn led everyone out into the bright sunshine to the KING TUT RULES / OUR HOUSE car and asked Tino's students where they'd discovered each piece of graffiti they had copied: on a bridge in Rock Creek Park, behind Senedu's parents' restaurant in Adams Morgan, on the side of a city bus in a Capitol Hill depot.

"I know enough from my sister to give you the basics, but we're on to science now, so stop bugging me about Angela." He pointed to a cutout Brie had done of a wrecking ball crashing into the words "Fight for Your Home." "This is stencil graffiti, just protest stuff, nothing too complicated," he said, then moved on to the hood. "And these are supposed to be wildstyle tags, but there's not enough life. Graffiti's got to flow. It should look like the cherry tops were breathing down your neck and you had no time to throw up your paint. The best tags are frozen motion. You want to know how it's done? Get me cans of red, orange, yellow and gold and I'll show you."

The class got all excited and rushed into the house to look for spray paint.

"Not on the car, though." Cinnamon stepped in. "This project is complete."

"And not in the living room, either," my father said.

"Go ahead and use our bedroom," my mother suggested offhandedly.

Quinn climbed the steps to join his classmates. Tino, Cinnamon and my mother followed in his wake. "Not so fast." My father grabbed my elbow. After everyone else had gone with Quinn up to my parents' room for the graffiti demonstration, my father led me to the corner of 16th and Hill. "We have some business to take care of with the Neighborhood Watch," he said.

We walked past Florida Avenue and took a right on V Street, where the whole block was lined with police cars parked in front of the Third District Station. Inside, my father caught the eye of Officer Trammell, who came over and gave him one of his bone-crushing handshakes. Trammell didn't bother to shake my hand or so much as look at me as he led us down a long hallway that seemed to narrow and darken the farther we went.

Officer Mazzocca, it turned out, was a lieutenant. He had his own office, decorated with trophies and plaques and pictures of Little League baseball teams. "I coach at the Boys' Club," he answered when my father asked about one of the larger trophies. "We took the ten-to-twelve championship last year, went nineteen and one."

"Congratulations," my father said.

Mazzocca beamed, sat behind his desk and folded his hands, suddenly serious.

Trammell ducked out of the room, and in his place, to my surprise, came Bailey, just back from the water cooler with a conical paper cup. He swallowed the water in one gulp, dropped the cup in Mazzocca's trash can and shut the door behind him.

"You want to meet a ballplayer?" Bailey asked. "Pete Truitt was the best third baseman you've never heard of."

"I had no idea," Mazzocca said.

My father brushed it off. "Sure, I used to play." He offered Bailey a seat, and just as I was fantasizing that they'd wile away the afternoon talking about baseball, my father added, "But that's not why we're here."

Since there were no other chairs in the room, I stood while the three men looked me over with a mix of perplexity and fascination, as if I were some reptile that had dropped its tail or changed color before their eyes.

"So I understand we're in the presence of a thief." Bailey loosened his tie and undid the top button of his shirt. He wore a camelhair blazer and tasseled shoes and had the rumpled, slightly put-out appearance of having stopped by the precinct on his way home from work.

I looked toward my father, who had said nothing about this ambush, only that we had some business with the Neighborhood Watch. "I thought we'd give you a chance to explain yourself, Daniel."

I didn't know what to say. I had learned from observation that lying only twisted one's life into knots. I recalled George Washington and the apocryphal story of chopping down his father's cherry tree. *I cannot tell a lie, Father, you know I cannot tell a lie! I did cut it with my little hatchet,* six-year-old George had said. *My son, that you should not be afraid to tell the truth is more to me than a thousand trees! Yes, though they were blossomed with silver and had leaves of the purest gold!*

But I was no George Washington, and I had overestimated my father, who apparently was not so quick to forgive. Faced with this jury of three, I made up a story, one of the first and last lies I'd tell. I said that I'd been walking through the Dornans' dining room that election night and the silverware drawer had been slightly open. Through the crack I'd seen a glint of the beautiful mother-of-pearl handles and had an inexplicable need to study them. So I opened the drawer and slipped some of the forks and knives into my pocket. I'd intended to shut myself in the bathroom and admire the pretty silver under the light, but the bathroom was locked and the party turned boisterous and before I knew it a bottle rocket was screaming toward me and my hair was on fire. After returning from the hospital and recuperating, I recalled the silver in my pocket, and so began months under the weight of guilt, not knowing how to give back the heirlooms. Only after seeing "The Treasures of Tutankhamun" did I come up with an idea. "It wasn't fair of me to ask for Cleo's help, but I did, and I'm sorry," I said.

"That's a crazy story." Bailey knitted his heavy eyebrows. "We've all been foolish teenagers I guess. It's part of the contract."

"But when you do something reprehensible you should have to pay for it," my father added.

"You're sounding like one of those law-and-order Democrats, Pete. You sure you don't want to come over to the Grand Old Party?" Bailey checked his watch and stifled a yawn with the inside of his elbow. I was astonished that he wasn't more upset. "So, do you need anything more from me? I should be getting home."

"The lieutenant and I have talked, and we thought you should know that the Neighborhood Watch takes petty theft seriously." My father nodded at Mazzocca, who got up from his desk and asked me to put out both hands.

"I'm sorry," I repeated, and thought for a moment that Mazzocca would understand why kids with no money might take from the rich. I remembered the Boys' Clubs of Indianapolis and Chicago; they were full of regular kids like me, whose parents both worked, whose sneakers came out of the discount bin at Turn Style, and who couldn't begin to imagine a house like Bailey's, with whole rooms shipped in from Africa.

The handcuffs pinched my wrists.

"You get one phone call," Mazzocca said.

I looked at my father. His face betrayed no emotion. I thought of my mother, at home watching Quinn spray-paint graffiti all over her bedroom. Tino, whose ass I was covering, leering at underage girls. Cleo would be returning from school around now, unaware of my predicament.

"So?" Mazzocca asked, handing me the phone.

I considered calling my mother but didn't want to disrupt the school or cause any more embarrassment. "I don't know anyone," I said.

My father tensed his jaw. Mazzocca put the phone back in the cradle, took off his Buddy Holly glasses and cleaned them with a handkerchief. Outside the window, a squad car pulled out and flipped on its siren.

"Well, it's time to take those last steps of freedom." Mazzocca got up from his chair. "You want to do the honors?" He handed Bailey a ring of keys, but Bailey passed them to my father.

We walked through a large room where policemen were digging into their takeout dinners. The precinct smelled like old newspapers and charred meat. I was grateful that none of the officers except Trammell seemed to notice us.

The holding cell, on the basement floor, sat at the end of a long hallway of spartan offices. It had a bench built into the wall, a toilet and a sink.

"Which key is it?" my father asked. None of us had said a word.

Lieutenant Mazzocca pointed to a key that could have been any office key, and my father opened the holding-cell door.

I stepped inside and stood behind the bars as my father clanged the door shut. I gazed at him steadily, but he did not look back.

Mazzocca reached through the bars into the cell and with a small key released my handcuffs. "Good night," he said, and the three men walked down the echoing hallway.

Years later, around the time I was in graduate school, at one of those holiday dinners where we brought up old stories, I asked my father if he and Mazzocca had planned to keep me in jail overnight. It couldn't have been legal, since no one had booked me or read me my rights. My father said no, they'd just wanted to give me a scare. But even now I can't be sure, because within a couple hours of the bars locking in front of me and the men retreating down the hallway, a new set of footsteps returned, and there in front of me were both of my parents and Lieutenant Mazzocca. My mother's cheeks were wet with tears—I almost never saw her cry—and when my father tried to explain, she said, "Shut up, you bastard! How dare you!"

By the time they'd brought me back to Our House, the rest of the school had gone home. My parents took me up to their room and shut the door, a weak effort at privacy in a place where nothing was private and all secrets eventually would be revealed. Quinn had spray-painted a word that I couldn't make out—*anthem, antonym, antipathy, anything*—just crabbed cacography, the letters dancing along the side wall like flame. My mother called my father a coward and said he'd thrown me under the bus just to satisfy Bailey. "How could you not talk to me first? You're always acting on your moral imperatives without consulting anyone. Have you forgotten why Lake Bluff let you go? No one likes surprises, least of all me."

"Daniel had to learn a lesson."

"You're one to talk about learning lessons. You've learned nothing for as long as I've known you. And how can you expect to run a free and equal school when you're locking your own son in jail? Imagine. What kind of hypocrite are you?"

My father said that Bailey would have called him about the silver before long. "It was a preemptive strike. I had to do something dramatic."

"Like deliver up your family?"

"I'm sorry," my father said, and he looked it. He seemed genuinely stupefied.

"You bet you are. Now both of you get out," she demanded, and

I went up to my room and my father went down to the sofa, where he would spend the next two nights.

Perhaps his exile would have lasted longer had he not received the good news in the mail from the Braitmayer Foundation: the grant he had applied for months before had come through. We were awarded eight hundred dollars, less than we'd hoped for, but enough to cover rent for May and June. Talk had begun about summer plans, and the prevailing idea was to open a coffee shop downstairs, charge admission for open-mic nights, and sell arts and crafts or anything else the students could peddle. "The trick is, have them do all the work, make the crap we're selling, and put the proceeds back in the till," Tino said one night at dinner.

"Spoken like a true Maoist," my father sneered.

"Tell me," Tino said. "When will we get another chance to screw the carriage trade?"

The good news about the grant cheered my mother only briefly. She spoke to my father in clipped sentences and threatened again to take a job, this time leaving a long message and our phone number with Linda Silvers's secretary in Senator Gaylord Nelson's office. To compensate, my father was extra solicitous: bringing my mother coffee in bed each morning before the students arrived, finding ways to steer conversations back to the grant award, cooking his bland pastas so she could relax and watch Hepburn and Tracy films on Channel 20 at the end of the day.

I regretted how my self-sacrifice had backfired, and not just because my parents' tentative détente had returned to a cold war. I wanted to announce to the whole school that Tino was a thief. On top of everything else, he'd taken to taunting me for returning the silver. "What kind of chickenshit goes sneaking into people's rooms like that?" he said to me one night in the third-floor hallway. "I know you took my Abbie bible, too. That you can keep, but you should read it more closely. You're supposed to stick it to the plunderers, not give back."

But I said nothing about these encounters or Tino's guilt, and as the days went by I began to harbor bitterness toward my father that only grew. It's taken nearly until now for me to recognize, but from that moment when he shut the cell door in my face and walked down the echoing hallway of Third District Station, a part of me knew that I could never trust or believe in him the same way again. My mother was right—he had thrown me under the bus—and I would never understand how he even came up with such a punishment, particularly against me, his steady aide-de-camp and confidant. Would he stop at nothing to please Bailey? Would he sacrifice his own family to prove to this old teammate that a small-town midwestern nobody could come to clubby, backbiting Washington, D.C., and make it? And what's more, he still didn't seem to grasp what he'd done, even after my mother had told him he'd betrayed me. He just seemed baffled, as if detached from all responsibility.

14

NATURE

SCIENCE AND TECHNOLOGY month had gone well enough that Molly agreed to finish out the year at our wild and woolly school. I told her she should be happy with so much freedom, but she said that going to Our House was like taking endless sick days, so my mother promised that she could explore other options for fall, perhaps Hardy, the public school where Amy Carter went.

We'd had a string of sunny afternoons, and I'd enjoyed watching Quinn get keyed up at the Air and Space Museum when he saw a rocket or plane he recognized. We went as a group to the Naval Observatory, peered at the stars through the huge refractor telescopes and laughed in spite of ourselves when the bishop's kid asked the resident astronomer if he could see the rings of Uranus. The twins brought in a record of Orson Welles's broadcast of "The War of the Worlds," and we talked about what we'd do if a Martian capsule landed in New Jersey and Martian machines rolled into our cities spraying poisonous gas.

I gave a report on Jimmy Carter's sighting of a UFO above Leary, Georgia, shortly after dark on the evening of January 6, 1969. He was standing outside waiting for a Lions Club meeting to begin when he spotted a single "self-luminous" object. "It was the darndest thing I've ever seen," he said later. "It was big, it was very bright, it changed colors and it was about the size of the moon. We watched it for ten minutes, but none of us could figure out what it was. One thing's for sure: I'll never make fun of people who say they've seen unidentified objects in the sky." Carter was the first president to report a UFO, and he believed we were not alone in the universe.

During the last week of April, the school discussed and voted on what the group project would be. The twins wanted to build a model rocket and enter the National Rocketry Contest, but Quinn's idea, a four-foot-long blimp advertising Our House, won in a landslide. Promising that we could learn science, art and marketing, all at the same time, Quinn appointed himself lead designer, with Linc and I spearheading the publicity campaign. Once we'd finished building the blimp, we would paint the Our House logo on either side in bright colors, fly it on a tether above 16th and Hill, and take it to festivals and parades or anywhere we could find a crowd. For our next school subject, my mother proposed Banned Books Month, but Brie said the weather was too nice to sit around inside and "read a bunch of boring stories. I want to go out barefoot and let my hair down and watch the flowers open up." And so was born Nature Month at Our House, co-taught by Tino and Brie. "Buckle your seat belts, kids," Tino said, "and get ready for a celebration of the senses."

I had spoken only a couple of times to Cleo since her mother had caught her returning the silver, but she called one afternoon to say that the orthopedist had removed her cast. She wanted to know if I'd help her celebrate by shooting baskets at Pierce Park. I'd been on the patio listening to Quinn try to persuade my father to exceed the budget on the Our House blimp. Quinn had run out of money after building the girder framework of his handmade model. He had yet to complete the nose and put the finishing touches on the fuselage, hadn't bought the canvas cover or the helium balloons that none of us knew for sure would keep the contraption afloat. He'd done elaborate drawings of the gondola, his pièce de résistance, complete with tiny figures looking out the windows. By continuing to fund the project, my father would have to dip into his grant, but I could tell as I left the back yard to put on my high-tops that Quinn was going to get his wish.

On my way to the playground, I noticed the sky darkening. I looked beyond the sooted clouds to a section in the distance that would have sat above the basketball court, and there, cut into the gray swath, was a round patch of blue. I took this as a good omen. Cleo had arrived first, and for a while we just shot around. A drizzle began to fall, and I asked her if she wanted to call it a day, but she said her favorite time to play was right after it rained. I knew what she meant—I loved shooting baskets after a spring shower, the way the net would hold the ball for an extra beat. That hour or so when the court fizzes, drinking up the rain, is the best time to get a good grip on the seams.

Cleo got to talking about the silver again. "I heard about your jail time. That sounds like something *my* dad would do."

"My mom was madder about it than I was. Sometimes my father makes these grand gestures without thinking them through. It wasn't a big deal," I lied.

Cleo was rusty, not having played in three months. Her left-handed jumper kept coming up short and she couldn't quite bend her wrist into that graceful swan's neck follow-through. Still, she looked lovely, her cheeks flushed in twinned crescents, her damp hair whisking around her forehead. The rain had soaked through her green tank top and white game jersey, *OLPH 13*. I loved that she wore a bad-luck number, as if to declare her allegiance with the misunderstood.

She rested the ball on her hip at the free-throw line, and I glimpsed her nipples through her shirt. "You have to explain something to me, Daniel. If you didn't take the silver, why did you fess up to it?"

I wanted to tell Cleo everything, but I couldn't allow the real story to get back to her mother and Bailey. "Part of our school's philosophy is all for one and one for all. When one does good, we all get credit, and when one does bad, we all take the heat."

"But why did *you* have to be the patsy?"

"Why not me?" I said.

"I think it's admirable." Cleo rattled a free throw home. "But I bet I know who stole the silver. It's that sleazy guy with the mustache. What's his name?"

I played dumb, but she pressed me. "Tino," I said finally.

"So you're admitting it was him?"

I grabbed a rebound off Cleo's miss and bricked a turnaround from the corner. "Let me try that again," I said, and she threw it back. I launched another for a *swish.* "Now, that's what I'm talking about."

"You're avoiding the question. Tino did it, didn't he?"

"Maybe," I said. It was exhilarating to withhold information, though I knew that this time, in spite of myself, I wouldn't suppress it for long. We did a pas de deux for a while until I yielded: "Okay, it was Tino. But I didn't want your dad to think our teachers are crooks."

"I wouldn't worry so much about that. I hear there are other problems." Cleo glided in for an off-hand lay-up. When the net released the ball, she caught it and stopped playing. "As long as we're giving away secrets, I have one for you. But you have to swear not to let anyone know I told you this."

I gave her my scout's honor, wondering again what made me the repository of everyone's confidences. In a house full of clashing personalities I'd been the one at the top of the stairs listening for trouble. I rarely asked for much and took up little space, so perhaps to compensate, people freighted me with the clutter of their lives. As a collector of facts and trivia I accepted their donations willingly, and though I sometimes suffered for it, in the long run I would be repaid for my curiosity.

Cleo crossed her hands over her chest. Goose bumps prickled her arms. "Tino and Brie are having an affair."

I was seized suddenly, less with shock than a powerful dread. "You're kidding."

"Dawn told me, and she's not a gossip."

I had nearly forgotten that Dawn, Cleo's new friend and fellow Charlie's Angel, was Brie's younger sister. Though I saw them most days at Our House, they never spent time together. Dawn and Stephanie were thick as thieves while Brie traipsed around like a second-generation flower child.

I put out my hands for the basketball, and Cleo passed it to me. "How did Dawn find out?" I asked.

"Brie told her. I'm sure she's proud of it."

My fingers were trembling. "You don't think she'll tell anyone else, do you?"

"She doesn't want it getting back to her parents, that's for sure. Her mother's wound tighter than a spring. But you know how rumors get around. That's a serious scandal, sleeping with your teacher."

"He's not really a teacher. He's a tutor-collaborator," I said in a rush of words, realizing as I spoke how ridiculous I sounded.

"She calls him her teacher. That's all I know."

I grew defensive. "But they couldn't be having an affair. They're never alone."

Cleo gave a wobbly smile. "Maybe not at school, but at night she tells her folks she's going to the library. Dawn told me they have a mattress tucked away under some bridge in Rock Creek Park. Can you believe it?"

I breathed deeply to quiet the thud of my heartbeat. Yes, I could believe it. Tino was capable of any transgression. Lying, cheating, impersonating a priest, ripping off the landlord's heirlooms, stealing his best friend's wife. Bedding a sixteen-year-old? Sure. "How long has it been going on?"

"A couple months," Cleo said.

I thought back to earlier in the year, when I'd first noticed that he and Cinnamon were having problems. The sounds from their bedroom had begun to subside around the time she got serious about teaching. At night she went to the library to study Rauschenberg, and he said he was going to a bar or to run an errand, only to slip off for his trysts. Tino needed constant attention, and when the door had been left open for even one moment, some teenager was there to satisfy his vanity.

Cleo pushed her wet hair out of her face, asked for the ball back, and took some easy shots inside the key.

"What do you think I should do?" I asked.

"I don't know. It's a tough one. I guess I'd tell my parents so they could put a stop to it."

"But you don't know Tino. He's a hothead. He's totally unreasonable."

Cleo made a flip shot across the lane, and something about her left-handedness, her lopsided smile and that jersey number 13 compelled me to admit for the first time that Cinnamon and Linc were still legally married, though Cinnamon and Tino, Linc's former best friend, slept in the same bed.

"Your poor uncle," Cleo said, but not with the judgment—*What's wrong with you people?*—that I might have expected of someone raised in the Bailey regime.

"So you see, he's capable of anything." I wiped the sweat from my forehead with the back of my wristband.

"But she's sixteen, Daniel. How old is he?"

"Thirty or so."

"I'm pretty sure that's illegal. He could get in big-time trouble for this. Your school could get in trouble."

"I know," I said. "You're right. I'm going to tell my parents."

But I didn't tell my parents at first. I kept the news to myself because I'd run out of people to believe in. My father had taken me to the local precinct and arranged a night in jail, and the more he lost control, the more he sought someone to blame. If my mother hadn't invited Linc to D.C., Tino would still be living in a tree house outside Mazama and many of our problems wouldn't have come to pass. What was the point in stirring up my parents when my father would say to my mother, *I told you the hippies would ruin everything,* and my mother would tell him, *I gave you one last chance and you're blowing it.*

So as soon as I got home I dove into my presidential biographies and tried to forget this latest news. Yet everywhere I turned reminded me of scandal. Even doing research I couldn't catch a break. I'd finished Woodrow Wilson and had begun studying the Warren G. Harding administration, arguably the most corrupt in history. He'd filled the White House with his friends, the "Ohio gang," and would forever be linked to the under-the-table leasing of government land to private interests, known as the Teapot Dome Affair. His officials and cabinet members were convicted of fraud, bribery, skimming profits, running underground drug and alcohol operations. While no one could prove that Harding himself broke the law, he'd done nothing to stop the shady business that swirled around him. "My God, this is a hell of a job!" he said. "I have no trouble with my enemies, but my damn friends, my God-damned friends . . . they're the ones that keep me walking the floor nights!"

It appeared as though his friends even sped his demise. In the second month of a PR trip across the country, his "Voyage of Understanding," in which he tried to defend himself and explain his unpopular policies, Harding fell ill and died in San Francisco. Some doctors called it a heart attack, others a stroke, but a conspiracy was born when the First Lady, Florence Harding, refused to allow an autopsy. After his body was returned to the White House she was reportedly seen speaking to his corpse. "They can't hurt you now, Warren," she said.

Following his presidency, the public learned of his numerous affairs. He'd had a long relationship with Carrie Fulton Phillips before his election, and when she'd threatened to tell the world, the Republican National Committee had paid her and her family fifty thousand dollars and sent them on a hush trip to Japan. There was also Nan Britton. As a girl living in Harding's hometown of Marion, Ohio, she had pasted pictures of the rising politician on her bedroom walls. In her tell-all book, *The President's Daughter,* published after his death, Britton claimed that she and Harding conceived an illegitimate child, Elizabeth Ann, in his Senate office, and later, when he was president, they continued their affair, using a closet off the Oval Office for their assignations.

Reading all this became too much. It didn't matter that it happened more than fifty years before, with a different cast of characters who held opposite beliefs from ours. The facts were too familiar: a self-governing community run principally by friends, a man in a position of authority swept up by a girl with stars in her eyes, a White House so rife with corruption that it seemed ready at any moment to cave in under its own lubricity. I had to put my research away and distract myself with other activities.

Ever since he'd conceived of the Our House blimp, Quinn had been spending long days in the back yard working on his project. Soon after my father was allowed to return to the bedroom, Quinn had even begun spending nights on the parlor sofa. He'd go to sleep late and get up early, and my parents didn't seem to mind so long as he put away his sheets and pillow and kept the doors and windows locked. I liked the idea of having an older brother, and recalled that time in the attic room when Quinn and I had talked a stream. But no sooner had I thought we'd become great friends than he took over the class, and now here he was, Count Ferdinand von Zeppelin incarnate.

Meantime, the rest of the school was wrapped up in the nature course. I kept a close watch on the students during the morning meetings, but everyone seemed so busy, and humming with spring fever, that I couldn't tell whether others knew about Tino and Brie. Though the pair were co-teaching this month, they kept a distance between them, careful, it seemed, not to give off electricity. Dawn and Stephanie would catch my eye and glance away, relaying the message with their furtive looks that they promised to hold their tongues. Cinnamon spoke cheerfully about the peonies, irises, azaleas and rhododendrons blooming in the front yard, and though she had stopped stroking Tino's hair at dinner, she still sat next to him and slept in the same room.

Returning one evening from the Neighborhood Watch, my father finally laid down the law about the marijuana plants, which Tino had put back in the side garden, and to my surprise Tino didn't bristle. He shoveled the plants into plastic bags and drove off in the art car, saying he knew just the place to take them. "So long as it's not on this property," my father said. I pictured Tino meeting Brie under the bridge and hiking to some sunny patch in the woods to replant their crop.

At last my mother had spoken to the elusive Linda Silvers, and the conversation had energized her. My father had guessed that Linda gave up her whole life to become Gaylord Nelson's chief of staff. But in fact she'd married an aide to the other Wisconsin senator, William Proxmire, and last spring, at the age of thirty-six, she'd given birth to twins. Double motherhood kept Linda at home for four months, and it was soon after this that she'd traveled to Milwaukee to get out the vote for Carter. She apologized to my mother for not returning her call right away, but already she was back to the same hours she'd kept before the pregnancy. "She's a superwoman," my mother told us at the dinner table. "And listen to this." She turned to Molly excitedly. "This superwoman is going to be the first guest lecturer at Our House. She's coming next week."

Molly seemed only vaguely impressed, so my mother emphasized what it meant to be chief of staff for a U.S. senator, not to mention a mother of twins. "And it's perfect that she's coming during nature month, because Gaylord Nelson *founded* Earth Day, and the environment is Linda's pet project."

At the time, I couldn't fully grasp what Linda Silvers meant to my mother. I knew only that I'd been waiting for some sign of legitimacy to grace our fly-by-night operation. I figured the visit was welcome news, but I didn't understand that for my mother it offered a chance to prove herself and show that she, too, had fulfilled the promise of her heady undergraduate days, when she and

Linda marched on the capitol in Madison. For all her complaints and apprehension, and in spite of her veiled threats about leaving or starting some new career, part of my mother was proud of what we were trying to accomplish, and she wanted to show her commitment to it. I could see her eyes illuminate with the thought that soon she could display our own homemade democracy.

I'm certain it was that same night—it could even have been in the middle of my mother's animated talk—that the phone rang in the kitchen and I picked up.

"This is your D.C. post office calling," said the gruff, fast-talking voice. "We're updating our records and would like to confirm that a Mr. Lincoln Gearhart resides there."

For a moment it occurred to me that the bishop's kid was making a crank call. The voice seemed staged, so I listened for giggles in the background. "He's right here." I hesitated. "Do you want me to get him?"

"No, that's okay. Just making sure he lives there," the caller said. "And can you confirm the address for us? Sixteen-oh-one Hill Street?"

"That's right," I said, and nearly added *as you well know*, but the caller hung up. I didn't hear laughter, so I assumed it really was the post office, and thought nothing more about it. I should have known better, should have remembered that Linc almost never got calls—and wasn't the post office closed at this hour? But I had too much on my mind.

The next day we took a field trip to the National Zoo, and again I kept running into signs of Tino and Brie's affair, as if the world were trying to tell me that all secrets are out in the open and it's only a matter of recognizing them. Tino had arranged a question-and-answer session with one of the keepers at the giant-panda cage, and the guy talked on and on about the sex lives of the bears. Only about two weeks remained of the mating season, and the keeper was frustrated that Ling-Ling had continually spurned Hsing-Hsing's advances, to the point where the male panda had given up and spent his days chewing bamboo in a muddy corner. Their failure to reproduce threatened the continuation of the species, the zookeeper said, and went on to explain the mating rituals of other bear species, like the male grizzly in the Rocky Mountains, who herds the female to the top of a peak so other males won't catch her scent. Instead of foreplay, grizzlies swat, claw and wrestle each other, before giving in to their nature and coupling for up to an hour at a time.

"Let's see a show of hands, everyone. What kind of bear are you?" Tino asked the class. "Panda or grizzly?"

I wasn't about to play along, but most of those who did raised their hands for pandas. Tino and Brie were among the few grizzlies in the crowd.

Besides the zoo, we visited Eastern Market and interviewed organic farmers, went to the Safeway and learned about the journey of food from seed to factory to table. Back at home, Tino told stories of life on the commune that sounded more like Maoist propaganda—*Long live the Great Leap Forward!*—than the tales of woe my mother had reported. He talked about their abundant apple harvests and the apple butters, pies and cider they used to make and sell from a roadside stand on the Cascades Highway. He was portraying a golden era when Linc suddenly spoke up. "You're leaving a lot out," he said. "We were living on food stamps and never once saw a bumper crop."

"Oh, come on. It was beautiful," Tino insisted, and rode right over Linc so the students wouldn't hear that in fact the only decent farmers had fled Freelandia within the first two years, leaving Tino, Cinnamon, Linc and a handful of unskilled hippies to raid dumpsters and make knockoff crafts that they couldn't sell. Cinnamon stayed out of the fray except to tell of certain characters who passed through Mazama, like the "tomatarian" who ate nothing but tomatoes, and thus could barely summon the energy to pull a weed in the fields. He was constantly stopping to munch tomatoes, which he kept in a pouch attached to his belt. There was the hunter who had a vision after shooting a ten-point buck—he swore the deer froze him in a stare and mouthed the words "Lay down your arms."

"It freaked the guy out so much he stopped eating meat for good," Cinnamon said. The former hunter joined Freelandia and taught the communards how to tan the hides of deer that piled up in the town dump at the end of hunting season. The hides brought in some much-needed cash, until the hunter came unhinged and started punching people who made eye contact on the sidewalk or in the checkout line at the grocery store.

"What happened to him?" Molly asked.

"Dunno," Cinnamon said. "He wandered into the woods one day and never came back. He's probably still out looking for that deer's family, hoping to apologize."

The students laughed but Molly sat on her pillow consulting her Casio Biolator as if it were a crystal ball. "I don't know what to think," she said out loud. "He wants to be nice to animals but then he goes and punches people."

"What does your calculator say?" Brie asked.

"I'm not feeling very well," Molly said.

Things only got worse for my decorous sister, because the next story Tino told was about his attempt to turn the commune into a nudist colony. "We kept getting all these hippie watchers, who'd come up from Seattle to groove on the scene and ogle us like we were a bunch of giant pandas. They wanted to see how we worked and played and made a go of our utopia. One couple—professor types from Bellingham—asked if they could pull up a chair and watch us ball. Now, I'm not one to get shy under such circumstances, but imagine trying to frolic when Alfred Kinsey and wife are over there scribbling notes on their steno pads."

"Can we stick to the subject?" my mother interrupted.

"I thought this course was called Nature: Earth, Man and Animals," Tino said. "There'd be no man if we didn't get animal once in a while. And what's the point of living on earth if we can't freely express our nature?"

Tino went on talking about his failed experiment with the nudist colony. Since the commune was getting tourists, he figured it might as well try to earn some bread along the way. "A smart zoo charges admission," he said. "So for a while we went 'clothing optional' and had a spike in visitors, who thought we were some kind of psychedelic pastoral play. A bunch of long-hair sun worshipers picking apples from a tree, bare-assed as Adam and Eve skipping in the Garden. Your uncle"—Tino turned to Molly, whose eyes were fixed on her Biolator—"had his picture in the *Seattle Post-Intelligencer,* one hand cupped over his twig and berries, the other giving a wave."

Cinnamon stood up from her pillow and stretched, exposing her pale midriff; her bellybutton yawned and the shirt fell back over the waist of her dungarees. "That's enough story time for one day."

"I want to hear more," Brie said.

"The colony failed when winter came. The commune fell apart. What more is there to tell?" Cinnamon sounded testy. "We have work to do. Who's in favor of a group project?" she asked, and a quorum raised their hands.

We went around the room talking about what we could do as a school that would help our understanding of nature.

"Orgy!" yelled the bishop's kid.

"Peyote ritual!" said the twins.

"What, please, are these things?" asked Senedu.

"That's enough." My father stepped in. "I say we make a garden. All in favor?" He looked around firmly, and the hands went up one by one, as if lifted by his glare.

We split into three groups: Cinnamon led the landscape architects, Tino and Brie the planters, and my father the laborers. Because we only had a rusty trowel and a snaggletoothed rake, each student was asked to bring in one tool from the family shed and contribute one flat of vegetable seedlings that the school would nurture. That afternoon Molly, Quinn and I went with my father to buy tomato plants, and late that night Tino, Cinnamon and

Linc took off with the van. By the time the sun came up, bags of fertilizer and wood-chip mulch had magically appeared in stacks on the patio. My father set his transistor on the back porch and cranked up his Top 40 hits, and we dug into the sunniest part of the yard to Rod Stewart's "Tonight's the Night," Thelma Houston's "Don't Leave Me This Way," Marvin Gaye's "Got to Give It Up" and the song we'd be hearing, like it or not, more than any other in 1977, Debby Boone's "You Light Up My Life."

After we had dug a wide trench around the perimeter of the garden, Tino bent down to inspect the soil, declaring it fit for planting. My father grabbed a handful of earth, and when he tried to crumble it the pieces fell in gobs and left a terracotta smear on his hand. "I'm no expert, but isn't there too much clay in this soil?"

"At the moment," Tino said. "But when we're done with the garden we'll build a compost bin. Put all that good stuff together with the fertilizer, and by the end of July you'll have enough beefsteaks to feed an army of tomatarians."

"What about the sun?" my father asked. "Aren't vegetable gardens supposed to get hours of direct sunlight?"

The morning sunshine latticed Tino's face as he looked up through the branches of linden and maple trees. "A little shade won't hurt anyone. By afternoon this garden's going to be catching some serious rays."

But a few hours later, when the sun had reached its apex and along with the rest of the laborer group I had hoed the surface weeds, removed the roots and stacked rocks in piles beside the garden bed, I noticed that the sunlight still strained through the leafy screen to touch the ground. I would have mentioned this to my father, but I realized that both the back and front yards were in heavy shade. The limbs of the trees were too high to reach, the branches too thick and entwined to try to trim them to let in more light. After an afternoon of turning over the dense earth, in which two shovel handles snapped and the laborers complained about the bossiness of the landscape architects, I took a long, hot shower and sat in bed flipping through *Steal This Book.*

Dear Abbie,

How do you make a garden grow when you have no idea what you're doing?

Dubious in D.C.

Dear Dubious,

You cadged the wrong book. What do you think this is, *The Whole Earth Catalog? The Encyclopedia of Better Homes and Gardens?* I'm no green thumb. I like to keep my thumb free for hitching, 'cause in the words of Che Guevara, "Eternal vigilance and constant mobility are the passwords of survival." But since you asked, my little brother, you've got to have good soil and light and level ground. If you're looking to grow some prime dope, don't forget to incubate your seedlings and plant the seeds three inches deep and two feet apart. If you're worried about your neighbors or if the pigs come sniffing around, you better hide your plants. Sunflowers make a nice shield, the way they grow tall and gaudy. Put in the dope just behind them where no one can see, and you and your friends will be firing up all fall long.

So Abbie Hoffman wasn't always helpful.

The laborers raked fertilizer into the clumpy soil; the landscape architects made a border of bricks around the garden; and the planters put in plugs of celery, cucumber, eggplant, pole beans, green peppers, lettuce, early cabbage, kohlrabi and, most of all, tomatoes. We covered the garden in mulch and watered it, each of us predicting that our plants would be the most robust.

I recall, one night that May, my mother giving us an assignment to watch President Carter's message to Congress on the state of the environment, so we'd be better informed for Linda Silvers's visit. In his speech, which would later result in "Global Report 2000," Carter asked the State Department to prepare a study of ecological and population issues facing the world through the end of the century. The report, which Carter would publish in his final year in office, predicted that the world of 2000 would be dramatically more crowded, more polluted, less stable environmentally and more in danger of catastrophic events than the already imperiled world of the late 1970s.

Carter's hundredth day in office had recently passed, and most editorials were giving him a low B or high C, his place in my art-car pantheon notwithstanding. The "cardigan speech" had been a success, though Carter had yet to implement much of his energy policy and the country was still reeling from winter heating bills and bracing for record-high gas prices during the summer driving season. He seemed committed to focusing on the "three E's": Environment, Energy and Economy. But the last E was the one that mattered most, and after thirty years of prosperity no one knew better than our austere, moral-minded president that the high times were over.

In preparation for Linda Silvers's visit, Dawn had been spending extra hours practicing the guitar. Now she was sitting on the stairs in the front hallway, playing simple Bob Dylan tunes—"Tangled Up in Blue," "Girl from the North Country"—while Linc, in his red *Hey, Kool Aid!* T-shirt, turned the pages of her song book.

A cheer went up when Linda arrived, as if the First Lady herself had stepped into our living room. It didn't matter that, in her sensible shoes, thick glasses and smock-like dress, she did not call to mind a superwoman. Linda Silvers was our first guest lecturer, which lent her a certain charisma. My mother embraced her and told her how wonderful she looked. "I can't believe you just had twins."

"Oh, I'm a frump. Look at you," Linda said. "You haven't aged a minute."

My mother clutched her friend's hand. "Gosh, it's good to see you. Has it really been this long?" Her eyes welled up. "Seems like yesterday that we were knocking on doors rallying the Madison homemakers to vote for Jack and Jackie. But that was, what, eighteen years ago?"

She took Linda on a tour of the house. "When I watched you being interviewed at the convention, I told Pete I knew all along we'd be hearing about you. Who would have guessed that national TV would bring us together?"

"I'm so sorry we fell out of touch, Val. I dove right in after school and never came up for air."

"It's not your fault. I was no better," my mother said. "We've moved a lot. The post office must think we're on the run from something."

Linda marveled at the size of the house. "Well, you've certainly arrived now."

"We like the place," my mother said, and I felt hopeful when she added, "It just might be a keeper." She took Linda aside and explained the mission of the school, how the council meeting was like convening a cabinet, where we could decide as a group, with equal voice, the future of our own little world. Linda said it all sounded ideal. "If only the government ran so smoothly." My mother smiled wanly, then introduced her friend around, giving an overview of our recent projects.

Tino showed off the back garden and Linda praised our work, though she did repeat my father's concern, urging us to cut back branches to let in more light. Quinn gave her a detailed report on the blimp, which he said was a week away from launch. Stephanie had completed five of the deadly sins, and hung her photocollages in a ring around the living room. Linda seemed most impressed with *Wrath*, since much of it focused on natural disasters—earthquakes, volcanoes, tsunamis and blizzards.

She used the picture as a prompt for talking about the environment. She said that Senator Nelson had gone on an eleven-state conservation tour with President Kennedy in September 1963 in an effort to bring the environment into the public consciousness. Though the press gave the tour good coverage, the senator couldn't capitalize on the issue, because before long the country fell into the turmoil of assassinations, riots and the Vietnam War. But six years after the conservation tour, during a Vietnam teach-in, the senator realized that Americans could organize a huge grassroots protest over what was happening to the environment. And so, in 1970, Earth Day was born.

My mother led the question-and-answer that followed Linda's talk, and I was pleased that even the bishop's son and the twins were behaving themselves. We were all discussing President Carter's address when the doorbell rang, and because he was sitting closest to the door, Linc got up to answer it.

At first we continued the discussion, assuming it must be a canvasser or a Jehovah's Witness—we'd had several solicitors since the weather had turned pleasant—but then the gruff voice at the door grew louder and we all stopped and listened.

"You didn't think I could find you, but here I am!"

"There must be some mistake."

"You said you're Lincoln. How many other motherfucking Lincolns could there be at Sixteen-oh-one Hill Street?"

"Okay, take the keys." We heard a jingle and the sound of keys passing hands.

"Doesn't matter. I have my own set. A good friend from Seattle sent them to me. Maybe you've heard of him: Rex Brisbee? Name ring a bell?"

"I can explain."

"You stole his car, Lincoln Gearhart, and you made a hippie-dippy mess out of it."

My father started to get up from his pillow in front of Linda Silvers, who appeared aghast. Linc was backpedaling into the living room, turning helplessly toward us. His tormentor must have been six foot five, in a red plaid shirt and work boots. He looked like Brawny the lumberman, back from chopping wood.

Before my father was on his feet, the guy had hauled off and punched Linc square in the jaw, sending him crashing into the circle of students, a foot away from me. I'd never seen Linc so startled. Blood slid down his face and onto his T-shirt, the smiling Kool-Aid pitcher rushing to the rescue.

15

LITERATURE AND CREATIVE WRITING

THAT ONE PUNCH had broken Linc's jaw, and for the second time since our arrival in D.C., we rushed en famille to the George Washington University emergency room. All I could think about during the drive was how it was my fault—why hadn't I steered the caller with the gruff voice off my uncle's trail?

Linc spent two nights in the hospital and had as many surgeries, to stabilize three fractures of the mandible. He came home with his jaw wired shut, and sequestered himself in his room. My mother bought a heavy-duty blender, Cinnamon returned from Fields of Plenty with bags of vegetables and protein supplements, and Molly and I provided room service, carrying tall glasses of pureed soups, fruit shakes and whatever else could be liquefied and sucked up with a straw.

The Brawny look-alike who'd laid Linc out had not been heard from since. After the punch, my father rushed down the front steps and threatened a citizen's arrest, but the lumberman flipped him the bird and hopped into the Bug, and that was the last we'd see of the KING TUT RULES / OUR HOUSE car.

While we flew off to the hospital, my father and Tino had remained behind, dealing with Linda Silvers and the stunned students. According to Dawn and Stephanie, who later reported back to me, even the St. Sebastian miscreants could only sit quietly as my father and Tino asked questions about Earth Day and President Carter's address, pretending that nothing had happened. After half an hour, class was dismissed. And when we got the news that Linc was going to need a second surgery, my father canceled school for the rest of the week. The term had been winding down anyway, and he needed time to come up with some explanation for why a vigilante had stormed into class, cracked a teacher in the face and stolen our school's art project. Linc returned in no state to explain himself—wincing, he garbled his words—so my father called a meeting of the Fellowship of Chester.

By now I'd grown weary of this ritual. Getting locked in jail had been the last straw on so many counts with my father. Wasn't I grown up enough that we could speak plainly, without reciting some artificial vow? In graduate school, the woman I'd eventually marry would tell me that in times of stress her own father was so uncomfortable talking directly to his sons that he resorted to pirate-speak:

Ay, me hearties, your mother wants to leave me.

Shiver me timbers! You don't say?

'Tis true, me buckos. The saucy wench is set to weigh anchor and hoist the mizzen!

As I look back on it, my father was not much better at getting his message across. We were in the kitchen, and he was washing dishes. Chester sat on the counter, stabbing at an injured roach. "You've been acting funny, Daniel. Is something on your mind?"

I filled the blender with banana, yogurt and honey and claimed to know nothing more than anyone else. I said the assault had to do with the cigarette car, a simple case of payback. Not long ago I might have told him about the letters Linc had showed me from Rex Brisbee and Rudy, the mail clerk at the Mazama P.O. I might have confided my guilt over the phone call that preceded the attack. But I no longer felt I'd do anything to protect my father, and the words that used to roll off my tongue stayed coiled as snails.

"What should we tell the students?" he asked.

"Say it was a car theft."

"But they could see it was personal. The guy knew Linc's name." My father put a plate in the drying rack. "And I don't want someone to call and get the police involved. I have a good thing going at the precinct."

"Say it was a misunderstanding."

"That's too vague. We have to brainstorm. I can't afford to have Bailey find out about this."

You don't know the half of it, I wanted to say. If Bailey found out we had a teacher sleeping with an underage student, all his preconceptions would be confirmed and he could shut down the school tomorrow. My father shooed Chester off the counter and sprayed the backsplash; the wounded roach circled the drain and disappeared; and it occurred to me that maybe Molly had been right all along about Our House. What kind of school was this, after all, where the kids were indistinguishable from the teachers, where there was no order and no one in charge? That my father couldn't recognize the signs of a looming crisis, that he stood by and counted on me, a thirteen-year-old with no experience in the world, to tell him what to do next, made me wish for someone I could look up to, like the presidents I'd been studying for years. Why couldn't my father be that kind of leader?

"What are you going to do, Dad?"

"I was asking you."

"I don't know. It's your school." I switched on the blender and the kitchen filled with a steady, piercing wheeze.

After I had fixed Linc's banana shake, I poured it into a glass and said I should be getting upstairs. Leaving the kitchen I caught a glimpse of my father with his back to the sink, his third baseman's forearms crossed over his chest and a weirdly vacant look on his face. He could have been lost, or lost in thought. It was anybody's guess.

That night, in the back yard, Molly and I helped Quinn with the final details of his zeppelin. The days were growing longer, and we worked—or, rather, Molly and I lifted the frame and tail assembly while Quinn tinkered with the gondola—until dusk wore down to dark. Quinn figured he was a week away from formally christening his airship and flying it on a tether above Our House, and he wondered aloud if the school would ever reconvene. "I've been through this kind of thing before," he said.

"What kind of thing?" I asked.

"You know, watching what happened to Anthony with his family. I couldn't take that again." Quinn put a tarpaulin over his blimp and we made our way inside.

It occurred to me that Quinn cared far more than I had realized. He poured as much energy into that silly balloon as I used to put into helping my father. "The school's going to be fine," I said, and felt a new resolve. "All the kids will be back on Monday, just like normal."

But when we reached the front hallway we heard the sound of my parents' arguing from Linc's room at the top of the stairs. Afraid to go up, we waited and listened:

MOTHER: Don't talk to him like that. He's in incredible pain.

FATHER: He brought it on himself. You can't drive off with a car and get away with it.

LINC: Uh here uhreddy. Got a hrolluh?

FATHER: Damn right I've got a problem. I've got a whole list. Want me to go over it for you?

MOTHER: Leave him alone, Pete. He shouldn't be talking.

FATHER: What am I supposed to tell the parents, huh? Guess who I got to speak with this afternoon? The bishop of the Episcopal diocese of Washington. And guess who else? Sister Donovan. I didn't know what to say, so I told them it was a freak incident, a random attack.

MOTHER: That wasn't very smart. We're supposed to be a safe

haven. How do you think we got students here in the first place?

FATHER: And you have better ideas?

MOTHER: You could have told them what I said to Linda—it was a lovers' quarrel.

LINC: (*muffled laughter*)

FATHER: Are you kidding me?

MOTHER: It worked. She said she'd come back anytime.

FATHER: This isn't my fault. It's your brother's. That's right, Linc. I'm talking to you, and I don't care about your jaw. I've had worse pain than that, buddy, and I didn't deserve it. You think I'm mad now? Wait till the hospital bills arrive, and you bankrupt us.

LINC: 'Ats not your hrolluh.

MOTHER: Quiet, Linc. Don't get excited. I'll call Mom and Dad. I'm sure they'll help out.

FATHER: They haven't talked to your brother in years.

MOTHER: They still ask about him. They're ready to reconcile.

FATHER: And what better way than to slap them with a bill for a couple thousand dollars. I used to have an inheritance—now it's gone. Got an education grant—that'll be up in smoke after next month's bills. A few days ago we had two cars for the entire school to share. Now we're down to one beat-up van in need of a tune-up that we can't afford. Thanks to you, Linc, I'm going to the Rent-A-Man as soon as the term is over to work a summer job. And I'm not the only one who better be seeking outside employment. You're going to have to get off your ass, too. Your sitting-around-plucking-the-guitar days are done if you have any desire to stay in this house.

This time my mother allowed my father to let off steam, and I thought his threats would turn out to be idle. But I didn't realize how dire our finances had become. The next week, the students did return, and when they asked Linc to explain why he'd been attacked, he struggled to speak and my father took over. But he hadn't come up with an adequate lie and was blabbing abstractly when Cinnamon broke in to save the day. She asked everyone if they remembered the story about the former hunter who taught the communards how to tan deer hides then wigged out and wandered into the woods. Somehow he'd gotten into his crazy head that Linc had done him wrong, and came all the way across the country to punch him out and take his ride. "The good news is, the cops arrested the guy and took him back to Washington State to lock him up."

"What's the bad news?" Stephanie asked.

"There was a high-speed chase, and he totaled the car."

On the last day of the term Quinn launched his blimp over Our House. It got stuck in the linden trees, and Tino climbed onto the roof from an attic window. Cinnamon and Brie cried out, "Be careful," as Tino inched nimbly across the roof tiles. He hacked at some branches with a broom and freed a space for the airship. It slipped up on its tether and snapped to rest above the trees, where it looked, for all purposes, less like a beacon than a distress signal.

Though the other faculty would have to get jobs from June through August, my mother was determined to teach and keep the school running through the summer. She called around soliciting students to take her literature and creative writing course, which would run through July, and to our pleasant surprise fourteen students signed up. Each of the four poets took charge of a different summer activity: the Our House coffee shop, the literary magazine, the book discussion group and the reading series. Linc was disappointed to learn that Dawn would be gone for the summer, particularly since she'd graduated to fingerpicking and was trying out her first Joni Mitchell tunes. The poets had wanted live music to be part of their reading series; now they'd have to look elsewhere for entertainment. Dawn said her parents had signed her and Brie up for a language camp in Aix-en-Provence, and had been late in letting the school know they'd be overseas all summer. "But we'll be back in the fall," Dawn promised. I could hardly contain my excitement when I heard that Brie would be out of the country for two months. With any luck she'd fall in love with a French swain and never come back to the States. Or at least she'd forget about grubby Tino during her rousing months abroad.

After a week of walking to 7th Street and standing in line at the Rent-A-Man office, my father ran into Mazzocca at a Neighborhood Watch meeting and the lieutenant got him an interview as a summer camp baseball coach. All he had to say was "first team Big Ten" and "Detroit Tigers farm system" and he was hired on the spot. After more than twenty years he dusted off his bats and gloves, slipped on his old cleats and returned to the field. The camp, the largest in D.C., drew junior-high- and high-school-age kids, so the job would bring in not just some cash but perhaps new recruits for fall.

My father told Cinnamon and Tino that they had to get jobs as well. "If we're going to make it next year we need to build up our savings. No more hand-to-mouth." They balked at first, but when he threatened to charge them rent, they gave in, signing up for seasonal work at an organic farm in Fairfax County, Virginia. Cinnamon helped out in the tomato and bean fields, and Tino worked in the mill, squeezing sorghum for molasses. They came home on the bus each day with bags full of vegetables, gained, for a change, by legitimate means. Despite his condition, Linc, too, went on the job hunt. After the medical bill arrived, even higher than my father's estimate, Linc started reading the *Post* classifieds. He sounded like Jaws from *The Spy Who Loved Me*, which didn't help his prospects, and over the six weeks before doctors could remove his wires, he grew ascetic-thin despite the protein shakes and starchy soups that Molly and I delivered. He put down the guitar, finished the last volume of *The Man Without Qualities*, and turned to more practical reading: *What Color Is Your Parachute?*

To make up for the loss of the Bug, Linc was determined to get work that came with a company vehicle. "CEO?" Tino mocked him. "You're going to be a fat cat in a stretch limo?" In fact, Linc hoped to drive a limo, or barring that, a cab, but getting a hack's license proved too much of a hassle, particularly through D.C.'s byzantine Department of Motor Vehicles. The best he could find was a street vendor job with the Jack & Jill Ice Cream Company. Each evening, after making his rounds through the posh neighborhoods of Chevy Chase and Bethesda, he'd park behind the Ben Franklin hydrant and sell ice cream sandwiches, nut cones, strawberry shortcakes, Screwballs and red, white and blue Bullet pops to the students and patrons of the Our House coffee shop.

I remember it was on one of these evenings, in late June, that I saw Cleo for the first time in more than a month. When she'd broken her wrist she had promised to stop by the school, but that hadn't happened, and I'd only heard about her from Dawn and Stephanie, who said she'd been lying low of late and seemed different, more reserved. Each time I went to the basketball court I felt Cleo's eyes on the back of my neck, but when I'd turn around, no one would be there. Not wanting to explain what had happened to Linc or why I'd never told anyone about Tino and Brie, I never got up the nerve to call.

She came to Our House for an art opening. Stephanie had recently completed her seven deadly sins project; her photos hung on the walls; and to celebrate, each of the fourteen summer students was to read one original poem based on a deadly sin. Several had invited friends, and Cleo said she was here for Stephanie, though I wanted to think she'd really come for me.

Tino, Quinn and I had gone around in the van at the end of the college semester and picked up three old couches, some sturdy wooden chairs and a La-Z-Boy recliner that some rich kid at Georgetown University had abandoned outside his dorm. Now the living room and parlor were almost comfortable. The only trouble had been the onrush of another swampy-humid D.C. summer. But the twins had concocted a makeshift air conditioner using garbage cans filled with ice water, coiled copper tubes and standing fans, a Rube Goldberg contraption that would have made Dear Abbie smile.

After admiring Stephanie's photographs, which covered three walls in our living room and one in the parlor, where Senedu manned the coffee shop, Cleo and I nestled on a lumpy sofa to listen to the night's event. My mother, standing in front of the mantel, introduced the students one at a time, the four poets first, and they all read in earnest, quavering voices:

GLUTTONY
he's walking down the street eating apple strudel not a care
in the world while
at the corner, another man waiting all night waiting
all his days for some kindness
says
please, I been down on my luck
spirit smashed
he's looking for another chance
but that man with the strudel keeps walking not a care not a stare
in the world for his brother on the corner
I'd like to ask him how much of that strudel can he keep on eating
when
the man on the corner gets no pastry, just these trivial words,
he waits, keeps waiting
while the man with the strudel walks on by
keeps going.

We applauded each poet until my mother invited Cinnamon to say some words about Stephanie, who was the last reader of the night. Cinnamon gave a warm introduction praising the deadly sins photographs, then Stephanie came up and thanked everyone for attending. She said the title of her poem, "Lust," and waited for the oohs and whistles to die down:

A girl sits on the bench
in the park.
She seems innocent yet

in the distance there is dark.
A torrid wind blows in from the west
Pulls at her skirt, acts like a pest.
The wind has desires . . .
and wants them met.
It lures the girl into its net.
Now the bench is empty and bare
And the girl and the wind
are who knows where?

Later, after nearly everyone had gone home, Cleo asked me what I thought of Stephanie's poem. "It was short, but not bad," I said. We were alone on the back patio, sitting on a wood-and-cinderblock bench beside the vegetable garden. Only the lettuce, kohlrabi and cabbage were growing; the celery, cukes, peppers, beans and tomatoes had barely peeked out of the ground.

"I thought it was pretty obvious." Cleo lifted a linden bract from the knee of her white jeans. "The wind is supposed to be Tino, and Brie is the girl."

I tried not to let on that I, too, had decoded the poem right away. It had taken a force of will for me not to look around the room while Stephanie read the words. I'd been dying to know if other students had heard rumors. "She should be careful," I said.

"It's been on her mind. Dawn talks about it constantly. She likes your school. She wants you to succeed." Cleo tossed the bract in the air like a boomerang and it spun to the ground.

"But now that Brie's in France, I'm pretty sure the whole thing is over—some other wind is blowing her skirt." I smiled but Cleo did not respond. "So how have you been?" I was eager for a change of subject, and relieved that she didn't badger me about whether I'd told my parents.

"I've been better."

"What's wrong?"

"Trouble at home. It's about Troy," she said, and went on to tell me about her family's ordeal with her older brother, whose drinking had gotten out of control. He used to organize parties at Battery Kemble Park, where kids from OLPH and St. Sebastian would gather at nightfall and shotgun beers on the hill in the headlights of their parents' cars. From being a weekend drinker he'd moved on to hitting the family liquor cabinet; he'd sneaked flasks into school until Factotum Frank and the maid began to notice that the booze had inched down to near empty. "When my folks were out of town around New Year's he threw a big party and I saw him take some pills. I told my mom about it, and she sent him to the school psychologist. Troy didn't talk to me for weeks after that."

But drugs were not his downfall, the psychologist determined. Bailey's son was an alcoholic. "He used to be a good student, too, but his grades have been slipping and this spring they went completely south," Cleo said. "Frank tried to keep an eye on him at home, and my mom put me on watch at school, but it was no use. He didn't do his work, and he was always disappearing." She sighed. "I've been following my brother around for months like some undercover agent. It's been awful."

"So what's going to happen?" I asked.

"My dad won't take it seriously. He keeps talking about 'the Fall of Troy,' as if by joking about it he can make it go away. My grandfather lost an arm in World War I, and the extent of his advice to my father was to stop whining and bite the bullet. It wasn't until Sister Donovan called to say Troy had failed all but two courses that my parents realized they had to do something."

"They're getting him treatment?"

"That's what my mom and I thought we should do. But my father doesn't believe in twelve-step programs—he's all about self-reliance. And my mom always caves in to my dad. He told Troy to get a job, make himself useful. He lasted three days as a bellhop at the Crystal City Marriott before he overslept and didn't bother to call in."

"I had no idea any of this was going on," I said. No wonder Bailey hadn't been coming around.

"My dad would rather you not know. So please don't tell your parents. Anyway, Troy went to France for the summer, on the same program as Dawn and Brie. It seemed the best compromise. He can get credit for the language classes, and I'll have a friend to keep an eye on him. He probably just needs a change of scenery, far away from my dad."

Last I'd heard, the French were not exactly teetotalers, but Cleo didn't need to be reminded of that. "Sounds like a good plan," I said.

Turning toward me, her lips still slightly purple from the Bullet pop she'd bought from Linc, Cleo took my hand and squeezed it. "Thanks for listening," she said. "I knew you'd understand."

Careful not to shatter the moment by uttering a word, I closed my eyes, leaned in, and then we were kissing, a taste of ozone and some sweet, indefinable fruit. I ran my hand down her back. Her shirt rode above her belt line, and my fingers brushed the arch of exposed skin. Entwined like this, I tried to summon the courage to cup her breast, seized suddenly with the presentiment that the chance might never come again. I was capturing this feeling in my memory when Cleo stopped and pulled back. "I should be going."

"Why?"

"It's late. I need to call Frank to pick me up."

"My dad can give you a ride. Or Linc. You can go in style in an ice cream truck. Can't you stay just a little longer?"

She touched her lips with the tips of her fingers. "The truth is, Daniel, I'm leaving tomorrow for Bethany Beach, and I haven't packed. They're putting me in a tennis camp there. I'll be gone all summer. That's really why I came here tonight—to tell you."

I didn't know what to say.

She kissed me again.

"Maybe I can visit," I said, aware that I sounded too desperate.

"Well—" Her voice trailed off and she stood up to go.

"I can take the bus, sleep on the beach and sneak over to see you."

"I don't think my mom will go for that."

"Oh, come on."

"I'll be back before too long," she said. "It's just for July and August." She took my hand and led me into the house.

Linc and my parents were talking and cleaning up the living room. While Cleo and I had been out back, Lieutenant Mazzocca had stopped by, answering a noise complaint. Mr. Unthank had called the precinct to say the poetry reading and Linc's ringing of the Jack & Jill bell had finally gotten to him. While I listened to my parents talk about Mazzocca's visit, Cleo slipped away to call Frank to take her home.

Apparently police complaints had been on the rise of late. People were on edge, particularly those with family in New York, ever since the news out of Queens that a serial killer using the name Son of Sam had shot two more people. Five had been killed and six wounded in seven attacks over the past year. This time, miraculously, the couple had survived. Moments before the shooting, one of the victims, Sal Lupo, had said to his girlfriend, "This Son of Sam is really scary, the way that guy comes out of nowhere. You never know where he'll hit next."

The fear seemed to have crawled up and down the East Coast. "The twins' parents almost didn't let them out tonight," my mother said. "I'm worried we're going to lose students unless this guy gets caught." It turned out she was right. Soon after Cleo left for Bethany, our numbers dwindled to nine, and business at the coffee shop tapered off so much that one day Molly abandoned her sandwich board on the corner of 16th and Hill and called our grandparents to ask if she could move to Wausau for the summer. "And I'm *not* going to this school next year!" She stomped up to her room and slammed the door.

Eventually Molly calmed down, and among the remaining students my mother did her best to keep up morale. She went over the top in praising their hackneyed fiction and poetry. She took them to old movies based on novels—*Breakfast at Tiffany's, Great Expectations, Doctor Zhivago*—and when she sensed their interest flagging she presented a list of "banned books"—*Animal Farm, Huckleberry Finn, Of Mice and Men*—and called for a vote. Stephanie suggested we read *Lolita*, and the class approved the choice unanimously. Worried that Tino and Brie would be the subtext of the whole discussion, I told my mother in private that we should read another book, but didn't explain why. Seeing that *The Great Gatsby* was playing at the American Film Institute, I persuaded her to put off *Lolita* for a while, and she liked the idea enough to bring it up in class. The students resisted, but one of the poets, a votary of all things gothic and macabre, took my side. She'd heard that recently the bodies of Scott and Zelda Fitzgerald had been moved to a Catholic cemetery in Rockville, a few miles beyond the Maryland border.

"We can read the book, see the movie and put coins on their headstone," she said. "A friend of mine left a martini glass and a pack of cigarettes."

"Hands up for a pilgrimage," I said, and because the poets formed a bloc and Quinn always voted with me, my idea won the day.

And so, on July 12, on a cloudy, blessedly mild afternoon that followed two solid weeks of ninety-degree days, nine of us plus my mother crammed into the clattery van and drove up Wisconsin Avenue to Rockville Pike, turning into the small parking lot behind St. Mary's Catholic Church.

We had seen the Robert Redford movie and read *The Great Gatsby* the previous week, and though it would take years and several rereadings before I'd understand why I identified with the book, I knew that something about those midwestern dreamers—one the lavish millionaire, the other the outsider looking in—who had come east to make their mark, moved me in ways that only biography ever had before. I felt an observer's kinship with Nick and forgave Gatsby his venality and recklessness, all in the name of love. I called up a romanticized picture of my own parents as a modern-day Scott and Zelda, in self-imposed exile, on a wild, headlong ride.

We opened the gate and walked into the small cemetery, and the macabre poet pointed out the grave. Scott and Zelda were buried under the same headstone, the only one in the place footed with a marble slab. The ten of us stood in a semicircle and noted the couple's ages: Scott had died of a heart attack at forty in Hollywood, leaving *The Last Tycoon* unfinished, not one of his books still in print at the time; Zelda was killed eight years later in a fire at Highland Mental Hospital in Asheville, North Carolina. Etched in the slab were the last lines from *Gatsby:* "So we beat on, boats against the current, borne back ceaselessly into the past."

This could describe the life I've chosen, every day a backward look over time, which in its lengthening makes sense of experience. A part of my teenage self was already honoring the past as I laid a quarter on the headstone, which was half-covered in French and American coins. The macabre poet added a ballpoint pen and a fresh pack of Pall Malls, and after the rest of the group offered their own quarters and dimes, we all tried to have a quiet moment. But the graveyard was only a couple of acres and surrounded by busy Veirs Mill Road and Rockville Pike. The steady rush of traffic and car horns and the distant sound of a jackhammer broke any sense of peace. Another of the poets complained, but my mother pointed out that the Fitzgeralds had lived a clamorous life, so this seemed an appropriate resting place.

We returned to the van, piled in and rolled down the windows. I sat in the far back with Quinn, who pointed to a plane crossing the sky and asked if I'd heard about the upcoming test flight of the NASA space shuttle. He was saying it would be the first to hitch a ride on the back of a jetliner, when my mother turned around from the driver's seat and announced, "Something's wrong."

"What?" I asked.

"I need you to call your father, Daniel."

"He's on the baseball field."

"I need you to go into that church and get someone on the phone." She gritted her teeth.

And that's when I saw that she was turning the ignition and the engine wouldn't start.

"Jesus Christ." She tried again, without any luck. "I told your father this thing needed to be serviced."

The other students turned around and looked back at me with expectant faces. I slid past Quinn, climbed up to the middle and let myself out of the van. Not knowing whom to call or what it would mean for us to lose our car, on top of everything else, I ran toward the church.

16

RELIGION

If the summer of '77 was a struggle for us, we were not alone. The day after our van broke down, a twenty-five-hour blackout hit New York City. Riots spilled across dozens of neighborhoods, more than a thousand stores were looted, and firefighters responded to hundreds of blazes. Within a few days, nearly four thousand people had been arrested, jamming the city's jails and holding cells. A month later, New Yorkers felt some relief when Son of Sam, David Berkowitz, was arrested, but the blackout and the killing spree had signaled a city in crisis, and this same sense of unease was spreading through the country.

It was the summer of the Johnstown Flood, James Earl Ray's brief escape from prison, back-and-forth nuclear tests between the United States and the Soviet Union, and in August the death of Elvis. The economy was stagnating, inflation and gasoline prices continued to rise, and Jimmy Carter's approval rating was slipping for the first time since he took office, thanks to trouble with his budget director, Bert Lance. A close adviser and one of several old friends from Georgia to whom Carter had given top appointments, Lance was being accused of shady banking maneuvers and abusing his influence for his own financial gain. Loyal to a fault,

Carter defended Lance, and with each new headline his credibility as the president who'd promised to bring trust back to the White House, the moralist who still taught Sunday school, suffered blows from which he would never fully recover.

Back at Our House we had our own lingering concerns. At first it appeared that the van only had a dead battery, but when a mechanic checked the car he found transmission problems and a leaky head gasket. We couldn't afford to replace the engine, so we drove the old clunker as little as possible, running most of our errands on foot or in Linc's ice cream truck. On the bright side, my mother salvaged her summer class, and the students who stuck with it seemed pleased with their work. To my relief, the discussion of *Lolita* did not expose Tino and Brie's affair, perhaps because neither party was there to face the jury. Though the Our House coffee shop failed, my mother looked back on the turbulent summer with a survivor's pride, proclaiming herself excited for fall, when the rest of the faculty would return, invigorated and with some money in their pockets. Enrollment was up, and remarkably, the coming term looked almost promising.

My father had been smitten by baseball again, and his enthusiasm had spread to the team, which went 14–6 over summer league and won its division. More important, he brought five new recruits to the school. Added to the returnees and a handful who had joined us by word of mouth, our numbers had now reached thirty. The hippies also had a good summer: Tino and Cinnamon returned from the farm, and Linc, his jaw healed and clean-shaven, reduced his Jack & Jill hours to weekends. He said he liked selling ice cream; in fact he'd begun to mix his own flavors; and I was happy to see he'd indulged in the merchandise and was back to his jolly, potbellied self. He looked forward to taking the reins of the fall's first course: religion.

Only two students would not be coming back: Molly, who got her treasured wish and enrolled in Amy Carter's class at Hardy Middle School, and Stephanie, who was on hand for the first week but then mysteriously dropped out. Dawn gave no explanation other than that her friend had done a year of photography and was ready to move on to other interests. At first I was happy to see Stephanie gone—the fewer people who knew about the illicit entanglement, the better. I was upset enough on the first day of school to see that Brie had not stayed in France but was back in our circle, throwing off her same radioactivity.

Stephanie's departure only made me think more about Cleo. She'd written me a note from Bethany Beach in June, signed *Yours truly,* and I'd sent her two long letters afterward. In the first I'd wished her a Happy Fourth and said I'd be spending the holiday in a pith helmet in the basement, far away from fireworks; in the second I went on about *The Great Gatsby* and told her what had happened to the van. But she'd taken three weeks to reply, and even then sent only a postcard, of the five-and-dime variety: *Greetings from Delaware.* She wrote in her big loopy cursive, using only the left-hand side, and mentioned tennis camp and the Rehoboth boardwalk and perfect waves for bodysurfing. *Looks like I've run out of room. Sorry about your van. Sincerely yours, Cleo.*

All summer I fell asleep replaying our last night together. I started or finished letters that I never sent, full of too much longing or turgid descriptions of the D.C. heat. The more I waited to hear from her, the more I wondered if she was angry with me, if she knew somehow that I hadn't told my parents about Tino and Brie. Or maybe there was another reason for her silence. I managed to get her phone number in Bethany from Factotum Frank, and often thought about ringing her up, making an expensive long-distance call that would infuriate my father. But when I went to pick up the phone, something told me that whatever was going on with her, I didn't want to know.

On the Monday of the second week of school, a new student showed up. We were in the middle of a guest lecture by two Mormon missionaries who had knocked on our door the previous evening while making their rounds of the neighborhood. Linc had told them *Thanks, but no thanks,* then got the idea that it might be fun to bring them to class. "What would you say to *thirty* potential converts?" he'd asked.

Now the missionaries, pert as Osmonds, were talking about the *Book of Mormon* in our living room. They were just getting into the story about Joseph Smith and the golden plates of the angel Moroni when the doorbell rang, and a second later in walked Bailey, his son Troy in tow.

"Don't mean to interrupt." Bailey looked around at the students arranged on couches and pillows on the floor, many jotting in notebooks. With these polite young men holding forth we almost had the appearance of a respectable school. "Seems you're making progress, Pete. Mind if I have a word with you?"

I was glad he didn't look closer at our guests and recognize their telltale white shirts and black nameplates. He already thought we were a den of Communists. What next? Champions of plural marriage?

He and Troy joined my father on the porch, and later that night, after the missionaries had left calling cards and copies of the *Book of Mormon*, agreeing to come back anytime, my father announced that Troy was our latest student.

"Not a good idea," my mother said. She was dishing out salad before our manicotti dinner.

"How could I say no?"

"You've got to learn not to mix business with friendship. Especially when it's not a friendship at all."

"We're living in Bailey's house. His *half-price* house." My father refilled his glass with Gallo Chablis. "Do I need to remind you that the lease comes up in October? Don't you want him to renew?"

"Sometimes yes and sometimes no," my mother said.

"Look, Troy's only a part-timer: Tuesdays and Thursdays after school."

"What's he into?" Tino asked.

"Bailey didn't say."

"I know what he's into," I blurted out. What was the use of covering for Troy when his problems would surely reveal themselves? I felt I had to warn people about *something.* "You all have to swear yourselves to secrecy," I said, and went on to repeat Cleo's story about her brother's struggles with alcohol, right down to the empty liquor cabinet and his academic slide.

"That's not what Bailey told me," my father broke in. "Troy's still at Our Lady of Perpetual Help. He's doing well but he needs a creative outlet."

"He failed two courses last term," I said.

"Bailey told me he gets straight A's."

My mother dropped the serving spoons into the salad bowl, which wobbled on the table like a spinning top. "Who are you going to believe, Pete? That S.O.B. or your own son?"

"I'm just reporting what I heard."

"And so is Daniel. I'd be a lot more inclined to listen to that nice girl than her megalomaniacal father. No wonder his kid has a drinking problem. Stuck in that 'spoils of Africa' house—it's his only way out. Can you imagine living with Bailey? My blood pressure soars at the sound of his name."

"Well, we're going to have to live with his son." My father took a big swallow of wine. "He starts tomorrow."

Molly said in a low tone, "I'm sure glad I go to Hardy."

Tino couldn't avoid putting in his own opinion. "Every teenager's an alcoholic. That's neither here nor there. You want to know the bigger issue?" He shook his grimy finger at Molly and me. "Espionage. Young Troy is his father's chief of Gestapo. Look out, kids, he's the young Heinrich Himmler. And you know what that means? Hide your dirty magazines and bury your dope. There's a bonfire in the town square and it's hungry for books."

"Oh, please." My mother sniffed.

"You watch," Tino said. "Because rest assured, he'll be watching you."

Though I'd grown used to Tino's self-dramatizing, I had to admit I was curious to know why Bailey would send his son to a school that he didn't approve of.

Later that evening, while my mother was in the dining room

helping Molly with her homework and my father was in the parlor watching an Orioles game, I called Cleo from the only semiprivate phone in the house, in my parents' bedroom. This time I didn't hesitate or think about it, just dialed her number, and was lucky that she was the one who answered, on the first ring.

"Daniel." She sounded surprised, and I wondered if she'd been waiting for a different call.

I tried to be casual, and act as if we'd been in touch all summer and everything was normal. "So what's up with your brother?" I asked.

She made a desultory effort to catch up, though she never apologized for taking so long to write back and not bothering to call, when *she* was the one who'd left, not me. And too quickly she moved on from talking about the summer to answering my question, when she should have known that I was really calling to talk to her. She reported that Troy was on probation at OLPH, and would be trying Our House part-time, for a change of pace.

"I'm just surprised your dad is letting him," I said, going along. "Or did Sister Donovan put in a good word for us?"

"No, it was Troy's decision. He's been pushing hard for it ever since he got back from France."

"That's odd. He doesn't strike me as the type for a democratic school."

Cleo tapped on the phone. "Hello? Anyone on here?" She paused for a moment. "Sorry about that," she said. "Sometimes Frank listens in. He doesn't think I can hear him unscrewing the whatchamacallit. But I don't care if you're on here, Frank. It's not like I'm saying anything the world doesn't know. My brother needs to maintain a B average. At least he's not drinking as much since he came back from France head over heels."

"He's got a girlfriend? Good." I figured romance was a far preferable form of intoxication.

"She's not exactly a girlfriend."

"But they were going out this summer?"

"Sort of—" Cleo hesitated. "Their status is unclear."

"What do you mean?"

"It would be unladylike of me to share the details, but suffice it to say that something happened, and for one of them the fun ended there, while for the other it was just getting started. My brother doesn't have much experience with girls, and this one in particular has plenty of experience. Are you listening, Frank? Because I don't care." Cleo sounded almost cynical. I wondered what had happened over the summer to sharpen her edge. Perhaps she'd met an older boy, someone with a motorcycle. The thought of Cleo, her arms wrapped around the leathered waist of some beach town heartbreaker, made me wish to be off the phone. It seemed years ago since we were kissing by the garden.

"Anyway," she went on, "Troy's obsessed with her, and he thinks he can make her fall for him, but that's not going to happen. The school psychologist said my brother has an addictive personality. If it's not one thing, it's another. He's just substituting the drink with misguided love."

"But she's in France. Won't he forget about her soon enough?"

"She's not in France. She's right here," Cleo said. "Why do you think Stephanie quit your school? She's had enough of the Tino and Brie situation. But she's too nice to say anything and screw you guys over."

"They're still together?" I shuddered.

"It's not obvious?"

"We've only been back in school a week. They seemed to be keeping apart. I thought it was over." Perhaps to pretend the whole thing wasn't happening, I asked, "But what does this have to do with Troy?"

"You're not getting it, are you? Brie's the one who Troy's obsessed with. They hooked up in Aix-en-Provence. She probably thought he was a rebel then got sick of him. Now she's back with teacher."

I didn't like Cleo's sarcastic tone. Her Bailey side had surfaced out of nowhere, and for the first time I grew annoyed with her. "If you knew about Brie and Troy, why didn't you call to tell me right away? We could have used a warning, you know. This is great, just great," I said, wondering how many love triangles one house could take.

"Don't blame me," Cleo snapped back. "You never told your parents, did you? Because if you had, this wouldn't be happening. They'd have fired that old creep long ago."

"You don't know Tino," I said despondently. "He's like a leech you can't peel off."

"If you'd told your parents in May, they could have done something."

"The summer came up fast and we got busy and everyone went their separate ways. I thought Brie would run off with some French guy and Tino wouldn't leave Cinnamon again." My words raced together. "I wanted to talk to my mom, but she was teaching the summer course and my dad was coaching baseball. I couldn't find the time—"

Cleo softened her voice. "I'm sure you meant to. It's not my business anyway. But you might want to try again."

After I got off the phone I stepped into the hallway, gathering the will to talk to my parents. I wanted to say something now, but hated to think of the fallout. They couldn't get rid of Tino without launching an inquisition, and I knew he'd put up a colossal fight. With the new term under way we couldn't afford this kind of disruption. Why had I held my tongue so long?

I needed to think this over, so I went upstairs. Tino and Cinnamon's door was closed. I waited and listened a moment but heard no sounds from their room. Sitting in bed distractedly I tried to decide what to do. My latest biography, on Calvin Coolidge, rested on my side table. I paged through it, casting my eyes over the life of the thirtieth president:

He kept quite a menagerie at the White House, including cats and dogs, a donkey and a goose that once starred in a Broadway play, and a raccoon named Rebecca that he walked on a leash.

Though Jefferson, Adams and Monroe all died on the Fourth of July, Coolidge was the only president born on Independence Day.

Stiff and laconic, his nickname was "Silent Cal." He was known to go an entire party without making conversation. But he justified his economy of speech in a famous quote that he often repeated: "The things I did not say never hurt me."

Good for you, Cal. I closed my notebook and paced my room. *Silence may have been your trick, but it sure hasn't worked for me.*

With Cleo's exhortation still ringing in my ear, I made my way downstairs, fully intending to talk to my parents. But on the second floor I saw a light from the bedroom where Quinn had set up camp. He'd brought an old mattress, a crate and a lamp, and was spending most of his nights at Our House. He said his parents didn't mind that he was a boarding student, so long as he came home occasionally to help out with the chores. I knocked and he invited me in. He was sitting on the mattress reading. "Got a minute?" I closed the door behind me. He put down the *Book of Mormon.*

"I need your advice," I began, and whispered everything I knew about Tino and Brie, from their apparent trysting place to the real reason why Stephanie had bowed out. I told him about lovesick Troy as well, and the catastrophe his arrival might bring. I felt relieved to be able to tell someone, though I realized, as I unloosed a breathless plait of words, that I still carried the burden.

Quinn blinked his starry eyelashes, and I sensed he appreciated my confiding in him.

"I'm going to settle this." He dropped the *Book of Mormon* and hopped out of bed. Before I could tell him to wait, he'd breezed past me and was climbing upstairs. As I reached the top step he was already knocking on Tino's door.

"Come in," Cinnamon said, and Quinn let himself inside.

"Is Tino here?" he asked.

"What do you need?" Cinnamon sounded groggy, as if she'd fallen asleep with the light on. She was braless in a tank top. A book with a red symbol in its center lay open on her freckled chest.

"I've got something to say to him." Quinn leaned in the doorway. "Do you know where he is?"

"Probably at Dan's." Cinnamon rubbed her eyes.

"Who's Dan?"

"Dan's Café. It's the neighborhood dive. Tino's friendly with the bartender."

"And you don't go with him?"

"It's not my scene." Cinnamon gave Quinn a look that seemed to ask, *Why all the questions?*

I stepped inside the room, nudging past Quinn, afraid he was going to tell too much. "What are you reading?" I asked.

Cinnamon held up the book: *The Divine Principle* by Sun Myung Moon.

"Moonies," Quinn said. "Did you hear about the mass weddings they do over in Korea? They're talking about doing them here, too."

I asked Cinnamon why she was reading a book by Reverend Moon. He'd been in the news since taking his Unification Church to the United States in the early seventies. He'd met with President Nixon, addressed both houses of Congress, and his "God Bless America Festival" was one of the biggest religious rallies in the history of D.C. It would be another five years before the famous mass wedding of two thousand couples in Madison Square Garden, but already the Moonies had struck fear in many parents.

Cinnamon reported that Linc had hatched a brilliant idea: he'd invited some Moonies to Our House to debate the Mormon missionaries about marriage and religion. "It's gonna be a trip," she said. "That's why I'm studying up." She flipped through *The Divine Principle.* "They're all coming tomorrow."

"Do my mom and dad know about this?" I asked.

"Linc checked it through with them. You worry too much, Daniel. You should take up meditation."

"I'll think about it," I said, and Cinnamon gave me a smile that made me weak in the knees.

We went back downstairs to Quinn's room.

"I bet that rat's with the girl right now," he said.

"Cinnamon knows, doesn't she?" I asked.

"Of course she knows. She's just letting it ride."

"I don't understand it," I said.

"Neither do I." Quinn grabbed the *Book of Mormon* off his bed and gestured with it. "I'm going to wait up for him, and when he gets home I'll give him a piece of my mind."

I was grateful for Quinn's support, but I told him that this was my problem.

"It's everyone's problem," he said. "I like it here, and I'll do anything to help."

"You have to promise to let me deal with this," I insisted. "I need to figure it out on my own. Let me talk to my mother and father first. I wanted you to know, that's all."

"Okay," he said, and on my way out of his room, just to be sure, I closed the door so he wouldn't glimpse Tino slinking back upstairs.

My parents and Molly were having a spirited talk in the dining room about Amy Carter. Molly said the First Daughter was shy and that she missed her old home in small-town Georgia. Sometimes, to get away from the First Family hullabaloo, she climbed up into the tree house her father had built her on the South Lawn. "If I'd only gone to Hardy last spring instead of staying here, I bet we would have been good friends. But she already has her group now," Molly lamented. "A bunch of them went to slumber parties in the tree house this summer."

"It's not too late," my mother said. "You can still make friends with her."

"I told her about Chester and Chairman Mao, and she told me about Misty Malarky Ying-Yang, but it's not like she invited me over. Maybe if *we* had a tree house, I could invite her over here."

This got me excited. I had visions of a great tree house up in the maples, near Quinn's airship. Jimmy and Rosalynn would come over and sit on the patio, talking with my family about world affairs. Imagine how many students we'd recruit if the president of the United States was a regular guest lecturer. We'd have to move to a bigger house, new and clean and insect-free. We'd be famous. My parents would get cabinet positions: co-secretaries of Health, Education and Welfare. I'd have full use of the presidential archives, clearance for every room in the White House. Jimmy was hardworking and thrifty—to save money for the country and set an example, he'd sold the presidential yacht and turned off the lights around the city's monuments. His family was humble, just like us. It wasn't hard to picture that we could all be friends.

"I don't know about a tree house," my mother said. "Your father's carpentry skills leave much to be desired. The last thing we need is the floorboards breaking and Amy Carter crashing to the pavement."

"I think it's a cool idea," I put in. "Tino's a good carpenter. He built his own tree house on the commune. And it was sturdy enough for lots of people." Somehow, in my fantasy about the Carters, I'd forgotten why I'd come downstairs, and instead of accusing Tino, here I was praising him.

Molly's eyes lit up, and she clutched my mother's sleeve. "Let's make Tino build a tree house."

My father rose from his chair. "It's late. You should be going to bed, Molly."

"But can we put a tree house in the back?"

"We'll talk about that later. You have to get up early for school."

Molly grabbed her homework, took my mother's hand and led her upstairs, no doubt to further plead her case that we absolutely had to have a tree house so she could be friends with Amy Carter.

After they were gone, my father asked, "Why did you have to open your big mouth?" His face was high-colored; he'd had more than his usual two glasses of wine and I knew this was not the moment to tell him about Tino and Brie. "We can't afford a damn tree house. And do you think we have all the time in the world?"

"It could be a school project," I suggested.

"What do tree houses have to do with religion? This is your uncle's harebrained course, and I plan to stay out of his way and let him screw it up."

"I'm sorry," I said, a misplaced apology.

The next day was bright and mild, a beautiful fall morning. We opened the downstairs windows, and the lily fragrance from the Moonies' bouquets brightened the dusty living room. Linc had asked the Mormons to arrive at midmorning so we'd first have a chance to meet Thomas and Ketzia, representatives from the Unification Church's enclave on Upshur Street. Thomas was thin and clean-cut in a throwback suit and skinny tie; Ketzia wore a sky-blue dress, her ginger hair tied in a bow. They were friendly and outgoing, but in the tight-wound way of flight attendants, fond of the word "wonderful," as in "It's so wonderful to meet all of you on this wonderfully sunny day. I just know we're going to have a good time." These were not the Manson family freaks that Sister Donovan had spoken of, unless they planned to kill us with kindness.

We went around the room giving our names. It worried me that Dawn was absent for the second class in a row, but this quickly left my mind when I saw that Troy wasn't here, either. I'd woken up late with a powerful dread. I'd missed breakfast and had come downstairs just as the students had begun to arrive. Was this my reprieve? Did Troy have a change of heart and decide not to come to our school after all?

Brie introduced herself, and last came Tino, who wasted no time attacking Reverend Moon and his support of Richard Nixon. "No offense, but your boss is a nutso fascist. He was for the Vietnam War right up to the bitter end, and after Watergate he took out full-page ads asking everyone to 'love and forgive' Tricky Dicky."

Linc turned to Tino. "That's no way to talk to our guests."

"How do you think Moon got his green card?" Tino continued. "He wrote Nixon a personal check for a hundred thousand dollars. What do you have to say to that?" He fixed the Moonies with a wicked stare.

Linc told Ketzia she didn't have to answer.

"It's all right," she said politely, as if Tino had asked for nothing more than a second bag of salted peanuts. Then, in one bubbly stream of zeal, she explained that Reverend Moon was the Messiah of the Second Coming, and his wife, Hak Ja Han, was the Holy Spirit. He was the "True Father" and she the "True Mother." Together, they were the first couple to bring children into the world without the curse of original sin. And since Communists do not believe in God, and thus deny the existence of the "True Father," His Holiness Reverend Moon, they are agents of Satan and must be defeated. "President Nixon was a wonderful man for fighting the spread of communism. He will always be a friend of the Holy Spirit Association for the Unification of World Christianity."

"Try saying that ten times fast," Linc said in an effort to cut Tino off.

But Tino rode right over him: "See, kids. It's just like I told you. Moon's a wacko fascist."

Thomas straightened his tie. "I bet it would be fun if we could see a show of hands. Who here likes communism?"

A couple of hands wavered, and Tino was about to tee off again when the doorbell rang.

My mother told me to answer it then turned to Linc, gritting her teeth. "You need to do something. This is getting out of control."

I went to the door, praying that it wouldn't be Troy, and breathed a sigh of relief when the Mormons greeted me with Pepsodent smiles.

"Are we early?" asked Brother Drexel and Brother Sidell.

"Just in time," I said.

But as I let them in and they walked past into the front hallway, I caught a glimpse of the street below. Double-parked beside the Ben Franklin fire hydrant was the champagne Cadillac. Two figures were inside, engaged in what looked like an argument.

I shut the door and, instinctively, locked it.

17

HISTORY

I COULD ONLY HOPE that Troy was telling Bailey he didn't want to go to our crackpot school. Sometimes you have to come right up to the threshold before you realize you'd rather not cross, and that's what Troy was feeling now, I said to myself. But then I wondered why he'd be arguing with his father. If anything, Bailey was making one last effort to keep him from Our House. Either way, what could be done about it now? I sat back on the sofa beside Quinn, and when some minutes passed without a sound from the door I began to calm down. If Troy did walk into this room, I'd still have a chance to tell my parents. I could do it today, after school, or take them aside at the lunch break. So what if Troy was obsessed with Brie? It's not as if he knew about Tino. Sure, it wouldn't be long before he found out, but if I acted fast and my parents made a decisive move and tossed the lech out on his ear, there was nothing, really, to worry about.

Linc was doing his best to reestablish order. He introduced the Moonies to the Mormon missionaries. "We were talking about communism, but let's not get into a political debate. This is supposed to be a religion class."

"Politics and religion are the same," Tino said.

Linc rubbed his chin where his beard used to be, a habit he'd had since shaving it. "We have separation of church and state. It's in one of the amendments."

"The *First* Amendment," I put in.

"Right," Linc went on. "We're here to talk about marriage, and I'd like to thank Brother Drexel and Brother Sidell, and Thomas and Ketzia, for coming this morning. I'm going to ask each of you to give a brief overview of your church's marital practices, traditions and ceremonies, and then we can all have a conversation."

The Mormons were quick to address polygamy, noting straight off that their church had abandoned the practice in 1890. They admitted that their founder, Joseph Smith, had more than thirty wives, and many of the original church leaders, including Brigham Young, had followed the polygamist tradition of Abraham, Isaac and Jacob. Smith had professed that no man was to take another wife unless the Lord directed it, and contrary to the stereotype, only a handful of Mormons in the early years practiced plural marriage. "Today you'd be excommunicated for it," Brother Drexel said. "It's absolutely, positively not tolerated. And that's a good thing, in our opinion, because one could argue that polygamy is a form of adultery. And adultery is a terrible sin."

It was not long after this, in the middle of Brother Sidell's talk about Mormon dating and courtship practices, that the doorbell rang again. I knew who it was and had no choice but to answer it.

Thankfully, Troy was alone; the champagne Cadillac pulled away as I was letting him in. His hair was greasy and his face had broken out. He looked as if he'd had a long night, and I detected the smell of alcohol emanating from his skin. Introducing myself, I reminded him that we'd met at the election party last year. He nodded but seemed not to recall. I caught him up on what was happening in class in a way that I hoped would convey that it was hardly worth his while.

Without a word he walked into the living room. The Mormons were just sitting down and the Moonies taking their place in front of the mantel. I offered Troy my seat on the sofa and took a pillow on the floor nearby.

Thomas and Ketzia were talking now. I had assumed they were a couple, but they said they had yet to go through the Gate of the Blessing Ceremony, and when their time came they would surely not marry each other. "The True Parents decide who we marry. They're the only ones who know the right match for us, and together with our partners we will create large families devoted to love and peace and a more wonderful world," Ketzia explained.

"And why do you think Reverend Moon decides who you end up with?" Tino asked rhetorically. "Because he charges each of you suckers a hefty arrangement fee. That's why he marries you off by the thousand. How do you think he became a multimillionaire? Good deeds?"

A vein swelled in the middle of Thomas's forehead, and he was about to respond when my father interrupted. "Let's be civil here. I want to pause a minute anyway to introduce our newest student. Troy Dornan is a junior and he attends Our Lady of Perpetual Help. He's going to join us part-time and I hope you'll all welcome him."

Everyone said, "Hi, Troy," then my father had us go around the room and give our names. "Don't worry. You won't be tested on this," my father continued. "But I bet you know some of these people already. Maybe you could say something about yourself, like how you came to be interested in Our House."

Troy had not spoken since he'd walked in the door; he was such a stranger to me that I didn't even remember the sound of his voice, which was vaguely adenoidal.

"I know Brie," he said. "And I know something else. She's fucking *that* guy." He pointed at Tino. "And I became interested in your school because I wanted to see for myself what kind of place lets students fuck their teachers."

I can't recall exactly what happened next, whether the Moonies and the Mormons just gathered their flowers and books and took off, or which of the kids quit school that day, or the next, or the day after that. I would have liked to see the expressions of everyone in the room, but I was sitting too close to my mother, father and Linc to glimpse their faces, and could only see Cinnamon, who registered little surprise, and a handful of students in profile who had turned their heads, as I did, toward Tino and Brie. In that moment everyone must have been searching their memories for retroactive signs: Brie asking Tino to be her tutor-collaborator, the way she followed him around, laughed at his jokes, nodded her head at his outrageous ideas, the furtive looks between them, the sexual charge that up until now most of the students mistook for an energy in the air, the freedom of knowing that here at Our House, unlike anywhere else they'd known, they could "Act first. Ask permission later." Those words, on the banner that Cinnamon had designed, rose like an epitaph over Tino's and Brie's heads.

I remember Brie getting up and running out the door, and Troy following behind her.

A long silence fell over the group before my mother asked, "Well?"

That's when Tino stood up, slowly, as if having to rise to his feet were a great inconvenience.

"Well?" My mother repeated, raising her voice.

Tino shook his head and tightened his bandanna, and for the first time since he'd arrived, he had no defense, no offense, nothing to say. He walked out of the room, and when he climbed the stairs to go up to the third floor, the house was so quiet we could hear his footsteps fade.

The next day our numbers dropped by half, and by the end of the week we had fewer than ten—things fell apart that swiftly—and the phone kept ringing.

"You answer it," my mother insisted.

"Why me?" my father said.

"It's your school. This was your idea. I'm done with all of this!"

My father went into their bedroom and shut the door, and a half hour later stormed out to find my mother and rehash the conversation, though she didn't want to hear it. He'd talked to the bishop and the headmaster at St. Sebastian, to Stephanie's mother and Sister Donovan, who took the OLPH kids back in a single sweep. Bailey's call, on the Friday of that week, sent my father into such a rage that he knocked all the books off his homemade shelves and left them in a pile on the floor. Walking into their bedroom, my mother tripped over the books and screamed, "You're such a child. You think a tantrum's going to get you out of this one?"

"He might take away our house or refuse to give us another lease," my father said.

I sat at the top of the stairs with Quinn. Lucky Molly was off at school. Cinnamon had shut herself in her room; I'd hardly seen her in days. Two nights before, after my father had threatened to pummel him and drag him to the precinct, Tino had disappeared, just slipped away, and hadn't been heard from since.

There was the sound of a book being kicked across the floor, then my mother's voice: "I can't believe you're worried about the lease right now. This isn't our house anymore. It was always a house of cards."

"What kind of attitude is that? You give up so easily. We can get the students back. Tino's off the faculty. If he tries to return, Mazzocca will bring him in on trespassing charges. I can call up the parents today."

"It doesn't matter, Pete. No one's going to let their kids back here."

"We still have some students. We can keep going."

"No we can't. You're worrying about a lease and a school that are doomed, that don't exist anymore," my mother said. "You want a real concern? We could be talking about statutory rape. Brie is sixteen, and if her parents press charges, Tino won't be the only one in trouble. They could sue us, too."

"They're not going to press charges. Stephanie's mother told me so. The relationship was consensual. That's why Brie's not letting her parents pursue this any further."

"What happened was illegal and incredibly wrong. I don't care how you look at it," my mother said. "There was exploitation."

"*Mutual* exploitation, maybe."

"There's no such thing. Tino took advantage."

My father paused for a moment. "That brings me to the major point—what did *we* do wrong?"

"Tell me you didn't just ask that question. You take no responsibility?"

"They hid it well. I had no idea."

"You should have. We all should have been paying better attention. You've known that Tino was capable of this. You should have kept an eye on him."

"*I* should have been watching him? What about you? That bastard would never have come here if you hadn't invited your brother."

"Either way, Brie's parents could sue us for failing to protect their child. You think we have money problems now? Imagine the legal fees."

"They're not going to sue," my father insisted.

"Why haven't they called? They're pretty much the only ones. I bet they're consulting lawyers."

"You're being rash and paranoid. Just give it a couple weeks. You watch, the storm will blow over."

"And you're being delusional. The school is finished," my mother said. "I don't want this anymore."

Their argument would haunt me for a long time. I'd known for months about the affair and had meant to say something. Even after it was exposed I planned to come clean. Who knows if speaking up would have made a difference? As my mother said, we were living in a house of cards. Still, I'd been afraid to tell my parents, and that fear had become a burden. Or perhaps a part of me was still angry enough with my father for setting me up and knocking me down that I'd wanted to pay him back, and did so with my silence. I'd never heard of statutory rape, and the shock of those words brought home for me the seriousness of the transgression, and my own culpability. It didn't matter that Brie was a flirt and had gone after Tino. One of our teachers had crossed a line. I'd known this and kept it to myself. It was one of the few secrets that I would keep to this day.

Toward the end of the weekend, my father called a meeting of the Fellowship of Chester, only without the cat, the fellowship or the veil of secrecy. He corralled me in the parlor and didn't seem to care if others could overhear us. He said he wanted me to take over the class on Monday. "No more Moonies and Mormons. No more mumbo jumbo. We need to get serious and move on to history. Can you work something up about the presidents?"

"But I'm just a kid."

"Science and technology was a hit. Kids get into it more when their peers run the show."

"I don't know, Dad." I was quickly losing faith in democratic education, and found myself longing for the old structures.

"Oh, come on. We're in D.C. The city's a virtual amusement park of American history. We've got to pull out all the stops, make it fun. I asked Molly to see if Amy Carter can get us a tour of the White House."

"What did she say?" This perked me up, however briefly.

"She's looking for a bargaining chip. She wants that damned tree house."

"But Tino's gone. It's never going to happen."

"Your sister has managed to stay out of most of this, and I want to keep it that way." My father looked older by the light of the window, as if gray hairs had sprouted overnight. "Let me handle this. You put your mind to that history class."

I watched my mother move around the house, quietly now, in a kind of trance. She put away dishes, books and knickknacks, wiped down shelves and countertops, made notes to herself, as if taking an inventory. Though I wanted to think she was bringing order back to the place, I knew it was just as likely she was making a new plan.

All I could do was wait and see and follow my father's wishes.

I'd begun reading about Herbert Hoover, and with only a day to prepare I figured I should go with my latest research. The following year would mark the fiftieth anniversary of Hoover's election, so he seemed a decent subject for my first time running the class. But as I filled out note cards for the talk, my mood darkened. Hoover had been in office just seven months before the stock market crash and the onset of the Great Depression, and he was one of the least popular presidents of all time, joining a shortlist that included his eighth cousin once removed: Richard Nixon. The 1929 crash was not Hoover's fault any more than the looming economic crisis was Jimmy Carter's. But people needed someone to blame, and rumors had swirled among the hungry and unemployed that Hoover was so callous that dogs whimpered at the sight of him and roses wilted at his touch. One woman summed up the country's exasperation in 1932: "People were starving because of Herbert Hoover. Men were killing themselves because of Herbert Hoover, and their fatherless children were being packed away to orphanages . . . because of Herbert Hoover."

When I told Molly that it was my turn to teach, she put her newest LP on the turntable: *Annie,* the Depression-era musical that was the current Broadway smash. I planned to play one of the tracks in class to liven things up: "We'd like to thank you, Herbert Hoover . . ."

But on Monday morning only four students came to school: Quinn, Senedu and two recent recruits from the baseball team. Too humiliated to hold a regular class, my father told us to hop in the ailing van, and we drove to the Smithsonian's National Museum of American History, where I'd never been but always wanted to go.

At first we took in the permanent exhibits as a group, but when the baseball kids began to linger too long at the sports memorabilia, my father gave up trying to keep us together and told everyone to meet at the Foucault pendulum, in the main transept, at noon.

• • •

I wandered around with Quinn, passing objects like Thomas Jefferson's writing desk, George Washington's waistcoat and breeches, Warren G. Harding's monogrammed silk pajamas, the top hat Abraham Lincoln wore to Ford's Theatre the night of his assassination and the coffee cup that had held William McKinley's last drink. I stopped to cast my eyes over the exhibits, but I wasn't transported back in time the way I'd thought I would be, this close to touching the past.

Quinn, too, had an abject look about him. I saw him walk right by the collection of Edison's electric lightbulbs and settle at the Foucault pendulum a good hour early. I joined him at the railing under the huge flag that had flown over Fort McHenry and inspired Francis Scott Key to write "The Star-Spangled Banner." We didn't mention the flag or say a word, just watched the heavy brass bob swing forward and back with the rotation of the earth. We stood there long enough for several tourists to tire of the pendulum and move on.

"So what are you going to do?" Quinn's voice echoed off the ceiling collars.

"Looks bad" was all I could say.

He gripped the railing with his slender hands. "I'm thinking of going back to Cardozo. It's still early in the year. I can catch up with the work. If I want to do something in this world, I have to go to school."

"I understand."

"I'd rather stay, believe me. But I've been through this before, and last time I stayed it didn't go so well."

"What do you mean?"

"I really appreciated what you told me the other night, Daniel, and I wish we could have stopped everything from going up in flames. I bet I'm the only one you've talked to, aren't I?"

"It's true," I said.

"Well—" Quinn cast his eyes downward and followed the lazy swing of the bob. "A year ago or whenever it was—has it only been that long?—I told you about my friend Anthony taking your flags and TV and then moving to Cleveland. I gave his whole story, from his mom falling off that bridge to all the families he stayed with over the years, and how the road always led back to Horizon Foster Home. I didn't tell you that the first thing he always did when he moved in with a new family was to find the nearest library and spend all his time there, because books were more like home to him than any house he knew. And remember how I told you that when the Kurtzmans came along all that changed?"

"Sure," I said.

"Well, it's a true story except for one thing. There is no Anthony. He doesn't exist."

"What do you mean?" At that moment I felt a shiver of recognition, almost like a double take, as if I'd seen someone I recognized passing on the street.

"You know what I mean." He was still watching the pendulum.

"You're Anthony?" I asked.

"I hope you're not mad," he said in a quiet voice. "I didn't like the way we were tossed out of that house, and I guess I blamed your family. But when I got to know you all and saw you were okay, I didn't want you to think I was some kind of criminal."

"So you don't live with your parents down the street? You made all that up?"

"I'm sorry."

"Where do you live?"

"The foster home down on Fourteenth, but I try to avoid the place."

"And what happened to your parents?"

"I told you about my mom. What I didn't say is that she was probably crazy. They have a name for it now, and I hope it doesn't catch up with me. She said my father could be anywhere or nowhere, and claimed to know only three things about him: he was light-skinned, he was from New York City, and his first name was Anthony. Sometimes I borrow his name, try it on for size. I figure he owes me that much."

I took a moment to gather my breath, then asked Quinn if he'd ever tried to look his father up. He rubbed his mustache, which hadn't thickened in the year that I'd known him, and I reminded myself that he was still a kid, not much older than me. He explained that every time he came back from a fostering arrangement that hadn't worked out, his caseworker would post a notice among the scores of similar pleas on the Family Court bulletin board at D.C. Superior Court. He saved the first of these, which read: *Unknown Father: You have an 8-year-old son. His mother, who passed on March 12, 1970, said your name was Anthony. You have light skin and you are from New York City. Please contact Horizon Foster Home, 1702 14th Street NW.*

"And Angela?" I asked.

"I don't have a sister," Quinn said. "I thought of Becca and Rachel Kurtzman as sisters. And maybe somewhere out there I have a half sister or something. But now it's just me."

"I had no idea."

"I'll be fine. In a few years I'll call you up to invite you on the maiden voyage of my zeppelin. We'll sip champagne over the Serengeti and follow the migratory herds. Don't worry about me."

"You can still stay at the house, you know, even if you go back to Cardozo. We've got the extra room."

"That's nice of you, Daniel. But I went all the way to Cleveland once, only to turn around and come back here. I can't follow you all wherever you're going."

"But we're not going anywhere—"

Quinn gave me a knowing look and said nothing more.

Below us the pendulum swung forward and back, like a slow-motion wrecking ball.

Quinn didn't leave right away. He waited until the end of the week, after the baseball kids had failed to show on Tuesday and Senedu had appeared with his mother on Wednesday, asking if everyone was playing a trick on him. My mother explained that it wasn't a trick; there had been a problem with the school and she was incredibly sorry but he would have to find some other place to go.

"You can still help me with my English?" Senedu asked.

"I can't," my mother said. "It's going to be impossible." She hugged him quickly and wiped her eyes.

Quinn reassured Senedu's mother and offered to walk him over to Cardozo and sign him up the following week. He even agreed to tutor him after school. "Where do you live?" he asked.

"Above the Blue Nile on Eighteenth Street," Senedu said.

"I'll pick you up on Monday."

On the same afternoon that Senedu and his mother had showed up to an empty school, Molly returned with the happy news that she'd gotten us a group tour at the White House.

"So you've made friends with Amy Carter?" I asked.

"I'd like to," she said. "But those girls just surround her. I had to get the tickets from a Secret Service man."

"Do you think the president will be there? Can we have our picture taken in the Oval Office?"

Molly played it cool. "I'll see what I can do."

Thrilled that I'd finally have a chance to step inside the White House, where every president since John Adams had lived, our travails momentarily slipped my mind; I wanted to tell someone right away, and my first impulse was to call Cleo. I ran upstairs and dialed her number—Factotum Frank answered—and I was waiting for her to come to the phone when I found myself sitting on my parents' mattress, looking at the graffiti Quinn had painted on the wall, and recognizing for the first time that the flame-like letters spelled *Anthony.* And that's when it hit me that Quinn really was going to leave, that the students had decamped already and weren't coming back, that when my mother said she couldn't tutor Senedu anymore, she meant she didn't know where we'd be in a month, a week, tomorrow. Brie's parents could call anytime to press charges, and Tino had vanished, leaving the rest of us to answer for his crimes.

I was going to invite Cleo to the White House, but now I didn't want to talk to her at all, didn't want to face the humiliation of what had happened to Our House, all in less than a couple weeks. She had warned me months ago, then warned me again: *If you'd just told your parents, they could have done something. You have to talk to them, Daniel.* But I hadn't listened, and the house of cards had fallen, and here I was waiting for Cleo to come to the phone. Why? So she could say I told you so?

I hung up but remained on my parents' bed.

A minute later the phone rang.

I thought about answering it. No doubt Frank had told Cleo it had been me on the line. I could pick up and say, *Sorry, our phone's been acting up,* ask her to meet me at Pierce Park in order to buy myself time to think. I'd called her too hastily. I needed to gather my thoughts. The phone was ringing a second time when I noticed, next to my mother's tilting wardrobe box, several more boxes, which she must have dragged out of the closet in her frenzy of organization. Next to the boxes was a roll of packing tape.

I picked up the phone but said nothing.

Cleo said, "Hello."

And then I gently put the phone back in the cradle.

My father, alone, hadn't given up. Linc and Cinnamon, who'd endured the long, slow failure of the commune and did not seem eager to hang around only to watch history repeat itself, had already sent out letters to friends, looking for leads. My father called them quitters, and with near fanaticism turned his attention to new recruits. He opened the yellow pages on the kitchen counter and went down the list of schools, cold-calling administrators one by one. He left messages on dozens of answering machines, and my mother called him a fool. "Before long, every headmaster in the city is going to know what happened," she said. "Even if you do round up a few strays, Bailey's going to shut you out of this house."

"He's more reasonable than you think, Val."

But on Monday Bailey called in a most unreasonable humor

and told my father that he'd known about the scandal for weeks but didn't want to get involved. "I'm just the landlord," he'd said. Recently, however, Brie's parents had started to bother him at work. They claimed that Troy was harassing their daughter, calling her three or four times a day and lurking outside their Georgetown home. On the night that Troy discovered Tino and Brie's affair he had secretly followed her from her house to the Georgetown University library, where she told her parents she went to do homework, then from the library to her trysting place.

The rumor about Tino's dragging a mattress under a bridge turned out to be untrue. In fact, he'd befriended a National Park Service employee who, perhaps in exchange for drugs, gave him a key to a historic building, the Old Stone House, so he could use it after hours. Bailey reported that Brie was still not willing to press charges, which had made her parents turn their frustrations on Troy. "It's not my kid who's been banging some teenybopper. It's your faculty, Pete. What are you going to do about it?" My father promised that Tino would never return, and asked Bailey if he could meet him for lunch to talk about the future; Bailey disdainfully agreed.

My mother asked when this meeting would take place, and my father said on Wednesday afternoon, which was the time we were scheduled to visit the White House. "You can go on without me," he suggested.

"I guess you don't care about Molly." My mother crunched down hard on a Tic Tac.

"It's not that I don't care. We're talking about our survival. Wednesday was Bailey's only free day this week. I'm going to flatter him like there's no tomorrow and see if he'll write us up a new lease."

"I don't want a new lease."

"We've come all this way, Val."

My mother had no reply, and on Wednesday morning I put on my best clothes—a striped oxford shirt, chinos and loafers, vestiges of my Lake Bluff Academy wardrobe—and hopped in the van with my mother, Linc, Cinnamon and Molly.

But when we arrived at the southeast gate of the White House, a sign was posted: NO TOURS TODAY.

Molly was already crying by the time my mother got to the security guard to ask what the hell was wrong.

"Important press conference," the guard said.

My mother shook the tickets. "But we have a special appointment. My daughter is a classmate of Amy Carter's."

"I'm sorry, ma'am. No tours. You'll have to call to reschedule."

When my mother badgered him, the guard did not say what the press conference was about, but we could see a flurry of activity—the bustle of journalists and cameramen—beyond the gate. And later that night we'd hear that President Carter's embattled budget director, Bert Lance, had resigned.

Back at the house, my mother told Molly and me to pack our bags. "We're leaving," she said.

"Where are we going?" I asked, still reeling with disappointment.

She ignored me and stormed upstairs.

"But I have school tomorrow," Molly whined. "I'm already in trouble for missing today."

After our mother had gone up to her room to pack more boxes, I assured Molly that this would only be another trip down Livid Lane. "We'll go to the Potomac River and watch the sludge drift by, and when Mom calms down we'll drive home and everything will be back to normal."

I packed a box of books and my biographies and filled my suitcase with clothes. So sure that my mother was bluffing, I left my portraits of the presidents on the walls. Molly and I hugged Linc and Cinnamon goodbye, but they didn't look as certain as I was that we'd see them in an hour or two. Then I helped my mother load her wardrobe box and the carriers with the meowing cats into the van.

I told myself this was all for show, unwilling to admit how much I shared my father's stubborn optimism. Before my mother pulled away and headed up 16th, I took one quick look—at Linc and Cinnamon waving on the porch, at my tower and Quinn's Our House blimp still high on its tether above the trees—refusing to believe that I wouldn't see this place again.

III

OUR COUNTRY

2000

18

IT'S FRIDAY, NOVEMBER 10, three days after the election in which no one was elected, and I'm at Washington National Airport waiting to pick up my parents. CNN replays the Florida recount on every TV monitor, and people are walking around in a daze, as if the present tense has been replaced by a perpetual limbo.

The other night, around eight o'clock, at the election party at Molly's house, my wife, Karen, popped a bottle of champagne after CNN and all the rest projected Gore the winner in Florida and for all intents and purposes the next president. But not two hours later new results came in from the panhandle, and the anchor said, "Stand by, stand by."

Karen had yelled at the television, "You can't do that. The White House is ours!"

This is my first time back in Washington in six years. As a grad student at UVA, I used to come here to do research at the Library of Congress and the Center for the Study of the Presidency. I'd stay with Molly, who's a lawyer at the Securities and Exchange Commission. She went to Georgetown Law then settled in the city to join a huge firm that worked the life out of her and made her realize that money can't buy happiness but does pay off the law school bills. Debt-free after five years as a corporate attorney, she hopped over to the SEC, and now, instead of representing multinationals, she gets to keep them in line, and when they misbehave, drag them to court.

In a way, Molly and I have never left D.C.—she always talked about returning and has been here since graduate school; and even when I'm far away, the books I read and write always bring me back in my imagination.

It was Molly's idea that Karen and I arrive a few days early to celebrate the election. We were sure that Gore would win, which seemed a fine excuse for a longer stay. Karen and I are both on the tenure track at the University of Oregon and had arranged to take research leaves next quarter because Karen is pregnant. She's a professor of community and regional planning and I teach modern U.S. history and am finishing my first book: *Crisis of Confidence: The Presidency of Jimmy Carter.* Some kids know what they want to be at the age of ten and hold to the rails like a steady train. That's me, I guess, though it hasn't been easy. Karen and I lived in apartments all over the country before landing thousands of miles from her folks in Boston, my sister in D.C., and the rest of my family, who have lived for the past twenty years in Madison, Wisconsin.

We're all gathering here this weekend for my father's sixtieth birthday, a bittersweet reunion that none of us could miss. Six months ago he woke up in the middle of the night unable to control his right arm, a spasm that went away until a few weeks later when the entire right side of his body froze. He was standing on the first-floor landing and lost his balance, blacked out and fell down a flight of stairs. At the hospital they did a CT scan and found a mass the size of a marble: a malignant brain tumor that I can't help thinking goes all the way back to the collision at home plate that ended his baseball career. The doctors dismiss my theory, saying the causes of brain tumors have never been known; why one person gets one and another does not remains a medical mystery. Either way, my father has been through months of chemotherapy and more than thirty radiation treatments, and while the marble has shrunk by half, it hasn't gone away.

He approaches the airport greeting area looking surprisingly well. Last time I saw him, at the end of summer, he was pale, but now his color is back and he's walking without a grimace. He wears a red baseball cap with a white W, for the Wisconsin Badgers, pulled low on his head.

A step behind him, my mother calls out, "You're moving too fast, Pete. Slow down." She's dragging a rolling suitcase behind her with a day bag balanced on top of it.

My father comes over and gives me a hug. He's frailer to the touch, rawboned, and up close the skin seems loose on his arms.

As she catches up, my mother complains, "I wish you had checked your bags."

"I don't trust the airlines." With a handkerchief he dabs at the sweat under his cap. "They're always losing things."

My mother says, "Hi, sweetheart," and gives me a kiss. She's let her hair turn mostly silver, but she's still lithe, and her only prominent wrinkles are parentheses on either cheek. "Here, help your dad with his luggage."

"I've got it," my father says.

"See what you're missing?" My mother passes me the handle of her suitcase on our way to the car. "He hasn't changed a bit."

I've stopped being amazed that my parents are together after all these years. They're like warring old cats in a studio apartment who've growled and hissed at each other for so long the routine has become a comfort. I spent much of my childhood worried that my parents would divorce. After we left Our House in the van and headed up 16th then onto the highway, stopping for the night at a Holiday Inn outside Pittsburgh, I was convinced that my mother had finally done it: she was going to leave my father for good. The next morning Molly and I climbed into the van and our mother refused to answer us when we asked, "Where are we going?" But then she turned the key and the van wouldn't start.

I remember sitting in the front seat and looking back at Molly, who had the hint of a smile on her face, and in that moment I knew we were both thanking the van for being a rusted old junker.

Now our mother would have to call our dad and scream at him for failing to fix the engine the first time around, and he'd rent a car or catch the next bus to Pittsburgh to pick us up and take us back to D.C. But this time we were the ones who caught a bus, a Greyhound to Milwaukee and then another to Wausau, an all-night ordeal that ended at our grandparents' house.

We would live there for a year and a half. Molly and I slept in Linc's old room, and my mother in her childhood room, which hadn't changed since she'd left for college, right down to the class pictures from Wausau High and archery ribbons from Camp Osoha. Molly and I went to the public schools and our mother taught social studies. Meantime, in D.C., my father grudgingly packed his bags and moved to Madison, two and a half hours downstate from us. Molly and I visited him every other weekend and slept on the foldout couch in his one-bedroom apartment, two blocks from La Follette High School, where he took a job as assistant baseball coach.

By the fall of 1980 my father had worked his way back into school administration, as associate principal at La Follette. He rented a two-bedroom house, bought a bunk bed for our visits and began to court our mother again. I remember the first few months when she'd drive us down, and instead of dropping us off she'd stay for the weekend. My father slept on the couch in the living room, and in the morning brewed fresh coffee and served us blueberry muffins that he'd made from scratch. In the summer before my senior year in high school we all moved to Madison and into my father's house. My mother was quick to say she was settling here for the sake of the kids and to look for a new job, perhaps in local politics. But as usual she diverted her own ambitions into those of someone else, assisting Uncle Linc, who himself had come to Madison the year before and opened up a business that would surprise us all.

Molly's husband, Anand, greets us at the curb of their house in Palisades, a neighborhood of bungalows and town homes between the Potomac River and MacArthur Boulevard not far from the Maryland border. It feels like a small town nestled in the far western corner of the city, with kids racing their bikes through the streets and barrel-chested chocolate Labs trundling after them. Molly and Anand have neither kids nor a dog, and joke that the neighbors are going to start picketing: YOU NEED TO BREED or ANY BREED WILL DO.

My parents embrace Molly and settle into the guest room to rest and get ready for the party. Anand sets up the bar and I help Karen set out the cheese and crackers and cold hors d'oeuvres. Molly reports that Linc called to say he's checked into his hotel and will be bringing a special guest, but might be running late.

My father thinks we're having a small party of mostly Molly and Anand's friends tonight, followed by the birthday dinner at Obelisk tomorrow, and maybe a museum visit or two. But Molly and I have rung up a few ghosts of the past, and who should show up first but Bailey Dornan, in a tuxedo, with his hair dyed black and what looks suspiciously like makeup on his face. He steps aside to make way for Ann, who's a Madame Tussaud's version of her younger self, down to the flowing clothes, which have cycled back into fashion.

"We can't stay long. We've got a fundraiser. So where's your dad?" Bailey asks. "I've brought someone here he might want to see." He introduces me to a man whose name I don't catch and his much younger wife, also dressed to the nines, who have come to the party with Bailey and Ann. I lead the group to my father, who is sitting on the living room sofa in a dress shirt and tie but still wearing his baseball cap. His eyebrows have thinned to a pale peach fuzz, and I know he's kept the hat on so he won't make people uneasy.

Getting up from the sofa he drops his jaw upon recognizing Bailey, who gives him a bone-rattling hug. Over his shoulder my father has a look of astonishment mixed with *what-is-the-meaning-of-this?* He hasn't seen Bailey in twenty-three years. The friend, it turns out, was the first baseman on the Wisconsin squad of '61; he used to catch my dad's bullet throws across the infield. He moved to D.C. not long after we left, rode in with the Reagan cavalry, and has been here ever since. He's a bigwig now with Fannie Mae and lives across the river in McLean.

Before inviting Bailey, Molly had screened him on the phone to see if he'd mellowed with age. He seemed dumbstruck when she told him about the tumor and prognosis. "I don't believe it," he'd said. "Not Pete. He's invincible." Molly had been a kid and had mostly forgotten the old, cantankerous Bailey, but she was pretty sure something about him had changed. All these years had passed, anyway, and Our House had loomed so large in our father's life; it had been his great adventure, and we figured any reminder of that time would be welcome.

I take drink orders, and when I return Bailey's making jokes about the baseball cap. He seems agitated to see my father looking frangible. Bailey stirs his gin and tonic with his finger, and when he takes a sip his hand is shaking. "I think we all know what that W is for." He points at the cap, nudging the first baseman. "George *W.* Bush. Looks like you've finally come around, Pete."

"Very funny," my father says. "But actually it's for *Winner* of the popular vote."

"Touché." Bailey clinks his glass with my father's and turns to his friend. "A lifetime ago Pete's family came to an election party at our house. Remember the place in Kalorama, the old embassy? We've downsized since then. But that was a helluva party. *You!*" He points to me. "Talk about losing your hair. This kid had giant hippie hair and it went up in smoke when some joker shot off fireworks."

We have a good laugh, then Bailey says, "That was the night Jimmy Carter beat Jerry Ford. That rocket was a warning flare for trouble ahead—" I worry that Bailey will make some snide remark about the demise of Our House, but instead he adds, "The Carter presidency."

This gives my father a chance to tell everyone about my work and my book in progress. I know he's proud that I've pursued a career in scholarship and teaching. Any educator would feel a certain *amour propre* to see one of his children take the same path. But I wonder sometimes: am I in this field as a tribute to my dad or to prove that I can do it better?

"A professor, huh?" Bailey says, as if surprised that a kid from that crazy school could amount to anything. "You remember Cleo? She got a master's degree in education and tried to save the world teaching in the San Francisco public schools. That job just about did her in. She got out of it but still talks about going back."

"What's she up to now?" I ask, and Bailey is sure to let us know that she got into Yale, Princeton, Columbia and Notre Dame before choosing Stanford, which doesn't surprise me, since it couldn't have been farther away from her parents. After getting her undergrad with honors, she stayed in the Bay Area for the M.A. at Berkeley, then taught for seven years at two inner-city schools—neither Bailey nor Ann can remember the names—one in Oakland, one in San Francisco. But then the guy she was dating, whom she eventually married, talked her into joining the online grocery business, where he's a junior executive, and ever since, they've been pouring all their time into that dream. "But these dot-coms are busting up all over the place," Bailey says. "I told Cleo and Matthew if you grow too fast and you've got a thin-margin business like groceries, you're asking for trouble."

"It's big risk, big reward, right?" I ask.

"Let's put it this way. A year ago their IPO was at fifteen dollars a share. Just this week the value dropped below a dollar. Cleo and Matthew are lucky they didn't sink a lot of their own cash into that company. Of course, I got fleeced for several grand, but family's family. I'll bet you dollars to doughnuts she goes back to teaching and Matthew comes down from the clouds and gets a real job."

I'm happily married with a child on the way—Karen's five months along; boy? girl? we've chosen to wait and see—but I feel a frisson of my long-ago affection for Cleo, hearing that she's an idealist after all. I imagine her in front of a classroom of restless kids, probably around the same age as the rough-and-tumble group from Our House. She would pace in front of the room, reading their desires and frustrations in how they slouch in their chairs or let their eyes drift toward the window. She'd hunt in the library after each class for the book or passage that would get this student to sit up today or that one to raise her hand tomorrow. Maybe a line from *The Great Gatsby:* "I was a pathfinder . . . an original settler."

I couldn't blame her for wanting to pan for dot-com gold; even Karen and I burned some hours trying to come up with Internet schemes back at the height of the boom. I think of Cleo in San Francisco, a straight shot on I-5 from where we live. I haven't spoken to her since the phone call that never happened, all those years ago.

"Do she and her husband have kids?" I ask.

Bailey looks at Ann, whose face is hard to read because her skin has been tightened and redraped, and she never had much expression to begin with. "They've been trying."

"He's shooting blanks," Bailey says.

"I don't know if Cleo would want that advertised." Ann forces a smile.

To change the subject, and without thinking, I ask about Troy.

"Right." Bailey sighs, breathing into his glass. Again, it's Ann who has to speak to anything nettlesome. She says that Troy has traveled the world and tried a lot of jobs and gone to a number of schools and is now living abroad. "He's into raw foods," she explains. "He's a vegan."

"All he eats is flowers and leaves. He weighs about a hundred pounds." Bailey finishes his drink and puts it down on the coffee table. "You might as well tell them—we haven't seen Troy in two and a half years. Can you believe this kid? We gave him everything and more, paid for his yoga retreats and the rest of it, listened to him go on about how we're all going to die eating cooked food. He told us, 'Animals don't cook their food.' I said, 'Great. You'd rather be a grasshopper?' Every winter he went off to some ashram in southern India—on my dime, of course. One year he decided to stay."

"It's just a phase." Ann slips her arm into Bailey's.

His scalp shifts forward and back. "He's thirty-nine years old," he says. "Some phase."

The first baseman's wife is thoughtful enough to ask Bailey how his business is going, and I take the opportunity to slip away.

I'm opening bottles of red wine in the kitchen when I see Quinn. I was surprised how easy it was to track him down. Before Karen and I left Oregon, I looked him up on the Internet, and he was the only Quinn Simmons listed in the D.C. phonebook. I called to invite him to the party, and we caught up on the years since 1977. I'd gotten so absorbed in the conversation that I found myself running late for school, before I'd even bothered to ask what he was up to now.

I knew that he went back to Cardozo and after a few months of tutoring moved in with Senedu's family in the apartment above their restaurant, the Blue Nile. "I'd never gotten to know the kid because his English was so bad," Quinn told me, "but once he got the hang of the language he was cool, and all that restaurant needed was public relations help." Quinn worked at the Blue Nile part-time and summers, then full-time after high school, and helped make it one of the more popular spots on 18th. "But working and living there, my whole being smelled like garlic and *wot kimem,* and I probably stayed too long because I wanted the place to do well."

In fact, Quinn worked as a waiter for twelve years before Senedu's family sold the business and fulfilled their longtime desire to move back to Addis Ababa. That was nine years ago, and I'm eager to know what Quinn's been up to since.

He looks mostly the same, though his mustache has filled in, his cheeks are a bit jowly, and he's gotten an early start on middle-age spread. He wears his pants high and his belt cinched tight over his midsection. We hug and compliment each other on how gracefully we're aging. He asks me more about my job and says, "You never did get to teach history at Our House. How long did you last? A day or two? Looks like you're making up for it now." He volunteers that he's taken night classes over the years at Howard but is far from earning his B.A., which takes me aback. Quinn had been such a confident kid—I'd figured he'd whiz through high school, win a scholarship to MIT or Caltech, and I'd be reading about him in the *New York Times.* But I was naïve to think that finishing near the top of his class at a D.C. public school would put him on a fast track. He had no money or support and couldn't depend on Senedu's family for his education. It took their returning to Ethiopia for him to think about starting college.

"After the Blue Nile, I got a job in the mailroom at the USPTO."

Washingtonians love their acronyms, but I have to ask what the letters stand for.

"That's the United States Patent and Trademark Office." He pulls out his wallet and shows me his ID. "I'm on the help desk at the Public Search Facility in Alexandria."

I'm wondering whatever happened to his zeppelin safari plan, and he must be able to read my mind because he starts reminiscing about it, then explains, "After you and your mom and sister left, I went by the place and your dad said he was getting ready to move out, and did I want anything from the house. I climbed on the roof and cut down the airship and took it back to the foster home. They wouldn't let me keep the thing unless I disassembled it. I've still got it, you know, packed in an old box. It doesn't inflate anymore, and the lettering has mostly faded, but it's a nice piece of memorabilia."

We get back to talking about the patent office, and I'm happy to hear that Quinn has never stopped coming up with ideas. During high school and afterward he made more zeppelin designs and became obsessed with flying cars, reading up on all the prototypes, like the Waterman Aerobile and the AVE Mizar, a cross between a Cessna and a Ford Pinto that crashed in a test flight in 1973, killing its inventor. Quinn made drawings and models of his own flying cars, eventually filing a patent for one with the USPTO.

"When I started working at the search facility and got to read all those patents, I figured I should get in on the fun. I've got thirty-one so far, and I'm running out of space, with all the notes and books stacked up in my apartment. A few years ago I realized flying cars and safari zeppelins were all well and good but if I wanted any of these inventions to actually get made I had to start small," Quinn says. "I was living—still live, actually—in a five-hundred-square-foot studio in Southwest, and man, that apartment got cluttered fast. So I started thinking about space-saving devices, and that's my new thing for now. I've got nineteen patents for the kitchen alone."

"For instance?" I ask.

He opens some cupboards in my sister and Anand's kitchen to show how inefficient most storage space is, then describes various apparatuses he's invented for hanging and stowing utensils. He talks about a cutting board that can lift out from the side of the sink and fit across the top to save counter space, a small dishwasher that fits beneath the sink, and a series of Ronco-like cutting gadgets folded into one neat package, like a Swiss Army knife for the kitchen.

He asks for my address and phone number and tells me he's going to send some Xeroxes of his designs. He's writing down his own contact info when Molly ducks her head into the kitchen and says, brightly, "Linc's here. And he's got a surprise."

It occurs to me that if Quinn's designs are as good as I imagine they might be, I could put him in touch with my uncle, who's always on the lookout for a speculative venture. But for now I say, "I'm sure you remember Linc," and leave it at that.

Linc has always been accident-prone, but sometimes there are happy accidents, and that's the story of his success. He went from the Midas of Mayhem in the sixties and seventies to simply Midas in the eighties, when he got in early on a craze and made a fortune.

After Our House disbanded, he turned in his Jack & Jill ice cream truck and hitchhiked with Cinnamon to Yellow Springs, Ohio, where some old friends from Freelandia had resettled on a communal dairy farm. There, they grew vegetables and made and sold their own granola and yogurt, and Linc, who had mixed ice cream in his free time at Our House, began experimenting with different flavors of frozen yogurt. Word got around Yellow Springs and Dayton, and soon his cart was among the most popular at the farmers' market. His marriage to Cinnamon, on the other hand, was not going so well. They had tried to revive their relationship in Yellow Springs, but when she ended up with a bright-eyed stargazer just out of college and talked about wanting to marry him, Linc granted her a divorce and moved to Madison.

This time, instead of selling at farmers' markets, he rented a small storefront on pedestrian-only State Street near the University of Wisconsin campus, bought some dispensing machines and planned to name his operation The Yogurt Pump. I recall one weekend when Molly and I were visiting our father, and he told us that Linc had picked a silly name, and no one was going to choose yogurt over ice cream in the heart of the Dairy State. What's more, Linc had terrible luck, so my father predicted the business wouldn't last a year.

Linc had ordered his signage and merchandise from the same company at a bargain-basement price, but when the awning, decals, menus, signboards and T-shirts arrived, the printing company had made a crucial misspelling. Instead of The Yogurt Pump, they'd written The Yogurt *Pimp.*

Linc called up the company in a rage and demanded they fix the spelling and reprint the materials. They refused, and blamed his poor handwriting on the order form. Unable to afford a new order through a more reliable company, Linc decided to stick with the name, and on the first day of work wore an extra-large purple T-shirt emblazoned with the moniker that would become legend, in our family and beyond.

The Yogurt Pimp was an instant success. College kids lined

up around the block to try Linc's thirteen distinctive flavors, and T-shirt sales were so brisk that he had to hire additional staff and move to a larger space up the street. It was my mother's idea to expand the merchandising end of the business, and when she moved us to Madison for good, that became her primary job. She sold T-shirts, hats, mugs, and key rings, and introduced Linc to a graduate student at the University of Wisconsin School of Business, a young divorcée named Maxine who had a lot to prove.

Maxine said the time was ripe for a frozen yogurt boom. In the hopelessly vain 1980s, Olivia Newton-John wasn't the only one getting physical; everyone was counting calories, and though franchising made Linc nervous, he put his faith in Maxine. By the middle of the decade The Yogurt Pimp had a hundred stores in twenty-two states, from Maine to California.

Maxine and Linc were married at their house on the shores of Lake Mendota in 1992. A few midwestern newspapers and business magazines sent reporters to the wedding, and couldn't resist such quippy headlines as YOGURT PIMP TAKES A BRIDE and HIS PIMPING DAYS ARE OVER.

If it weren't for Maxine's good advice, he might have held on to the business too long, past the expiration date of the frozen yogurt craze. After they sold the company they went into various investment ventures and put my mother in charge of TYP Foundation and its large endowment for educational philanthropy.

I asked my mother once if she'd ever offered a start-up grant to my father, who at this moment is on extended medical leave from La Follette High, where he's still associate principal. "Of course," she said. "He could have created his own curriculum, had a brand-new building and grounds, and called it Our House Two or Pete Truitt School or anything he liked. But your father is going to do things his way—I learned that long ago—even if he knows he's only hurting himself."

Now I'm headed with Quinn back into the living room. Bailey, Ann and their friends have left for the fundraiser, replaced by Maxine and the Yogurt Pimp himself, both looking stout and blowzy and more like each other every day. Linc's in one of his trademark Hawaiian shirts; he wears them all year round—in Madison through Thanksgiving, then in Key West, where he and Maxine spend the winter. Between them is their special guest, and I'm taken back to that long-ago arrival at Our House of the Salem Cigarette Car, when I realized we were facing a love triangle.

But this time there will be no such drama. People embrace and grow teary-eyed, and we all sit around the living room listening to Cinnamon talk about Yellow Springs and her life on one of the oldest active farming communes in the Midwest. Just beneath her leathery tan and her unraveling bun of russet and gray hair is the woman of my adolescent dreams, still sexy, with a throaty Lauren Bacall voice from too many hand-rolled cigarettes. Cinnamon's the true believer, the last hippie standing, a fixture in a community that she says she'll never leave. She talks about her carpenter boyfriend, with whom she's lived for five years. Wringing her hands, her fingers crooked as parsnips from tending the earth, she tells us how her second marriage hit the skids when the stargazer ran off with an Antioch coed. "Remind you of something?" Cinnamon says.

My mother asks about Tino. Has anyone seen him? Is he living or dead? Cinnamon has no idea; he vamoosed and that was that. "He could be a carnie or a venture capitalist. I wouldn't be surprised either way."

"He once called me out of the blue," Linc says. "Jeez, it must have been fifteen years ago. Claimed he was working at The Yogurt Pimp in Missoula, had been for months, when the manager told him that some old hippie from Wisconsin owned the whole shebang. Tino looked up the old hippie and discovered it was me."

Maxine gives Linc a nudge. "It's too much of a coincidence. He had to be bullshitting you."

"Probably."

"I'm sure he was looking for a payout."

"So what happened?" I ask.

"I agreed to meet him. I guess I was hoping he'd apologize. And, yeah, maybe he wanted some dough or a better job. We set a date for the next time I'd be traveling out west—to Seattle, of all places. We picked a time and a coffee shop off Pioneer Square where I used to kill the day when I was supposed to be selling cigarettes. But that son of a bitch never showed. Can you believe it?"

I can. Tino is nothing if not perverse.

"So who's up for a tour of the old school tomorrow?" my father asks, and all hands in the room go up but Quinn's. Sitting next to me, Quinn leans over and whispers, "I can't make it," before adding, "You may not like what you see."

I keep this to myself, not wanting to be a downer. My mother told me years ago that Bailey had sold the house not long after we left, but I haven't been by the place since my graduate student days. I recall that it did look a bit shabby then—but really, how bad could it be?

Plans are made to convoy at noon tomorrow to the corner of 16th and Hill. I open a bottle of champagne left over from the election party and give the first of the weekend's toasts. "To Albert Gore Jr., the forty-third president of the United States of America. Here, here!"

Cinnamon crosses her fingers. "God, I hope you're right."

Then Molly says, "To Jimmy Carter, who only gets better with age. Good luck with your book, Daniel. It's going to be amazing."

Linc raises his glass. "To old friends and family." He clinks flutes with Cinnamon, Quinn and Maxine.

"To Pete Truitt." My mother chokes up. "To many years of health and happiness."

My father has the last word of the night. "And to Our House," he says. "A very, very, *very* fine house."

On the morning of my father's sixtieth birthday, the election news isn't good. CNN reports a discrepancy in Florida between the nonpartisan Voter News Service tally, which says Bush's lead has narrowed to 300 votes, and the official tally of the Republican-run Office of the Secretary of State, which puts the lead closer to 1,000.

Meanwhile, 20,000 hanging, dimpled or pregnant ballots have been invalidated in heavily Democratic Palm Beach County.

"The fix is in," my father says as we take off in Molly's Subaru. "Looks like Bush has got it."

"That's not like you, Dad. You're the optimist in this family." Molly heads out on Nebraska Avenue, with Anand and the others in a second car behind us. We go all the way to the top of 16th Street, near the Maryland border, and take the long route south into the heart of the city, the same drive our father made in the old tan van when he moved us here from Lake Bluff.

Sixteenth looks familiar, with its mature trees and grand corner houses. In the distance to the east, tall cranes peer over the tree line, signs of a housing boom on the horizon. I'm sitting next to Karen in the back seat; the slight curve of her pregnant belly brushes against my arm. She asks Molly when she last saw the house, and my sister admits it's been a while. "I checked it out about three years ago, and the place was an unholy mess."

She says the white paint had peeled in strips down the side, the yard was a tangle of weeds, and the porch, filled with old furniture and rolled-up rugs, had warped with weather and age. But a year or so later she went by again, and though the house was still in shambles, she saw a Sold sign out front and a well-dressed woman leaning in the doorway, talking on her cell phone. "I pulled over at the curb and nearly got out of the car," Molly says. "That was the closest I'd ever come to asking for a look inside, but the woman seemed preoccupied so I didn't go up and talk to her."

My father turns to Molly, his mood lifting. "I bet they did a complete restoration. A beautiful Victorian like that? Can you imagine how spectacular it would be with new floors, new paint and windows, all the fine detailing refinished? That house must be worth a fortune now."

"I wouldn't be surprised," Molly says. "The whole neighborhood has changed. There's new construction everywhere. Shaw is getting gentrified, Starbucksified, for better or worse. There's a neat strip of shops and bars at Fourteenth and U, and the park across Sixteenth is cleaned up. People play soccer there now, and have picnics."

My father touches the brim of his baseball cap. "Maybe the new owners will let us inside for the price of a story or two. Your mother brought her camera."

We crest the hill after Columbia Road and can see all the way down beyond Scott Circle and Lafayette Park toward the White House.

"They're sprucing it up for Al," I say hopefully. "Only a couple more blocks to go."

Molly nearly drives right past the house because it's no longer white. The exterior wood looks saturated, covered in a greenish patina, like a coastal shanty. Molly turns onto Hill Street and goes a little ways up the block to leave room for Anand's car to pull up behind us. We climb out of the Subaru, unable to take our eyes off what's become of Our House.

At first I tell myself that the owners have stripped it for repainting, but as we get closer I see the first-floor windows boarded up. Newspapers and beer bottles litter the yard. A temporary chain-link fence circles the property, and behind it a dumpster brims with scraps of wood and old wallpaper. Three boards cover the parlor windows. The lace-like brackets have come loose and now dangle along the porch supports.

A No Trespassing sign has been threaded to the fence, which blocks the entrance to the house. We peer through at a sign posted on the front door in large red letters: NOTIFICATION OF INTENT TO RAZE.

"They're just tearing it down? That's it?" my father says. His face is ashen and he has a panicked look, as if he's just come home from a trip to find that his property has been condemned.

Molly notices another sign, farther along the fence: CAPITAL CITY DEVELOPMENT CORP.

She points down the block to what used to be Mr. Unthank's house, and three more houses beyond. They all have the same demolition signs. "Everything's going condo these days," she says.

My mother takes her camera out of her purse. "How about we get a picture anyway?" She starts to line us up—Cinnamon, Linc, Maxine, Molly, Anand, Karen and me. "Come on, Pete. I want you in the middle."

"No pictures," my father says.

"But honey, it won't be here next time we visit. This could be our last chance."

"Maybe *I* won't be here next time."

"Pete—" My mother's voice trails off.

"No pictures, Val."

A light wind rustles the leaves on the sidewalk, and we look at one another, wondering what to do.

"Let's go," my father says.

And we turn around because no one wants to make him any more upset.

But as we're headed back to the cars, I notice the fire hydrant by the curb, the one that got us a parking ticket on our very first night here. To my amazement, it hasn't been repainted since the bicentennial. "Look." I point it out to everyone.

Rust covers the base and cap, and though the paint has faded I can make out the same blue waistcoat and square glasses of Benjamin Franklin.

And there's something else.

Leaning against the fire hydrant is a large box. I kneel down to read the writing across the top. FOR THE TRUITTS, it says in bold black marker.

I know just who left this here. Who else could it be? He could be watching us, even now, as he used to watch the strange people who had moved into his house. I know what's in this box, too. What did Quinn call it? *A nice piece of memorabilia.*

I pick it up. Today's my father's sixtieth birthday. "It's for you." I hand him the box.

Behind him the tower of Our House rises. In the broken window of my old room, a red curtain, caught on a piece of jagged glass, waves in the breeze.

Acknowledgments

This novel has its origins in some of the most eventful years of my childhood in the 1970s, when my parents received a start-up grant to open an alternative school. Along with my uncle and a handful of his hippie friends, who had just returned from a long stint on a commune out west, my family taught a series of experimental courses and tried, against all odds, to keep the school running. In my novel, I have used the real name of the school, borrowed from the Crosby, Stills, Nash & Young song "Our House." But beyond that, and a few anecdotes based on actual events, this is entirely a work of fiction. I want to thank my parents and my uncle, Jeff Richards, for sharing their experiences and supporting me, as they always have.

I am grateful to the Purdue Research Foundation for a Summer Faculty Grant and the Purdue Center for Artistic Endeavors in the College of Liberal Arts for the generous fellowship that allowed me to complete this book. I would like to thank the Purdue University English Department, particularly my colleagues and students in the Creative Writing Program.

This novel contains bits and pieces from two short stories I wrote some years ago—"The Eloquent Exterminator," which appeared in *Witness,* and "Neighborhood Watch," first published in the anthology *Tales Out of School.* The quote "We're not a college prep school, we're a life prep school" comes from the Second Foundation School in Minneapolis, and the motto "Act first. Ask permission later" comes from the Albany Free School. I found a number of books to be invaluable, especially *The American Presidency,* edited by Alan Brinkley and Davis Dyer, which provided the Herbert Hoover quote; *Jimmy Carter: American Moralist* by Kenneth E. Morris; and *The Seventies: The Great Shift in American Culture, Society, and Politics* by Bruce J. Schulman. I also quote from Abbie Hoffman's *Steal This Book* and draw on it to create an imagined correspondence between Hoffman and my narrator.

I am enormously grateful to my editor Jane Rosenman, and also to Janet Silver, Ben Steinberg, George Hodgman, Sasheem Silkiss-Hero, Becky Saletan, Andrea Schulz, Ken Carpenter, Lori Glazer, Megan Wilson, Carla Gray, Larry Cooper and everyone at Houghton Mifflin, my agent Tim Seldes, my family in D.C. And most of all, always, to Bich Minh Nguyen, my partner in this craft and life.